D1414731

WITHDRAWN

AS
LOVE BLOOMS

Books by Lorna Seilstad

THE GREGORY SISTERS, BOOK 3

AS LOVE BLOOMS

A NOVEL

LORNA SEILSTAD

Revell

a division of Baker Publishing Group
Grand Rapids, Michigan

© 2015 by Lorna Seilstad

Published by Revell
a division of Baker Publishing Group
P.O. Box 6287, Grand Rapids, MI 49516-6287
www.revellbooks.com

Printed in the United States of America

All rights reserved. No part of this publication may be reproduced, stored in a retrieval system, or transmitted in any form or by any means—for example, electronic, photocopy, recording—without the prior written permission of the publisher. The only exception is brief quotations in printed reviews.

Library of Congress Cataloging-in-Publication Data
Seilstad, Lorna.
    As love blooms : a novel / Lorna Seilstad.
        pages ; cm — (The Gregory sisters ; Book 3)
    ISBN 978-0-8007-2183-1 (softcover)
    1. Sisters—Fiction. I. Title.
PS3619.E425A93 2015
813′.6—dc23   2014047671

Scripture quotations are from the King James Version of the Bible.

This book is a work of fiction. Names, characters, places, and incidents are the product of the author's imagination or are used fictitiously. Any resemblance to actual events, locales, or persons, living or dead, is coincidental.

Published in association with Books & Such Literary Agency, 52 Mission Circle, Suite 122, PMB 170, Santa Rosa, CA 94509-7953.

15 16 17 18 19 20 21   7 6 5 4 3 2 1

To Parker, Caroline, and Emma.
If I had a flower for every time you've each
made me laugh or smile,
I'd have a garden to walk in forever.
Watching the three of you grow to love the Lord
has been my greatest joy.

As ye have therefore received Christ Jesus the Lord, so walk ye in him: rooted and built up in him, and stablished in the faith.

Colossians 2:6–7

1

"Flowers have an expression of countenance." Tessa Gregory whispered the words she'd once read. She studied the blooms in the Como Park planter and shook her head. If the author was correct, then these pansies were suffering from a severe case of melancholy.

Why hadn't a gardener tended the velvety flowers after the frost the other night? If the shriveled, damaged blooms weren't removed, fungus might grow on them and spread to the rest of the healthy flowers. Should she help the poor things or simply keep going?

They seemed to cry out to her, but it wasn't her job to take care of the pansies.

Not yet anyway.

She read the sign posted with large block letters. PICKING FLOWERS IS AGAINST THE LAW. Excellent! Perhaps the staff did care about their plants.

The colorful faces of the pansies—violet, yellow, orange, magenta, and white—winked at her, daring her to risk a few moments with them.

She sighed, sat down on the edge of the planter, and removed her gloves. Deadheading the plants wouldn't take long, and then she could be on her way to meeting the park superintendent.

Humming to herself, she plucked the withered blossoms, leaned back, and examined her handiwork. How much better the array looked already!

A shrill whistle startled her.

"Miss! Put down the flower!"

She whirled. Was the policeman speaking to her?

"Now, miss." The park officer rode his bicycle nearer, dismounted, and leaned the bicycle against the planter. He approached Tessa with a stern scowl on his face. "Miss, it's against the law to pick flowers." He pointed to the sign. "Do you know I can arrest you?"

Tessa stood and held out the frazzled bloom. "For picking this? I'll have you know I was helping the plant, not hurting it."

"Helping it by picking its flowers?"

"I'm telling you the truth. I'm a horticulturist and—"

"You might be the queen of England, but you still can't pick the flowers. Now, move along and I'll ignore your ordinance breach."

"But I'm almost finished." She swept her arm toward the beautified planter. "See? There are only a few of the ugly blooms left."

His glower spoke volumes. "Keep your hands off the flowers. Understand?"

Tessa didn't flinch.

The officer remained until she turned to leave. As soon as she heard the bicycle's clatter against the planter, she spun around. Hurrying back to the flower bed, she grabbed the remaining spongy blooms as fast as her fingers could pluck them. Hands still full of the withered blooms, she stood and surveyed the tidy planter as satisfaction warmed her.

Someone with a deep voice cleared his throat behind her.

Slowly, she turned.

The policeman took hold of her upper arm. "Miss, you'll be coming with me now."

Inhaling, Reese King drew in the familiar scent of the freshly turned earth. He plunged the shovel back into the ground and heaved yet another load of rich dirt beside the hole. Planting this shrub was taking far too much time. He had a long list of things to do today, and if he wanted to continue to impress the Saint Paul park superintendent, Fred Nussbaumer, he'd need to finish every item.

His father might not see Reese's future as a gardener, but Mr. Nussbaumer seemed to. He'd even given him an area in the park in which to develop a new garden. Now if he could get done with his list, he could start designing it.

At least he wouldn't have to deadhead the pansies. He'd spotted a pretty young lady, with hair the color of poppies, taking on that task a few minutes ago.

Once the hole was deep enough, he leaned against the shovel's handle and noticed a group gathering around one of the nearby planters. What was all the commotion about?

"Unhand me this instant!"

Uh-oh. The pretty young lady he'd been watching deadhead his pansies attempted to pull her arm free from the police officer's hold. This couldn't be good.

He dropped the shovel and rushed over. "Officer, what's the problem?"

"Caught this young lady picking your posies, Mr. King."

The fiery-haired girl fought against the officer's grasp. "I was not picking them. Not the live ones anyway. How many times do I have to tell you that?"

"Settle down, Little Miss Polecat." He gave her a little shake. "I'll take care of her, Mr. King. She won't be bothering us here again."

"Wait." Reese barred his way with an outstretched arm. He glanced at the onlookers and leaned in close. "Officer, I believe we can sort this out without arresting the young lady." He turned to the girl. "I was watching you. You were deadheading the pansies, right?"

Her eyes widened, and for a fleeting second relief washed over her face, only to be replaced with indignation. "That's what I've been trying to explain to this lout."

"Why, you little—" the policeman growled.

"Officer, clearly the young woman is beside herself with fear. Perhaps she's had too much sun."

"Too much sun?" she squeaked. "More like—"

Reese silenced her with a stern look. "Why don't you allow me to show her to the shade, and we can forget this whole unfortunate matter?"

The officer moved his gaze from the young lady to Reese as if he were considering a life-altering decision. The girl kept her chin high, clearly unwilling to back down. After a long moment, the policeman sighed. "Are you sure you want her, Mr. King? She's a handful."

"We'll be fine. How much trouble could one young lady be?"

The park officer released her. "All right. She's all yours."

Reese met her gaze, and her eyebrows arched over twinkling hazel eyes. Was she daring him?

Good grief. What had he gotten himself into?

2

Tessa held out the withered blossoms. "I believe these belong to you." Mr. King extended his hand, and she deposited the blooms. "You really ought to be ashamed of yourself for not tending to those poor beleaguered pansies. Hadn't you noticed them?"

Mr. King tossed the handful of flowers into a trash can. "Dead-heading the pansies was on my list of things to do today, Miss . . ."

"Tessa Gregory." She tugged on her gloves. "And thank you for your assistance. Now, if you'll kindly direct me to the office of the park superintendent, I'll be on my way."

"I'm off to see Mr. Nussbaumer myself. You can walk with me." He motioned toward the path, and the two of them fell in step together. Neither spoke for the first few minutes, but finally Mr. King broke the awkward silence. "Why do you want to speak to our park superintendent?"

"I'm seeking a position."

"I don't think you'll find Mr. Nussbaumer in need of a stenographer. He does all the record keeping himself."

Tessa glanced in the young man's direction and saw he was serious. "An office girl? I realize we've only known each other a short time, but do I seem like the kind of person who'd be content filing papers?"

Mr. King chuckled. "Not really."

"That's certainly correct." The wind whipped at the rolled-up garden prints she carried, and she tucked them under her arm. "I'm a horticulturist. I've spent the last two years at the University of Minnesota studying horticulture, and I'd like to secure a position as a gardener."

His eyes widened. "From Fred Nussbaumer?"

"Yes, he has a stellar reputation."

"Indeed, but do you know anything else about the man?" He slowed as they neared a brick building.

"Like?"

"He's German, he's brilliant, and he works harder than two men on any given day."

"Are you trying to scare me off?"

Mr. King met her gaze and held it. "Not in the least, but I don't want you to get your hopes up. He's a great man—a great *opinionated* man."

"Once he sees my ideas, I'm sure we'll get along famously."

"He may never look at your plans." Mr. King held the door to the small building. "But I wish you Godspeed, Miss Gregory."

After introducing herself, Tessa flashed Mr. Nussbaumer a broad smile and glanced around his office. Open volumes bearing sketches of plants littered one table in the corner. Another table bore several pots beneath a window, and she recognized the plants they held—milkwort, curled mallow, wild peppergrass, rock cress, and columbine.

Mr. Nussbaumer motioned her to a chair. "What can I do for you, Miss Gregory?"

"I'd like to speak to you about securing a position at one of Saint Paul's parks." She laid her rolled-up plans in her lap and took a steadying breath. "I would be happy to work at any of them, but I must admit a particular fondness for this one, Como

Park. It's truly magnificent, and I could learn a great deal by working here."

The man's bushy eyebrows drew close. "Working here in what way?"

"As a gardener, of course. I studied horticulture in college, so I'm well qualified. I've had classes in fruit and vegetable growing, greenhouse practices, plant breeding, floriculture, systemic pomology, ornamental horticulture, and my favorite—landscape gardening."

The man threw himself back in his chair and laughed. "You want to work in my gardens?" His mustache wiggled as he spoke. "The work here is man's work. There is a great deal of lifting and digging in the dirt. You are a fine lady. You can't be serious."

"But I am serious."

His eyes sparkled with merriment. "I wouldn't have you here as a flower girl, Miss Gregory, let alone a gardener. Surely you can find things to keep you busy at one of the many ladies' flower clubs."

Disappointment pricked her heart and welled inside her. "Mr. Nussbaumer, I want to design gardens. If you'll only take a look at my plans . . ." She held out her papers.

Mr. Nussbaumer waved them away. "I'm sure you are a lovely young woman. Go design your own garden in your backyard. Perhaps it will keep you entertained until you find a young man to marry you, *ja*?"

"Entertained?" Her voice rose. She had to make him understand. "Gardening is not a hobby for me. I take it very seriously. I want to work for you."

"That is not going to happen, Miss Gregory." Although his eyes were kind, his words were firm. She'd heard her father use the same tone. "Perhaps you can be of use to the parks in some other way. We are always in need of community support. Maybe you'd be willing to speak to your lady friends about becoming patrons. We can work together to make our city beautiful."

The nerve of this man. First he wouldn't take her seriously, and now he wanted her to help him secure funds?

Don't say anything you'll regret.

She forced a thin smile. "I'll do what I can to help."

"Now there's a good girl." He picked up his pencil and opened a ledger. "Good day, Miss Gregory."

Reese leaned against the wall and waited for his turn to speak to Mr. Nussbaumer. If he was honest with himself, he was waiting for Miss Gregory. He'd overheard part of the conversation, and he worried about how the young woman would handle having her hopes dashed. There was something about her that made him want to help her.

Miss Gregory shut the office door with a solid bang, then glared at him. "Mr. King, have you been eavesdropping? Did you stay here so you could gloat?"

"N-n-no, of course not."

"While I appreciate your assistance in that rather unfortunate exchange this afternoon, I do not see how it gives you the right to listen to my private conversations." She marched toward the exit.

For all her bravado, Reese sensed the woman's hurt and defeat. "I'm sorry Mr. Nussbaumer wouldn't consider you."

Her eyes glistened. Would she cry? Instead, she lifted her chin, drawing attention to the freckles dotting her nose, and squared her shoulders. "I don't give up easily, Mr. King. I always find a way to get what I want."

Reese smiled and watched her leave. "I bet you do, Miss Gregory. I bet you do."

During the short walk from the streetcar up Summit Avenue to Aunt Sam's mansion, Tessa rehearsed what she was going to tell her two older sisters. If she was going to make her dream come true, she'd need their help. Aunt Sam, of course, would be willing to lend a hand as well.

The butler greeted her at the door. "Welcome home, miss."

"Thank you, Geoffrey. Are my sisters still here?"

"They're in the parlor."

Perfect. She'd tell them all about her unfruitful morning. They'd understand. Both had fought to get where they were today. Her oldest sister, Hannah, was an attorney, and her other sister, Charlotte, was the chef in charge of City Hospital's kitchen. Together the three of them would come up with a plan that Mr. Nussbaumer would never see coming.

Tessa scurried through the parlor's double doors. Hannah, who sat in a winged chair with a tablet of paper in hand, looked up. "Oh, Tessa, we're glad you're home. Come join us. We want to tell you about the plan we've come up with."

Tessa took a seat on the divan next to Charlotte and smiled when her three-year-old niece Ellie climbed up in her lap.

Hannah's daughter held up her porcelain doll to Tessa's lips. "Kiss my baby."

Tessa obliged and gave the doll a peck before Ellie slid off her lap. "You'll never guess what happened this morn—"

"What do you think about the three of us arranging an excursion to surprise Aunt Sam for her birthday?" Charlotte captured Tessa's hand. "Wouldn't it be fun?"

"Yes, of course, you know I love surprises. How can I help?"

Hannah waved her pencil in the air. "You don't need to worry about the details. Charlotte and I can manage those. All you need to do is pitch in the day we tell her—and of course keep our secret. You can do that, can't you?"

"Don't treat me like a child. Of course I can keep a secret."

Charlotte poured Tessa a cup of tea. "We simply don't want her to find out, and with you living here in the house with her, it might be more difficult for you to keep our surprise under wraps."

"I won't let on to the trip." Tessa dropped two lumps of sugar into her tea. "And why would we put you in charge of the details, Hannah? If you'd had your way, we'd have all been on the *Titanic* last year."

"They said the ship was unsinkable." Hannah jotted down a note on her tablet. "I hardly think that precludes me from deciding our next venture."

Tessa shrugged. "Now, can I tell you about what happened to me this morning?"

"All right." Hannah set the tablet down on the table.

Tessa relayed the experience with Mr. Nussbaumer, doing her best to reenact his German accent, and leaving out the part about almost being arrested. Neither of her sisters seemed to appreciate her dramatic interpretation of the events. Didn't they realize how difficult it was to improvise a performance?

"You weren't honestly expecting him to welcome you with open arms, were you?" Hannah hurried to still Ellie from pounding on the piano keys. "It's like I warned you. There are women gardeners at private estates, but I doubt if there are many working in the city parks systems."

"But a woman helped design the gardens at the Saint Louis World's Fair, and there's the City Beautiful Movement. Sure, everyone associates men with the effort to bring beauty to the cities, but we all know it's women volunteers who've made the most difference. It's simply not fair he dismissed me because I'm a woman."

Charlotte patted Tessa's hand. "I'm sure you'll find something else to catch your fancy. After all, you've already passed through the journalist, photographer, librarian, and Pinkerton agent phases."

"Horticulture is not a phase!" Tessa set her cup down so hard some tea swished out onto the saucer. First Mr. Nussbaumer and now her sisters? Didn't anyone understand? "This is the profession I've chosen, and you both need to realize I'm not a child anymore.

I'm almost twenty years old, and in case you've forgotten, when Mother and Father passed away, we promised to help each other achieve our dreams."

Hannah shared a knowing look with Charlotte, then came round the back of the divan and placed her hands on Tessa's shoulders. "You're right. We did. But is this *really* your heart's true desire?"

"Yes, Hannah, it is." She shrugged her sister's hand away, stood, and squared her shoulders. "But I don't need your help. I'll make my own dreams come true—with or without you."

3

Refreshed after her suffrage meeting, Samantha Phillips entered her home and passed her wraps to the butler. Raised voices from the parlor drew her attention. She turned toward the French doors only to see Tessa storm out of the room.

Oh dear. What had upset her niece?

Her lips curled in a smile. She truly thought of all three of the Gregory girls as her blood relatives even though they were not. It was only because her true nephew Lincoln Cole had married Hannah that she'd even been blessed to have the three delightful young ladies in her life. Thank goodness Tessa had agreed to stay with her during her summers home from college. She'd missed the young woman's pluck and creativity a great deal during her time away, and now that she was back, this massive house felt like a home with her flitting about.

Sam swung the French doors wide as she entered the parlor. Charlotte looked up. "Aunt Sam, you're early."

Hannah stuffed a tablet beneath a pillow—a sure sign the two ladies were up to something. "How was the meeting? I hated to miss it."

"I believe the women's suffrage parade in Washington last March has infused the cause with new vitality. The ladies were positively bubbling over with ideas." She picked up a stack of envelopes from a small writing desk in the corner and thumbed through them. "Now, would the two of you like to explain why your sister left the room in such a huff?"

"You saw that?" Charlotte rolled her eyes. "You know how Tessa is."

"No, I don't think I do know." Sam sliced through one envelope with a letter opener.

"Well, today she's enthusiastic about securing a position as a gardener in the public park system, but you know tomorrow she'll probably want to be a ballerina."

Sam sat down on the divan, unfolded the missive in her hands, and smoothed the creases in the paper. "A ballerina?"

"Or a butcher," Charlotte added.

"Or a pilot." Hannah gathered Ellie into her arms and chuckled.

"Oh my, don't let her hear you say that." Charlotte glanced toward the door as if she expected Tessa to appear any minute and lowered her voice. "It'll only give her ideas."

"I'm ashamed of you two." Sam looked up from her letter. "Your sister has worked hard at her horticultural studies. Do you blame her for wanting to use her education?"

Hannah stroked Ellie's hair as the girl nestled against her shoulder. "Of course we don't blame her, but we all know how Tessa doesn't exactly have a history of sticking to one thing for any duration."

"Even if that is the case, did you not all promise to support one another's dreams?" Sam drew in a deep breath as she watched both women nod. "I know Tessa is young, and I know you have always been the older sisters. I also realize Tessa is a dreamer, but will you support her only in the dreams you believe are worthy? Do other people think it's fitting for you, Hannah, to work as a lawyer? And Charlotte, I remember all too well how difficult it was for you to enter the man's world of being a chef."

"But Tessa lacks a single-minded purpose."

"Does she?" Sam walked to the vase of tulips Tessa had picked and placed on the mantel, and fingered the cut glass. "Ever since I met your sister, she's worked in my garden as if it were her own. Even when she wanted to be a photographer, then an actress, and then a Pinkerton agent, she never stopped gardening. By the way, I talked her out of learning how to fly an airplane." Sam turned toward the two sisters. "She told me your mother liked to garden. I believe becoming a horticulturist is her connection to her mother. In her world, where flights of fancy are a regular occurrence, working with the earth literally and figuratively grounds her."

Charlotte swiped at the tears gathering in her eyes. "Aunt Sam, you're right. Hannah, remember Mother's roses and how Tessa insisted we dig them up when we left the farm?"

Hannah nodded. "She's worked so hard to keep them alive so we each could have one of the bushes."

"We owe her an apology." Charlotte stood and shook out her dress. "But I'm afraid it will have to wait. If I'm going to be home when Alice Ann gets home from school, then I need to leave."

"Then go, dear. You can speak to Tessa later." Aunt Sam walked over to Charlotte and took hold of her hands. "You two have blessed that child of yours more than she'll ever know."

"Adopting her has been my greatest joy, but she might be the only child we have."

Sam patted the back of Charlotte's hand. "Give it time. I'm sure a baby will come."

"We've been married for two years. That seems like plenty of time."

Hannah eased a sleeping Ellie down onto the divan and whispered, "What does Joel say? He's the doctor."

"He said as advanced as medicine is today, doctors still don't have all the answers. But he also reminds me that God does. So we keep praying. If I'm not with child by the end of the summer, though, I'm going to speak to him again about adopting a sibling or two for Alice Ann. She's already seven, and I want her to have sisters. I can't imagine growing up without them." She smiled at Hannah, then turned to Sam. "I'll speak to Tessa tomorrow and see what we can do to help her."

"I can go up now," Hannah offered.

Sam shook her head. "No, I think Tessa might need some time to calm down. Besides, actions speak louder than words. Perhaps you two can come up with a way to demonstrate your support."

Charlotte kissed Sam's cheek and hugged her sister before leaving the parlor. After Sam was certain she was out of earshot, she turned to Hannah. "When are you going to tell her your news?"

"I can't. Not yet." Hannah placed her hand over her abdomen. "I can't bear to see the disappointment on her face."

"She loves you. She'll be happy for you—in time."

"It's not fair, Aunt Sam."

"Life seldom is." Sam glanced at the photograph of her husband beneath the rounded glass of a mahogany frame. How she missed him, but God had filled her life with a new family. Lincoln and Hannah, Joel and Charlotte, and of course, the effervescent Tessa.

She cupped Hannah's cheek. "But as a woman whom God did not bless with her own children, I can assure you that you can come to love those not born to you as your very own."

"Thank you, and I feel the same."

"But you need to tell your sister. Eventually, news like this has a way of making itself obvious, and the fact that you've kept it a secret will hurt her all the more."

"I'm sure you're right. I simply need to find the right time." Hannah sighed. "Please don't tell Tessa yet either."

"I won't, but if anyone can sniff out when someone is keeping something from her, you know it's our Tessa."

The long, mournful face stared back at Reese with accusing eyes. "What? You need to wait your turn. This is my supper." Reese forked the last bite of pork chop and tossed the bone to the blood-hound, Lafayette.

"You spoil him." Mrs. Baxter, the owner of the boardinghouse, took his empty plate. "He's more your dog than mine now, you know? Someday when you leave, you'll have to take him with you."

Reese stood and grabbed the remaining dishes. "I'm never leaving you, Mrs. Baxter." He gave her a wink.

"Cheeky young man."

A ruckus in the foyer drew their attention, and Mrs. Baxter frowned. "Dear me, it sounds like the Henderson boys are home, but they must be in a sorry state."

Peachy. Those two had been nothing but trouble since they'd moved in, but Mrs. Baxter, God bless her, believed they'd been put on her doorstep for a reason, and she intended to save their sorry souls.

Reese put a hand on her arm. "You should send them both packing. This is the second time they've come home like this."

"But at least they joined us for evening prayers the other day. What if God sent them here for a reason?"

Reese couldn't argue with that, nor could he dissuade the kindly older woman. She might seem like she was made of marshmallows, but Reese had learned she was as tough as leather deep down.

They both jolted at the sound of glass breaking. Lafayette raised his head and barked.

"Stay here. I'll see to them," Reese said.

"Reese, you're a good man."

"God just puts me in the right places at the right times." He flashed her a smile. "At least that's what you've been telling me."

With a set of garden plans once again tucked beneath her arm, Tessa left the house early and headed for Como Park. Mr. Nussbaumer was not going to turn her down without at least taking a look at her work, and she'd keep coming back every day until he took her seriously. She had to secure this position. It was the only way to keep her secret.

The streetcar ride gave her time to put her plan together. She would go to his office and introduce herself again. After a few minutes of park flattery, she'd get down to business. If he turned her out today, she'd return tomorrow. Eventually, he'd look at her work either out of curiosity or to be rid of her, and then he'd see the promise in her garden designs.

She'd be the first to admit she still had much to learn, but her professors had praised her work and encouraged her to continue— right up until that unfortunate curfew breach. And when she finally was an employed horticulturist, people—especially her sisters— would start to take her seriously. No one would ever have to know what really happened.

A spring breeze kissed her cheeks as she stepped off the streetcar. The paved walkways throughout Como Park made traversing the rolling hills quite easy. Despite being tempted to stop and take in some of the current displays, she made a beeline for the park office. There'd be time enough for looking around once she secured the position.

"Whoa!" The gardener from yesterday stepped in her path. Mr. King, wasn't it?

"Excuse me, Mr. King, but I'm headed to speak with Mr. Nussbaumer."

"Call me Reese, and that's what I was afraid of." He tugged his cap out of his back pocket and pulled it in place. "What's your plan?"

"I don't think that's any of your business, Mr. King." She had no intention of becoming familiar enough with this gardener to call him by his given name. Reese? A different name, but she liked it. At least his parents showed some creativity. She'd met enough Johns, Walters, and Franks to last a lifetime.

The man nodded. "It may not be any of my business, but you seem like a smart, resourceful young lady, and given that, I figure you're willing to accept the counsel of those who might know Mr. Nussbaumer better than yourself."

"If you think because I'm not a man, I should stop trying to work here, you've got the wrong idea."

"Are you finished?" He smiled, revealing slight dimples like parentheses around his mouth. A jolt of anger fired through her. He was too cute, and way too distracting.

"No, I'm not a bit finished." She pointed to him with her rolled-up plans. "I am not going away until Mr. Nussbaumer sees what I can do, and no one—and that includes you, Mr. King—is going to stop me."

"I have no intention of stopping you."

"And I'm going to come back every day until he looks at these." She jabbed him in the chest with the plans.

He snatched the roll and held it aloft. Tessa swung at it, but her feeble attempt did not yield results. Short of kicking him in the shin, she had little recourse than to wait for him to give back the plans—and then she could make him wish he'd never touched them in the first place.

"You cad!" She crossed her arms over her chest. "Taking a lady's belongings is beyond ungentlemanly. I insist you return them this instant."

"After I look at them." He lowered the papers but kept a firm hold. "I want to see your work. If your plans are any good, then I'll see what I can do to help you get Mr. Nussbaumer's attention."

"You want to help?"

"That's what I've been trying to tell you." He tapped her nose with the cylinder.

She batted the plans away. "But you said Mr. Nussbaumer wouldn't . . ."

"Never mind that. Let's go have a seat and take a look at these, Miss Gregory."

"Tessa." She fell in step beside him. Her sisters would be mortified. "You can call me Tessa."

They stopped at a walled planter. Mr. King—Reese—unrolled

the plans and spread them on the bricks. He leaned over them, securing the sides with his arms.

Tessa held her breath. If she couldn't impress this gardener, one of Mr. Nussbaumer's underlings, how would she ever impress the master gardener himself?

Without a word, Reese moved on to the next page. After what seemed like an hour, he finally turned to the last set of plans. Still, he said nothing.

Tessa couldn't wait any longer. "Well?"

He rolled up the plans and turned to her. "There's only one thing I can say, Tessa."

Like a cactus, disappointment pricked her. Now what would she do?

"These are amazing. You have the ability to look at a garden like a blank canvas, but . . ."

"But?"

"Mr. Nussbaumer still won't take you seriously. He's too old-fashioned about what women should do."

Anger threatened to erupt, but she held it in check. "That's not fair."

"No, it's not." He paused and seemed to study her for a while. "But I've got an idea. I said if you had talent, I'd help you, and I will, but you're going to have to trust me."

"Trust you?" Her father always said you could tell if someone was trustworthy by looking in their eyes. The famous detective Allan Pinkerton said that too. She gazed into Reese's blue eyes and noticed the color matched the faded denim trousers he wore. Mesmerizing. She blinked. *Focus.* Yes, he had pretty eyes, but was he trustworthy? Could she trust this man with her future? What if he had ulterior motives?

If she made the wrong choice, what would her sisters say when she had one more thing to explain?

4

Reese was insane. Somehow being around this fiery little redhead had made him completely loco. He looked past her toward the mosaic garden and thought of how many hours he had spent working on the carpet bedding display. Sure, it lacked Tessa's artistic flair, but Mr. Nussbaumer had expressed pleasure with his work. After that, Reese had been given even more responsibilities, and then finally he'd been offered the chance to prove himself. Some had even started to refer to him as Mr. Nussbaumer's second in command. So what had possessed him to offer to help Tessa Gregory? He could be risking everything.

While his mind screamed for him to withdraw the offer, his mouth had other ideas. "What do you say, Tessa?"

"I'd like to hear your plan before I fully commit. It seems only sensible."

He nodded. Smart girl. "All right. Here's what I'm thinking . . ."

For the next hour, Reese had Tessa walk with him. As he performed his morning duties, they discussed his ideas, which entailed using Tessa's plans on an area Mr. Nussbaumer had recently assigned him to create a garden of his choosing. When the work was done and Mr. Nussbaumer seemed pleased, he'd give Tessa the credit, thus opening the door for her work to be taken seriously by the German park superintendent.

Tessa agreed to the plan but insisted he allow her to come help plant the garden. Keeping her presence a secret would be quite difficult, but he had to admit having a working companion would be a nice change. Seldom were the other park gardeners assigned to the same area, and when they were, he usually had to work with Nels, a man who seemed intent on making himself look good by pointing out every fault he could find in Reese's work. But what would Mr. Nussbaumer do if he found out Reese was letting Tessa work at Como?

"Um, Reese, I think that hole is deep enough." Tessa's voice broke through his thoughts.

He leaned on the handle of his shovel. Yep, she was right. This little bush didn't need the crater he'd dug. She reached for a gunny sack filled with soil, and Reese laid a hand on her arm. "Let's get one thing straight. I don't mind if you dig in the dirt and plant things to your heart's content, but as long as I'm around, you don't need to be lifting anything heavier than a rosebush. Agreed?"

"I could manage."

"I'm sure you could, but it doesn't feel right. Give me that, okay?"

She grinned. "I'll do my best."

"Your best not to carry things or your best not to let me catch you doing it?"

She shrugged. "Guess you'll have to wait and see. Can we start now?"

"Not until tomorrow." He glanced at her fancy outfit. "And I hope you have something more appropriate for a lady gardener."

"Naturally I have several dresses for that purpose."

"Dresses?" If the sharp tan jacket and skirt she was wearing were any indication, she'd stick out in an upturned garden like a rosebud in a pigpen. He wouldn't even start on the lavish hat with a brim wider than her shoulders. And how on earth did she do up all those buttons on the front? There had to be at least thirty of the little things all lined in a straight row from the hem to the—

She cleared her throat. Good grief. Had he been staring?

"I have serviceable skirts and shirtwaists to work in, if you must know."

"Uh, yeah. That'll have to do, I suppose." Many of the girls who worked as teachers, clerks, switchboard operators, and stenographers wore black skirts and white shirts, so the other gardeners might simply look past her and think she was visiting Como on her lunch or a break. "The hardest part will be to keep your role here a secret. If the wrong person sees you working in the garden, they might say something to Mr. Nussbaumer and that will ruin our plans, so you'll have to be on your guard all the time."

"I guess I'll have to work incognito. Mr. Pinkerton said—"

"As in Allan Pinkerton, the famous detective?"

She nodded and placed her hand on her heart. "'A friend to honesty and a foe to crime.' Anyway, he said working incognito is a detective's most difficult challenge."

"We aren't solving a train robbery, but I'd agree." Tessa Gregory certainly had a flare for the dramatic. "We'll just have to be careful."

A smile bloomed on her face. "It will be a grand adventure, Reese. I can feel it. You'll see."

Somehow he doubted that. "We'll start at nine sharp. Meet me on the hill I showed you, where the new garden is to be planted."

"I'll be there, and I promise, I won't let anyone see me." She pulled her enormous hat down until it nearly covered her eyes. "Incognito, see?"

If he had to guess, Tessa Gregory would have a hard time becoming invisible. This idea was doomed. "I wish I knew a better way to keep you hidden, Tessa, but I don't."

"Don't look so glum. I'll think of something. I always do. A grand adventure, remember?"

He wanted to believe her, and looking at the glint in her hazel eyes, he almost did.

Almost.

Nine times out of ten, Tessa loved shopping at the Golden Rule almost as much as attending a moving picture show, but today her stomach quivered as she entered the unfamiliar boys' department. Like she'd promised Reese, she'd come up with a better way to hide—to disguise herself completely.

She eyed the trousers neatly stacked in wooden cubby holes. On the other side of the room, knickers were stacked in a similar manner. Which should she get? Only younger boys wore knickers, but they might fit her frame better. How would she figure out what size she wore without tipping off the salesman?

She fingered the fabric on a rack of suits—tweeds, worsteds, serges, and cashmeres. None would work for a serious gardener.

"May I help you, miss?" The salesman straightened a jacket on the hanger.

"I need a pair of heavy trousers."

He looked down his long narrow nose, where his spectacles balanced. "Not for yourself, of course."

"No, uh . . . for my brother. My younger brother." If she had a brother, she would surely purchase clothes for him. It wasn't her fault God had only blessed her with sisters.

"In that case, I think you'll want to look over here, where we stock the work pants and overalls."

She followed him around the corner. He gestured to the wall of dark blue, black, gray, and brown work trousers. "What size is your brother's waist?"

"His waist?" She bit her lip. What had Madam Dubois measured her waist at last time she'd had a dress made? "Well, he's about my size."

"I see." The salesman seemed to be trying to guess her measurement. "Is he taller than you?"

"No, about the same height too."

"Truly? That's unusual." The salesman took a step back and rubbed his chin. "Then, I'm guessing his inseam would be about twenty-nine inches."

"Inseam?"

The salesman's cheeks colored. "Miss, is your mother here? Perhaps shopping in another department? Mothers usually have a good idea about such things as measurements."

"No. My mother is gone." There. That was the truth. "She died of influenza."

"Please accept my condolences." He moved to the shelf and pulled out three pairs of trousers. He held up the dark blue first. "This is a nine-ounce York denim."

Tessa took the pants and held them up to her body. She wouldn't look like a girl in these—except for her top half.

"Are you certain these are for your brother?" The salesman seemed to be studying her. "We don't sell trousers for young women to wear. It's simply not appropriate. Our store owner frowns on such sales."

A prickle of anger nudged her, but she tempered it. This man couldn't possibly know if the trousers were for her, and besides, what business was it of the department store if she wore the pants or not? Aunt Sam had been wearing bloomers for years and was always praising them for their comfort. As of late, she'd taken to wearing cropped pants, tall boots, and a long jacket for motoring about.

Tessa smoothed the velvet lapels of her fitted jacket. "I'm offended. Do I look like the kind of girl who would go around in a pair of work trousers?"

"Pardon me, miss, but those suffrage girls are everywhere these days."

Tessa pointed to the black trousers. "What can you tell me about those?"

The man ran his long fingers over the fabric as if trying to decide if he should continue the sale. "These fine pants are called Texas Ranger Overalls. They are made of ten-ounce duck, and they're very sturdy. I'm assuming your brother is doing some farm work, so these pants would be perfect. Or he might like a pair of these bibbed overalls. A lot of men like having the bib in the front so there's no need for suspenders."

"Yes, those would be perfect." The bib would hide her most obvious feminine part. "I'll take two pairs—one blue and one gray. Please charge them to my account."

"And what's the name?"

"Tessa Gregory. My name is under my Aunt Sam's—Mrs. Samantha Phillips. She lives on Summit Avenue." Tessa would have to pay Aunt Sam back as soon as she could.

"Yes, miss." Clearly impressed with the address, the salesman grinned and picked up the clothes. "And you'll probably need some shirts to go with those. May I suggest the blue and white percale over here?"

"Excellent. And I'll take that white linen one as well." She pointed to her selection. "In my—I mean his—size."

The salesman's brow furled. Oh no. He'd caught her slip. Would he turn her away now?

His furl lessened, and he looked at her with a twinkle in his eyes. "I'm certain your *brother* will require work boots too. We have a nice selection in the corner. If you'd like, you could go over and select a pair while I write these up."

So a pair of boots was the price of his silence? She had shoes that would have served her well, but the boots would be a small price to pay. To her great relief, the salesman ignored her while she tried on a few pairs. After she selected a soft kidskin pair, she slipped her own shoes back on, found an appropriate straw hat to buy as well, and carried her purchases to the counter.

The salesman's eyes widened. "Excellent choices, Miss Gregory. Excellent indeed." He wrapped up the shoes and boxed the hat before tying the parcels together. "I'll have your packages delivered this afternoon, and I do hope your *brother* doesn't work too hard."

She smiled. "Nothing too strenuous. Just a little gardening."

And a little subterfuge. A thrill shot through her as she imagined Reese's face when she arrived dressed in her bibbed overalls and straw hat. Maybe he wouldn't even recognize her.

Cheese and crackers, this was going to be fun.

5

Reese lifted the handles of the supply-laden wheelbarrow and directed it toward the area where he'd be implementing Tessa's design.

He stifled a yawn. No wonder he was tired this morning. He'd pored over the plans late into the night. Tessa truly had a gift. As with Mr. Nussbaumer, the garden was her canvas, and the plants she'd chosen were her paints and textures. If only he possessed that creative ability, then maybe he could be as successful as his father.

But that wasn't his forte. Hard work was his gift. With renewed vigor, he pushed the wheelbarrow up a steady incline and left the path. He reached the area and looked around. Where was Tessa? As eager as she had been yesterday, he'd imagined she would be there before him.

He studied the area, allowing the plans Tessa had created and he had studied to take shape on the empty land before him. In the end, he'd selected her design for an Arts and Crafts garden. She'd included a nice selection of flower groupings in intense colors. Most of the flowers needed were already propagating in the greenhouse.

Her design featured separate garden rooms, which would give each area of the garden a different feel. The little areas, partitioned off a larger garden, would have different schemes. Some would have ornamental additions, some water features, and some hard landscaping.

He spotted a boy pilfering through his wheelbarrow. "Hey! What do you think you're doing?"

The boy looked up.

Only he wasn't a boy.

"Tessa?"

She stepped back and hooked her thumbs in the buckles of her bib overalls. "So, what do you think? I told you I'd think of something. "

"I must admit I'm a little dumbfounded." Reese scratched his forehead. What kind of young lady went around in overalls? "I know I said you had to remain hidden as much as possible, but I didn't mean this. What would your mother say if she saw you in that getup?"

"I can assure you my mother will not say a thing. My sisters, on the other hand"—she flipped her right wrist—"might have a few words for my costume choice. Then again, they seem to have a few words about everything I do."

"Is that so?" He did nothing to disguise the sarcasm in his voice. But could this work? He took in her appearance. From the straw hat on her head to the boots on her feet, Tessa Gregory had transformed. From a distance she'd pass for a boy, but up close—she was still all lovely young lady. A wave of protectiveness swept over him. "How did you get here? Did you ride a streetcar like that?"

"Heavens, no. I had my Aunt Sam's driver bring me."

"Your aunt has a driver?" He sucked in his breath. Would the surprises never end with this girl?

"Yes, his name is Henry and he's worked for her for years. Since I'm living with her right now, it wasn't any problem."

"You live with your aunt, who has a driver?"

"Yes, I just said that. And yesterday you said no one could know I was a girl"—she spun in a circle—"so I thought this should take care of it. Problem solved."

Was it that easy? It was true most of the other gardeners wouldn't give her a second look if they passed by, but what kind of man would allow a young lady to continue this charade? Sure, he didn't cotton to keeping women "in their place," but was this going too far? Still, she was so excited, and the itch he had to get started told him her exuberance was contagious.

Before he had a chance to decide if he should allow it, she tugged work gloves out of her back pocket—heavy leather ones, not pretty white ones—and slipped her hands inside. "Ready to get started, Mr. King? Time is wasting."

Tessa held a wooden stake in place as Reese pounded it into the ground, then he stepped back and surveyed their handiwork. Already they had the plots staked, and they'd removed the grassy sod from the border areas and marked where they'd build raised planters. She could picture them spilling over with a rainbow of blooms by summer.

The more she thought of this project, the harder her heart pounded. Even though she'd worked many hours in a garden, this was the first time she was part of transforming a large green space into one of her own creations.

As she worked alongside Reese, more and more questions formed about him. Why didn't it bother him to work alongside a woman? What kind of man was he? Perhaps the bigger question was why was he willing to risk so much for her? If given a chance, she aimed to get some of her questions answered.

"We'll bring the hand cultivator over after lunch." Reese's hammer dropped with a thunk into the wheelbarrow. "It'll take most of the afternoon to till the soil, so if you want to call it a day, I can do that myself."

"No, thank you. I'm staying with you every step of the way. From now on, you're stuck with me." Even though it was only May, the noonday sun and the work had warmed her cheeks. She could almost feel the freckles popping out. She removed her hat and fanned her face.

"Then let's go eat."

"Is there a place I can purchase lunch?" She glanced down at her clothes. "Oh wait. Never mind. I guess I can't do that."

He chuckled. "I brought lunch for both of us. Nothing fancy. I hope that's okay with you."

"Bless you, Reese King! I'm starving." Her cheeks grew hot. "Pardon me. I think it's the hunger speaking."

"I knew the concessions weren't open yet for the season." He grinned. "Why don't you go sit down in the shade, and I'll be back in a few minutes with our food."

Tessa found a spot beneath an oak tree, brushed some acorns aside, and sat down. She watched Reese go and was struck by the way he carried himself. He walked briskly, like a man who knew what he wanted, but his relaxed broad shoulders showed how at ease he was with this park.

He had certainly worked hard, but he'd said little. Her questions about him resurfaced. What was Reese's story?

Despite the rough bark pressing against her back, Tessa closed her eyes. The morning's hard work had left her more tired than she expected. A few minutes of rest would do wonders for restoring her energy.

"Tessa?"

A deep voice stirred her. Where was she? Her eyes flew open and Reese came into view. Embarrassment streamed through her. How could she have fallen asleep?

"Did you have a nice nap?" He passed her a waxed paper–wrapped sandwich. "It's egg salad. I'm not much of a cook, but it's one of the five things I've mastered. Do you mind if I say grace?"

"Please do." His sincere prayer added another thing for her to consider about Reese. Had he offered to help her because of his convictions?

Tessa unwrapped her sandwich and took a bite. His egg salad was almost as good as Charlotte's, but she wouldn't dare tell her sister that. "This is delicious."

"Thanks." He blotted his mouth with a napkin and began to discuss what they'd accomplished and what their next steps would be in creating the garden. "It'll take us at least two weeks to get it all set up. I have some other obligations here at the park I'll have to see to besides working on this."

"Are there other things you need to work on today? I could help."

"No, no other jobs today. I did them before we got started." He pulled two apples from his sack and handed one to her. "I can see questions are running amok in your head. What do you want to know?"

"Mr. Pinkerton would not be impressed if he knew I was easy to read."

"You mentioned Allan Pinkerton yesterday. What's with the references to him?"

"I went through a time when I considered becoming a Pinkerton detective."

"You would have been good at that, I bet." He bit into his apple with a loud crunch.

"You think so?" Tessa rubbed her fruit with the napkin until it became glossy. "Most people thought it was silly."

"It sounds dangerous. Gardening is much safer, but somehow I don't think that was the reason you turned to it."

She took a bite and then dabbed the juice from her lips. "I've always loved gardening. My mother and I used to do it together."

"Used to?"

"When I was fourteen, she and my father died." She went on to explain how they'd lost the farm and how her sister Hannah had had to drop out of law school and become a switchboard operator to provide for them. "But when we left the farm, I took three of my mother's rosebushes, and I'm happy to say all three are thriving."

She swallowed the emotion clogging her throat and changed the subject. "Reese, have you always wanted to be a gardener?"

"You might say I was born with a hoe in my hand." He glanced toward the garden they were planting. "My father is the park commissioner for Chicago."

"Samuel King?"

He nodded. "And he's almost as well-known as Fred Nussbaumer. Maybe gardening runs in my blood."

"Why don't you work for him?"

"Sometimes a man needs to make a name on his own. I don't want other people to think I'm successful because I'm related to the man in charge. I want them to think I'm successful because of my own work."

"Does Mr. Nussbaumer know about your father?"

"Sure." He tossed his apple core into the bushes. "I told him from the start, but he said I'd have to prove myself, and he's certainly meant it."

"He's a hard man to please?"

"He's fair, but his expectations are high. He's an artist—like you."

"And you're not?"

"Mr. Nussbaumer sees the big picture." He stood and pulled out his pocket watch. "Time to get back to work—unless you need another nap."

"You just try to keep up." She jumped up and hurried toward the cultivator Reese had brought.

Rough beneath her ungloved hands, the wooden handles bit into her skin as she shoved the cultivator in deep and directed it down the path. The metal wheel on the front creaked. The tiller turned the soil, filling the air with the earthy scent of dirt. Expecting Reese to stop her after a few yards, she glanced back only to find him seated, his back against a tree and his ivy cap down over his eyes.

He pushed it up and grinned at her. "You want to do it? Go right ahead. It's my turn for a nap."

No one had ever left Tessa speechless.

Until today.

Reese King was so different from every other man she'd ever met. He seemed too good to be true. Maybe she'd have to put some of her sleuthing to work and uncover some of the dirt on him.

Strong hands suddenly gripped her shoulders. She jolted and grabbed for her hat to keep it from flying off. She turned to find Reese, his jovial expression gone. "Reese, what's wrong? You frightened me."

Reese inclined his head toward the sidewalk. "Hide, Tessa. Now."

6

Tessa looked in the direction he indicated and gasped. "Oh no. I think he's already seen me."

"Then go over there and start digging in the far corner. Keep your back to him, understand?"

She nodded and started to race away.

He jogged alongside her. "Don't run like a girl. Go slower. Stomp a little." She did as she was told, and he turned to the approaching park superintendent. Would their ruse be uncovered already?

"Mr. Nussbaumer, a pleasure to see you this afternoon."

"*Ja*, and a fine afternoon it is." The man lumbered up the incline. "Your Arts and Crafts garden is already staked. *Gut*. *Gut*." He stopped and glanced toward Tessa. "Who do you have helping you? William?"

"No, William is tending the Japanese Garden. This is a boy from the neighborhood who wants to learn about gardening. I thought the extra hands would be helpful. He's volunteering to work, and I'm teaching him along the way."

"*Gut* idea, Reese." He nodded toward the garden stakes.

Reese glanced at Tessa, who lowered her head even further. He pointed to the center of the garden, causing Mr. Nussbaumer to turn away from her. "There will be a picnic area and a pond. Do you want to see the plans?"

"No, I trust you. If I did not, you would be pulling weeds with William in the Japanese Garden." He chuckled and headed back to the paved sidewalk. "It's *gut* to see your progress. Even with help, this will take some time to complete, but I must admit, I am anxious to see the finished garden."

Reese fell in step beside him. "Thank you, sir, for the opportunity. I pray I don't disappoint you."

Mr. Nussbaumer waved his words away. "You've earned the chance to prove yourself, but you realize this will be your only one. *Gut* luck to you, Reese. And by the way, we'll want to put the banana trees out next Thursday. Perhaps your young apprentice would like to help."

"I'll speak to him." He watched the park commissioner trek down the hill, then turned to Tessa, who remained with her back to him. He shook his head. That had been close. Too close. Guilt nudged him. Keeping this secret about his "boy" apprentice was, in essence, lying to Mr. Nussbaumer.

Maybe this risk was too great and the cost too high. One chance to prove himself and he was spending it on Tessa Gregory and her garden plans. But he could never tell her no—especially now. He'd seen a damsel in distress and rode in to save her.

Who was he kidding? Tessa was no damsel in distress, and he needed her as much as she did him.

Dirt beneath her fingernails, smudges on her face, and clumps of hair having escaped her straw hat—and Tessa had never been happier. She chuckled to herself, and Henry glanced back at her from his driver's seat.

"Something wrong, miss?"

"No, Henry. I'm thinking about what my sisters would say if they could see me right now." For a week, she'd spent her days with Reese working on the Arts and Crafts garden. Things were really taking shape. They had only one section left to cultivate. After that was done, Reese said he'd sneak her into the hothouses to help pick out plants.

Henry pulled into the driveway. "It looks to me as if you might find out what at least one of them might say. That's your brother-in-law's automobile, I believe."

Tessa moaned. Henry was right. And if Lincoln was there, most likely he'd brought Hannah too. If she hurried upstairs and changed, perhaps no one would be the wiser to her apparel.

Henry opened the door for her. How strange it felt to step out of the eye-catching Oldsmobile Touring car in her overalls. After thanking him, she slipped inside, every footfall so soft it was as if she were walking on some of Charlotte's whipped cream. Voices came from inside the parlor. She recognized Hannah's, Lincoln's, and Aunt Sam's, but there seemed to be two unfamiliar male voices present as well. Peachy.

She eased past the parlor doors and laid her hand on the end of the banister. *Please don't let them hear the creaky first step.*

"Tessa, is that you?" Hannah called from the parlor. "Come into the parlor. We have someone we want you to meet."

Oh, cheese and crackers. Why did things always happen to her like this? "Let me go freshen up first. Then I'll be right down."

"There's no need." Hannah's voice was closer. She was headed her way.

"Hannah, let your sister have a few moments." Aunt Sam to the rescue. Bless her soul.

"But . . ." Hannah stepped into the hallway and gasped. She hurried to the steps and hissed, "Where is your dress?"

"In my armoire, and if you let me go, I'll put it on." She glanced at her dirty fingers. "I've been working in the dirt."

"More like wallowing." Hannah put her hand on Tessa's back and called to the others, "We'll be right back. I'm going to help Tessa get ready for dinner."

"Dinner? With whom?"

"Senator Ferrell." Hannah gave her a little shove to get her moving. "And I'm trying to help you make your dream come true, but you're about to ruin everything."

Thirty minutes later, Tessa appeared, scrubbed and appropriately dressed for dinner with someone of the senator's stature. Hannah had chosen her dress while she bathed—a sapphire-blue gown with a black lace overlay. It hadn't taken her long to pin Tessa's curls in place with a beaded comb, but she'd used every moment to lecture on how the senator should be treated.

"When the time is right, I'll bring up the subject of gardening. Understand?" Hannah squeezed Tessa's hand. "Please be quiet about it until then. I truly want to do this for you."

Together they made a grand entrance into the parlor. Lincoln joined his wife, then introduced Tessa to Senator Ferrell and his grandson Edward.

"I've already called for dinner to be served. Shall we?" Aunt Sam took the senator's arm when he offered it to her. Lincoln and Hannah filed in second, leaving Edward and Tessa to walk in together.

Tessa wasn't surprised she was also seated with the young man. If she had to guess, he was about her age. But where was Mrs. Ferrell?

Once their plates had been filled with the entrée, chicken à la king served over rice, small talk was dismissed in favor of earnest conversation.

"So, Senator." Aunt Sam set her fork down. "The Minnesota Women's Suffrage Association will again be putting an amendment before you granting women the right to vote. Can we count on your support?"

Tessa sighed. There it went—any chances she had for her dreams coming true. Whatever Hannah had meant by that.

The senator chuckled. "Even if it passes the senate, it will have to pass the house."

"I well remember that was what happened in 1893 when it passed the senate, thirty-two to nineteen, but failed in the house. However, I'm asking if you, sir, will be voting in favor of women's suffrage—as so many of your contemporaries have agreed to do."

He leaned back in his chair. "And you've probably contacted each one of them personally, haven't you, Samantha?"

Hannah sucked in her breath, and Tessa met her gaze. He'd used Aunt Sam's Christian name, which was hardly proper.

It was Aunt Sam's turn to laugh. "Don't look so scandalized. James and I have been friends for years." She patted his arm. "We've had this discussion hundreds of times, and finally I believe I've won him over."

He covered her hand with his own. "You have indeed."

Beside Tessa, Edward shifted in his seat. Was he embarrassed by his grandfather? Tessa hadn't been paying the young man his due attention as a dinner companion. "Mr. Ferrell, do your interests lie in politics like your grandfather?"

"Not really. I'm a law student at Drake, and I'll be returning for my senior year in the fall. I also have some other interests and hobbies I'd like to pursue, but for the summer, I'll be serving as a law clerk."

"With Lincoln?"

"No, I'm with another firm." He took a sip from his cup. "And you? What do you enjoy doing?"

"Garden—" The word slipped out before she could pull it back. She looked at Hannah. Had she heard her?

Hannah smiled. "Yes, our Tessa is studying horticulture at the University of Minnesota. She's very talented."

"Is that so?" The senator forked another piece of chicken. "Just today I was meeting with Fred Nussbaumer. Do you know our city's park superintendent? He has a grand new idea."

"Are you at liberty to tell us about it?" Hannah asked.

He shrugged. "I suppose it won't hurt. He'd like to build a botanical conservatory. It's like a gigantic glass house for plants. He says San Francisco has one, also New York and Baltimore."

"Oh, there are many more. One of the most famous is in Palm House at the Kew Gardens in London." Tessa's heart pounded. Did Reese know about this?

"I think that's the same one he mentioned modeling it after."

Tessa clasped her hands together in her lap to keep from applauding. "It's a marvelous idea. When can they begin building it?"

The senator held up his hand. "Hold on a minute, Miss Gregory. Fred's been talking about this for a while, but he's yet to persuade enough people on the park commission to get the funding. It's an expensive endeavor. He'll need to garner a great deal of support from influential community members."

"I see." Her hopes sank. She glanced at Hannah, who lifted her eyebrows in a knowing manner.

That was it. That was what Hannah was trying to do by inviting the senator here. If she could gather the kind of support Mr. Nussbaumer needed, maybe he'd take a second look at her as a candidate to work at Como Park.

Thoughts raced through her mind. Because of Aunt Sam, she had a myriad of wealthy contacts on whom she could call. If she used her acting and persuasive skills, surely she could garner their interest in such an altruistic endeavor. It would mean she'd have to spend a great deal of time hobnobbing with their neighbors.

There she had it. A new goal. Gardener by day and deal maker by evening. This grand adventure was only getting better.

As soon as the senator and his grandson left, Tessa wrapped her arms around Hannah. "Thank you! Mr. Nussbaumer will never be able to turn me down once I've helped him secure the support he needs for his conservatory."

Lincoln laughed from his seat in one of the parlor chairs. "And how do you plan to garner that support, dear Tessa?"

"Since I've been home, I think I've received nearly a dozen invitations a week to join various functions. I may have to begin attending a few of them."

"Are you serious?" Hannah took a seat in the other parlor chair. "From the time Aunt Sam started sending you to finishing school, you've avoided those engagements. If I recall, you said the girls were stuffy and condescending. You said you didn't feel like you fit in."

"That doesn't mean I don't know how to act like them if I have to." She tipped her chin up and waved her hand dismissively. "This is one performance for which I've been well trained."

Hannah sighed. "Tessa, you're too old for games. If you're going to go to these functions, be yourself. Don't pretend to be anything you aren't."

Why couldn't her sister simply embrace her idea? Would she never realize she was an adult now?

Any further discussion was cut short by Aunt Sam's return to the parlor. After a short while, Hannah and Lincoln said their goodbyes.

Aunt Sam kissed Tessa's cheek, said good night, and left for her own bedchamber.

Tessa flopped on the divan and picked up the latest issue of *Redbook* magazine. She read the same column twice because Hannah's words kept plaguing her thoughts. She'd said to be herself. But who was she? Sometimes Tessa wasn't so sure.

Fitting in seemed hard everywhere right now—at the university, with her family, in the park, and in social circles where she should have felt at ease. Playacting was simply easier. She would take on a role, immerse herself in the character, and become someone everyone could admire and respect.

Including Mr. Nussbaumer and her sisters.

And it would start tomorrow.

With a Remington Pump pressed against his shoulder, Reese eyed the cloud in the sky and took a steadying breath. "Pull!"

The trap snapped and a clay pigeon vaulted into his line of sight. Lightning fast, he lifted the barrel of the shotgun and fired. He grinned at the faint familiar sound like the ring of bell, signaling a hit, and watched the pieces rain down.

Nineteen for twenty. Not too bad. Not perfect either.

He turned to his puller and teammate. "You're up, Erik."

They switched spots, and Reese loaded the trap with the clay disc while Erik Swenhaugen readied his shotgun.

Reese looked at his Norwegian friend. The robust man would have made a good Viking. They'd met at the Saint Paul Rod and Gun Club two years ago after he'd moved to the area, and had been fast friends ever since.

"You ready?" Reese grabbed the cord of the trap.

"Don't rush me." Erik cocked his gun. "Pull!"

Erik missed and the disk fell to the ground. He hit the next three, then missed another. In the end, he came in at seventeen for twenty shots.

"Not bad. I wish the trap boys weren't busy. I'd like to try my hand at doubles." Reese picked up his shotgun and glanced toward Erik's nine-year-old son Kristoffer, who was working as one of the trap boys. Several of the other club members had yet to complete their practice, so he motioned Erik toward the clubhouse door.

Erik stopped. "What's Kristoffer doing out there?"

Reese followed his line of sight and caught a glimpse of the boy skirting around the end of the field. Did he think he could get a start on retrieving the clay pigeons? Didn't he hear the men still shooting?

"Hold your fire!"

7

Reese raced toward Kristoffer, his heart thundering in his ears, while Erik barreled down the line, shouting to his fellow club members over the din of the shotgun peals. Most lowered their shotguns immediately, but a few seemed slow to catch on.

Pausing at the end of the line, Reese glanced at the men to see that all had lowered their weapons, then ran onto the field. He grabbed Kristoffer by his shirt collar. "Why are you out here?"

The boy swung his arms and tried to wrench himself free. "Let go of me!"

Reese gave him a firm shake. "I asked you why you're out here on the field."

"I was picking up pigeons." Kristoffer squirmed some more. "Now let me go."

"Not until your dad gets to talk to you." Reese hauled the young man back behind the firing line.

Erik met them and clamped a beefy hand on his son's shoulder. "Thanks, Reese. I'll take it from here."

"He's all yours." Reese stepped back and leaned against the wall of the club. From this short distance, he could easily hear the exchange between father and son. He chuckled. Who was he kidding? Probably half the county could hear it. Kristoffer protested that he hadn't thought he was in any danger because the men were done shooting on his end. With his booming voice, Erik made sure his son was well educated to the contrary.

How would Reese's father have handled such an experience? He was not a man given to displays of anger or affection, but he managed to express his approval or disapproval in quiet ways. A frown or scowl spoke volumes, and a pat on the shoulder could make Reese's day, but something like this? Reese could only imagine how his father might have reacted.

When the men began to file into the clubhouse, Reese followed and took two Cokes from the cooler. He returned with the drinks in time to see Erik release Kristoffer to finish his work on the field. Reese popped off the caps of the Cokes and passed one to Erik.

He took a long swig from the bottle. The cold liquid hit the spot. "It was a childish mistake."

"It could have gotten him killed." Still red faced and out of breath, Erik seemed to be fighting his churning emotions. "*Uff da*, my Sonja will never forgive me."

"You wouldn't have to tell her."

"And then when it slipped someday?" He swallowed some of his Coke. "No, Reese, secrets always have a way of coming out. It's best to be honest from the beginning—especially with the woman you love." He sighed. "But I am guessing tonight will not be a good one at our house."

"Makes me glad I don't have a wife and children."

"You don't know what you're missing." Erik chuckled. "And if my Sonja has her way, she'll find you a wife by year's end. She wants you to meet a nice girl."

"I meet nice girls." His work at Como Park did keep him busy, but there were always young ladies at church. The only problem was none of them seemed to have any spunk. He liked a girl who was more than pink frills and parasols. A girl like—

"Recently?"

"As a matter of fact, yes." A girl like Tessa? Good grief. Sure,

Tessa had spunk in spades, but the last thing he needed right now was to look at her any way other than as a friend.

Erik set his Coke down on the fence rail. "Oh? What's her name? Or does she even exist?"

If he told Erik about Tessa, he'd have to get into the whole story. Somehow he imagined Erik would see more in their garden arrangement than it was.

"Well?" Erik chuckled.

Why had he opened his big mouth?

"You haven't met anyone, have you?"

"Yes I have." Reese rubbed the back of his neck with his hand. "Her name is Tessa—Tessa Gregory—but she's simply a friend."

"Friendship is a good place to start." Erik downed the rest of his Coke. "Sonja will be thrilled to hear this. Maybe she'll forget all about Kristoffer on the field when I tell her your news."

"It's not news. You asked if I met any girls, and I have. That's all."

"I know. You're just friends." He clapped Reese on the shoulder. "You say that with your mouth, but your face says something else."

Since Reese had to move the potted banana trees from the hothouse this morning at Como Park, Tessa planned to stop by Lincoln's office before heading to meet him. She wanted to know the names of the men on the park commission and figured if anyone could find out, it would be Lincoln.

She stepped off the streetcar and began the trek to his office on Wabasha. Tessa tipped her face up to view the Ramsey County Courthouse. The large Romanesque Revival–style stone building seemed to symbolize unfailing justice. Was Hannah inside, arguing a case before a judge? Her hours varied now, as she took on fewer clients. She might also be at home or even at the office she shared with Lincoln. If that was the case, Tessa hoped Hannah wouldn't be in a lecturing mood.

The ornate oak door to Lincoln's office bespoke of his clientele. The clerk, a long-faced fellow with spectacles, looked up when Tessa entered. "Good morning, Miss Gregory."

"Is my brother-in-law in?"

"Yes, he is. He's with a law clerk from another firm, but I'll let him know you're here." The clerk left the room. He returned a minute later and told her to go on in.

Tessa smiled when she saw the visiting clerk was Edward Ferrell, her dinner companion from last night. Both men stood when she entered.

"Well, to what do I owe this pleasant surprise?" Lincoln asked.

Tessa sat down in a leather-clad chair. With Mr. Ferrell present, she'd have to choose her words carefully. "I know Hannah believes my plan may be flawed, but I want to help Mr. Nussbaumer by soliciting more support on his behalf. A conservatory is an excellent idea, and if I can help by encouraging members of the park commission to agree with his plan, then I'd like to do so."

Lincoln raised a skeptical eyebrow. "And what do you need from me?"

"I need the names of the park commissioners and any other information about each of them you can provide. Otherwise, how will I know who to reach out to?"

"And what makes you think these men will have anything to do with you, Tessa?"

"I won't contact them directly. I will try to influence them through their wives and daughters." She stilled her hands in her lap. "Please, Lincoln. I need your help."

Lincoln leaned back in his chair and steepled his fingers. "Let me talk to your sister first. If she agrees, I'll drop the list by later."

Tessa swallowed her disappointment and stood. Hannah would never agree. She'd have to get the names elsewhere. "Thank you."

"I'll walk you out, Miss Gregory." Mr. Ferrell opened the office door. "Lincoln and I were finished anyway."

Lincoln chuckled. "More like at an impasse. Do you think you can get Johnathon to consider my client's offer?"

"Absolutely." Mr. Ferrell shook his hand. "For at least ten minutes. Miss Gregory, shall we leave your brother-in-law to his next victim?"

Tessa giggled and told Lincoln goodbye after putting in one more plea for the names and information. Out on the sidewalk, Mr. Ferrell offered to walk her to the streetcar stop. Automobiles beeped at one another on the busy street, and patrons bustled from business to business.

"Miss Gregory, I may be of help with your endeavor."

"You want to help?" Tessa paused and looked at the law clerk. Dressed in a chocolate-colored three-button sack suit that complemented his dark eyes, he was the epitome of affluence. Still, he lacked a pretentious demeanor, and she found his deep, rich voice hard to ignore.

"I have those names you want, and I'm familiar with the men and their families. If you'll do me the honor of joining me for lunch, I'll be happy to provide the information you requested. I believe there's a get-together this weekend, and many of the wives and daughters you spoke about will probably be in attendance. I'm sure you'll want to begin preparing for that as soon as possible."

Tessa clapped her gloved hands together. "That's a wonderful idea!"

He motioned down the next block. "Let's make a detour by my office so I can make the list. Then we can have lunch and go over those details."

Oh dear, if she went out to lunch with Mr. Ferrell, then she'd be late to meet Reese. What would he think?

"And Miss Gregory, please call me Edward. All of my friends do, and we may be seeing a lot of one another."

A friend like Edward could prove invaluable. Surely Reese would agree when she told him about Mr. Nussbaumer's plans.

She smiled and picked up her pace. "I'm indebted to you for your help."

Where was Tessa?

Reese looked over his shoulder at the sidewalk for the tenth time since he'd begun tilling this section of the garden. She should have been here at their garden an hour ago. Was she sick? What if she had gotten hurt on her way? He didn't even know how to contact her.

He shook his head and put his weight into pushing the cultivator. From what little he knew of her, she had probably gotten sidetracked watching butterflies and forgotten all about making them a garden.

No, that wasn't fair. Tessa seemed to be taking this garden project seriously, and she'd worked as hard as any man. A picture of her in her overalls took shape in his mind, and he chuckled. She'd even gone to the extreme of disguising herself to protect her identity and his job.

So where was she?

8

Another glance down the sidewalk yielded a figure jogging in Reese's direction. Although the clothes said the jogger was a young man, the manner was all girl. All Tessa.

Relief swept through him, followed by a surge of anger. She didn't look injured or ill. So what was her excuse? He needed to slow down and hear her story.

He brought the tiller to a halt, crossed his arms over his chest, and waited for her to reach the garden. "Where have you been?"

Out of breath, she whipped off her straw hat and waved it in front of her face. "I'm sorry. I didn't mean to worry you. I was having lunch with a man . . ."

She was having lunch? With a man? Instead of coming here to work with him?

"I wasn't worried about you. I was worried about this project. I thought you took this opportunity seriously." He stomped back to the tiller.

"I do." She trailed behind him. "If you'll let me explain—"

"I don't need to hear your excuses. Put your hat back on before someone sees you."

She grabbed his sleeve. "Reese, you need to listen to me."

He didn't look at her. "The only thing I need to do is get this garden tilled, which I've been doing all afternoon—alone."

Her hand slipped from his arm, and he fought the urge to turn and stop her from walking away. Had he been too hard on her? No. What was she doing agreeing to lunch when they had work to do? And who was this fellow anyway?

Jealousy pricked him like the thorns of a rosebush. He grimaced. He needed to get out his clippers and give this particular rosebush a good old-fashioned pruning.

Tessa patted the ground around the pussytoe plants. Soon the plant would sport white flowers that looked like tiny cat's paws. *Antennaria plantaginifolia* might be their official name, but *pussytoes* certainly fit them better.

She fingered a velvety leaf and glanced at Reese. All afternoon she'd felt as if she were walking on cats' feet around him, and she was getting tired of it. She took off her leather gloves and knocked the dirt from them, then went to retrieve one of the jars of cold tea she'd brought. Perhaps a peace offering would help.

"Reese?"

He ignored her, so she marched to the plot he was working and positioned herself beside the cultivator. He still refused to look at her. She jammed her hands on her hips. "Reese King, you need to hear me out."

"Let it go, Tessa. I'm not sore at you anymore. Girls are flighty. They can't help it."

Before she could stop herself, she tossed the tea into his face.

She gasped and her hand flew to her mouth. What would Reese do now? Send her away?

Without a word, he withdrew a blue handkerchief from his back pocket and swiped his face. "I reckon I deserved that."

"Reese, I'm so sorry. I don't know what came over me."

"I do." He tucked the handkerchief away. "I was rude."

"It's just that I had a good reason for being late. It involves the conservatory Mr. Nussbaumer wants to build, but you wouldn't let me explain."

"How do you know about the conservatory?"

"Senator Ferrell came over for dinner. He told me about it."

"A senator came to your house?" He drew in a breath and released a slow whistle.

"Well, not mine. Aunt Sam's—where I live for the time being."

He rubbed the back of his neck. "Come on, Tessa. Let's go start picking out some more plants. I think we have a lot to talk about on the way."

A gentle breeze blew across Reese's damp shirt front. Given how hot under the collar he'd been all day, it was a welcome change. Now, walking alongside Tessa, he found it hard to believe he'd let his anger get hold of him like that. It wasn't his usual way. Even when kids in school tried to provoke him, he'd always managed to stay calm. After only a few days with Tessa Gregory, she'd managed to irritate him like a patch of nettles.

He glanced at her. What kind of family had senators over for dinner? And hadn't she mentioned her aunt had a driver? The pieces began to fall together. He should have seen she was from a wealthy family from the clothes she wore the first day they met. The ivory and green dress with its enormous ostrich-feathered hat had shouted money. Still, Tessa hadn't seemed like some of the society girls he'd met. She didn't seem like she expected things to be handed to her—she seemed like a fighter.

"I really am sorry about the tea." Tessa stuffed her hands into her pockets.

"And I apologize for saying girls are flighty. That sounds like something my dad would have said, not me. Now, suppose you tell me about this aunt of yours."

For the next five minutes, Reese listened as Tessa explained how

Hannah had met her husband Lincoln and how Aunt Sam was actually Lincoln's aunt.

"I guess she always wanted girls, because she's sort of taken us all in. She treats us like her own, and I couldn't love her more if she were my actual aunt. But I admit, she does spoil me."

"The old maid type, huh?" Reese navigated the cultivator around a bend in the walk.

"Heavens, no." Tessa giggled. "More like the bicycle-riding, bloomer-wearing, suffragette kind."

"You must be like two peas in a pod." Reese leaned against a tree. "And she's wealthy?"

"Yes, her husband was in the railroad business before he passed. She lives on Summit Avenue."

"So that's where you live too." He snuck a look at her only to find her taking an interest in her shoes. Was she embarrassed? Did she think he might renege on his offer to help her? Even though he was sorely tempted, that wasn't his way. "Why aren't you going to balls instead of digging in the dirt?"

Her head snapped up. "Why can't I do both?"

He chuckled. "Good point. Now, tell me about the senator."

Since he was already aware of Mr. Nussbaumer's dream of building a grand conservatory, he wasn't surprised by the news. However, he was concerned the senator believed some members of the park commission wouldn't support the plan.

"Can't you see how this could help me get a position here? I can use my connections with the park commissioners' wives and daughters to encourage each of them to work hard at persuading their husbands or fathers to vote for the conservatory." She stopped and turned to him. "Between our garden and the help I can give him, surely he'll see how seriously I take this job."

"You can fit into that world?"

"I'm a very good actress." She grinned. "And I went to school with many of their daughters. So you see, when I ran into Senator

Ferrell's grandson Edward, who's a lawyer like Lincoln, I had to say yes to lunch because he said he'd help me with my plans. He provided me with the names of the park commissioners. How else was I to get them? Lincoln wasn't going to help me unless Hannah said it was all right, and I know she wouldn't have agreed."

"And you didn't think I'd know who those men were?"

"No—I mean yes, of course you do, but I needed to know more about them. Edward knows each of the families well."

"And how old is this Edward?"

"A year or two older than you, I'd guess. He told me he may be able to help even more in the future."

"I bet he did," Reese mumbled.

"Pardon me?"

"Nothing." He shook his head. He might not like this on several levels, but the worst one was the position she could be placing herself in. "Tessa, the circle these men travel in is filled with all kinds of politics. Each man has his own motive, and many of them will do anything to get what they want. It would be easy for you to get in over your head, and it could even be dangerous. Just be careful. I'd hate to see you get hurt."

She laughed. "Don't worry. Careful is my middle name."

9

What a treat it was for Sam to have all three nieces with her this bright Saturday morning, although it meant attending a stuffy social function.

From the backseat of the Oldsmobile Cadillac, Tessa laid her hand on Sam's shoulder. "Thank you for taking me to the Ladies' Gardening Society, and Hannah and Charlotte, thank you for coming along. It's like old times—spending the day together."

Sam patted the back of the girl's hand. "You don't need to thank me, dear. Everyone is invited."

"But we all know that isn't really true. Without your introduction, the members wouldn't truly welcome us."

Sam turned to look at Tessa and lifted her eyebrows. "I'm not sure how much good an introduction from me will do with these ladies. I believe I've been referred to as a 'crazy old troublemaker' more than once by the club's president. You might be better off simply attending with your sisters." She glanced in the rear seat and smiled at Charlotte and Hannah. "You two don't have to hold your tongues. You both know I'm telling the truth."

Charlotte bit back a chuckle. "It's always an honor to go out with you, Aunt Sam, and it will be fun to spend the morning supporting our sister."

"And keeping an eye on her." A mischievous glint sparkled in Hannah's eyes.

Tessa frowned. "Hey, I don't—"

"She's teasing you, dear," Sam said as the driver pulled the automobile to the curb. He climbed out and came around to open Sam's door. She surveyed the area. The gardening society met near the Elks Club, across from the post office. She was familiar with the Rice Park area since her suffrage meetings were near here.

She noticed a friend standing on the porch of the Elks Club. "Why don't you girls go on in? I see someone I'd like to speak to. I'll be right up."

Once the sisters entered the hall, she made a beeline for the columned Elks Club. Her friend came down to the sidewalk to meet her.

"Hello, Samantha. I was hoping you'd come over to speak to me."

Her lips curled up at the sound of his deep voice. "James, how did you know I'd be here?"

"You mentioned you might attend the club meeting with Tessa. I had my clerk find out when the next meeting would be."

As if she were a schoolgirl with a crush, a tiny thrill fired through her, but that was silly. She was too old for this nonsense.

He motioned toward a bench. Once she was seated, he took his place beside her. "I know I've asked several times already, but will you have dinner with me, please?"

Should she? They'd been friends for years, but somewhere along the line, things had begun to feel differently. Their once-a-week lunches seemed to take on a life of their own, filled with innocent flirtations. Both of them had been widowed a long time now, but would their families approve? Dinner seemed to be a big step forward, and what if it ruined the friendship she'd grown to cherish?

She licked her dry-as-cotton lips. "I'm not sure we should take the chance."

"Where's the crusader? The woman who learned to ride a bicycle at fifty, who wears bloomers to every social function she possibly can, and who's intent on saying what she thinks on any given subject? I know my risk taker Sam wants to say yes to dinner."

She looked into his coffee-colored eyes, fanned by wrinkles much like her own, and smiled. "But your friend Sam isn't so sure it's a good idea."

"One dinner. Then, if you want, we can go back to weekly lunches, and I won't bother you anymore."

Hope radiated from him, making her traitorous heart swell at the thought of an evening alone with him.

"One dinner. Next week." She stood. "I'd better go before the girls come looking for me. I'd like to keep our friendship private, all right?"

He grinned. "For now."

Tessa nearly bounced up the stairs of the hall. A gardening society. Surely this would be a place she'd find several kindred spirits. She could share her knowledge of horticulture and garden design, and participate in hours of flora and fauna discussions. What could be better?

She scurried inside with Hannah and Charlotte on her heels. She paused in the foyer and glanced upward. Her heart skipped. Oh my, even the light fixture sported periwinkles.

"May I help you?" The lady at the desk looked as if helping them was the last thing she wanted to do. She pulled what Tessa guessed was the club's logbook closer to her and guarded it like a sentry.

Tessa approached with all the grace and dignity she'd been taught at the finishing school. "Yes, ma'am, you can. We're here to join the gardening society."

"You?" The lady's nasally voice echoed in the foyer.

"Yes, my sisters and I." Tessa's back stiffened. "The club is open to all, is it not?"

"Of course, but there is the matter of the yearly dues of two dollars. For each of you." Her gaze swept to Charlotte and Hannah.

"Two dollars?" Hannah stepped forward.

Tessa clenched the chain of her purse. Although she had the money inside it, the price seemed a bit steep to her. Were all new members quoted that amount?

"If it's a problem, there is a Community Garden Club on Snelling for which the dues are only twenty cents a year. Perhaps that would be more fitting."

Anger began to flicker inside Tessa. This woman didn't know if they had twenty cents or twenty dollars, but since she didn't recognize them, she judged them unworthy of her club.

The creaking of the front door drew Tessa's attention. Aunt Sam, thankfully wearing a tasteful lavender suit rather than her cycling bloomers, breezed inside. Only a slight limp remained from her apoplexy. "Dears, why aren't you meeting the other members already? I'm sure the program is about to begin."

The lady at the desk sucked in her breath. "Mrs. Phillips?"

"Yes, that's me." Aunt Sam removed her tan kid gloves.

"Thank you for joining us," the lady gushed. "Are these lovely young ladies with you? I was explaining about our club's dues."

"Oh?" She eyed each sister. "Is there a problem?"

"She thought we might be more comfortable at the Community Garden Club," Tessa said.

"Is that so? While I'm sure you ladies would fit in anywhere, I think we'll join this club. It's closer to home. Now, about those dues."

"It's"—the lady coughed into her gloved hand—"two dollars per person, ma'am."

"Then ten dollars will more than cover all four of us." Aunt Sam opened her purse, pulled out a bill, and dropped it onto the desk. "Girls, shall we?"

The lady pushed the logbook forward. "But you need to sign—"

Aunt Sam waved the book away. "We'll take care of that after the meeting. We don't want to miss anything. You've delayed us long enough."

Like ducklings, Tessa and her sisters followed Aunt Sam into the meeting room. They found four empty seats in the center. Many ladies noticed their arrival, but only a handful introduced themselves. Tessa sighed. Breaking into this circle was going to be harder than she'd thought.

The club's president, Eleanor Bates, stepped to the podium and pounded her gavel more times than necessary to draw everyone's attention. Then her gaze landed on Aunt Sam. Disapproval flickered across her face, but she quickly seemed to stem it. "I see we have some new members. Mrs. Phillips, would you care to introduce yourself and the ladies joining you?"

Aunt Sam stood. "With pleasure, Eleanor. I'm Mrs. Phillips, and these three young ladies are my nieces—Mrs. Lincoln Cole, who's an attorney, Mrs. Joel Brooks, who's the chef in charge of City Hospital's kitchen, and Miss Tessa Gregory, who is studying horticulture at college."

Polite applause echoed throughout the hall.

"So pleased you could join us." Mrs. Bates's words struck a false note, making Tessa flinch. "Now, ladies, it's my honor to introduce today's guest speaker. Leroy Boughner of Minneapolis is part of the American Civic Association. Last February, he spoke at the organization's national meeting, outlining a program he began in Minneapolis known as the vacant lot gardens campaign. I'll let him tell you the rest."

Mr. Boughner didn't stand behind the podium but addressed the ladies from the stage. His broad hand gestures displayed his enthusiasm for the project, and from the way he self-consciously tugged at his lapels, Tessa surmised he was probably more comfortable in work clothes.

"By the end of 1911," he said, "we had planted vegetables and flowers in 360 vacant lots. We gave out 28,000 cabbage and tomato plants and 22,000 packets of nasturtium seeds."

He went on to explain how with the garden club acting as intermediary, every vacant lot on Hennepin Avenue had been cleaned and planted with grass and flowers.

The more he spoke, the more excitement bubbled through Tessa. What a wonderful idea!

"We'd like to expand this program to Saint Paul. The city will be divided into six districts, and a student from the Minnesota Farm School will serve as an assistant gardener. We're asking clubs like yours to help. We need people who are experienced with gardening to teach those in the communities how to plant and tend their gardens."

Tessa clasped her hands together and smiled at her sisters.

Mr. Boughner's gaze swept over the club members. "Would any of you like to volunteer to help work in these gardens?"

Tessa's hand shot up.

Alone.

She shot a plea toward her sisters. They looked at one another, shrugged, and raised their hands as well.

"Thank you, ladies. Anyone else?"

Nervous chatter indicated how uncomfortable the ladies were at the idea.

Mrs. Bates rose from her seat on the front row. "I believe I can speak for the club in offering a ten-dollar donation to the cause."

The ladies applauded.

Ten dollars? That was all? Besides, Mr. Boughner had asked for gardeners, not money.

Aunt Sam lifted her hand in the air. "I'd like to make a challenge. I will give five dollars to this most worthy endeavor for each lady in this room who actually gets her hands dirty by assisting in this civic project."

Tessa did a quick calculation. There were nearly forty women in the room. If half of them helped, Aunt Sam was committing to a hundred dollar donation.

"Ma'am, that's an incredibly generous offer!" Mr. Boughner grinned like a fool. "Now, I'd like to ask again, who would like to volunteer?"

A dirt clod–sized lump formed in Tessa's stomach. What if no one else volunteered? If this made the ladies feel guilty, they might ostracize her. Then how would she ever influence them in the conservatory's favor? *Please, God, make them volunteer.*

One by one, hands went up until Tessa was certain more than half had agreed to help. Mr. Boughner directed them all to leave their names and telephone numbers with him so he could organize the efforts. As soon as the meeting was dismissed, he hurried over to speak to Aunt Sam. "Ma'am, thank you again for your pledge."

"It's my pleasure, young man."

He turned toward Tessa. "And thank you for being the first brave soul to volunteer. I heard your aunt say you are studying horticulture. We can certainly use your talents to organize the others. May I call on you to help me organize the ladies into teams?"

Oh no. Not another commitment. Tessa looked to her two sisters, her eyes begging for assistance in getting out of the predicament.

Hannah grinned. "It is a worthy cause, Tessa."

"Yes, very." Charlotte linked her arm with Tessa's. "She'll be glad to help."

"Thank you. I look forward to working with you."

After Mr. Boughner said goodbye to all four of them, Tessa turned to her sisters. "Why did you say I'd be glad to help?"

Charlotte placed her hand on Tessa's arm. "You're the one who's so anxious to be taken seriously. This will be a great chance to show the club how important gardening is to you."

"And the busier you are, the less apt you are to get into trouble," Hannah added with a grin.

Aunt Sam pulled her gloves back on. "You should be thanking them. I thought he was rather cute."

Charlotte giggled. "And I think he liked you."

Good heavens, another man in her life was the last thing she needed right now.

Mrs. Bates strutted toward their circle. Every nerve in Tessa's body seemed to pulsate as the president approached.

"Miss Gregory." Mrs. Bates elongated her name in an unnatural fashion. "I hear you're going to be heading things up on the club's behalf. You're a rather ambitious young lady, aren't you? You must be a great deal like your aunt."

Tessa flashed the woman a saucy grin. "I'll take that as a compliment. Thank you. Thank you very much."

Toasted almonds scented the air. Reese drew in a deep breath and smiled as Sonja Swenhaugen set a piping hot piece of cake before him and another in front of her husband Erik.

Reese cut a bite with his fork, speared it, and slipped it between his lips. The butter-rich delicacy melted on his tongue and he moaned. "You're spoiling me, Sonja."

"If you get yourself a wife, I won't have to." She lifted an enameled pot from the stove and refilled his coffee cup.

"I could never find someone who can bake like you." Reese raised the corner of his lip in a cheeky smile.

She wiped her hands on her apron and sat down at the table. "I'm sure you'd find my neighbor's daughter Inga to your liking. I only wish you'd let me introduce the two of you. She's such a sweet girl."

"And she's plump, so I bet she can bake quite well—or at least eat quite well." Erik laughed and downed his coffee. "Momma, leave poor Reese alone and let him enjoy his *fyrstekake*."

Reese set down his fork and took a swallow of coffee. "Fristakaka?"

"It means royalty cake, and it's my favorite. I could eat it every day."

"And if you did, you'd look like Inga." Sonja patted her husband's arm. "Now, Reese, about finding you a wife."

Erik pushed his chair back from the table and stood. "Momma, let him be. He's already met a girl."

"You have!" Sonja's eyes widened. "Tell me about her. Is she pretty? Does she have a pleasant disposition? Can she work like a man if she needs to?"

Reese chuckled to himself. Tessa could even look like a man—or at least a boy—if she needed to. He took in Sonja's hopeful expression and wished Erik wasn't so incredibly honest with his blonde-haired bride of fifteen years. "I mentioned to Erik I'd met a girl named Tessa, but she's just a friend."

"And is she pretty?"

Reese swallowed the last of his coffee. "Even in overalls."

"Overalls?" Sonja scowled. "What kind of girl is this Tessa?"

"Tessa knows no limits." He chuckled. "But don't worry, Sonja. She's just a friend."

"Friends sometimes become more."

Erik laid his hand on her shoulder. "Let him be, Momma. He came over here on his day off to help me put a new roof on the shed, not answer all of your questions."

"That may be, but someone has to look out for him." She paused as Reese stood. "Promise me you'll be careful with this girl. She may bring you great happiness or she may bring you terrible grief."

Erik swung the back door open and laughed. "Or she may bring you a little of both."

How true, but that was enough talk about Tessa. She invaded his thoughts enough without Sonja's help.

Reese thanked his hostess for the cake, then headed outside. He located the ladder and propped it against the shed. Erik opened the shed's door to reveal the shingles they'd be using. Reese heaved a bundle onto his shoulder and began the climb to the roof, and Erik followed behind him with a bundle of his own. They worked in silence for nearly half an hour with the steady ring of a hammer filling the warm spring air.

Erik leaned back and wiped his brow with the sleeve of his shirt. "You've grown quiet, my young friend. Did Momma's questions bother you? You know, she was only teasing about your Tessa."

"She's not *my* Tessa, and yes, I know Sonja was teasing me."

Erik moved to the ladder. "We need another bundle, but when I get back, I want to hear about why your young lady friend was wearing overalls. There must be a story in there."

Reese grabbed another shingle. "There is, but for the time being, I think I'll keep it to myself."

Thank goodness Erik honored his request, because if he'd pressed him, Reese probably would have spilled everything about the overall-clad girl who filled his dreams.

10

Why Reese found himself at Como Park after church services this morning was a mystery even to him. A niggling feeling had surfaced every time he thought of the park, and he'd grown to appreciate those moments as coming straight from the Lord. But why had the Lord prompted him to come here today on his day off?

Still dressed in his blue serge suit, he began a trek down Banana Walk. The fruit trees and other palms were adjusting well to being moved from the hothouse outdoors, even if the days weren't quite hot enough yet to keep the plants truly happy.

He paused to touch the soil of the ferns. It needed more water. He needed to check on who'd been assigned to use the pumper on Friday.

After turning in the direction of the park office, he stopped on the path. Tessa? He watched the young lady approach. Gone were her overalls. They'd been replaced by an attractive ivory dress with a belt that accentuated her small waist. A huge matching ivory hat—decked with more silk roses than the east garden and bearing an enormous matching bow—dipped alluringly to the right.

He whistled softly. Today Miss Gregory was all young lady, and if he were honest with himself, he'd have to admit he liked what he saw. A lot.

But why was she here?

Their gazes connected, sending a jolt through his chest. She flashed him a wide smile and walked toward him. "Reese, isn't Sunday your day off?"

"I could say the same thing to you." He cleared his throat. Normally words came easy when he was with her. Why was it so hard to talk to her today?

"I wanted to check on our garden. I know it's silly, but I had a feeling I should come to the park today."

Chill bumps crept up Reese's neck.

"What about you?"

"No reason." Reese stuffed his hands in his pockets and looked down at his shoes. "Shall we go take a look together? Then maybe I can show you some of the other parts of the park."

She clasped her hands together at her waist. "Oh, Reese, I would love that."

"Good."

Good? That was the best he could do?

He offered her the crook of his arm. She didn't hesitate before slipping her hand in place. He covered it with his own and tucked her arm against his side, his chest warming at the contact.

What was Tessa doing to him? No girl had ever affected him this way. He'd stepped out with more than one girl in the last few years, but none of them turned him into a blithering idiot. Tessa simply had a way about her that drew him in.

She squeezed his arm. "I'm so excited. I've yet to explore the whole park."

"It's twenty-two acres, Tessa. I don't think we can explore all of it today."

"Then you'll just have to promise me more days like this one."

For some reason the idea of doing that made him much happier than it should have. He'd better be careful or Tessa was going to have him under her spell by the end of the day.

But magic was only an illusion, and he wanted the real thing.

Dust motes danced in the air, suspended in a May sunbeam. Tessa released a contented sigh from her seat on a park bench beside Reese. Strains of "The Land of Golden Dreams" came from the bandstand. The round, open building was built on pilings and set out in the water of Lake Como as if on giant stilts.

The trills of the flutes echoed off the water, and Tessa let the music feed her fantasy. She imagined the dust motes as fairies, flitting around on the wind.

She glanced at Reese, and a smile crooked her mouth. She doubted he ever thought about such whimsical creatures. As much as she was given to a flight of fancy, he seemed rooted to reality, and she found that quiet strength oddly attractive.

So far, their day had been entrancing. He'd shown her the Schiffman Fountain with its cast-iron mermaid spouting water from the seashell in her hands, and the Mannheimer Memorial. The wooden pergola, resting on marble columns, sat on a hill and held a sparkling white fountain.

They'd laughed at the children running through the recently constructed playground. He'd shown her the statue of Henrik Ibsen, donated by the Sons of Norway, and the elephant topiary, situated on an island in the center of Cozy Lake. When the band concluded, he told her they would return to Cozy Lake, south of Lake Como.

Reese had proved a most attentive, almost flirtatious companion, but he was probably being kind. A solid man like Reese wouldn't find a whimsical girl like her of any great interest.

"Tessa?" Reese waved his hand in front of her face.

She blinked and laughed. When had the music stopped? "Sorry. I was distracted."

"By?"

By you. Her cheeks warmed. She stood and adjusted her skirt. "I was thinking about the dust motes."

"Dust motes." He didn't pursue the topic but instead directed Tessa down the long, classical concrete pergola west of the lakeside pavilion. They passed beneath the canopy of red and yellow climbing roses, their sweet fragrance cloying the air.

"Okay, I may regret asking this, but I have to know. Why were you thinking about the dust motes?"

"They reminded me of fairies." She grinned. "Do you regret asking me already?"

"Not yet. Go on."

"I was once in a production of *Peter Pan* at the Metropolitan Opera House. Don't look so impressed. I was only the nanny, so my part was small, but the specks floating in the sunbeam reminded me of Tinker Bell and her fairy dust."

He chuckled. "And what would you sprinkle fairy dust on right now? Would you have the fairies carry us away to Paris or the Orient?"

"No." She looked at him from beneath the brim of her hat, butterflies colliding in her stomach. "This day is perfect as it is."

His lips curved and his eyes sparkled like the sun off the water. He seemed to want to say something, but instead he inclined his head toward the lake. "Come on. I want to show you something."

She brushed away a twinge of disappointment and reminded herself to quit imagining things where they weren't. They were friends—partners, even—but nothing more.

Fairy dust? The way his heart was pounding, Reese would have sworn Tessa had sprinkled fairy dust all over him.

Focus. Show her the park. Tomorrow they could get back to work on their garden. Back to normal. He didn't need a relationship with someone like Tessa. He needed someone predictable, solid, normal.

But why did "normal" hold so little appeal right now?

Tessa seemed quieter than before. Had he offended her somehow? No, she'd said the day was perfect, and he'd have to agree. Tessa was effervescent—bubbling like the fountain. She delighted in everything she saw, and she made him look at things through fresh eyes.

Maybe she was the kind of girl he needed after all. Carefree. Fun. Creative.

Then again, maybe she wasn't.

He'd made a poor choice once before and allowed a girl to manipulate him, and he promised himself he'd never let that happen again.

But Tessa wasn't Laura.

After a few minutes of walking, they reached Cozy Lake. Reese led them to a tall bamboo gate shaped like two conjoined capital Ts, which announced the entrance to the area. Reese explained the gate was called a *torii* gate. "Mr. Nussbaumer said that according to the Japanese, the gate divides our world from the spirit world."

Tessa tucked a strand of hair behind her ear. "It's peaceful here."

He had to agree. They turned a corner on the path and Tessa gasped. "The cherry trees are exploding with blossoms."

Reese pulled one of the pale pink blossoms down lower for her to sniff. "Haven't you been to the Japanese Gardens before?"

"Not when the trees were blooming." She drew in a deep breath and closed her eyes. "Reese, this is beyond words."

"Don't you want to see the rest?" When she didn't follow him, he reached for her hand. The contact sent a jolt through him. He tightened his grasp and led her over the concrete footbridge. "When Dr. Schiffman attended the 1904 World's Fair in Saint Louis, he fell in love with the Japanese tea garden. He arranged for the gardener to re-create the tea garden here. The gardener was from the Japanese Imperial Household. I wonder what he thought of our Minnesota winters."

"If he was lucky, he was back home before he endured one."

The path weaved through the unusual shrubs and plants that surrounded the small pond. He stopped at one of the large stone lanterns dotting the landscape. "These are lit most evenings."

"Oh, I'd love to see that. The light reflecting off the water would be so enchanting."

Enchanting. The word wrapped around his heart like a creeping vine and squeezed. That was the best word he had to describe Tessa. Of course, *strong willed*, *overzealous*, and *stubborn* were good words too, if he wanted to be honest with himself.

But he didn't.

He smiled at her. "Maybe we can come back and see them later."

She glanced at the sun. "I'll need to go home soon."

"What time is your driver coming?"

"He's not. I'm taking the streetcar."

"I can take you home."

"You have an automobile?"

He shrugged. "Who needs a motorcar? I thought I could toss you in a wheelbarrow and push you home. Wouldn't that be all right?"

"Reese . . ."

"Yes, Tessa." He chuckled. "I have an automobile. It's not brand new, but it will get you home."

"In that case, I accept your invitation."

Since they now had more time, they dallied in the Japanese Garden for a while before Reese persuaded Tessa to join him at one of his favorite spots—the lily pond.

Her eyes grew wide. "Those are the biggest lilies I've ever seen."

Tessa's reaction to the pond's huge Victoria water platters did not disappoint him. "You've not been here either?"

"I've mostly visited the park's gardens. Sorry."

"These lilies are from the Amazon River. They get to be about four or five feet in diameter."

"How can they survive here in Minnesota? It's not warm enough."

"The water is heated by huge boilers and piped in."

She moved closer to the water to smell the blooms, then grabbed Reese's arm. "What are they doing with that little girl? Stop them!"

Reese chuckled at the common sight. "The lilies can support her weight as long as she sits down." The father of the girl, who was probably about five or six, gently lowered his daughter onto one of the platters. The girl clapped her hands.

"By sitting, her weight is distributed over the whole platter. See?"

"Look at her face. She is absolutely delighted." Tessa turned to him. "I wish I were that little. I'd love to be on one of those. It's like a magic carpet. Have you ever tried sitting on one?" She tipped her face up to him, the glint of a challenge in her eyes.

"I can't say I've ever considered it."

"Have you no imagination, Reese King?"

Her words pricked him like a thorn. Unbeknownst to her, she'd pinpointed the truth. He knew it. His father knew it. And if he had to guess, Mr. Nussbaumer probably had suspected it as well. When it came to creativity, Reese was sorely lacking.

Wait a minute. He might not be creative, but he was a good problem solver. An idea took shape in his mind, and he grabbed Tessa's hands. "Will you stay here while I go get something? It'll only take a few minutes, but I promise it will be worth it."

Waiting wasn't one of Tessa's strong suits. She stared at the path Reese bolted down after his rather obscure request. What was so important that he'd leave her like that?

She sighed and sat down on a large rock. His sudden departure confirmed what she'd feared. Any spark between them was strictly the product of her ever-active imagination. She'd mistaken his polite company for the possibility of something budding between them.

A boy tossed a rock into the pond, narrowly missing one of the platters. Lightning fast, his mother grabbed his earlobe and hauled him away from the edge, scolding in the process. Tessa giggled. She may have been in trouble more than her sisters, but her parents had never had to take her by the earlobe.

"I've got a surprise for you," Reese whispered into her ear.

She jumped, then pressed a hand to her chest. "You scared the life out of me."

Reese came around so she could see him. He held up a square piece of wood and grinned.

"What is that for?"

"To make your wish come true." He drummed the board with his fingers. The twinkle in his eyes made her stomach somersault. He took her hand and drew her to the water's edge. "I'll put the board on the water lily. It will distribute your weight so when you step on it, you won't sink."

"I'm really going to do it?"

"I certainly hope so. It's not every day a handsome man offers you a magic carpet." His lips curled in a crooked grin. "Now, let me put this board in place." He stepped across several partially submerged stones until he selected a large lily. He crouched and gingerly placed the board on the plant's center, then returned for Tessa.

He held out his hand. "Careful. The rocks are slick."

When they reached the lily, she drew in a deep breath. "Do I simply step on?"

"Unless you'd like to hop." He chuckled. "Just step on the board's center. Go ahead. I won't let go."

If she slipped, this would not end well. And if Reese was wrong, this could prove disastrous. But a little water had never frightened her before.

She lifted her right foot and held her breath. As soon as it made contact with the board, she brought her left foot alongside it. She wobbled, but Reese kept hold of her hand. She released her breath and looked around. With the sun dipping in the sky, the white, saucer-sized water lily blossoms opened, emitting an intoxicating pineapple-like fragrance.

She squeezed Reese's hand. "You can let go now."

To her surprise, he didn't argue like she imagined most men would, but released his grip. She immediately wavered and the lily dipped, but she regained her balance. She glanced at the shore, where a cluster of people watched them. One woman looked mortified while her husband appeared to find the whole thing quite entertaining.

Reese followed her gaze to the spectators. "Maybe it's time for your magic carpet to land?" He held out his hand and she took it. "Easy."

She meant to move gently, but in order to get off the lily, she had to put a bit of bounce in her step. Her weight shifted and her foot slipped on a mossy stone. She gasped. Her arms flailed.

Reese caught her around the waist and pulled her close, knocking her wide-brimmed hat off in the process.

The hat plopped into the water, but she didn't care. The warmth of his solid chest and his work-honed arms seeped through her dress and wrapped around her heart.

"I've got you," he breathed into her hair.

Oh my, he most certainly did. But what if he didn't share her feelings?

11

Gravel crunched in the driveway. Sam closed her book and peeked at the clock. Tessa's afternoon outing had extended into the evening. She glanced at Hannah, little Ellie, and Alice Ann, then rose and went to the window to see who had delivered her niece home at this hour.

A young man came round to Tessa's side of the white Model T Torpedo and helped her out. Unwilling to spy any longer, Sam returned to her seat.

"Was that Tessa?" Hannah smoothed her sleeping daughter's hair. "I thought she was taking the streetcar home. Did she catch a ride with someone?"

How could she help this well-meaning older sister understand that Tessa was growing up? "Apparently a very handsome someone brought her home."

Alice Ann, Charlotte's seven-year-old daughter, stood up behind the dollhouse in the corner. They'd had a delightful afternoon with the girl while Charlotte and Joel enjoyed a day to themselves. "A boy?"

Aunt Sam smiled. "I'd say he was more of a man than a boy."

Alice Ann set a miniature table in the dollhouse's parlor. "Is Aunt Tessa in trouble?"

"No, honey." Hannah eased her arm from beneath Ellie's head, tucked the blanket around her daughter, and moved to one of the parlor's winged chairs. She leaned in close to Aunt Sam. "Are you going to say something to her or should I?"

"Neither. She has a right to her privacy." Sam settled back into her chair and opened her book again. After a few seconds, she looked at Hannah and smiled. "It's 1913, you know. Young ladies have more freedoms."

Hannah picked up a magazine from the side table. "Giving Tessa more freedom is a scary thought."

"True." Sam laughed. "But she's old enough that if she constantly bumps against a list of don'ts, I think she'll stop trying to please anyone. Trust me on this, dear. She's no longer a little girl. Tessa may push boundaries, but she has a good head on her shoulders and she knows how to use it."

"I only hope she does use her head."

"And not her heart?" The murmur of voices on the front porch stopped her. "Hannah, dear, where would you be if you'd followed that advice? I think the best matches come when a lady's head and her heart come to an agreement. Don't you?"

"Yes, but we're talking about Tessa. I don't want her to make a mistake."

"Why not? In your law practice, haven't you learned as much from your mistakes as your successes?"

Hannah sighed. "How did you get to be so wise?"

"By making a lot of mistakes." Sam quirked a hint of a smile and watched the worry lines slip from Hannah's brow. As the oldest child, she carried a great deal of responsibility for her sisters. "Relax. Tessa and I have few secrets."

Secrets. As soon as she said the word, Hannah's brow creased again, and she pressed a hand to her stomach.

Sam touched her arm and whispered, "You didn't tell Charlotte yet?"

"I will, but I need the right time."

"Don't wait too long. This is hard on you and the baby. Besides, keeping things hidden tends to hurt families." Guilt nudged Sam even as she said the words. But she wasn't really keeping a secret. One outing—which she'd not yet taken—was hardly news.

The front door creaked open, and Tessa stepped into the parlor. She held a limp and soggy ivory hat in her hands, its ostrich plume having lost all its bravado.

"Tessa, what happened to your hat?" Hannah's eyes darted to Sam. "Of course, you don't have to tell me what happened if you don't want to."

"It fell in the lily pond." Tessa tilted her head. "Hannah, why are you and Ellie here? And why is Alice Ann here? Where's Charlotte?"

"Well, little sister, Lincoln is in the billiards room. We came for the afternoon. I offered to take Alice Ann so Charlotte and Joel could have an afternoon alone." Hannah glanced at the clock. "I'd hoped to visit with my sister."

Sam scowled at her.

Hannah seemed to catch on and smiled. "But instead, I spent time in Aunt Sam's wise company. And what did you do this afternoon?"

Tessa sat in the other wing chair and folded her hands. So different this young woman was than the girl of yesterday who would have plopped down without a second thought.

"I was at Como Park. One of the gardeners I met there earlier offered to show me some of the park's attractions." Her eyes glittered as she spoke. "We had a pleasant afternoon together."

Hannah glanced at Sam, and they shared a knowing smile. "What is this gardener's name?"

"Reese King." Tessa straightened. "His father is the superintendent of parks in Chicago, but he came here to make a name for himself—all on his own."

"And I saw he escorted you home." Sam set her book on the table. "That was kind of him."

Alice Ann stood by the dollhouse with her hands clasped behind her. "Did he kiss you?" She swayed on her tiptoes as she spoke.

Hannah spun in her niece's direction. "Alice Ann!"

Tessa's cheeks turned crimson. "No, sweetheart, he didn't. We're friends."

The little girl crossed her arms over her chest and gave a firm nod. "Good. Boys are yucky."

"That isn't kind." Hannah's tone still held a note of amusement. "And not all boys are yucky."

"Well . . ." Alice Ann scrunched her brow. "My daddy isn't—and I like Uncle Lincoln, but Jimmy Wilson is as mean as a rattlesnake." Her eyes filled with tears.

Sam looked from Hannah to Tessa. Hannah shrugged. Apparently both were unaware of this boy.

Tessa walked over to the dollhouse and knelt on the floor beside her niece. "What does Jimmy do to you? Pull your braids? Tease you?"

"I can't say. It's a secret."

"That doesn't sound like the good kind of secret." Tessa wiped the tears from the girl's cheeks. "You can tell us, honey. We're your family. We love you no matter what."

"Momma won't."

Hannah joined them and laid her hand on Alice Ann's shoulder. "Your mother won't love you? Why do you say that? Honey, please tell us. That's the only way we can help." She glanced at Sam. "Families share things. You shouldn't carry burdens alone."

Alice Ann sniffed. "Jimmy says my real mother didn't want me. He says Momma will get tired of me when she has a baby of her own, and then Daddy will send me back to the orphanage."

"Oh, honey." Tessa pulled the little girl into her arms. "That would never happen. Your momma can love you and any new babies that come along just like she loves me, Aunt Hannah, and Aunt Sam all at once. And your daddy would never send you back to the orphanage. Families don't give up on you when you make a mistake. No one knows that better than me."

Alice Ann pulled back and wiped her nose with the sleeve of her dress. "Really?"

Tessa grabbed her niece by the waist and tickled her ribs. "Absitively. Posilutely."

"Aunt Tessa, you're silly."

"And being silly is one of my favoritest things." She tickled her again. "So when does this nasty Jimmy bother you? At school?"

"No, when I'm walking to school. He lives five houses away from mine."

"And is he ugly as a fence post?"

"Tessa." Hannah's voice held a note of censure, but Alice Ann giggled.

"He's not ugly, Aunt Tessa, but he has ears that stick out like this." She placed her hands by her ears and waved them.

Tessa squeezed Alice Ann's hand. "But you never tease him about that, do you, sweetie?"

"No, Mommy says Jesus wouldn't want me to do that."

"He certainly wouldn't." Tessa smiled at the little girl. "I want you to tell us if he bothers you anymore, okay?"

Sam took in the scene before her. Her family. God had given her what she never thought she'd have. They probably deserved to know her undisclosed news, but what difference would it make? It wasn't as if there were any understanding between James and her. Besides, she had a right to her privacy, in the same way Tessa had a right to hers.

Stares didn't bother Tessa, and it was a good thing. When she'd hopped on the streetcar wearing overalls, boots, and a straw hat this morning, more than one lady gave her a lecture with their eyes. Still, she wouldn't let their disapproval bother her. She had something more important to do.

Tessa stepped off the streetcar where Charlotte and Joel lived and walked down the sidewalk. As she neared their home, she counted five houses down and then leaned against a tree a short distance away and waited.

It didn't take long for a boy in knee pants to exit the home and skip down the steps. Alice Ann had described Jimmy's ears quite well.

"Jimmy?"

He stopped and turned toward her, his eyes wide.

"I'm Alice Ann's aunt, and I want to talk to you."

His face scrunched. "You're her aunt? But you look like a boy!"

She swallowed a chuckle. Laughing would certainly limit the effectiveness of her threats.

"Listen, Jimmy, I heard that you've been saying some unkind things to Alice Ann." She kept her voice firm. "I've come to warn you to stop. If you don't, I'll have to come back and speak to your parents."

Fear flashed across Jimmy's face, but it was quickly replaced with a quizzical tilt of the head. "You gonna wear that?"

"I don't know. Why?"

He crossed his arms over his chest. "Then I don't have a thing to worry about, 'cause my momma wouldn't let you through the door."

"In that case, I'll wear my prettiest dress. So you think long and hard about what your momma would say if she knew you'd been mean to a girl." She tapped the bill of his cap. "And remember, I'll be watching you."

Reese hated to disappoint Tessa—especially after yesterday.

He stood waiting for her at the Como Park streetcar station. She'd told him her aunt would need the motorcar this morning, so she'd be coming by streetcar. He could only imagine how the other passengers would react to her gardening clothes.

83

He glanced at the station's fireplace, where only embers remained glowing. They'd probably needed the heat last night. By the time he arrived home from delivering Tessa to her aunt's house, the air was ripe with a chill.

Tessa's aunt's house. Wow. What a home. It was dusk when he pulled up to the home on the corner of Chatsworth and Summit, and despite the diminishing sunlight, he could tell the place screamed money. The enormous brick mansion, set back from the street, sported at least six chimneys. He could only guess how many rooms it had. Even the wraparound porch, with its tiled floor and inviting wicker furniture, told him Tessa's aunt surrounded herself with the finest things.

It was hard to believe that anyone who lived in a place like that wanted to spend her life digging in the dirt. But Tessa did. There were a lot of things about Tessa he was unsure of, but her desire to garden wasn't one of them.

The streetcar bell clanged as the trolley came to a stop. Tessa descended the steps a minute later, wearing her overalls and straw hat. She spotted him, and a wide smile lit her face.

He sighed. Now he'd have to break the bad news.

"Good morning." She tugged the brim of her hat down. "Ready to work? It's planting time. You said we could put in the bushes today."

"I have some bad news, Tessa."

Her smile faded. "What's wrong?"

"We can't work together."

She paled. "Why? Did I do something wrong?"

"No!" She was taking this all wrong. "Mr. Nussbaumer assigned me to a different task, and it'll take a few days."

"Oh." Relief filled her voice. "Then I guess I can work on the garden alone, or I could help you."

Reese rubbed his chin. "Mr. Nussbaumer did say I should ask my young apprentice to join me."

"You have an apprentice?"

"He means you. I told him the boy working with me wants to learn about gardening." He motioned her toward the exit. "But I don't know. If we're discovered, it could ruin everything."

"We'll have to be careful, but if I help you, it will go much more quickly. Then we can get back to planting the rest of our garden. What are we going to be working on?"

"I didn't say yes yet."

"You will. Resisting me is impossible."

He chuckled. He should show that her wiles didn't work on him, but then again, she had a point. So far she'd proven hard to resist more than once. "All right, you win. We'll be planting the Gates Ajar according to Mr. Nussbaumer's plans. It'll be messy. We'll have to apply a lot of mud to the walls, so you can take back your offer if you want."

Tessa shook her head. "It's going to be great fun."

"Is everything entertaining to you?"

"Mostly." She chuckled, then wrinkled her nose. "Scratch that. I don't find lectures, quilting circles, or long train rides the least bit enjoyable. Everything else is pretty much fair game. Come on. Let's hurry." She skipped down the walk, leaving Reese to follow.

Good grief. What if someone saw her right now? From the way she walked, they'd know for certain she was a girl in boy's clothing. He didn't dare call out to her, so he had to hurry to catch up. He grabbed her arm. "Tessa, you're a boy, remember?"

She tipped her face up to his with a coy smile. "Surely you realize by now I'm no boy."

His neck warmed. Did she know what she was doing to him with that look? "Uh . . . of course I know that. I mean you need to act like a boy, not walk all bouncy like a girl. At least right now. Understand?"

"Sure. How's this?" She walked in front of him and added a swagger to her step.

He watched from behind. Nope, still all girl—at least to him. He shook his head. He had to stop this. *She's a friend. A friend. A friend.*

"Yeah, that'll do." His voice came out gruff, but she paid it no heed. She prattled on about the sun-drenched morning, the blooming tulips, and a play at the Metropolitan Opera House she hoped to see. He found himself half listening to her words and half watching the way her lips moved when she spoke. His lack of attention to walking nearly cost him a fall when his boot caught on a crack. Tessa laughed at the acrobatic feat it took to stay upright.

A genuine, warm laugh—not the kind girls made when they wanted to seem ladylike.

By the time they reached the hill east of the bronze Schiller Monument on which the floral sculpture would be displayed, he'd heard all about her niece's troubles with a rotten kid named Jimmy, who'd teased the little girl about being adopted.

A bully. He'd never liked them. What would he do if he caught his son bullying someone?

His son? Where had that come from? He wasn't married or even courting anyone. He glanced at Tessa and squared his shoulders. Until he proved himself to Mr. Nussbaumer, that was how it needed to remain.

As they approached the wood frames, Reese was pleased to see that wire netting had already been attached and vats of mud had been delivered by a couple of the workers. He walked around the structure, checking on the quality of the work. This showpiece was important, and the fact he'd been entrusted with it showed Mr. Nussbaumer's faith in him.

Tessa sat down on the wood frame, which would later make up part of the floral carpeted staircase. "Tell me about the Gates Ajar."

"Every year since 1894, Mr. Nussbaumer has planted the sculpture. It changes a little with different designs on the gate or different colors of flowers." Reese tacked a piece of wire in place with a hammer, then turned to her. "Even he thinks it's a bit showy. Have you seen the Gates before?"

"I have. I come to see it every year. I always wondered how he came up with the idea of an open gate with stairs leading up to it. It made me imagine all sorts of things, like what I would do if I saw a gate slightly ajar."

He laughed. "Who are you kidding? Unless the gate was chained and padlocked, you'd go right on through it."

"I would not."

He raised his eyebrows.

"Okay, maybe you're right." She hopped up. "So, what design goes on this year's gate?"

Reese picked up a trowel. "In the drawing Mr. Nussbaumer gave me, it almost looks like a snowflake."

"Appropriate for Minnesota." She moved to stand beside him. "What do we do first?"

He dipped the trowel in the bucket of mud, then held it up. "We have to put this into the holes in the frames. Then we smooth it and trace his pattern on the mud. The hardest part is that we have to keep the soil moist or it will crack on the frame. You can simply watch if you want."

"Hey, I do my best cooking in mud pies." Tessa grabbed the second trowel and loaded it with mud.

They worked hard most of the morning. Conversation between them came easily. He asked about Tessa's parents, and she shared memories of her life on the farm—fishing with her dad and gardening with her mom. He could only imagine how difficult it had been on the three sisters to lose both their parents and their home. Thank goodness her sister Hannah had taken care of them.

When she asked about his parents, he figured he needed to respond in kind. He told her about his mother, who herself had loved to garden, and explained that he thought she actually loved flowers more than his father ever had. When she asked what kind of person his father was, he tried to put into words how his father was a strong but quiet man who was not given to emotional reactions. "He's very calm on the outside but very passionate on the inside."

She looked at him through the wire. "Who are you most like?"

"A little of each, I suspect." He came around to her side, picked up the watering can, and watched the spray saturate the mud he'd applied.

Running his hand along the surface, he smiled. They'd done good work and accomplished a great deal already.

A chunk of mud landed squarely on his cheek.

Tessa giggled. "Oh, Reese, I'm so sorry."

"You don't seem a bit sorry." He brushed it away with his finger and shook it off.

"I promise to be more careful."

Seconds later, she tossed another handful in his direction, and it hit him on the chest. Apparently unable to suppress a bubble of laughter, Tessa released a telltale giggle.

He glanced from the watering can to the mud. Either would make good ammunition, but perhaps he should respond in kind. With mud clenched in his fist and a grin on his face, he approached her.

She backed away. "You wouldn't dare."

"Oh?"

"Reese, you can't!" She spun and raced away from him toward a grove of trees.

He followed and caught her about the waist. He pulled her to the ground but was careful not to let her hit too hard. Her chest rose and fell beneath his arms. She laughed as she fought his grasp and pleaded with him to let her go. He held up his mud-fisted hand.

"You're not—"

"But I am."

She stilled and looked at him with a strange wonderment. Dressed as a boy, she lay there and let him draw four muddy fingers down her silky cheek—and she'd never looked more beautiful.

He couldn't tear his gaze from hers. Lord help him. He was a goner.

Try as he might to keep it closed, the gate to his heart was certainly ajar.

12

Lifting her carnation-pink ball gown, Tessa descended the grand staircase. Aunt Sam and her escort for the evening both waited for her at the bottom.

Heat pooled in her stomach as she imagined Reese—not Edward Ferrell—waiting to take her to the Chattingworths' dinner party. But the truth was Reese hadn't kissed her. When the perfect moment had come, he'd jumped away like he'd been stung by a bee, and worse, he'd hardly said two words to her the rest of the afternoon.

In that moment on the grass, perhaps Reese had thought of her differently, but his further actions showed he did not plan to act on any attraction between them. No fairy dust here—but she wasn't imagining things. There had been an undeniable pull between them. She'd seen it in his eyes and felt it in every pore, but he'd resisted the attraction. He'd resisted her.

She sighed. She had to bury her hopes and refocus on her goals. Even if they were designed to encourage suitors, social events like tonight's birthday dinner party for Catherine Chattingworth were the best way she could garner support for Mr. Nussbaumer's conservatory. She should be thankful for Edward's invitation. She and Catherine had been friends in high school, but not close ones. When Edward had called and invited her, he'd said he was a family friend.

She placed her gloved hand on the newel post and took the final step down.

"You look lovely." Aunt Sam kissed her cheek, now washed clean of the mud.

She forced a smile. Water had washed the dirt off, but it hadn't dimmed the memory of Reese's caress.

Stop it, Tessa. It didn't mean anything to him.

Not-a-hair-out-of-place Edward flashed her a broad smile, his crisp white shirt accenting his perfect teeth. "Your aunt is right, Tessa. You do look lovely."

"Thank you. I'm sorry for taking so long to get ready. Shall we go?"

He offered her his arm, and she placed her hand in its crook. A sickening feeling of falsehood washed over her, and she pressed a hand to her midsection.

She could do this. She was an actress.

Taking a deep breath, she lifted her chin and slipped into the role everyone expected her to play—Samantha Phillips's wealthy niece.

And tonight she'd play the role with aplomb. She had to.

Tessa slipped the last bite of her chicken in brandy and cream sauce between her lips and stared at the centerpiece on the table. Only the final course, the birthday cake, remained, and like most of the young women at the table, she'd nibble on dessert and declare she was simply too full to eat another bite.

Did any of the five other young women present or their escorts know the dinner table was massed with Jacqueminot roses? More importantly, did anyone else care?

Beside her, Edward was having a conversation with jade-eyed Susan Frazier, who was seated on his right, about her father's political ambitions. On Tessa's left, nasally William Riley seemed enthralled with his dinner companion, Elizabeth Periot. However, Tessa didn't think the flaxen-haired maiden shared his enthusiasm.

The frosted birthday cake was set on the table, resplendent with candles. Catherine blew out the candles in one full breath, and the guests followed with a chorus of "For She's a Jolly Good Fellow."

Slices of the lemon sponge cake were served on china dessert plates bearing tiny roses whose color matched that of the center-piece.

"Miss Gregory." Mrs. Chattingworth, the hostess for the evening, set down her fork. "We expected your aunt to host a coming-out for you this last season. We were surprised when she didn't."

I didn't want to be put on the market. Tessa smiled politely. "You are probably aware that my aunt is a little unorthodox, so when I said I'd rather attend college than spend the season attending parties and balls, she supported my wishes."

"I see. Are you studying art or music?"

"Neither, ma'am. I'm studying horticulture."

"Flowers?" Elizabeth Periot nearly choked on her cake. "And dirt?"

Tessa slid a piece of dessert onto her fork. "I study vegetables too, and trees. My favorite courses, however, include garden design."

"Fascinating." Mr. Chattingworth lifted his glass in her direction. "I myself am on the park board."

Now was her chance. She glanced at Edward, who gave her a slight nod of encouragement. As Henry had driven them here, she and Edward had discussed using this opportunity to speak to Mr. Chattingworth. Edward had pledged to help her should the subject come up.

She turned to her gray-haired host. "Thank you for serving our community in that capacity, Mr. Chattingworth. Do you enjoy your work on the park board?"

"Most of the time." He leaned back in his chair and folded his arms over his broad chest. "I must admit, I tend to spend a great deal of time helping my fellow board members understand that not every project is worthy. Many of them think that whatever Fred Nussbaumer wants, he should get. I'm more practical than that."

"I imagine that it's difficult to determine which things deserve the board's financial support." Tessa paused. Everyone at the table was now listening. She'd have to tread carefully lest she offend the guest of honor, Catherine, by stealing the spotlight.

"Catherine," Tessa said, "what about you? Do you enjoy Como Park?"

"I most certainly do, and I have been growing chrysanthemums from seeds for several months. I want to enter them in the fall show. Perhaps after dinner you can give me a few pointers on them."

"I'd be happy to." Tessa smiled. This was going better than she could have imagined. "And Mr. Chattingworth, I'm sure another difficult part of your job is considering how Saint Paul will keep up with the parks of the other important US cities. For example, in my coursework I learned Saint Louis, San Francisco, New York, and Baltimore all have botanical conservatories."

"They do?"

"Oh yes. Even Columbus brags about their grand Franklin Park Conservatory."

Mr. Chattingworth swallowed and leaned forward. "What about Chicago?"

She tapped her finger against her lips. "Hmm. I believe the Garfield Park Conservatory was built five or six years ago." She slowly ate a second bite of her cake, then dabbed her lips with her napkin.

"I do hope there are plans for Saint Paul to follow suit soon." Catherine gave her father a slightly pouty look that said she expected her wishes to be met. "I'd hate for us to fall behind other important cities."

Edward placed his arm on the back of Tessa's chair. "Your daughter and Miss Gregory have made a good point. Under the board's direction, Como Park has become the crowning glory of Saint Paul, and a conservatory would be the jewel in her crown."

"I believe plans are already under way to that end." Mr. Chattingworth cleared his throat. "And if not, I'll be looking into it. We can't very well fall behind the other cities."

"I'm sure you'll take care of it, dear." Mrs. Chattingworth's gaze swept over the other ladies, and then she stood. The guests rose as well, and the ladies followed their hostess to the drawing room with the gentlemen close behind.

The carpet had been rolled up and removed to allow for dancing, and a pianist and violinist struck up a waltz called "Come My Hero."

Edward turned to Tessa and held out his hand. "Would you care to join me?"

Obviously well trained, Edward proved to be an accomplished dancer. It was too bad she could only allow him three dances. If she permitted him more, she'd be cut off from this group entirely, and with the progress she'd made in one night, she didn't want that to happen. She couldn't wait to share the news with Reese.

Reese. She frowned. She was dancing in the arms of one handsome man while thinking about another.

"Someone will think I stepped on your toe." Edward smiled down at her.

"I'm sorry. I was lost in thought."

"I noticed. I'm amazed you didn't miss a step, however." He leaned in a bit closer. She could feel his breath fanning her cheek. "You handled that dinner conversation perfectly. I'm impressed. You're quite good at manipulation, Miss Gregory."

She lowered her lashes. "I prefer being thought of as an actress. Thank you for your help."

"My pleasure. Now that I've helped you meet your goal, I hope you'll help me meet mine."

"And what is that?"

"I'll tell you later." The pace of the music quickened. "For the moment, I simply want to enjoy this dance with you. I'm glad we have an understanding."

A what? Tessa's corset drew tight. "Edward, I hope you don't think I've been leading you on, but I—"

"Whoa, Tessa. That's not what I meant. You're a lovely young woman, but I have a girl back at college I'm crazy about. The understanding to which I was referring is our ability to mutually aid one another in reaching our goals."

Tessa exhaled a slow breath. "Thank goodness."

"Excuse me?"

"Did I say that aloud?"

He grinned. "It's all right. I know what you mean."

An hour later, Tessa had danced with two of the other young men at the party, including nasally William Riley, who was surprisingly light on his feet. Edward then claimed her for a two-step to "Baby Rose," which he said seemed like the perfect dance for a lady gardener. Later, when "Court House in De Sky" was played, she met his gaze across the room and smiled. But unless he wanted their last dance of the evening to be another two-step, he'd have to take his turn with Catherine, the birthday girl.

She took the opportunity to sneak away with Catherine for a few moments to see the young woman's chrysanthemum seedlings. Tessa praised the tiny plants and complimented her hostess on meeting the chrysanthemums' every need. She promised to visit again once the plants had grown more.

Edward claimed her for the last song, "Garden of Roses." Catherine had kept the theme of the songs she'd chosen well distributed throughout the program, and this final waltz with its sweet and sweeping melody ended the evening perfectly.

As the last notes died in the air, she stepped away and looked up into Edward's dark eyes. For a brief moment, desire sparked in them. Cheese and crackers, she didn't want to encourage that—not yet anyway.

But Edward schooled his features, and they said their goodbyes to the rest of the guests. Once they were outside, Tessa turned to her escort. "So, what is it that I can do to help you?"

"It's quite simple, really, and I believe it will help us both." They stopped at the waiting automobile.

"Mr. Ferrell, you have piqued my curiosity." Henry held the door while she slid into place.

Edward sat down beside her and arched his dark eyebrows. "Good. I think we will make excellent partners."

Partners? A stitch of excitement mingled with a sharp stab of guilt. Reese was her partner—at least in the park—but somehow she didn't think he would like her connecting in any way to a man like Edward. He would probably be skeptical of Edward's motives, and a part of her would agree, but what Reese couldn't understand was the importance of connections among those of society. Edward had the connections to help her. He'd been an excellent companion this evening, and he'd already helped her twice. She needed to respond in kind.

Reese would probably not agree with her decision. He'd already cautioned her about these men sometimes being more than they seemed. But she could handle it, and he didn't even need to know. Actually, he had no right. She could balance both worlds and Reese would never know.

She laid her hand on Edward's arm. "What do you need me to do?"

13

After planting the last of the hen and chickens, or *Papaver som-niferum*, Reese stepped back from the Gates Ajar and eyed the structure. He could almost picture what it would look like when it was done. Almost. Maybe some of Tessa's imagination was rubbing off on him.

He glanced at her as she knelt with a pointed hand spade, embed-ding Joseph's coat plants on the staircase. When the small plants matured, the foliage would make a deep burgundy, textured carpet on the stairs.

She'd been unusually quiet the last two days. He'd tried to start a few conversations, but he stumbled over his words. Why had it always been easier for him to do something other than put two sentences together? Up until now, though, speaking with Tessa had been easy. Suddenly it seemed especially hard. Why?

Deep down, he knew the answer. Something had happened between them the other day, and instead of seizing the moment, he'd run from it. As much as he liked Tessa, something held him back. Something made him not trust her completely, and he'd been taught not to tinker with a young woman's affections. If he was going to start something, it wouldn't be to steal a kiss. It would be to win her heart.

Still, he'd been angry with himself ever since that night, and he didn't know how to fix the rift now. Maybe he should go ahead and tell her how he was feeling about her—about them.

Tessa pushed up from her position and wiped her hands together. "It's going to be beautiful. Don't you think?"

He nodded. "I think Mr. Nussbaumer will be pleased we finished it so soon."

"Speaking of finishing soon, I'll be leaving early today."

"Oh?" What else could he say? She didn't answer to him. She could come and go when she wanted.

"Did I mention my visit to the Ladies' Gardening Society the other day? The speaker that day, Leroy Boughner, enlisted the club's help in creating vacant lot gardens in Saint Paul, and I volunteered to help in the effort. I'm meeting Mr. Boughner this afternoon."

She was meeting a man? Alone? He swallowed hard. "Anyone else coming?"

She giggled. "I doubt it. I can't imagine the ladies I met actually working, but one can hope."

"Vacant lot gardens sound like a great idea. Where are you starting?"

"Oh, somewhere on University." She pushed her straw hat up and wiped her brow with a handkerchief. "Anyway, I'll see you tomorrow." She started down the sidewalk.

"Tessa, wait. I'll walk you to the depot." *And I'll get as much information about this Boughner fellow as I can.*

"No need. I'll be fine." With a flick of her wrist, she waved goodbye and hurried off.

He stood there and watched her go, then kicked a dirt clod across the ground. Why was he so stupid?

For the second time this week, he'd let her get away.

Sitting in the backseat of Aunt Sam's Oldsmobile, Tessa giggled and pulled on her sleeve protectors. What would the women from the Ladies' Gardening Society say if she showed up wearing overalls and a straw hat? Although she'd been sorely tempted to shock them all, she'd chosen an appropriate outfit. Even stuffy Eleanor Bates would approve of the moss-green day dress she wore with its intricate embroidery work.

Henry slowed the motorcar, and Tessa looked around the vacant lot for Leroy Boughner or any of the ladies from the club. She spotted a man who could be Mr. Boughner lifting crates full of seeds from the back of a Maytag Light Delivery Car.

She grabbed her basket of garden tools and hopped out as soon as Henry stopped.

"Miss Gregory," Henry called. "It's not ladylike. Let me help you out."

She waved her fingers in the air. "Sorry. See you in an hour or so."

The uneven ground on the vacant lot made it difficult for Tessa to hurry, but she did her best. Charlotte and Hannah were supposed to join her, but she wanted to have things well in hand before they did. That way, they'd see she could manage on her own.

Mr. Boughner spotted her. "Miss Gregory, you're right on time."

She eyed the crates. Onion sets, cauliflower and cabbage seedlings, and seed packets filled them. "It looks like we're going to be busy."

"We sure are. It's a good thing we've got another volunteer." Mr. Boughner motioned to the man carrying a crate toward them.

Tessa's breath caught. "Reese?"

He set down the crate with a thud. "It sounded like a worthy project. Thought you could use some help."

"We certainly can." Mr. Boughner picked up a shovel. "It will take three of us quite a while to get these in."

"I think Tessa's got more than three volunteers here." Reese took her by the shoulders and turned her around.

A dozen ladies, led by Catherine Chattingworth, marched across the grass. Tessa recognized them from the Ladies' Gardening Society. How had Catherine convinced the women to lend a hand?

The ladies lined up in front of Tessa, and Catherine smiled. "So, tell us what to do first. We're *all* going to get dirty today. Right, ladies?"

Only a few of them nodded. Clearly not everyone was here by their own free will. But she had a job to do. She had to make them believe in this cause and their value to it.

Tessa drew in a deep breath. It was time to step on stage.

As hard as it was to believe, Tessa's speech had worked. There were no more disdainful glances at the garden tools, and some of the ladies actually looked excited. The exuberance was catching, and once Catherine picked up a hoe, the others followed suit.

Tessa turned to Mr. Boughner. "Where do you want us to start?"

He laughed. "You're the boss, Miss Gregory. You decide."

She glanced at Reese, who gave her an encouraging nod. Could she do this? Could she really organize all these women? Most of them didn't know a weed from a flower.

After dividing them in three groups, she assigned one group to Reese, one to Mr. Boughner, and one to herself. She then directed each group to plant one of the cool weather–tolerant vegetables in the boxes. She and her group took the onion sets.

"Look at that." Reese leaned against his hoe when they neared one another. "You got all of those ladies organized and working like they've been gardening all their lives. I still can't believe you got Mrs. Hammerston to dirty her hands. I got the distinct feeling she'd never touched a watering can, let alone a spade. How did you get to be such a convincing speaker?"

"Don't tell anyone, but I was acting." She patted the soil around the last of her onion sets.

Reese offered her a hand. She took it and let him pull her to her feet. Heat sizzled through her at the contact. He locked his blue eyes on hers and held them.

Please, Lord, make him see me as more than a friend.

He let go of her hand and inclined his head to the right. "I think those two ladies are searching for someone in charge. I think that would be you."

Tessa turned and smiled. "Those are my sisters. If you'll excuse me."

He took hold of her wrist. "I'd like to meet them, Tessa."

"Oh, Reese, my sisters can be overwhelming. Hannah's an attorney, and she might cross-examine you. And Charlotte, she's a chef, and by the time she's done, you'll probably feel like your goose is cooked."

"I'm sure it wouldn't be that bad, and if they're anything like you, I'm sure I'd love them."

She blinked. What had he said? If they were like her, he'd love them? Love?

If he loved her, he had a pretty strange way of showing it.

"Tessa, sorry we're late." Hannah took her hands. "How are things going?"

Tessa's mind whirled. Why couldn't she form a coherent thought? Now of all times.

Charlotte laid a hand on her shoulder. "Is all this too much for you to handle?"

"Are you kidding? Look at all these ladies." Reese motioned around him. "Tessa organized all of them."

"Of course, Catherine Chattingworth deserves the credit for getting them here," Tessa said.

Hannah smiled. "Aunt Sam said you attended Catherine's dinner party birthday celebration with Edward. Did you enjoy yourself?"

Don't look at Reese. Play it cool. Maybe he didn't hear.

"A dinner party?" Reese stepped back and jammed his hands into his pockets. "You didn't say anything about that."

Cheese and crackers, now what was she going to do?

"Tessa, aren't you going to introduce us?" Hannah used her eyes to motion to Reese.

"Hannah and Charlotte, this is Reese King. Reese, these are my sisters, Hannah Cole and Charlotte Brooks."

"It's a pleasure to meet you, Mr. King." Charlotte offered him a pleasant smile. "And how do you know our Tessa?"

Tessa squeezed her eyes shut. *Don't let him tell them. Don't let him tell them.*

"We both enjoy gardening."

Good answer, Reese.

"How did you meet?" Hannah asked in a much too sweet voice.

Oh great, she was onto them. "Reese sort of got me out of a jam at Como Park."

"A jam?" Hannah's tone switched to big sister.

Why had she admitted that?

"Nothing serious." Her oak tree, Reese, steeled her with his gaze. "Something involving pansies. Do you both like flowers as much as your sister?"

Excellent, Reese. Change the subject. But he was still no match for the two of them.

"Why don't we let Reese get back to work?" Tessa said. "I'll show you what we've done, and then you can decide where you want to work."

"Very well. It was a pleasure to meet you, Mr. King." Charlotte dipped her head.

Hannah smiled. "And hopefully we'll get a chance to speak again soon."

No need, my dear sisters. Reese and I are just friends, and if it's up to Reese, it looks like that's how it's going to stay.

Reese tossed the last of the crates in the Maytag Light Delivery Car and scanned the garden for Tessa. Only a few ladies remained, but she wasn't one of them. A few moments ago she'd been speaking with Catherine Chattingworth, so where had she gone?

Then he noticed her sisters had also disappeared.

"Lost something?" Mr. Boughner collected a bunch of rakes and tossed them in with the crates.

"Some*one*." Reese handed Mr. Boughner the last of the rakes. "Did you see Miss Gregory leave? I didn't get a chance to say goodbye."

Mr. Boughner chuckled. "I figured you didn't show up to volunteer by chance. She and her sisters got in some fancy car a few minutes ago."

Was this a sign that it wasn't the right time to make his intentions clear?

No. He'd come here today with that purpose foremost in his mind, and he wasn't stopping yet.

After saying goodbye to Mr. Boughner, Reese rushed to his Model T, cranked the engine, and hopped in. If he hurried, he might catch her before she went inside. Knocking on that Summit Avenue home uninvited wouldn't be his favorite thing to do, but he'd do it.

He wasn't going to let Tessa slip away again.

Lights sparkled in the mirror above the soda fountain, casting a sugary spell over the patrons. With a grin on her face, Tessa slurped the last bit of her root beer float from the glass. She eyed the frown on her sisters' faces and giggled. They were so easy to annoy.

Hannah exhaled through disapproving lips. "Really, Tessa. When are you going to grow up?"

"Hopefully never. I like having a good time. You remember fun." She let her spoon clink against the glass. "Oh wait, you were the responsible big sister. Maybe you don't remember having fun."

Charlotte tried to suppress a smile but failed. She laid her hand on Tessa's arm. "Tell us more about that handsome Mr. King. He seemed to know you fairly well—at least well enough to call you by your given name. You said you met at the park. Have the two of you seen each other often?"

Like an unruly vine, Tessa's stomach tangled. How was she going to get out of this? She didn't want to lie or even twist the truth. *Think, Tessa.* "You think he's handsome? I hadn't noticed."

Charlotte chuckled. "How could you not?"

"Why, Lottie, you're a married woman. Shame on you."

"I may be married, but I still have eyes. Speaking of which, Mr. King's eyes were the first thing that struck me. What color would you say they were, Tessa?"

Her lips curled. "I think they match the denim of his trousers."

"So you have noticed?" Hannah grinned and slipped a slice of strawberry into her mouth. "He seems like a nice young man, and I know he brought you home the other day. Why don't you go ahead and answer Charlotte's question?"

Tessa sighed. She might as well get this over with.

"We've been working together at Como Park." As briefly as she could, she explained how she and Reese were planting an Arts and Crafts garden using her garden design. "When it's finished and Mr. Nussbaumer expresses his pleasure, Reese is going to tell him the truth about the whole thing."

"Oh, Tessa, you're taking a big chance." Hannah dabbed her lips with her napkin. "What if things don't go as you want?"

"What could possibly go wrong?"

"Mr. Nussbaumer could dislike what you've done behind his back, for one thing."

Charlotte folded her hands on the table. "I think what Hannah's worried about is this whole thing backfiring."

Tessa shook her head. Why couldn't her sisters have a little faith in her? "You both worry too much. It'll be fine."

"And what if Mr. King's interest has grown from your garden designs to designs on you?" Hannah asked. "What are you going to do then? It would hardly be appropriate to spend all day, every day, unchaperoned with a man who has expressed an interest in stepping out with you. I guess Charlotte and I could take turns—"

"No!" Her corset tightened. A chaperone? For garden work? "If—and I do mean if—something develops between Reese and me, it will not affect our work in the park. Neither of us can afford it to. You both are going to have to trust me on this." She glanced at Charlotte, then Hannah, hoping for some sign of acknowledgment. "Besides, we are only friends."

For a long moment, Hannah's lips were pressed thin, then they slowly began to curl. She shared a knowing look with Charlotte. "In the words of our sister, the former actress, I think she 'doth protest too much.' What do you think, Charlotte?"

"Methinks you may be right." Charlotte laughed and squeezed Tessa's hand. "Don't worry, Tessa, we won't spoil your fun. Just promise us you'll be careful."

"Careful of what? It's a park, not a lions' den." Tessa stood and laid her hand over her heart. "Very well. I promise to be wary of every posy, peony, and possum, and to be on my guard at all times in case some great gardening catastrophe should strike." She lowered her hand and slid off her stool. "Now, can we get home? I have a long day tomorrow."

Hannah headed toward the door. "Yes, you'll need your beauty rest before you meet your *friend*."

14

Reese knew he shouldn't be spying. Parked on the street across from Tessa's aunt's home, he waited. He'd come to speak with her aunt, but that couldn't happen right now.

Who were the people on the front porch? If he had to guess, the elderly woman in the bloomers was Tessa's aunt, but the man? Tessa had never said anything about an uncle, and from the Packard in the driveway, he imagined the older, distinguished man was a guest, and a wealthy one at that.

But where were Tessa and her sisters? The robin's egg–blue Cadillac he'd come to recognize as belonging to her aunt was nowhere in sight. Perhaps they'd not come home, or maybe there was a garage around back. He would wait a while for them to come home, and then he'd go speak to her aunt and ask for permission to see Tessa.

The sound of their muffled conversation mixed with the song of a mourning dove and the rustling of the leaves on the trees.

Tessa's aunt stood, and the distinguished man followed suit. He took her aunt's hands in his and held them. Did Tessa know her aunt was involved with this man?

Reese rubbed his forehead. He should not be watching this.

"I'll see you tomorrow, Samantha, at the Ryan Hotel," the man called when he reached his automobile. "Tell your driver I'll bring you home."

Tessa's aunt laughed. "Senator Ferrell, I will not do that. My driver will take me and bring me home."

"This time." The senator waved, tipped his hat, and got inside.

The older lady waved too. She watched the senator back down the driveway and pull out onto Summit Avenue. Then she glanced around as if she were worried about being seen. Her gaze landed on Reese.

He looked away, then tipped his head back and closed his eyes. So much for making a good first impression. How was he going to explain this? *Yes, ma'am, I was spying on you and your gentleman caller, and yes, I do want to step out with your niece.*

Yep, that ought to make Tessa's aunt think the world of him.

Maybe he'd better head home tonight and hope the woman wouldn't recognize him later.

"Excuse me, young man."

He jolted and turned to find Tessa's aunt standing next to his motorcar.

She crossed her arms over her chest. "You're the young man who brought Tessa home the other night. Would you care to tell me why you were watching me?"

"I didn't mean to, ma'am. It was an accident. I mean, that's not why I came tonight. "

Her eyebrows lifted, and she placed her hands on the car door. "Keep going."

He swallowed hard. How was he going to explain his presence? "I came because I hoped to speak to you about Tessa, your niece."

"I'm aware that Tessa is my niece." She drummed her fingers impatiently on the automobile's door. "And what has Tessa done now that made you drive all the way to my home? Surely, whatever her transgression, it can't be as bad as spying on someone."

"Ma'am, I didn't mean to spy on you and your—your friend."

His mouth, as dry as clay, didn't seem to want to form words. "And I certainly didn't come to tell you anything bad about Tessa. In fact, it's the opposite. I wanted to ask you for your permission to see her."

Tessa's aunt didn't answer. Instead, she began to laugh.

Reese gripped the steering wheel. If she'd said no, he would have offered to prove this first impression wrong. If she'd said yes, he'd have thanked her profusely, but to laugh? It stung him to his core. How insensitive could a woman be?

"Does Tessa know you're here?" the older woman finally asked.

"No, ma'am."

"And does she know your intentions? Have you made them clear at any time?"

"No, ma'am."

"Then you don't know Tessa very well. Do you realize how angry she'll be that you spoke to me without allowing her to make the decision for herself? Yes, it's noble of you and all that, but Tessa should be the first to know you care about her, not the last. After all, it's her heart you want to win. Not mine."

Reese moaned inwardly. Tessa's aunt was right.

She chuckled again and shook her head. "I believe you and I, Mr. . . ."

"King, Reese King."

"You and I, Mr. King, need to strike a deal."

"A deal?" Reese's voice cracked.

"Yes. It will be most advantageous to us both." She leaned in close. "If you forget what you saw tonight, then I'll forget what I saw. Tessa doesn't need to know about either situation. Agreed?"

He scratched the side of his head. Why would Tessa's aunt want to keep her guest a secret? But did it really make a difference? She was giving him a way out of a situation that could ruin everything.

"Well?" The tapping began again.

He gripped the steering wheel and nodded. "Agreed. My lips are—"

"Hopefully going to be put to good use soon." She patted his shoulder and winked. "Good luck with my niece. You're going to need it."

Exhaustion grabbed hold of Tessa and hung on like a sand burr. Her head throbbed and her body ached. As soon as she told Aunt Sam good night, she was going to draw a bath, then head to bed. Maybe her dreams would star someone extra special tonight.

The butler took her wrap. "Miss Gregory, you had a telephone call while you were out—a Mr. Edward Ferrell. He said he was looking forward to Saturday and would pick you up at eleven."

The news sucked the last remaining shred of energy out of her. Why had she agreed to help Edward? Oh, she knew the reason, all right. The only problem was she didn't want to spend a Saturday with him, even if it helped her cause. She wanted to spend the day with Reese doing something fun.

But that wasn't going to happen.

With a sigh, she trudged into the parlor, and Aunt Sam looked up from her book. "Hello, Tessa, did you enjoy the time with your sisters? How did the beautification project go?"

"Very well, thanks to Catherine Chattingworth. She's quite a champion of horticulture. Did you know she grows chrysanthemums for the annual show?"

"No, I didn't." Aunt Sam stood. "You look like you're ready to drop. Why don't you head to bed and we'll speak in the morning?"

Tessa agreed and hugged her aunt good night. Upstairs, she drew a bath and slipped into the tub full of bubbles. It was heaven to be in one of the modern homes where hot water came right from the tap. Her bathroom even had a wall-mounted shower ring, a rubber curtain, and a hand shower if she chose to use them. She, however, preferred a long, soaking bath.

She tipped her head back and let the water ease the tension in her muscles, but her head continued to ache. Sleep would be the only cure.

Half an hour later, she crawled into bed and rang for the maid. She seldom summoned her, but tonight she requested two Bayer aspirins. Aunt Sam often touted the medicine as a miracle drug, and Tessa could sure use a miracle of her own tonight.

While she waited, she considered what her sisters had said about Reese and her plan. Could it backfire? She could deal with it if Mr. Nussbaumer still turned her down. She'd be sorely disappointed, and she might have to confess to her family about what happened at college, but she'd land on her feet somehow. But what if Mr. Nussbaumer punished Reese for their plan? She hadn't even considered this could cost Reese his job.

Reese. Why had he come to help today? He'd seemed different. Tessa couldn't put her finger on it, but she liked it.

Who was she kidding? She liked *him*. A lot more than she should.

And then there was Edward. Being seen with him on Saturday at such a public affair might cement her in society, but was she leading him on? No, it was a business deal. They both knew that.

The maid finally brought a glass of water and the aspirin, but the headache drummed on. With a cold cloth pressed against her eyes, Tessa finally succumbed to a fitful sleep.

In the morning, she threw on a periwinkle housedress and wandered into the breakfast room. The French doors opened into the garden, and she prayed that being there would refresh her.

"You look horrible." Aunt Sam set her coffee cup down and studied Tessa. "Mary said you had a headache last night. Is it still there?"

"Yes, ma'am."

"Then back to bed with you." Aunt Sam shooed her with the back of her hand. "I'll have Mary bring up your breakfast. You've been working too hard and need more rest."

So Tessa did something completely out of character. She did exactly as she was told.

Reese surveyed the area as he walked toward the superintendent's office. Como Park would be in fine form by the time the Memorial Day crowds arrived next week. If he were lucky, he'd be able to enjoy the festivities along with everyone else, or at least with a special *someone* else. He'd already planned to ask Tessa to accompany him, and if things went as he hoped, he'd ask her today.

He tugged off his work gloves and opened the door to the office. The hallway smelled of soil, but didn't everything at the park? He knocked on Mr. Nussbaumer's door.

"Reese, *gut*, you're here." He rolled up a set of plans and tied them with a string. "The mother of your young apprentice called—a Mrs. Gregory. She said he wouldn't be here today. He was ill and didn't want you to be worried about him."

Tessa was sick? He fought the urge to go to her aunt's house and check on her. If she had made the telephone call, which she would have had to, then she wasn't that ill. Reese swallowed. "Did she say what was wrong?"

"No, I don't think so." Mr. Nussbaumer tucked the plans under his arm. "I hope such a responsible fellow shows some promise for horticulture."

"He certainly does."

"When you believe the time is right, bring your young apprentice to me, and I'm sure we can find a place for him." He walked to the office door. "Come. We can talk as we go. I have some things I'd like to discuss with you."

Reese trailed his boss out of the office, his mind still on Tessa.

"So," the German began, his accent thick and his voice deep, "I've been corresponding with your father."

Reese paused midstep. "Is there a problem with my work?"

Mr. Nussbaumer laughed. "Why would you think that? I wrote him because we have similar positions. I wanted to know how he persuaded the Chicago park board to build the conservatory."

Air whooshed from Reese's lungs.

"Some of the park board members are not in favor of the venture. They feel it's too expensive, and I thought your father might have some ideas."

"Did he?"

"Nothing that will work here." Mr. Nussbaumer stopped and pulled a weed along the sidewalk. "He asked how you were doing."

"Oh?"

"He wanted to know if your vision had improved. Are you having eye troubles, Reese?"

"No, sir." A weight settled on Reese's chest. Nothing like having your father point out your flaws to your mentor. "My father was referring to my lack of creativity."

"You?" Mr. Nussbaumer's eyebrows rose. "I guess you don't have a flair for the dramatic in your gardening approach, but that Arts and Crafts garden you're creating shows strokes of genius."

It did, but it wasn't his genius. It was Tessa's.

"I didn't realize you were a student of Gertrude Jekyll's work. I myself have found her work quite inspired."

"But she's a woman."

Mr. Nussbaumer's belly shook with laughter. "That she is. A woman who's been commissioned to design gardens all over England. She paints gardens like an artist paints portraits."

"But I thought you didn't approve of lady gardeners."

"Ah, you must have overheard me turning down that young lady who came to visit me, *ja?*"

Reese nodded.

"Our garden requires men like you who can do the work and have the vision. I'm afraid the work is too taxing here, but I think working in private gardens is a *gut* place for a woman. That's what I told that young lady. We all must find our place in the world."

"That's not so easy."

"No, but you are getting there. Your greatest strength seems to lie in your horticultural skills. Everything you touch blossoms under your care."

"My father doesn't see it that way."

"At some point, a man must decide for himself who he is." Mr. Nussbaumer thumped his own chest. "I am a gardener. All that I am is played out in this park for everyone to see."

Reese glanced at the whimsical elephant on the island of Lake Como. He recalled the vast areas Mr. Nussbaumer had devoted to natural trees and shrubs, the formal gardens, the Banana Walk, the Japanese Garden, the aquarium, and even the lavish floral displays. All of these reflected something else about this brilliant man— another layer to who he was. Nature under man's control.

Tessa had those facets too. The whimsy and the grasp of beauty mingled with drive and determination. But what about him?

"My predecessor, Horace Cleveland, hated theatricality in landscape gardening. He felt all should be in harmony with the climate and sky." Mr. Nussbaumer chuckled. "He would be sorely disappointed in parts of this park, but I am not him. I believe the park must balance what the people love and what we must learn to love. You will decide your own path."

They walked for several more minutes with Mr. Nussbaumer pointing out a few areas he'd like Reese to address. They stopped by the Palm Dome. Mr. Nussbaumer's own two-story house was attached to this greenhouse where the banana plants and other palms wintered.

Reese followed him around to the other eight greenhouses. All nine of them were in need of repair and severely overcrowded.

"You may or may not be aware that at its May meeting, the park board agreed to allocate fifty dollars for a general set of plans for new greenhouses."

"You mean the conservatory? That's wonderful."

Mr. Nussbaumer smiled. "That is not what the board voted on. Not everyone sees a conservatory as a *gut* thing, but the plan I'm going to present to the park board would include destroying all of these greenhouses in favor of a new conservatory and a large production greenhouse. It will be hard to convince everyone, but since you have a vested interest in the project's success, I value your input."

Reese's brows scrunched. What did he mean, a vested interest?

Mr. Nussbaumer clapped him on the shoulder. "Surely you realize I am considering you or Nels to be in charge of this new conservatory. That's why I gave you each an area to develop. I'm watching you both to see who I believe would be the best fit and who can handle the great variety of demands."

Reese's face went lax. In charge of the new conservatory?

"Don't look so surprised." Mr. Nussbaumer squeezed his shoulder. "So now you'll understand my next request. I've been invited to join some of the park board members and their families at a garden party. I'd like you to join me. It will be an excellent way for me to see how you interact with these men."

"Certainly, Mr. Nussbaumer. When is it?"

"On Memorial Day—next Friday. I'll get you the time and place later."

Like the fluff of a dandelion, his hopes for the perfect day with Tessa blew away on the wind.

Mr. Nussbaumer hiked up his britches. "Now, what do you think about getting back to that garden of yours?"

"Yes, sir." Reese gave him a firm nod. "I'll make you proud, Mr. Nussbaumer."

"*Gut*, but please God, Reese. Not me and not your father."

That was easier said than done.

15

The spring breeze kissed Tessa's cheeks. When she'd awakened, her headache was nearly gone. It had taken a while to persuade Aunt Sam that she was fit enough to visit the park. She'd chosen a pink walking dress so she wouldn't look pale, and packed a picnic lunch. Aunt Sam didn't need to know she'd added her sleeve protectors and an apron so she could assist with some of the planting.

Reese looked up as she approached. "What are you doing here? I thought you were sick."

"I'm much better, thank you."

He set his hand spade aside, pushed to his feet, and met her. He lifted her chin to look beneath her satin-trimmed hat. "Your eyes tell a different story."

"I only have a little headache." She held up the picnic case. "I brought lunch. After we eat, I'll help you."

He took the case from her and started toward the shade trees. "You're not going to work in the dirt in that pretty dress."

"Aunt Sam wanted me to stay home, but we compromised. I wore the dress to prove to her I wouldn't work, but I brought my apron and sleeve protectors, so I'll be fine."

He set the case on the grass and took the blanket from her. "You're not helping today. After we eat, you can rest here in the shade."

She propped her hands on her hips. "And what am I supposed to do while I'm resting?"

"Watch me?" He took her hand and helped her settle on the blanket.

"You're not that entertaining."

"I'll try to throw in a few tricks."

"Cartwheels or somersaults?"

He chuckled. "I don't think I can do either one."

"It figures."

"I can juggle some spades or something."

"Never mind." She grinned and unlatched the lid of the picnic case. Unlike a traditional basket, this hard-sided suitcase held plates, napkins, silverware, and even salt and pepper shakers, all attached to the lid with leather straps. The deeper bottom part of the case had a square metal box to hold food, a jar for canned goods, another jar for drinks, and a spot for four enameled cups.

She unbuckled the plates and gave him one before pouring milk into a cup for each of them. "I hope ham sandwiches are all right."

"Fine with me."

Tessa opened the glass jar containing canned peaches. "I can't cook like Charlotte, but I did bring dessert."

"Really? What is it?"

"Only the best thing ever made." She lifted the lid on the metal box. Inside, next to the sandwiches she'd wrapped in waxed paper, lay a tin of Nabisco's new Oreo biscuit.

"What are those?"

"You haven't had an Oreo? Oh, this is going to be fun, but lunch first." She plopped a sandwich in his hand, the paper scrunching.

After Reese said grace, he told her about a meeting he'd had that morning with Mr. Nussbaumer. Excitement swirled inside Tessa as she heard Mr. Nussbaumer's plans for Reese. "I'm sure he'll pick you, Reese. You're the kind of man any superintendent would want responsible for his prized possession. You're smart and trustworthy and grounded and dependable."

"You make me sound like someone's faithful dog, Tessa."

She playfully slapped his sleeve. "That is not what I meant and you know it. I simply meant you're a man of integrity and your roots run deep. A salt-of-the-earth kind of fellow. Mr. Nussbaumer has got to see that too."

"If I'm a salt-of-the-earth fellow, what are you?"

"A reach-for-the-stars kind of girl, of course." She opened the tin of Oreos and held one out to Reese. "But that doesn't mean I don't need someone who keeps my feet on the ground."

He met her eyes and reached for the biscuit. When his fingers touched hers, electricity fired through her hand and up her arm. Her gaze shot to his. He looked as unnerved as she felt.

Lifting the cookie to his mouth, he started to pop the biscuit in.

"Wait a minute!" Tessa grabbed his wrist to stop him. She then took an Oreo for herself. "You can't just eat them. You need to twist them open first and dunk them in the milk."

"I have to?"

"Well, yes. That's the proper way to eat one, I'm sure of it."

He chuckled. "Or is it the way you prefer?"

"That too." She twisted her Oreo open, dunked one half in her milk, and then took a bite. She closed her eyes and savored the mingling of dark chocolate and creamy filling mixed with the cold milk. "Ah, perfection—but don't tell Charlotte. It would hurt her feelings to be outdone by Nabisco. And now that I've demonstrated the proper way, it's your turn to try them."

Reese grinned. "First, I twist." He copied her movement in an exaggerated manner. "Then, I dunk." He took a bite. "Wow, Tessa, these are great. I have to admit the milk seals the deal."

Laughing between cookies, they each devoured three or four, but when Tessa spotted an unfamiliar man approaching, she froze. "Reese, do you know that man?"

He turned and sighed. "Yes. That's Nels Anderson, the other fellow Mr. Nussbaumer is considering for that position."

"What's he doing here?"

"Probably looking for a reason to get me in trouble. He's that kind of fellow."

"A snitch?"

"No, not necessarily. He just doesn't mind stepping on someone to get what he wants." Reese stood up. "Wait here."

As soon as Reese walked away, Tessa scrambled to her feet and hurried to join him.

"Hello, Nels." Reese crossed his arms over his chest. "What brings you to my garden area? Need some advice?"

"Thought I'd come see how your work was going, but I see you're not actually working. Who's your lady friend?" He nodded his head toward Tessa, who was standing behind Reese.

She stepped forward. "I'm Tessa Gregory, and Mr. King has been gracious enough to educate me about the plants in his garden."

Nels sniffed. "I saw how he was educating you."

Reese took a menacing step forward. "Why, I ought to—"

A smile bloomed on Tessa's face, and she stepped between the two men. "Sir, I don't believe I caught your name."

"Nels Anderson."

"Well, Mr. Anderson." She linked her arm through Nels's. "Why don't you join me over here and I will demonstrate what Mr. King has so aptly taught me?" With a tug, she urged him toward the garden. "According to Mr. King, this is to be an Arts and Crafts garden. Because much of England's climate can be so similar to Minnesota's, he felt like the same plants would do well here. He said that he was inspired by the works of Gertrude Jekyll." She swept her arm toward the plot. "This area will contain bergenia, better known as elephant ears, and here he intends to plant dicentra. In this spot, I believe he said he was planting African orange marigolds with pale anthemis behind them. Need I go on, Mr. Anderson?"

"No, miss. Apparently you learned your lessons well."

Releasing his arm, she stepped away. "And is Mr. King not allowed a lunch? I offered to share mine in exchange for him taking the time to educate me. Isn't educating the public part of your job as gardeners, Mr. King?"

He nodded. "It is."

"Well then, I shall have to write Mr. Nussbaumer a letter commending you." She pressed the back of her hand to her brow. "Now, if you men will excuse me, I feel a terrible headache coming on."

Reese took her arm. "Are you all right, Miss Gregory?"

"Would you be so kind as to assist me to the shade?"

"I can help you, miss," Nels offered.

Reese shot him a glare. "I've got her." He led her away. "That was quite a show."

"Did he buy it?"

"He's probably scared not to." He helped her settle on the blanket. "Now rest—for real. I mean it."

She sighed and batted her eyelashes at him. "How can I rest when the scenery is so fine to look at?"

Cheeks flushed red, Reese walked away with his shoulders held a little stauncher and his walk showing a bit more pride.

Tessa leaned against the tree. Yes, she'd enjoy this scenery a great deal.

Tessa walked over to the garden and bit into an apple. The loud crunch broke the silence. "As much as I've enjoyed watching you work, I'm bored. Either you let me work or I'm leaving."

Reese dipped his hands in a bucket of water and scrubbed them clean. He straightened and turned toward Tessa standing beside the empty wheelbarrow with her hands on her hips. He chuckled and pulled out his watch. "It's time to call it a day. What do you say to a nice, leisurely stroll by the lake?"

"I suppose that will have to do."

"I'll throw in a ghost story."

She tossed him an apple. "Well, Mr. King, you're full of surprises."

Reese flung his jacket over his shoulder, and they headed toward Lake Como. He'd suggested they leave the picnic suitcase by the wheelbarrow and he'd retrieve it later.

The breeze off the lake contrasted with the late afternoon sun, bringing uncharacteristically warm spring temperatures. Gray clouds had begun to thicken on the horizon, but so far nary a drop had fallen.

Only a few park visitors seemed to be enjoying a quick reprieve after work. One family had spread a picnic, and some other patrons sat on the benches along the veranda. Hopefully, any rain would hold off and not drench the visitors.

"Hungry?" Reese slipped his jacket on and nodded toward the concession stands in the pavilion.

"I could be." She flashed him an impish grin, but he didn't respond. Was he completely unaffected by her?

Quit teasing him. He isn't interested in you that way.

The concession stand owner recognized Reese and presented him with two mustard-topped frankfurters wrapped in fresh, soft buns and an opened Coke for each of them. Reese paid the man and tucked the two Cokes into the crook of his arm and then picked up the frankfurters.

Raindrops began to speckle the sidewalk. Patrons scattered like mice to their automobiles or to the streetcar station, but Tessa shrugged and glanced up at Reese. "I love the rain."

He chuckled. "Of course you do, but why don't we wait this shower out in the bandstand?"

Wide and open, the octagonal bandstand stretched from the shore. Tessa spun inside, her shoes clicking against the oak floorboards. "This place is amazing." She glanced at the rafters of the

pergola and sang a few lines of "Amazing Grace." "Listen to how
the sound bounces off the roof and water. No wonder the concerts
are so grand." She hurried to the railing, leaned as far over as she
could, and studied the lake below. "It's almost like being on a ship."

"Be careful, Tessa."

Whipped by the wind, the waves crashed against the bandstand's
footings, sending a misty spray in the air, but she didn't pull away.
"Oh, Reese, can you smell the rain? It smells like summer."

He joined her at the railing, and she stood back up and leaned
against one of the pillars. He passed her one of the frankfurters
and set the Cokes on the wide handrail. "Speaking of summer, do
you have plans for Memorial Day?"

"I'm marching in the parade with my Aunt Sam and the other
ladies to support suffrage. You do support a woman's right to
vote, don't you?"

He grinned and took a swig of Coke. "If I didn't, would you
make me walk the plank?"

She covered one eye as if she were wearing a patch. "Argh, I
would, matey."

"You make a mighty fine pirate, Miss Gregory."

"Thank you. Now, where were we?" She tapped her finger against
her mouth. "Oh, Memorial Day. After the parade, I think we'll
attend Senator Ferrell's commemorative address on the steps of
the capitol to honor those who've served." A flicker of recognition
showed on Reese's face. "Do you know the senator?"

"How would I know a senator, Tessa?" He cocked his head.

Odd. It was the first time she didn't believe him.

"So, Reese, what are you doing for Memorial Day? Do you have
to work?" She took a bite of her frankfurter.

"No, but Mr. Nussbaumer asked me to go to some function
with him."

"Oh." She could hear the disappointment in her own voice.

He began to chuckle.

"Why are you laughing?"

He chucked a finger under her chin and thumbed something away. Mustard? "There. Perfect once again."

Perfect. If only he meant it.

A crack of thunder startled her and she jolted. The earlier heat from the day seemed to have vanished in a whoosh, and she shivered against the chill.

Reese took his jacket off and draped it around her shoulders. "Better?"

She nodded and let the warmth of the jacket hug her. As wonderful as it was, it was a poor substitute for Reese's arms. "I believe you promised me a ghost story."

"You don't believe in ghosts, do you?" He took her hand and drew her toward one of the band's benches.

"Of course not."

"Good, because this isn't really about ghosts. It does, however, involve bones." He washed down the last bite of frankfurter with a swallow of Coke. "Years ago, a man named August Robertson was out hunting muskrats in the winter. He found a box sticking out of the ice in the middle of Lake Como."

"The bones were in it, right?" She twisted on the bench so she could face him. "But how did they get there?"

"Be patient and I'll tell you." He glanced over her shoulder toward the lake. "You're right about the box containing bones. The news of the discovery spread all over. There was a lot of speculation about murder and such. They even opened an inquest."

She leaned forward. "And?"

"And someone stepped forward to explain the whole story." He shrugged and leaned back against the bench.

"That's it?" She swatted his arm playfully. "There has to be more."

"It might scare you to know the truth."

"Do I look like someone who is scared of anything?"

His eyes crinkled with his laughter. "No, I can't say that you do."

"Then spill the rest of the story."

He stood and walked toward the railing. "Apparently the bones had been given to a young doctor by the Minnesota surgeon general. The doctor was the surgeon general's nephew, and he was fresh out of medical college and in need of a skeleton."

"But who did the bones belong to?"

"Charlie Pitts."

"Should I know that name?"

He returned to his seat and draped his arm over the back of the bench. "No, but you'll recognize who he ran with. Charlie rode with the Jesse James gang."

"The very one?" Tessa pressed her hand to her chest.

"Is there another?" Reese laid his hand on her shoulder. "After they robbed the First National Bank of Northfield, Charlie was one of four of the gang members who a posse caught up with near Madelia. He was shot, and they packed his dead body in ice and put it on display at the state capitol."

"But how did the bones end up here?"

"The young doctor had left the bones in Lake Como for a year to bleach them clean, but then he went West, and they found the box while he was gone." He squeezed her shoulder. "And yes, some say Charlie Pitts's ghost still haunts the lake."

"That's ridiculous."

"It is. But you know how a person's imagination can run away with him or her."

Did she ever. Her own had let her believe this man had feelings for her, and yet here in this romantic spot, he'd done little to indicate that.

He stood and offered her his hand. "The rain's stopped. I'd better get you home."

She let him pull her to her feet. "I can ride the streetcar."

"No, Tessa." He held her hand tighter. "I *want* to take you home. There's something I need to ask you."

"What?" The question slipped out before she could stop it. He'd said he *wanted* to take her home, and she was not imagining he'd stressed the word.

He tapped her nose. "Be patient."

"Sorry. I have an insatiable desire to know things."

He offered her his arm. "Really? I hadn't noticed."

By the time they pulled into the drive at Aunt Sam's, Tessa had almost forgotten Reese intended to ask her a question. Well, not really, but she'd tried to put the thought out of her mind.

Conversation came so easily to the two of them—as if they'd been friends forever. Friends. There was that word again. Did she dare hope they might be moving beyond that?

After parking the Model T, Reese came around to her side and helped her out. He followed her onto the porch, and she turned to him when they reached the enormous front door. "Thank you for the ride."

"Tessa, don't pretend you've forgotten about the question I wanted to ask you, because we both know you haven't."

Air whooshed from her lips. "Oh, cheese and crackers, I've tried to be good and not question you, but it's so hard."

He laughed, a full, warm sound that made her smile. "I may not be able to enjoy Memorial Day with you, but I was hoping I could take you to the Indian Mounds tomorrow."

Tomorrow! Tessa felt the blood drain from her face. Please, not the day she'd promised to help Edward. Her mind whirled. How could she get out of her plans with Edward?

Reese jammed his hands in his pockets. "Listen, if you don't want to—"

"No, no, I do, but I have a prior commitment for tomorrow."

"I see." He seemed mesmerized by the diamond tile pattern on the porch.

"What about Sunday?" she blurted out. How desperate could she sound?

A slow smile spread across his face. "Sunday would work fine too. Do you want to join me for church services? Then after lunch, I want to take you someplace I think you'll enjoy."

"The Indian Mounds?"

"Not this time. I have something else in mind." He swallowed. "Is that a yes?"

"Reese, that sounds delightful. I'd love to."

He tucked his knuckle beneath her chin again.

"More mustard?" She bit her lip.

"Not exactly." His look gave her goose bumps. He brushed her lower lip with the pad of his thumb. "See you Sunday, Tessa Gregory."

She watched him drive away before turning toward the house. Touching her lips, she sighed. This was not a figment of her imagination. It was 100 percent real.

16

Tessa would wonder where Sam had gone, but the fact her niece had been late getting home had proved quite advantageous. Sam stilled her hands in her lap and watched the buildings in downtown Saint Paul pass by—the Pioneer Press Building, the Germania Bank, and the Federal Post Office and Court House. She willed her breathing to slow and reminded herself she'd eaten with James Ferrell many times. But that had been lunch, and this was dinner. Why did this seem like such a significant difference?

Sam glanced down at her Grecian-style evening gown. Was it too dated? She'd not purchased a new one in quite a while. She smiled. Why was she worried? James would probably be thrilled when she arrived not dressed in bloomers.

Henry pulled the Cadillac to a stop in front of the Ryan Hotel on Sixth and Robert. Dressed in a black dinner suit with satin facings, James opened her car door and helped her out. "I was beginning to fear you weren't coming."

"I was beginning to fear I wasn't coming either." She turned toward the car. "Return for me at nine, Henry."

James leaned over the window. "But if we're not here, don't wait for her."

"Senator Ferrell, I told you—"

"I know exactly what you said. I hang on your every word." He took her gloved hand and bowed over it. "Have I told you that you look stunning, Samantha?"

"I find that hard to believe, but I do like the sound of it, so thank you." She touched the coif she'd allowed her maid to subject her to. At least her hat with its mass of plumes was new and covered most of her silvery hair.

James tapped the door of the Cadillac, and Henry drove away. "It looks like you're all mine for the evening, Samantha." He offered her his arm. "Are you ready to go inside?"

"And if I say no?"

"Then I'll have them bring a table out here so that we can picnic under the stars."

"You will not make a spectacle of me. I reserve that particular right for myself." She placed her hand in the crook of his arm. "And you can turn off the charm, James. We've known each other far too long for all of that."

He covered her hand with his own and escorted her into the hotel. "Ah, but you secretly love it."

She gave him a humph and he laughed. But inside her heart swelled. It had been so long since she'd been treated like a lady. And she did love every word.

Lord, please guard my heart.

Where was Aunt Sam?

Tessa searched the parlor and Aunt Sam's bedchamber, but to no avail. She'd even questioned the maid, but the girl insisted that Aunt Sam had simply gone out for the evening. What if something was wrong? What if Aunt Sam was being held hostage by some nefarious character? Didn't the maid realize that her aunt didn't go places at night without leaving some sort of message?

Message. That was it. Tessa hurried to the writing desk in the study and glanced at the papers on its surface. Aunt Sam was fastidious about keeping a calendar. It had to be here somewhere. She rummaged through one stack and then another. Maybe she should phone Hannah or Charlotte. They'd want to know Aunt Sam was missing.

She pulled open the desk drawers one by one. In the upper left-hand drawer, a leather-bound book caught her eye. Complete with gilt decorations, the calendar had a page for each month of the year. She flipped to today's date, Friday, May 23, and scanned the page.

Dinner with old friend. 7 p.m., Ryan Hotel

Tessa closed the calendar and put it back in the drawer. She sank into the desk chair and released her breath in a whoosh. At least Aunt Sam was safe.

Questions began to swirl in Tessa's mind like the waves in the lake earlier today. Who was this old friend? Why hadn't she written the person's name down? And most of all, why hadn't she said anything to Tessa earlier?

Something felt off, and Tessa itched to find out what it was.

Awakening in the library, Tessa stretched her arms above her head. She must have fallen asleep while waiting for Aunt Sam to come home, and the book she was reading, *The Emerald City of Oz*, had given her the most colorful dreams. Someone, probably the maid, had draped a soft blanket over her.

The grandfather clock in the hall chimed ten times. Surely Aunt Sam had returned by now. She set the blanket aside and hurried into the drawing room, intent on getting some answers.

"Hello, Tessa." Aunt Sam smiled from her seat on the divan and set down her crochet work. "Did you have a pleasant day?"

"Yes, thank you." Enough pleasantries. Tessa plopped into a winged chair. "Okay, I'm going to come out and ask this. Where were you tonight?"

"I was out with a friend, and before you ask whom, may I remind you that you too may want me to extend you some degree of privacy." She pointed to Tessa's limp hat on the marble-topped table. "Exhibit one."

Heat crept up Tessa's neck. She didn't want to tell anyone, including Aunt Sam, about her budding feelings for Reese. They were still too tender to expose for others to trample on.

"You have a point." Tessa released a slow sigh. Even though Aunt Sam was right, she really wanted to know who her aunt had been with tonight. "I guess we should each have a right to some secrets."

"If they aren't harmful."

"Can you tell me about where you went?"

Aunt Sam laughed. "Yes. We ate at the Ryan Hotel, and I must take you someday. You'd love the airy dining room. It has decorated columns, stenciled walls, and painted murals that give it a fanciful feeling."

"And the lights?"

"Bronze and glass chandeliers. Truly lovely."

"Would Charlotte have approved of the food?"

"I think so." She picked up her handwork again. "I had chicken croquettes in béchamel sauce, asparagus, and baked mashed potatoes."

"And for dessert?"

"Lemon sherbet and truffles."

"Ooh, you're making me hungry."

Aunt Sam pointed to a white lace handkerchief on the table. "I snuck a truffle home for you."

Tessa popped the decadent candy into her mouth and let the chocolate slowly melt on her tongue. She moaned with pleasure. "Thank you for thinking of me."

"I'm always thinking of you, and praying for you too."

"What do you pray for when it comes to me?"

"It's always the same thing. That you'll be rooted in Christ. There are many things in this world that Satan tries to make us believe will give us the nourishment we need."

"I'll need to think about that." Tessa stood and grinned. "And since I can't ask you everything I want to, I guess I'll head to bed. Edward is picking me up at eleven."

"Edward?" Aunt Sam's eyes widened.

"You seem surprised." Did she know Tessa had feelings for someone else?

Aunt Sam pretended to lock her lips. "You have a right to your privacy. Good night, dear."

Tessa slipped into a cotton nightgown and eased between the crisp sheets. She opened her Bible to the familiar passage in Colossians that Aunt Sam had alluded to. "As ye have therefore received Christ Jesus the Lord, so walk ye in him; rooted and built up in him, and stablished in the faith."

The word *rooted* stood out. She'd studied root systems. It was through the roots that the whole plant was fed. If the roots were too shallow, the plant would wither when times of stress came, like drought. But if the roots ran deep, the plant could handle all sorts of hard times.

What was she rooted in? Was it Christ? Just before her parents died, she'd obeyed the gospel. Her own father had baptized her in the lake, but had she let her roots grow deeper? And what did Aunt Sam mean about Satan trying to persuade us to get our nourishment from other places?

Her eyelids drooped and she nearly dropped the Bible. She'd have to ponder all of this later. Right now her dreams were calling.

The Twin City Motordrome? Tessa couldn't believe Edward's plans for the day included a trip to the wooden track to watch motorcycles race. Sure, she'd seen the Motordrome on University and Snelling before. How could she miss it? It was smack-dab between Saint Paul and Minneapolis, but she'd never even considered going in.

Well, maybe once or twice.

She read the advertisement posted on the box office promising "a thrill every minute."

This was her kind of place.

Edward paused at the entrance. "Are you sure this is all right with you? The motorcycles can travel up to ninety miles an hour."

Tessa smiled. "I'm so excited I'm ready to burst."

"But I know it's not the most appropriate place to take a lady. I'm considering making a substantial investment in a company that makes motorcycles. My potential business partner will be racing one of his own machines there today and asked me to attend and watch. He said his wife would be there too, so you can see why I needed a lady to join me, and you're the only one I know who wouldn't be scandalized by a motorcycle race."

She laughed. "I think it's all very exciting."

"It would be more exciting to be an investor in a company that makes millions." They stepped up to the counter, and Edward paid for their tickets. "My friend has hopes of a company that would rival Henry Ford's."

"Truly? And you honestly want to be part of making motorcycles? You're a law student."

"I am, but this is something that has caught my interest, and it's more than money. For as long as there have been horses, men and speed have gone hand in hand. Don't tell my parents, but from my first ride on one, I've been hooked."

Excitement churned in Tessa's stomach. She'd love to ride on a motorcycle, but maybe she should keep that fact to herself.

She followed Edward inside the Motordrome. They climbed a set of stairs and wound around the walkway along the bottom row of the bleachers. Edward pointed to an empty row. "That's Mrs. Walker."

Despite the cacophony coming from the crowded bleachers, Edward managed to introduce Tessa to Mrs. Marjorie Walker, who couldn't be more than a year or two older than her. Mrs. Walker insisted Tessa call her by her given name.

"I'm glad you came." Marjorie's voice rose over the din. "Women are definitely outnumbered here."

A marching band struck up a chord and made their way to the center of the field. Tessa took the opportunity to study the Twin City Motordrome. On the bottom half of the open area, a steeply banked board track had been constructed. It rose to about ten feet all the way around the oval. How many hours had gone into placing the narrow boards so carefully?

The top half, where she sat, sported rows of bleachers with a sturdy railing separating the spectators from the track. At least she hoped it was sturdy.

Following the third song, the band marched off the field, and the drivers pushed their motorcycles into place for the first of the afternoon's races.

Edward leaned close to her ear. "That's my friend Joe Walker on the end—number eight. The two bikes next to him are the ones he needs to beat. Number six is riding an Indian and number seven an Excelsior."

"What does Mr. Walker call his?"

"The Orbit." He drew a circle with his hand. "They have to go two times around the track."

The announcer called for the men to start their engines, and a roar filled the Motordrome. A flag was dropped, and the motorcycles surged forward. Tessa sucked in her breath. What if someone wrecked? Other than a leather helmet and leather chaps, there was little to protect the driver.

As if he'd heard her, a driver in the back lost control, and he and his cycle skidded on the rough wood surface. Tessa squeezed Edward's arm as a group of men hurried forward. Some carried the man off the track, and others took care of his motorcycle.

Tessa had never seen anything move as fast as the racing cycles. Even a train did not move at speeds of eighty or ninety miles per hour. As they gained speed, the motorcycles climbed high on the wooden track and jockeyed for the front spot. The Indian took the lead with the Excelsior right behind. But Mr. Walker's Orbit had already managed third.

Mr. Walker raced around the Excelsior. Marjorie grabbed Edward's arm. "He's doing it!"

With only half a lap left, the Indian still had the lead. Then Mr. Walker leaned down even closer to his handlebars and surged forward. The two motorcycles rode neck and neck for what seemed like forever. Tessa applauded and Edward whistled, but Marjorie closed her eyes and appeared to be praying.

"He did it!" Edward grabbed Tessa's waist and lifted her off the ground.

She grabbed her hat to keep it from flying off and cheered along with him. The Orbit seemed to be everything Edward hoped.

Ten races later, Tessa and Edward joined the Walkers for an early supper at Carling's Café. Even before they ordered, Edward and Joe began to recount the races.

Tessa smiled at the two men. Mr. Walker certainly deserved to be excited. Blood was still drumming through her own veins. What she wouldn't give to ride on a motorcycle!

More than thirty total riders had competed during the thrilling afternoon, with Mr. Walker participating in a total of three races on his Orbit. In the other races, he placed second and third, alongside the Excelsior and Indian riders.

"I'm telling you, I had men asking me all day about how fast I could produce new cycles." Joe grabbed Marjorie's hand. "This is going to work, honey. You'll see."

Marjorie beamed at her husband with adoration in her eyes. "I know it will. I'll do whatever it takes to make sure it does."

"She worries about money." He kissed her cheek. "But I've promised her I'll always keep bread on the table. Right, honey?"

Tessa was certain she saw anger flicker in Marjorie's eyes, but why? Was she not in favor of her husband's plan?

"As soon as I get the start-up funds, I can start filling orders." He patted his wife's hand, then grinned at Edward. "You're still interested, aren't you?"

"Wild horses couldn't keep me away. But my capital alone won't be sufficient." Edward glanced at Tessa.

"Don't look at me." She laughed. "I don't have any money."

Edward's smile slid away, and his voice grew intense. "But your aunt does."

"I seriously doubt Aunt Sam will invest in a motorcycle company."

"But you could persuade her—"

"Edward, you've met Aunt Sam. Does she seem like a woman who can be persuaded by anyone, including me?"

"No, I guess not. I suppose I'm getting ahead of myself." He picked up his menu. "Shall we order?"

Tessa took in Joe's disappointed face and Marjorie's searing glare. Anger simmered inside her. How dare Edward put her in such an awkward position? She'd thought she was returning his favor of helping her by joining him at the race, but now she wasn't so sure. Had this been Edward's plan all along? To coerce her into getting Aunt Sam to invest in Joe's Orbit?

When her food came, she picked at the beef and noodles and managed to swallow a few bites of the dry roll with a great deal of water. Marjorie made no effort at small talk, which was fine. Tessa couldn't muster much conversation either. The two men didn't seem to notice. They continued to rattle on about the business.

Tessa caught bits and pieces of their plan. Apparently they'd met at the Motordrome after Edward had come with his motorcycle to race for the first time. He'd been an abysmal failure, but he'd fallen in love with this new sport and, more importantly, the motorcycle itself.

Joe had not only taught him about racing, but he'd taught him about how to maintain and care for his new two-wheeler. When Joe had mentioned the desire to go into business, Edward had encouraged him and promised his support. Edward had offered to put up one-third of the start-up money. Joe had saved one-third already, but they'd not found a third investor for what remained.

"Maybe I could take out a loan for the rest," Joe offered.

Edward frowned. "And what collateral would you put up? Give me a chance to see what I can do. I'm sure I can think of something"—he glanced at Tessa—"else."

"What do you mean by that?" Tessa's fork slipped and banged against the plate. "It is not my fault that you haven't thought this plan through. Why don't you ask your father or grandfather to invest? They both have money."

Joe looked at Marjorie, then they both looked down at their plates.

"Don't they?"

"Lower your voice," Edward hissed. "Yes, they have money. But my parents said that if they ever catch me on a motorcycle again, they'll disinherit me. They do not condone what they refer to as 'dangerous and base' behavior."

"But you still ride?"

"Not where they can see me."

What were Edward's parents like? His grandfather, the senator, had seemed amiable enough. While she supposed a lot of messengers and delivery people had taken up the motorcycles, and obviously quite a few risk takers, that hardly made them immoral.

Edward dabbed his lips with the linen napkin. "Because your aunt is so vocal about her thoughts, I thought perhaps she would be more open, but I understand you're not willing to speak with her. I'm sure that given some time, I'll find another way."

"Good." She leaned back in her chair and folded her hands in her lap. She refused to feel guilty about this.

"But if you were to change your mind—"

"Enough." She held up her hand and turned to Joe and Marjorie. "I apologize if my decision affects your plans, and I do wish you well in this endeavor. Personally, I find motorcycles to be fascinating, and you appear to know what you're doing with them. In time, I'm certain you'll find the right investors. It's been a pleasure to meet you both, and Mr. Walker, it's been an even greater pleasure to watch you race."

She stood and, without a word to Edward, marched away.

17

Reese drew his paintbrush down the length of one of the porch's balusters, then paused when the screen door banged open. The Henderson brothers, Albert and Clem, strode out.

"Boys," Mrs. Baxter called from inside. "A minute, please."

"We're in a hurry, Mrs. B." Albert elbowed his brother's side and chuckled.

Reese dropped the paintbrush in the bucket and stepped into Albert's path, stopping the two young men. "Gentlemen, I think Mrs. Baxter wants to speak with you."

Out of breath, the older woman waddled through the door. "Oh good, you're still here, boys. I'm sure it slipped your mind, but your rent was due on the tenth."

"Is that so?" Clem glanced at his brother and grinned. "How could we forget to give you our rent?"

"Then, you do have the money?" The wrinkles around her eyes deepened with her smile. "Did you both find employment?"

Albert shoved his hands in his pocket. "We've . . . uh . . . got some possibilities."

Her smile slid away, and her brow creased. "Now, boys, I try to be understanding, but I do need the rent as soon as possible. All right?"

The Henderson brothers both gave her a halfhearted agreement, then turned to leave, but Reese didn't budge. "Gentlemen, let's sit on the porch and have a chat about those possibilities. Maybe I can help."

Mrs. Baxter clapped her hands together. "Wonderful! If anyone can help you secure a position, it will be Reese. I'll let you boys be so you can have a nice chat."

As soon as she'd gone, Reese pointed to the two rocking chairs. "Have a seat."

Albert and Clem glared at him and then sat down. "Say your piece, King. We have places to go."

"Oh, I know what kind of places you are going to, and they can certainly wait."

Albert stood, took off his hat, and hit it against his leg before putting it back on. "Is that all?"

"No." Reese crossed his arms over his chest. "Mrs. Baxter may not send you packing, but I wouldn't hesitate to do it, so I suggest you stop frequenting those places you mentioned and put your money toward rent instead."

"And?" Anger sparked in Albert's eyes.

"If you do want a job, I can talk to Mr. Nussbaumer." He tried to soften his tone. They wouldn't hear a word if he continued down this path. The Henderson brothers might be young men, but they were still men, and he needed to treat them with as much respect as he could muster. "With the summer coming, he'll need some men to do general maintenance. You know, keep things looking neat."

Clem's eyes widened. "You want us to pick up trash?"

"That might be part of your job, but not all of it." Reese sat on the section of the railing he'd yet to paint and leaned against the newel post. "It's honest work, and it will keep a roof over your head."

"Thanks, but no thanks. We'll find our own work."

"Suit yourself." He shrugged. "But if you don't have Mrs. Baxter's money by next week, you'd better pack your bags or I'll pack them for you. Do I make myself clear?"

"Abundantly," Albert growled.

Clem followed Albert to the porch steps. "What happened to all that Christian charity you and Mrs. Baxter are always preaching about?"

"The Bible says if a man isn't willing to work, he shouldn't eat." And they'd certainly done their fair share of the latter at Mrs. Baxter's table. "My dad always said that without hard work, nothing grows but weeds."

Shoes pounding against the sidewalk, Tessa steamed past the storefronts toward Edward's parked automobile.

"Tessa, wait!"

She ignored Edward's pleas. Didn't the man realize she needed some time to cool off?

He caught her arm. "Why did you leave like that?"

She whirled toward him. "Why? You don't know?"

"It was a business deal, Tessa. That's all."

"That's all it is to you, but to the Walkers, it's their dream."

"It's my dream too. If Joe and I can make a go of this, I won't have to get my parents' blessing to marry Eve. They'll never approve of her, so I know they'll cut me off when I tell them I want to marry her."

Tessa wasn't ready to let her ire soften. A few other patrons on the street turned to watch them, but thankfully continued on their way. "Do you realize what an awkward position you put me in?"

"I'm sorry." He dipped his head and stuffed his hands in his pockets.

"Is this why you befriended me and offered to help me? Because you wanted to use me to get to my aunt's money?"

"No!"

Tessa refused to let it go. She'd sensed no romantic sparks between them, so that couldn't be it. "Then why?"

He lowered his voice. "Well, maybe your aunt's money was part of it, but you have to hear me out."

She tapped her foot. "I'm listening."

"You were the most unconventional young lady I'd met. I knew the motorcycles were certainly something not everyone could appreciate, especially my parents, but I thought you would understand my desire to be part of something like this. It's new. It's different. It's not predictable like the law."

"Go on."

"I also knew that I couldn't go to anyone my parents might know to secure the financing or it would get back to them. You were a safe person to go to."

"So, let me get this straight. You used me because, one"—she counted off the number on her gloved fingers—"my aunt has money, two, because I'm unconventional, and three, because you're too cowardly to tell your parents about your fascination with motorcycles or about this girl you want to marry. That sure makes you a stellar individual, Edward."

"Tessa, let me explain."

"I'm done with your explanations." She started for the motorcar again.

"Then let me apologize." His voice was soft, genuine.

She turned. "I want the truth."

"Okay, yes, at first I may have befriended you with the intention of getting your aunt to invest in this business. After all, she is even more unconventional than you. But as I got to know you, I truly wanted to help you. There's another big society thing on Memorial Day, and you should be there. I'd already planned to ask you." He held his hands out, palms upward. "What can I do to make it up to you?"

Tessa studied him. He did seem genuinely contrite now, but her own anger had barely ebbed. Make it up to her? He had to be kidding. What would make her forget an experience like this?

On the other hand, one thing might.

140

Her lips began to curl. "Are you serious about making this up to me?"

He rubbed the back of his neck. "Yes, anything."

"Then teach me how to ride your motorcycle."

Laughter, loud and hard, rumbled from his chest. After a few seconds, he looked at her and suddenly stopped. "You mean it. You want me to teach you how to ride a motorcycle."

"I do." She'd obviously caught him off guard. "A lot of adventurous women have tried them."

"But not the proper young ladies of society. If any of them saw you—"

"Then we won't let them see me."

"What would your aunt say?"

She cocked an eyebrow. "Really? That's the best you can do to dissuade me?"

"No, I mean yes." He took her elbow and directed her toward the automobile. "Even if she applauded you, I doubt Lincoln would appreciate it." He gave an exasperated sigh. "Tessa, this is crazy."

"But you'll do it?"

"Do I have a choice?" He opened her car door. "But this is going to make us more than even, Tessa. If I do this, you're going to have to help me get that financing."

Stepping onto the running board, she said, "I won't ask my aunt."

"I know, but if I need your assistance in some other way, you have to do what I ask. Agreed?"

Excitement zinged through her. She was going to learn to ride a motorcycle.

She nodded to Edward. "It's a deal."

With her suffrage sash draped across her cycling outfit, Sam mounted the steps to the meetinghouse. Charlotte and Hannah walked beside her. It was too bad Tessa had to miss today's meeting. She'd have liked her youngest niece to be there.

Once inside, they paused to let their eyes adjust, then hurried to join the others. Sam led them toward her dear friend Clara Ueland. The Minnesota Women's Suffrage Association was lucky to have a vivacious, up-and-coming leader like Clara, and Sam had vowed to encourage the woman any way that she could.

After a minute of general greetings, it was time to get to work. Sam turned to Clara. "Do you have any ideas of what our next step should be?"

Clara pulled out a clipping from her pocket. "Have you seen this?" She passed it to Sam, then tucked an errant strand of white-blonde hair behind her ear. "Last year, a suffragette army marched from New York City to Albany, led by Rosalie Jones. They spoke to people along the way from a yellow wagon. What do you think? Should we try something similar?"

Sam skimmed the clipping and passed it to Charlotte. "The article says they had great success in reaching the women of New York."

Clara's eyes lit up. "I know. I find that so many people think suffrage is a terrible thing when it's not. Perhaps if they could see all of the women already supporting it, we could bring suffrage home to those who really don't understand why it's so important."

"So back to what you're thinking." Hannah returned the clipping to Clara. "What is it?"

"I've been thinking that we need a huge march from Minneapolis to Saint Paul. You know, thousands of women. That would get everyone's attention. What do you think?"

Sam nodded. "Excellent idea, but it will take time for you to organize."

"Me?"

"Who else? It's your idea." Sam smiled at the young woman, a few years older than her nieces. Did Clara realize that her new ideas were exactly what the Minnesota Women's Suffrage Association needed? "A march like that would make lawmakers see our commitment to the cause too. Not to mention it would show them we're capable of organizing an army, as you said, and we intend to continue this fight as long as necessary."

"I don't think I could get it organized this summer."

Sam shrugged. "Then why not next summer? This has been a long fight, and while I'd love to see women receive the right to vote tomorrow, I fear we still have a ways to go."

The president hammered her gavel against the podium. "Ladies, will you please take a seat?"

Sam, Clara, Hannah, and Charlotte sat down in nearby chairs, and the chatter in the room died down.

"Ladies, it gives me great pleasure today to introduce our speaker, Samantha Phillips." The president's gaze swept over the audience until she found where Sam was seated. "Mrs. Phillips has been a tireless leader in our suffrage fight. For twenty-five years, she has been instrumental in helping the cause in Minnesota. So let's give a warm welcome to our suffrage sister, Samantha Phillips."

Sam came to the podium and splayed the pages of her speech across the surface. She'd worked on the speech most of the week, but now that she was here, she realized it wasn't what these ladies needed to hear. They already knew suffrage was inevitable for any democratic society. They knew that their country was founded on the principle of "government by the people, for the people," and that logically women were people. They knew women across the country had been granted the right to vote in many states, but what they didn't know was why they needed to stay the course.

Squaring her shoulders, Sam looked at her nieces. This fight was for them. It was for their future. As long as women didn't have the right to vote, they had no voice. They could be overlooked or, worse, treated as a man's doll.

"Ladies," she began, "many have grown indifferent to the cause of suffrage. The novelty of the topic has worn off, and many already believe they've taken their position either for or against it, but I'm here to tell you that your voice is needed in this world—now more than ever."

The audience applauded, and Sam went on to explain how there was great power in educating the public that women's suffrage was a fundamental right of a republic. She conceded that at times she too had wanted to give up, but when she was sorely tempted to do so, her dear husband had told her the Lord said, "It is not good for man to be alone."

"Ladies, that's why we are here tonight. Man should not stand alone in governing this great country. When our progress grows slow, we mustn't tire. Women are needed everywhere human problems need to be solved—in homes, in schools, in businesses, and in government." She looked at Hannah and Charlotte. "And who knows, perhaps someday we'll be casting our vote for one of you."

Apparently buoyed by Sam's speech, Clara stood and presented her idea for a march next summer, and it was enthusiastically received.

Sam closed her eyes and said a prayer of thanks. Women's suffrage would come sooner or later as long as people like Clara Ueland, Hannah, Charlotte, and Tessa were fighting for it.

Now, if she could get a certain stubborn senator to see things her way. If she didn't, there could never be anything more than friendship between them.

18

Three dresses and four hats later, Tessa descended the staircase of her aunt's home, where Reese waited. In the end, she'd chosen a buttercup-colored dress. It wasn't too fussy, but its narrow skirt, broached satin belt, and lacy bodice accentuated her feminine side. She did not want Reese to think of her as a boy today—or even as a friend. She wanted him to see her as a lady offering him her heart.

She took a deep breath. Over the years, Aunt Sam had often cautioned her to be careful and to guard her heart. Reese was kind. It was his nature, and even though it seemed like he wanted more, he might not.

Friends. They were friends.

Dressed in a fine pinstriped outing suit, Reese looked up at her as she reached the last steps and smiled. He gripped the straw boater beneath his arm like a lifeline.

"Has Aunt Sam been pressing you with questions?" She hurried down the last two steps. "I'm sorry I'm running a bit late."

"The wait was worth it." He met her gaze and swallowed. "You look . . . beautiful."

Chills enveloped her. Surely he meant that. This wasn't her imagination. He was here for her.

Aunt Sam cleared her throat from the doorway, where Henry

held the door for her. "You two had better go if you intend to get to church on time."

They both chuckled and hurried out the front door. Less than a half hour later, they arrived at the church building and soon were seated side by side, singing "Tell Me the Story of Jesus."

She did not miss the covert glances sent in their direction from a number of young ladies in the congregation. Apparently Reese, the most handsome bachelor in the building, had caught the attention of more than one of them.

"You okay?" His breath fanned her cheek.

She smiled up at him from beneath the wide brim of her hat and nodded. "Perfect."

After the congregation celebrated communion together, the minister stepped to the pulpit. If Tessa were quizzed on what the man said later, she'd probably fail, but she heard bits and pieces about having faith the size of a mustard seed.

She'd seen mustard seeds, and like many other seeds, they were tiny. One could fit on the tip of her finger. She also knew mustard germinated rapidly, and the black mustard plant grown in Bible lands grew into a large, shrub-sized plant.

But Jesus hadn't said they needed faith the size of a four-foot shrub. He'd said if they had faith the size of that tiny seed, they could move mountains. She had a few mountains she'd like moved— like the stubborn one in Mr. Nussbaumer's heart keeping her from working at Como.

The minister's voice grew soft. "The apostles asked for more faith, but Jesus said a little faith was sufficient to do great things. A small amount of genuine faith is enough to produce great hope." He stepped in front of the pulpit. "Brothers and sisters, the burden is not on Christians to muster faith, but to have enough faith to focus on the One who has the power to perform whatever needs to be done."

As soon as the services concluded, several church members came up to greet Reese and her. Reese introduced her as his friend, and she politely met each of them. The older ladies gushed over Reese's attributes—"He's such a nice young man." "He works so hard." "You can always depend on Reese if you need something." Then they started to question her, asking how she and Reese knew each other or where they met.

"I feel like a circus novelty," Tessa whispered to Reese when they were finally alone.

"I thought you liked being on stage." Reese grinned and took her hand. "But let's get out of here."

Outside, a matronly woman flagged them down. "Reese!"

He stopped. "Do you need something, Mrs. Baxter?"

"No, no. I wanted to make sure you were bringing your lovely guest home for Sunday dinner today. It will be such a treat to have another lady around."

He glanced at Tessa. She mouthed, "Home?"

"Mrs. Baxter, this is my friend Tessa Gregory. Tessa, this is Mrs. Baxter—she owns the boardinghouse where I live. She's a wonderful cook, and I usually have Sunday dinner with her and the renters, but—"

"That sounds delightful." Tessa smiled at Reese, then the elderly woman. "I'm looking forward to it."

Mrs. Baxter clapped her hands together. "Perfect. I'll meet you at home."

She turned to leave, but Tessa elbowed Reese and nodded her head in Mrs. Baxter's direction. "We can take her home, right?"

Reese rolled his eyes. "Mrs. Baxter, wait. You can ride home with the two of us." He then turned to Tessa and took her elbow. "This is not what I had planned."

"So we improvise. Life is full of surprises."

Tessa took the backseat of the Model T so that Mrs. Baxter could ride up front with Reese. It gave her an excellent vantage point to watch their interaction. Clearly the older woman had come to think of Reese as a son, and he treated her with dignity and respect.

Reese opened the front door, and a wrinkled bloodhound barreled toward him. "Easy, Lafayette." He gave the dog a rubdown and turned to Tessa. "This fine fellow is Lafayette. He belongs to Mrs. Baxter, but we sort of both claim him now."

"Can I pet him?"

"Sure."

Tessa squatted in front of the dog and held out her hand. She missed having pets. On the farm, she'd had a slew of them growing up. So, like her father had taught her, she waited for the dog to make the first move. Lafayette sniffed her hand and then allowed Tessa to pet him. "I think he likes me."

"He has good taste." Reese motioned to the other room. "Shall we wash up? It's time for dinner."

Lafayette took his place on the floor by Reese. Man's best friend probably got more than a few table scraps from his master, but who could blame him? That forlorn-looking face begged to be loved.

Four other housemates joined them at the table. Two were older men in town on business for a few months, and two were brothers, Clem and Albert Henderson. After introductions were made, Mrs. Baxter asked Reese to offer grace.

Mrs. Baxter laid a fine table of roast beef with potatoes, carrots, and cabbage. Her dinner rolls were light and fluffy, and the cherry pie she served for dessert would rival one of Charlotte's.

Tessa was pelted with questions about where she grew up and where she lived now, but she was careful not to reveal too much to any of these men. Whenever people found out she lived with her Aunt Sam on Summit Avenue, their demeanor changed, so she kept that part to herself.

As soon as dinner was over, the other residents departed, but Reese began to gather the dishes. Although not used to clearing the table nowadays, Tessa joined him and brought the leftover plate of roast beef and the bowl of potatoes to the kitchen.

"Reese, you leave those dishes for me to wash." Mrs. Baxter

hurried in with the rest of the bowls. "You and Tessa go enjoy your afternoon."

"I think we'll do exactly that." Reese took a final swig from his coffee cup. He thanked Mrs. Baxter for the delicious dinner and planted a kiss on the woman's cheek. Tessa thanked Mrs. Baxter for opening her home to her and making her feel so welcome.

"Come back anytime, Tessa." Mrs. Baxter took Tessa's hands. "And if you come while Reese is working, I'll tell you all of his quirks."

"I'll have to do that." Tessa squeezed Mrs. Baxter's hands. "And thank you again. The pie was especially delicious."

"Reese, I think she's a keeper."

"Because she likes your pie?" He took Tessa's elbow. "Come on before she hoodwinks you into staying for her cinnamon rolls."

They hurried to the automobile, and Tessa hopped inside. "Where are you taking me?"

Reese shut the car door. "I'm impressed. You've waited half the day to ask me that."

"So?"

"It's a secret." He chuckled and started the car. "You'll find out soon enough."

"What if I guess?"

"Hmm." He drummed his thumb on the steering wheel. "Go ahead. Give it your best shot."

Unfamiliar streets and buildings greeted Tessa as they drove to the edge of the city. A whiff of freshly mowed grass caused her to look around, but she couldn't find its source.

"Are we going to the Indian Mounds?" It was her tenth guess, but Reese simply shook his head no. "To Fort Snelling?"

Reese glanced at her and grinned. "We're almost there."

At long last, Reese parked the car in front of an attractive building with a brick and plaster façade. He reached into the back of the motorcar and removed a shotgun. She tensed. Why would he need that? He gave her no information from the time they exited the Model T until they reached the door.

"Reese, the suspense is killing me. Please, tell me what's going on." She eyed the weapon in his hands. "And more specifically, why are you carrying a gun?"

"It's part of the fun." He grinned and held the door to the club for her. "Have you ever shot one of these before?"

She paused. "You're going to let *me* shoot a gun with real bullets?"

"No, I thought we'd let you shoot marshmallows." He flashed her another grin. "Shotguns use shells, or you can call it *shot*."

"And what are we going to shoot? I don't think I could kill a bird or a bunny, and certainly not a bear, even though I'd love to climb a mountain and see one."

"Tessa, is life ever dull with you around?" He pressed his hand to the small of her back and nudged her inside. "This is a shooting range, and I'm going to teach you how to trap shoot."

All eyes turned toward them as they walked through the club to the shooting range. A thrill fired through Tessa. Reese was sharing something with her that was important to him. They got along well while gardening, but what about outside Como? Today they'd find out the answer.

He directed her toward one end of the shooting range, away from everyone else. "I'll pull for you."

"Pull?"

"Sorry, I'm getting ahead of myself." He loaded the trap with the clay disc and explained how the trap worked. "When the shooter says 'pull,' you tug on this string, which flips the lever, and the disc flies across the sky."

"And you just point and shoot?" She whipped the shotgun up as if she planned to fire it.

"Sort of."

She let the barrel drop downward. "Reese, do you have a smaller gun? This one is heavy."

"Yes, but the heavier the gun, the less recoil it has. I don't want you to hurt your shoulder."

"But you don't care if my muscles ache?" She gave him a teasing grin, then tipped the shotgun to the side and studied the mark. "What kind of shotgun is this?"

He pushed the barrel downward, away from his chest. "Never point at anything you don't plan to shoot. Okay?"

"I can see the merit in that." She giggled. "But maybe I'm planning to shoot you at some point in the future."

"Then why don't you think of it as never point at anything you don't plan to shoot right now."

"That works for me."

"And to answer your question, this is a 12 gauge Remington." He set the box of shells on the fence rail. "And that box holds the shot we're using."

"Can I watch you first?"

"Sure. Step over here and pull when I give the signal." He loaded the shotgun, took his stance, and drew in a deep breath. "Pull."

The trap mechanism clicked and the clay disc shot out.

In a lightning-quick, fluid motion, he raised the shotgun and fired. The disc exploded in midair, and Tessa burst into applause. "You did it!"

He lowered the shotgun. "Are you ready to give it a try?"

"Absolutely." Excitement coursed through her veins. She tugged off her gloves and tucked them into her satin belt. As soon as he moved out of the way, she stepped into his spot and held her hands out for the Remington.

Reese gave her the shotgun and watched her take her stance. "Move your feet apart a little more. Shoulder width."

"Like this?" She moved her feet outward as much as her narrow skirt would allow. "Now what?"

"There are two tricks to mastering trap when you're starting out. First, always, always keep your eye on the target and not on the gun." He paused and watched her nod. "Second, you want to move in a smooth motion. Practice that, okay?"

Tessa attempted to move the shotgun into position, but her motions seemed unfamiliar and jerky. He stepped behind her and covered her hands with his own. "Here, let me help."

She sucked in her breath. Did he think this would make it easier for her to concentrate?

"Let's do it in slow motion, Tessa. Nice and easy."

Her corset cinched as he helped her raise the gun from her side to her shoulder. If he didn't step away soon, she might faint in his arms. That mental picture brought a smile to her face.

"Focus, Tessa."

So much for romantic notions. Mr. Practical was on duty. Mr. This-is-my-friend-Tessa.

"Put your left hand here, under the fore-end." He moved her hand to the correct place. "Press the stock into your shoulder. Lift your elbow a little to keep it where you want it." He placed his hands on her waist. "It's important to be balanced. Is that how you feel?"

Balanced? Was he kidding? With his hands on her waist and dizzying waves rolling in her stomach, *balanced* would be the last thing she'd use to describe how she felt.

She shifted under the weight of the gun.

"Careful. I've got you."

Boy, did he.

Reese stepped back, and she immediately missed the warmth of his body against her back.

He stepped in front of her. "Now, lower the gun and then raise it. Let's see how smoothly you can do it on your own."

Tessa did her best to comply, but it still felt awkward.

"Try it again." He stepped in front of her and made a rolling motion with his hand. "Good work, Tessa. You're a natural."

"I haven't shot anything yet."

"You will." He picked up the cord on the trap. "Remember, keep your eyes on the clay pigeon, not on your gun. When you think you're ready, take a deep breath, then yell 'pull.'"

One, two, three deep breaths. She swung the shotgun into place. "Pull!"

The click of the trap told her the disc had released. She caught sight of the disc, swung the gun barrel to the left, and squeezed the trigger. The shotgun slammed into her shoulder, but the disc continued its arch.

A miss.

She lowered her gun and sighed. "I don't know if this is my gift, Reese."

"You're doing great. Try again."

Squaring her shoulders, she repeated the process. *Deep breath, smoothly raise the shotgun, yell "pull."* She kept her eye on the clay disc and fired the shot. A clang sent a surge of excitement through her. "Did I hit it?"

"Yes!"

"Can I do it again?"

"As much as you want."

Half an hour later, Tessa's shoulder ached, but she'd found a new thrill. Every time she hit the clay pigeon, she felt it, and the effect quadrupled when Reese flashed her one of his grins, his eyes full of pride.

They went inside the club, and Reese brought over two bottles of Coke. "What did you think?"

"I loved it. Tell me, how did you get into shooting trap?"

"My best friend Erik introduced me."

She glanced around the room. "Is he here?"

"No. He and his wife are at her mother's this weekend. He'll be sore he wasn't here. He wanted to meet you."

"He knows about me?"

"Yes." Reese twisted his Coke bottle in his hands. "He does."

"I'm sure you tell him about all of your friends."

"No, not all of them."

Her hopes dove. Reese didn't correct her reference to the word *friend*, and he had mentioned other people to this Erik. She had to quit wanting more from their relationship. Change the subject. Do something else.

She sat up straighter in her chair. "I have to admit I would have thought you a baseball man before I would have pictured you as a trapshooter."

He shrugged. "I like baseball. I'm a decent third baseman, but I love shooting trap."

"And from what I saw, you're good at it."

"I hit 90 percent." He slanted a smile toward her.

"You mean you hit nine out of every ten pigeons?" From her experience today, that was incredible. She'd probably hit one out of ten.

He chuckled. "There are men who shoot much better than that, Tessa."

"And women?"

"Yes, there are those too." He downed the rest of his Coke. "I read something recently about the world champion ladies' trapshooter giving an exhibition in Arizona."

"Well, if gardening doesn't work out for me, maybe I can head to Arizona."

Reese scowled. "You're not going anywhere. You're my partner."

Partner. Friend. Yes, that was her. She steeled her heart and forced a smile. "I should probably be getting home."

"Oh, yeah, sure." Reese stood and offered her his hand.

She pretended she didn't notice and stood on her own. Now, if she could only pretend he hadn't captured her heart.

19

Somewhere between attending church services together and leaving the shooting range, something had gone amiss with Tessa, and Reese had no idea what it was. As he drove through Saint Paul with Tessa seated beside him, he replayed the conversations in his mind. They would be reaching her aunt's home soon. This was not how he wanted their first outing to end.

Tessa sighed.

"Didn't you like shooting? What's wrong? You've sure gotten quiet."

"Nothing."

He placed his hand on her arm. "Why are you hiding things now? I thought we were friends."

"Friends, sure." Her voice sounded full of resignation.

Why? They were friends, and like Erik had said, friendship was a great place to start a relationship.

Realization hit him. How many times had he referred to her today as his friend? Five or six? No wonder her demeanor had suddenly changed direction. He'd done nothing to let her know beyond a shadow of a doubt that he wanted more.

He pulled the car to the curb.

"What are you doing?"

"Making something clear that I should have a week ago." He

came around to her side of the automobile and opened the door. Once she'd climbed out, he shut the door but didn't give her room to step away. He moved closer until she was forced to lean against his Model T, and then he cupped her cheek. "I want you to be my friend, Tessa, but not just my friend."

Then he covered her lips with his own and did his best to chase away every thought of being only friends.

No magic carpets were needed tonight to carry Tessa inside Aunt Sam's mansion. Just thinking about Reese made her float right through the door. She felt as if she'd been baptized in fairy dust.

"Well, Charlotte, look who finally decided to grace us with her presence," Hannah teased.

Charlotte tipped Tessa's chin upward. "And from her dreamy expression, I think she has a lot to tell us about."

With a sigh, Tessa leaned against the wall of the foyer and closed her eyes. "As much as I love you two, I think I'll keep this secret to myself."

"Uh-uh-uh." Hannah wagged her finger. "After all these years of you pestering us after we spent time with a fellow, you are not getting away without spilling the beans."

"I know how to make her talk." Charlotte snaked her arm through Tessa's and pulled her close. "Let's go in the kitchen. I think there's a piece of chocolate cake with your name on it."

"Really?"

"Hot out of the oven."

Charlotte delivered generous slices of cake to each of them, then began to pour glasses of milk to go with it.

Tessa licked her lips. Charlotte's chocolate cake ranked right up there with Oreo biscuits. She picked up her fork, but Hannah yanked the confection away before she could snag a bite.

"Details, little sister," Hannah said. "Did he kiss you?"

Tessa's cheeks flamed, and she tried to douse them with a swallow of the ice-cold milk.

Hannah winked at Charlotte. "I think that's a yes. What do you think?"

"I think you may be right." Charlotte pulled out a chair and sat down at the small, rectangular table. She forked a bite of cake and waved it in front of Tessa's mouth. "What I want to know is, was he a good kisser?"

"And you two call me immature." Tessa gave them a mock glare, then began to laugh. "And he was an excellent kisser, not that I have many to compare him to, mind you."

"No, of course not." Hannah pushed Tessa's plate back and then began to eat her own cake. "Tell us about the whole day, and don't leave out a moment."

Tessa told them about the church service, about eating with Mrs. Baxter, and about learning to trap shoot, but she didn't tell them *everything*. Some secrets were meant to be tucked away in her heart.

"What did you discover about Reese you didn't know before?" Charlotte picked up her empty plate and set it in the sink.

"Several things. Besides being an excellent trapshooter, he is like a son to the lady who runs his boardinghouse, and her dog now thinks Reese is his owner."

Hannah shrugged. "A man who has a dog can't be all bad."

"All bad? Reese is all good." Tessa leaned back in her chair and touched her lips. "He's sweet and kind and—"

"And you, my sister, are smitten." Charlotte returned for Tessa's empty plate. "But remember, no man is perfect. Every man has his flaws and his secrets."

"Reese isn't like that. He's genuine. He has his feet planted firmly on the ground."

"That's a good thing, because your head is clearly in the clouds." Hannah stood and squeezed Tessa's shoulder. "I'm thrilled for you,

Tessa, but like Aunt Sam always says, guard your heart. You can only fall in love for the first time once."

Love? Is that what she was beginning to feel? Her sisters slipped from the room, but she remained. She stared out the window and watched the electric lights flicker in the house across the way.

She touched her fingers to her lips. After the kiss, they'd sat on the porch and talked another hour. What had she learned about Reese? That he'd been drawn to her from the first time they'd met, and he intended for them to be much more than friends.

Secrets? Not her Reese. Flaws? Nothing she couldn't handle.

A future together? She certainly hoped so, both in the park and outside of it. Her full heart strained at the seams.

Thank you, Lord. Thank you. Thank you. Thank you.

It was hard to live a lie.

A cold, irritating rain drizzled around Reese as he surveyed the garden he and Tessa were planting. It trickled down the back of his neck and beneath the collar of his shirt. He raised the collar of his jacket and tugged it closer, then glanced at Lafayette. The bloodhound plopped on his paws as if he'd lost patience with Reese.

Normally, Lafayette didn't accompany him, but he'd seemed so restless after three days of rain that Reese thought a day in the park, even a rainy one, would do him good. Now he wasn't so sure.

He wasn't sure about a lot of things.

Since Tessa wouldn't be coming today, he should go into the greenhouse and work, but he had some serious thinking to do, and he needed to do it here in his garden.

Mr. Nussbaumer had given him this area to create *his* garden, yet it bore little of his mark. All around it he could see bits of Tessa shining through, but his personality? It simply wasn't there, and pretty soon Tessa was going to see that too. Would she say anything? If she did, how was he going to tell her that he hadn't been truthful from the beginning?

That first day, she'd blown in like a breath of fresh air, and even before he saw the garden plans, he'd wanted to help her. But his offer to use her garden plans to impress his boss? That had been a lie too. After he viewed the plans, he knew he needed her creativity as much as she needed the chance for Mr. Nussbaumer to discover her talent.

"It made sense at the time." He squatted and rubbed Lafayette's head. "She got what she wanted, and I got what I needed. But now that I like Tessa, I don't think she'll be impressed to learn I've been using her to make up for my inadequacies. And if there's any chance she could be the one, I'll need that job in the conservatory to support a wife."

Lafayette cocked his head at him.

"What? You think I'm jumping the gun? Well, you're the only one I'll admit this to, but I can't get that girl out of my thoughts." He stood. "Come on, boy. Let's go somewhere and warm up. Maybe if we get busy, I can make sense of all this."

Sure, hard work. His father always said it was all he was good for.

Rivulets of water trailed down the windowpane, and Tessa traced the path with her finger. Enough windows were open in Aunt Sam's house to let in the rain-scented breeze.

Three long days without gardening. Three lifetimes without Reese.

"Tessa, dear, how long are you planning to sit there staring out the window?" Aunt Sam sat down at her writing desk. "You can't make the rain stop by sheer will."

"I wish I could." Tessa crossed the room and plopped down at the piano with a sigh. She plucked out a series of discordant notes.

"It isn't like you to be unable to entertain yourself. Why don't you do something you enjoy, like reading a play or one of those Munsey books you're so fond of?"

Tessa snagged the May issue of the story paper from the table and thumbed through it, but even Zane Grey's *The Light of the Western Stars* failed to keep her interest for more than a few minutes.

She heaved a long sigh.

"Tessa, find something to do, or I shall put you to work cleaning ashes from the fireplaces."

"You wouldn't do that."

Aunt Sam arched her brows.

"You would?" Tessa hurried from the room before her aunt could make good on the threat. Several minutes later, she returned with her collection.

Aunt Sam looked up. "What on earth are all of those?"

"My scrapbooks." Tessa thumped them down on Aunt Sam's desk. "And the box on top holds the mementos I've yet to include. I thought I'd put them in."

"An excellent rainy day activity."

"I thought I'd spread these things out in the parlor. Do you mind?"

"Not at all, dear."

Tessa picked up the stack and jostled the albums onto her left arm. "Can you hand me the glue?"

With a nod of her gray head, Aunt Sam opened a drawer on her desk, removed a bottle of glue, and deposited it in Tessa's hand. "Enjoy your project."

It didn't take long to cover the table with clippings and programs she wanted to include. She opened the glue and caught a fishy whiff. Before she was done, the whole room would reek.

"Tess," Aunt Sam called from the adjoining study. "Why don't you put some music on the Victrola?"

"Great idea, Aunt Sam." Tessa opened the doors to the cabinet where the heavy records were kept. She pulled one out of its paper sleeve and slipped it onto the Victrola. After winding the player, she flipped the switch and set the needle down on the spinning turntable. Soon, strains of "When the Midnight Choo-Choo Leaves for Alabam'" filled the two rooms.

Halfway through the song, Aunt Sam came into the parlor, dancing a little jig to the music.

Tessa giggled. "You might be almost sixty-five years old, but you don't act like it."

"I think we all have two ages. One that we actually are, and one that we feel like we are. Inside, I have been sixteen forever."

"Me too," Tessa admitted. "No matter how old I get, I think I'll never feel old."

"Then dance with me." Aunt Sam restarted the record. Amid a flurry of laughter, they moved to the silly song like schoolgirls.

The butler stepped into the doorway and cleared his throat.

Aunt Sam turned and frowned at the interruption. "What is it, Geoffrey?"

"There's a Mr. King here to see Miss Tessa, ma'am. Shall I send him away?"

"No!" Tessa put a hand on Aunt Sam's arm.

"Even I expect some modicum of decorum, dear." She turned to Tessa and winked. "After you introduce me, I shall retire to the study—with the doors shut."

"Thank you, Aunt Sam."

Geoffrey bowed slightly. "I'll show the young man in, ma'am."

Tessa glanced around the room. What a mess. She hurried to the table and began to assemble her supplies. She hastily gathered the scraps of paper and lifted a pillow on the couch, stuffing some of the scraps beneath it.

"What will Reese think if he finds my things scattered from here to eternity?" she whispered.

A familiar male hand stilled her efforts. Heat searing her cheeks, she looked up into Reese's face.

"What will he think? He'll think he should have called ahead like a true gentleman." He grabbed a waste paper basket from beside the desk and held it out to her. "Sorry about that, but I didn't want to wait another day to see you."

Tessa dropped the contents in her hand into the wastebasket and smiled sheepishly. "Aunt Sam, this is Reese King." She motioned her hand toward her aunt. "Reese, this is my aunt, Mrs. Samantha Phillips."

Reese set the wastebasket down. "It's a pleasure to meet you, Mrs. Phillips."

"And you as well, Mr. King." Aunt Sam gave him a slight nod, a hint of smile on her lips. "Now, if you two will excuse me, I have some work to attend to."

After she'd closed the double doors, Reese swallowed. "Is your aunt upset that I've called on you like this?"

"No, not at all. She's giving us some privacy—but not too much." Tessa dipped her head. Shyness was a strange sensation she couldn't recall ever feeling before. She motioned to the couch. "Shall we sit?"

The maid entered the parlor. "Miss Tessa, would you care for refreshments?"

"Yes, Mary. Please bring us some of that chocolate cake Charlotte made and—" She turned to Reese. "Do you prefer coffee or tea?"

"What do you like with your chocolate cake?"

"Honestly?" Tessa's lips curled. "I want milk."

"Nothing goes better with chocolate cake than milk. Make that two milks, please, Mary."

After the maid scurried away, Tessa asked Reese about what he'd done the last three days in her absence. When the conversation lulled for a second, Reese reached for one of the scrapbooks. "What's all this?"

"My collections."

"Of?"

"Well . . ." She pointed to the one he was holding. "This one is a collection of newspaper headlines from when I wanted to be a reporter." She indicated the next on the stack. "This one holds all of my photographs from when I thought I wanted to become a photographer. This little notebook has information I gleaned from my study of Allan Pinkerton."

"From when you wanted to be a Pinkerton agent?"

She nodded. "This thick leather one holds all the clippings and pictures I've collected of actresses, and programs from the plays I've been in. The one beneath it holds photographs, postcards, letters, suffrage clippings, and other memorabilia that doesn't fit anywhere else."

"And this one?" Reese pointed to one off to the side.

She ran her hand over the gilt flourishes decorating its cover. "This is my garden scrapbook. It has all the etchings I've made."

"Can I see them?"

"The gardens?"

"No, all of the scrapbooks. It's like a museum about you. I want to go through every one."

"That's hardly fair. You'll know all about me, and I won't know anything about you."

"Tessa, I think I could spend a lifetime and still not know everything about you."

Her heart danced. He could spend a lifetime with her?

Slow down. Don't let your imagination run away with you.

Oh, but it was awfully fun to let her imagination run free.

Flipping one of the volumes shut, Reese leaned back on the couch and smiled at the woman beside him. He'd discovered so much about her. Whatever she was interested in, be it crime or the stage, she became passionate about it and immersed herself in it. Still, one thing had seemed to span the test of time—her love of flowers and gardens.

"This is the last one." She shoved her plate of half-eaten chocolate cake to the side and lifted the last scrapbook. "It holds all of the odds and ends."

He patted the empty spot beside him on the couch. "Scoot over here so we can both look together."

She complied and spread the scrapbook on their laps. "You have to promise not to laugh. Some of these things might seem silly that I kept them."

He covered his heart with his hand. "You have my word."

As soon as she opened the tome, he chuckled at the family photograph on the first page. A baby dressed head to toe in frills sat on her mother's lap. "Is that you?"

"You promised not to laugh."

"It's not my fault you were so cute." He leaned closer and peered at the photograph. The family of five had been posed outdoors, and all three little girls appeared to be wearing white Sunday dresses. "So these are your parents. Was this your house?"

"It was taken on the front porch."

"Your mother was beautiful. Which one of these girls is Charlotte and which is Hannah?"

Tessa pointed to the girl on the right. "That's Hannah. Charlotte has the big bow in her hair."

"I'm feeling sorry for your dad. He was surrounded by women." He chuckled. "Did he ever say anything about not having a son?"

Tessa touched the edge of the photograph, then turned to him with glassy eyes. "He said the Lord had blessed him with girls because there were enough foolish men in the world. He planned to raise smart daughters to make up the difference." She smiled at the memory. "He always told me, 'You'll never know if you don't try. The future belongs to those who dare.'"

Reese's respect for the man grew tenfold. Tessa had surely lived by those words. How well he must have known her. "And what did you mother always tell you?"

"She told me a lot of things. She constantly reminded us that friends would come and go, but our sisters would be our sisters forever." She glanced at him. "Do you have siblings? I can't believe we haven't talked about that."

"Two, actually. Like you, I'm the youngest. I have an older brother named Robert. He and his wife live in Chicago, and he works in insurance. They have four kids. My sister Tilly and her husband have one on the way. My mother loves being a grandma, so she's thrilled."

"So you're the only one who followed in your father's footsteps."

He sighed. "You can't become the sun, Tessa. You can only live in its shadow."

"Is that what you think? That you can't outshine your father? Reese King, that's the most ridiculous thing I've ever heard."

"You don't know what it's like to live in someone's shadow."

"Honestly?" She flipped ahead a page to a portrait of Hannah. "May I present exhibit A. My sister the attorney, who can take on anything and win." Then she jabbed a finger at a second picture of Charlotte. "And here's exhibit B. No one can out-cook or out-nice Charlotte. She warms up a room simply by walking into it." She looked him in the eye. "Don't you see? I can't be better than them at what they do, but I can be *my* best. They still think I'm the girl who tried something new every other month, but I'm not her anymore. That's why I want the job at Como so much—to prove to them I can be as good at what I love as they are at what they love."

Reese stood and paced the room. "I understand what you're saying, but I'm in the same field as my father. Do you know he's famous for his method of prairie gardening? I can't even—" He stopped short and turned to the fireplace. He raked his fingers through his hair. Good grief, he'd almost blurted out that he couldn't even design a garden on his own. Here he was falling for an incredible girl, and he was about to blurt out his biggest weakness.

Tessa crossed the room and put a hand on his shoulder. "You're not your father, but God doesn't want you to be. Where would the fun be in that?"

He cupped her petal-soft cheek. "Ah, Tessa, do you look for fun in everything?"

"Absolutely." She smiled, and he felt it against his palm.

Then, out of nowhere, she smeared his cheek with chocolate frosting.

"You're going to get it now, Tessa Gregory!" He dove for his remaining cake and grabbed the last couple of bites. He walked toward her, a handful of icing behind his back.

He backed her toward the corner.

"Truce?" To her credit, the offer almost sounded as if she were doing him a favor.

"Not today, sweet pea." He reached for her. She squealed and dodged beneath his arm with only a small smear of frosting marring her creamy skin.

"There's something you need to learn. Never mess with a Gregory girl."

She snagged the rest of her own half-eaten cake as she raced by. He caught her waist, and the Chocolate Cake War of 1913 was on.

20

Chocolate cake fight cleaned up, Tessa followed Reese out onto the front porch. If he didn't leave soon, he said she'd be working alone tomorrow.

The mention of his father earlier had led into a long talk about their childhoods. Being so much younger than his siblings, Reese said he was a bit of an only child. Tessa had no doubt this was why he didn't mind working alone for hours.

But if it was up to her, his days of solitude were history.

Holding hands, they reached the top of the stairs and turned toward one another. Tessa drew in a deep breath. "I love how the air smells after the rain. I wish I could capture it in a bottle and wear it every day."

"If you did, maybe it wouldn't be as special."

"You're probably right. It's like lilacs. We have their luscious scent for such a short time, it makes them a star in the spring." She glanced up at the night sky sprinkled generously with stars. "It looks like the clouds have finally gone, so we can get back to work on our garden tomorrow."

"I'm glad. I've missed it—and you." His gaze dropped to her lips. "You've got some frosting on your face."

"Where?"

"Right here." He tucked a knuckle beneath her chin and lifted her face to his. Then he kissed her cheek. "Oh, and here too." He pressed another kiss to her corner of her lips. "And a little here."

Her skin tingled beneath his touch. "Anywhere else?"

"Now that you ask . . ." He slipped his hand around the back of her head and threaded his fingers through her hair. "I think there's some right here."

His lips claimed hers in a burst of chocolate-infused sweetness. Warmth pooled inside her, and she leaned into his strong embrace.

She'd never felt so desired, so cherished, so grown-up.

He broke off the kiss and leaned his forehead against hers. "Tessa, you're intoxicating. I think I'm falling in love with you."

Her heart soared. He loved her!

It was too much to believe. All of the seedlings she'd planted were beginning to bloom—her relationship with Reese, her work at Como, and her plans to help Mr. Nussbaumer with his conservatory. Even her sisters had begun to see her differently.

And at the center of all those things was Reese King. He loved her and she loved him.

Hope took root. If she had a job at Como and had a wedding to plan, she'd not be able to go back to college. Everyone would understand, and she could avoid telling Reese or her family her secret.

"Reese, I think I'm falling in love with you too."

"Senator Ferrell to see you, ma'am."

Sam looked up at Geoffrey. "So early?" She smoothed the side of her hair and asked the butler to send the senator in.

When James appeared in the parlor's doorway, she rose and greeted him. "James, I'm surprised to see you."

"We have a standing lunch date, correct?"

"Yes, of course, but not at this early hour."

"Today I thought we could have an early lunch and attend a matinee." He raised his eyebrows. "I'll even throw in ice cream."

"Are you bribing me, Senator?"

"Is it working?"

"Yes, I believe it may be." She smiled. "Give me twenty minutes to change."

"If you'll wear a dress, you have a deal." He gave her a lilting grin.

Of course she'd wear a dress to the theater. "Did anyone ever tell you that you're a bit bossy?"

"It comes with the job description." A flash of humor crossed his face. "And I wouldn't talk if I were you, Samantha."

"I'm not bossy." She smirked. "I'm a revolutionary." And for his little comment, she'd put on a lovely pair of bloomers and see what Senator Ferrell thought of that.

With her niece Ellie's favorite doll tucked beneath her arm, Tessa hopped off the streetcar and began the trek to Hannah and Lincoln's Craftsman brick home. While she and Reese had been cleaning up after their cake war, she'd found the doll beneath the couch. She imagined Ellie was quite distressed about her missing "baby," so she decided to leave early enough to make a special delivery.

Hannah's housekeeper, Mrs. Umdahl, opened the door and directed Tessa into the dining room, where Hannah and Ellie were eating breakfast. They both looked up as she entered.

"Look who I found." She waved the doll back and forth.

"My baby!" The three-year-old launched herself from the chair and grabbed the doll's skirt.

"Careful, Ellie." Tessa squatted down to Ellie's level. "You don't want to break her."

"Give your Aunt Tessa a hug, sweetheart." Hannah set down her coffee cup. "It was kind of her to bring your baby home."

The little girl wrapped her arms around Tessa's neck and squeezed hard. "Thank you." She scampered back to her seat at the table and plopped the doll down beside her.

"If that poor doll survives the year, it will be a miracle." Hannah nodded toward the empty chair beside her. "Can you join us? Mrs. Umdahl said the muffins are almost ready."

"I can only stay for a few minutes. I have to get to Como."

"To see Reese?"

"To garden with Reese." Would her sisters ever truly take her work seriously?

The housekeeper brought out two plates filled with sunny-side-up eggs, cooked apples, and muffins and set them on the table before Hannah and Ellie.

Hannah looked at the plate and her face paled.

"What's wrong?" Tessa took Hannah's fork and pierced the center. Orange yolk oozed all over the place. "See? The yolk's just the way you like it."

Without warning, Hannah covered her mouth with her hand and bolted from the room. What was the matter with her? She hadn't looked sick a few minutes earlier. It was only a runny egg yolk. Why would that make her stomach churn? She hadn't been that sensitive since—

Realization dawned. Cheese and crackers, her sister had to be in the family way again. Her pulse quickened. What wonderful news! But why hadn't she said anything?

The housekeeper scooped up Ellie and told her it was time for her bath. Tessa took the opportunity to search out her sister. She found her lying down on her bed.

Tessa found a washcloth in the bathroom, dampened it, and returned to lay it on Hannah's forehead. "How are you feeling now?"

"I've been better. Don't worry. It'll pass."

"Yeah, in about nine months."

Hannah's eyes popped open.

"Don't look so surprised. I keep telling you I'm not a child anymore." Tessa sat down on the side of the bed. "Besides, it didn't take any of my super sleuthing skills to figure out your secret after that little display, but I do have one question."

"What's that?"

"Why am I the last to know?"

Hannah squeezed her eyes shut and rubbed her temples.

"I'm not the last, am I?" Why was Hannah keeping this exciting news to herself? Was there some kind of problem with the pregnancy? "Is everything all right with the baby?"

"Yes. I've been fine except for this morning sickness."

"Does Lincoln know?"

"Of course."

"Does Charlotte?"

Silence.

"Hannah, we're your sisters. We have a right to know these things." Tessa stood and closed the bedroom door. "Why aren't you telling her?"

She laid her hands across her stomach. "You wouldn't understand."

Tessa jammed her hands on her hips. "Try me or I'll tell her myself."

Hannah sat up and swung her legs over the side of the bed. "That's blackmail."

"I know."

An uncharacteristically long sigh told Tessa that Hannah didn't have the strength to fight her. "I'm protecting Charlotte. She wants a baby so badly, and I'm afraid my news will hurt her."

"But she'll be more hurt that you kept this a secret." Sure, Hannah had a point, but she wasn't thinking this through. How could Tessa make her understand? "What if the roles were reversed? Would you want Charlotte to keep this kind of news to herself?"

"No, but I'm not Charlotte, and she's going through enough without dealing with my condition."

"You think Charlotte would be jealous? Our Charlotte?"

Hannah shrugged. "Maybe. At the least, she might feel this isn't fair."

"But we're sisters. Sisters share everything. That's what you've always told us."

"Don't be naïve, Tessa. Of course there will be things from time to time we'll each choose not to share, and this is one of those times. I'll tell her eventually, but if I can keep this to myself for a little longer, maybe Charlotte will discover she's expecting a baby by then too."

"I haven't said this often, but you're wrong. Dead wrong." Tessa placed her hand on the doorknob, her heart hammering in her chest. A surge of protectiveness on Charlotte's behalf seemed to overtake her. "You don't want to hurt Charlotte, but that's exactly what you're doing. She'll be as excited about this baby as I am. It might take her a little time to get there, but she will. Deep down, I think you already know that." She pulled the door open.

"Tessa?"

"What?"

"You won't say anything about my news?"

"It's not my news to tell."

Guilt jabbed her. This was one time she wasn't sure staying silent was a good idea. Would her own silence only add to Charlotte's pain?

Lord, please help my stubborn sister see the error of her ways.

To Sam's surprise, James said nothing about the bloomers she wore. In fact, he'd complimented her on her fetching hat. When his driver reached the corner of Fifth and Saint Peter, James signaled him to stop in front of Saint Paul's Orpheum Theater.

Sam sucked in her breath when she saw the playbill in the display case. *Mon Amour?* Her French might by rusty, but she was fairly certain *mon amour* translated to *my love*. Surely that was simply a coincidence.

"I hope you like operettas." James held the door for her. "This one is a comedy, and it stars Miss Amelia Stone and Armand Kalisz. I hear they are quite the musical treat."

Similar to its sister theater in Minneapolis, Saint Paul's Orpheum welcomed patrons with a posh foyer. Stepping inside took Sam back about ten years. She remembered visiting it with a young Lincoln to watch her first vaudeville performance. Today, however, her escort was considerably older.

Inside the theater, they selected a seat in the middle, not far from the front. She heard a woman gasp as she passed, which made her chuckle. It was always fun to shake things up a bit. If she weren't with James, she might have spoken to the woman about how things were changing in America for women. In fact, the vote for women's suffrage should be coming up before the legislative session ended.

Sam turned to James. "By the way, how did you get away from the legislature today?"

"The finance committee is meeting later this afternoon and into the evening, so I suddenly found myself free for an extended lunch. Unfortunately, the committee has some things to hammer out, which could mean a very long night for me." He captured her gloved hand. "But enough of that. We're here to celebrate *amour*."

As if on cue, the lights dimmed and the curtains rose. With her hand still clasped in James's, Sam settled back to enjoy the operetta.

It began with a young composer, played by Mr. Kalisz, who had written an operetta that critics felt lacked depth of feeling and soul. The morning after the first production, a young prima donna, played by Miss Stone, called to order a new opera. Each time she visited, she sang different styles of songs she wanted the composer to write for it, and he began to fall in love with her. At last he was inspired by her to write an ardent love waltz called "Mon Amour" and finally won her heart.

James squeezed her hand as the two lovers kissed, leaving no doubt he'd carefully chosen this production, and her heart leapt at the thought. She ached to give in to her feelings, yet her head told her to hold back. But why? What was keeping her from enjoying James's attention and, more importantly, his advances?

James leaned close as the lights came up. "*Mon amour,* what kind of song must I sing to win your favor?"

His tone was light, but she turned to see his eyes were full of sincerity. Her chest constricted. What indeed was she looking for?

Her husband would not have wanted her to spend the rest of her life alone, and another chance at love might not come again. She did love James as a friend and had for many years. That love would blossom if she gave it half a chance, but she couldn't. Not yet.

"I'm still not ready, James."

"I know." James stood and pulled her to her feet. "Samantha, I won't give up easily, but I'm not sure you'll enjoy my singing as much as the composer enjoyed hers."

Sam wasn't so sure about that. Every time he said her name, her resolve to hold back weakened a little bit more.

21

Memorial Day dawned warm and sunny, and Tessa pictured a perfect day. That is, it would be perfect if Reese were her companion rather than Edward. Oh, she enjoyed Edward's company for the most part, but now the thought of being with him instead of Reese rubbed her like sandpaper. Still, it was for a good cause.

Yesterday Reese had told her that Mr. Chattingworth had expressed his support of the conservatory project. Since he'd seen Tessa speaking with Catherine Chattingworth at the vacant lot garden the other day, he'd surmised Tessa might have had something to do with garnering that support. Mr. Nussbaumer had confided in Reese that he was short only a vote or two of the plan passing the park commission on Monday. After today's soiree, she hoped to seal the deal for Mr. Nussbaumer, so she guessed that she could handle one more outing on Edward's arm.

She pinned her suffrage banner in place, put on one of her favorite hats, and hurried down to join Aunt Sam. Following the Memorial Day parade, where Hannah and Charlotte would join her and Aunt Sam to walk with the suffragists, she planned to meet Edward at the capitol steps to hear Senator Ferrell make a speech.

By the time they arrived, band members had begun warming up their trumpets, flutes, and tubas. The infantry and cavalry units would follow the military band, and the suffragists, who'd not truly been invited to march, planned to follow them all.

Tessa searched the crowd of banner-clad women for her sisters, but it was Aunt Sam who spotted them first. Together she and Aunt Sam zigzagged their way through the ladies to reach them. After a few minutes, the military band struck up a song and the parade began.

They'd gone only a short distance when Tessa glanced at Hannah to see how she was handling this early morning exertion. Perspiration beaded on Hannah's upper lip, but she dabbed it away with a handkerchief.

Tessa leaned close. "You okay?"

"Shh." Hannah scowled. "I'm fine."

The crowds cheered as they passed. At least most of the people cheered. A few people who'd yet to step into the twentieth century expressed their lack of support with rather ugly catcalls. Unfortunately, from her position on the outside edge of the group, she heard every jeer.

"Tessa!"

She turned toward the male voice calling out to her and spotted Reese. Warmth spread from her head to her toes. Giving him a wide smile, she waved back.

Aunt Sam linked an arm with hers. "Was that your young fellow?"

"Yes, I can't believe he even found me."

"I can."

Tessa glanced over her shoulder to get a final glimpse of him. Perhaps she could find him after the parade and before he left for his afternoon with Mr. Nussbaumer. Stealing a moment together was better than nothing.

By the time the parade concluded at the capitol, a crowd had gathered at the foot of the stairs to listen to James's speech. Sam noticed a podium had been set up with a few chairs behind it for the speakers, who had not yet arrived.

Edward, Lincoln, and Joel spotted them and motioned her and the ladies to the front to stand with them.

After they exchanged greetings, Edward touched the banner on Tessa's shoulder. "Why does this not surprise me?"

"The world is changing, Edward, and I intend to be in the forefront."

He chuckled. "That doesn't surprise me either."

James and three other men stepped from the capitol and took their seats behind the podium. He scanned the crowd and his gaze fell on Sam. A flicker of excitement seemed to be quickly replaced by a scowl. Was it her sash he disliked? Or was she reading his expression wrong?

The military band began to play "My Country, 'Tis of Thee." Then, after a lengthy introduction, James walked to the podium. He explained how the first Memorial Day was held at Arlington National Cemetery to honor the fallen soldiers, and he spoke about the high cost of freedom. The longer he spoke, the louder he became.

"The men"—his gaze locked on Sam—"who fought so bravely to preserve the freedom of this great nation deserve more than to have flowers strewn across their graves. They deserve to be remembered with a deep sense of gratitude." His strong baritone struck a chord with the audience, and he was rewarded with applause.

Sam's heart swelled with pride. Unlike with so many politicians, every word James had said seemed heartfelt. As he was a veteran himself, Sam knew how much he truly wanted the fallen soldiers honored for their sacrifice.

After another speech by the mayor, a minister offered a prayer of thanksgiving. The crowd began to disperse to the final march played by the military band.

James descended the stairs to shake the hands of onlookers,

but instead of making his way in their direction, he took a turn to his left.

"I think he'll join us in a few minutes," Edward told the group. "At least that's what he told me earlier."

"Where are your parents today, Edward?" Charlotte tucked a strand of windblown hair behind her ear.

"They're in Chicago for a week." He craned his neck. "I believe my grandfather is coming now."

Sam smiled at the approaching senator, but he scarcely gave her notice. As the group walked away, he chose to fall in line beside Lincoln rather than her.

This did not seem like the same man who'd taken her to a matinee yesterday. Had she angered him somehow, or was he simply trying to honor her wishes of keeping their relationship a secret?

If he was, he was doing an excellent job. Today no one would ever guess he had feelings for her.

To Tessa's surprise, Edward whisked her away soon after the conclusion of his grandfather's speech, and they arrived at the Noyeses' mansion on Virginia Avenue before most of the other guests.

Edward made no move to exit his motorcar. "I wanted to be able to point out who's who as they arrive, so you'll know which person to be sure to speak to."

"Thank you for helping me even though things didn't turn out how you hoped."

He hiked a shoulder. "It was an inconsiderate plan, but once I teach you to ride that motorcycle—"

"I know. I know. I'll owe you."

He chuckled. "You sure will."

Tessa glanced at the impressive colonial-style house. Painted buff with white trim, it sported a wrought-iron fence and columned porches. She could only imagine what its gardens looked like.

"You probably already know that Charles and Emily Noyes have made a trip around the world and have returned to the West Indies several times. That's a good place to strike up a conversation with either of them. He's also a coin collector and is interested in archeology and history. Know much about any of those things?"

"No, but I can act like I do."

"I bet you can." As the couples filed in, Edward provided her with names and other information that would help her speak with each influential person. After a short while, he came around and opened Tessa's car door. "Remember, once the park commission passes the plans, they will have to acquire funding through a bond issue, so all the support you can garner is important."

She stepped out and smoothed her skirt. "I'll keep that in mind."

The Noyeses' home opened to a large backyard complete with a rose-covered trellis. Paths curled amid flowering shrubs, and heathers and petunias bordered the croquet court. At the center of the lawn, a dance floor had been constructed and draped with oak boughs. As lovely as it was, the gardens lacked a cohesiveness that would make it stunning, and Tessa mentally began imagining it with a few changes.

Like an arrow aiming for the bull's-eye, Edward directed Tessa toward Mrs. Reynolds and Mrs. Oldham. "We can hit them both at the same time."

Since these two women both competed in the annual chrysanthemum show, it didn't take long for Tessa to work her way into their conversation and turn it to the subject of flowers and parks. When she brought up the subject of the conservatory, the women were both more than willing to encourage their husbands to support Mr. Nussbaumer in the endeavor.

"You were amazing." Edward offered her his arm, and together they walked toward Mrs. Brokaw, the last specific person to cross off her list. "With the ability to manipulate a conversation like that, maybe you should have been the attorney and not your sister. I'm not sure I trust you now. Are you manipulating me?"

"Manipulating?" She frowned. "I'd never do that. I was simply acting for a good cause."

Edward chuckled. "Come on. I'll introduce you. Mrs. Brokaw will be a great person for you to connect with. If you ask her about her children, you'll be an instant friend forever, and she'll probably introduce you to everyone she knows. I'll excuse myself, but when you need to be rescued, nod at me." He took two glasses of lemonade from a waiter's tray and passed one to Tessa.

"If it isn't two of my favorite ladies." Edward flashed a sparkling smile at the middle-aged women dressed in fine frocks. "Mrs. Brokaw, Mrs. Goddard, may I introduce my friend Tessa Gregory? She's the niece of Mrs. Phillips."

"Is she now?" Mrs. Brokaw raised her eyebrows.

"How is your aunt, dear?" Mrs. Goddard sipped from a glass of lemonade. "I heard she suffered an apoplexy."

"Quite some time ago, but she's recovered remarkably well." Tessa noticed Edward begin to step away.

"If you ladies will excuse me, I see someone with whom I need to speak." He patted Tessa's hand. "Enjoy yourself. I'll return shortly."

She fought the urge to tug him back. No, she could do this on her own.

Tessa caught a whiff of lilacs on the breeze, and it reminded her of why this was so important. Not only did she need for this conservatory to go through, the city needed it. Aesthetically pleasing cities, according to the City Beautiful Movement, possessed "civic virtue." Tessa tended to agree with the idea. When people were able to stay connected with nature, their world was bigger, brighter, and better in every way. Naturally, that would spill over into the residents' behaviors, so it was good for the people all the way around.

And the only way to enjoy nature all year long in Minnesota

was by having a conservatory, so after the project passed the park commission, she'd reveal her hand in making it happen.

She smiled. "Mrs. Brokaw, Edward was telling me about your exceptional children. What are they up to now?"

The floodgates broke, and Mrs. Brokaw spilled forth all manner of boasting. If Tessa didn't know better, Mrs. Brokaw's four children would single-handedly save the world from famine, pestilence, and scourge, and do it with aplomb.

But by acting impressed by Mrs. Brokaw's offspring, Tessa seemed to gain the woman's favor. When Mrs. Goddard excused herself to speak to a friend who'd just arrived, Mrs. Brokaw suggested she and Tessa sit down at one of the garden tables to chat. "I think my son Gilbert would have found you fascinating, Miss Gregory, but alas, he's engaged now to Miss Justine Wilshire. Why didn't we see you among the girls coming out this season or last?"

"I'm attending college. I'm studying horticulture."

Mrs. Brokaw frowned. "Plants?"

"Yes, ma'am, and garden design."

"Is that so? I guess young ladies are into all sorts of things nowadays." Mrs. Brokaw sipped from her lemonade. "Speaking of parks, I'm sure you're aware Saint Paul has a wonderful park system. Did you know my husband is on the park board?"

Tessa cheered inside. "Is he? It must be fascinating work."

"To hear him tell it, it's not, but he says a city without parks isn't keeping up with the times. It's bad for commerce to not be on the cutting edge."

"He's right. Most of the big cities have invested extensively in their park systems." Tessa glanced at Edward, who offered her an encouraging smile. "So he must be supporting Mr. Nussbaumer's plans for the new conservatory?"

Mrs. Brokaw waved her hand dismissively. "They can play music in the bandstand, dear. They've no need for one of those."

"A botanical conservatory, ma'am. It's a rather fancy greenhouse."

Tessa leaned forward. "It will be a divine location for all sorts of gatherings—perhaps even weddings."

"Weddings?" The woman's eyes lit up.

"A one-of-a-kind venue. You could suggest it to your son and his fiancée." Tessa leaned back and sighed. "That is, if Mr. Nussbaumer's plan passes."

"I'll speak with my husband regarding it. We can't fall behind the other large cities, now can we?"

"No, ma'am. We wouldn't want to do that." She tipped her head in a slight nod, a signal to Edward she was done here. He appeared on cue and told Mrs. Brokaw he'd come to claim Tessa for the first dance of the afternoon.

Edward motioned toward the dance floor, and they walked toward it. Off to the left, a small group of musicians began warming up. "How did it go?"

"Splendidly." Tessa smiled up at him. "You were right about her children. She loves to talk about them."

"Talk or brag?" He chuckled. "But what about the conservatory?"

"I think I can honestly say we have her wholehearted support."

"I won't even ask how you managed that."

Several couples took their places on the dance floor as the band struck up a lively two-step. Edward turned to her. "Shall we?"

Her heart thudded against her rib cage. Should she dance with Edward now? It really was no different than the other day at the dinner party. Edward had a girl back at college, and she'd never felt the least bit romantically attracted to him, but now that she was seeing Reese, somehow it all felt differently.

"Tessa? Is something wrong?" He frowned. "I told Mrs. Brokaw I wanted to dance with you. I know you have Reese and I have Eve." He touched her arm. "It's to keep up pretenses."

Pretenses. Such an innocent-sounding word. She pushed the troubling guilt deep inside. Edward was right. Besides, this was a garden party, and she loved to dance.

She'd whirl and twirl and think of nothing other than the moment she took her place beside Reese at Como.

Tucking a finger beneath the stiff collar of his shirt, Reese swallowed hard, then glanced at Fred Nussbaumer walking beside him. The park superintendent didn't seem the least bit concerned about fitting in with the guests at this garden party, even though everything about them bespoke affluence.

As they crossed the lawn and headed toward a group of men, Reese drew in a deep breath.

It wasn't like he hadn't seen his share of wealthy homes or spent time among the elite. His father's position had seen to that, and his own family wasn't exactly paupers, but today seemed different.

Perhaps it was because he sensed this was a test. If he had to guess, Mr. Nussbaumer wanted to see if he could handle the political side of a superintendent's work. His brother always said he could charm their mother out of her last penny, but could he work a group of men? His lips curled. Certainly not like Tessa could.

Mr. Nussbaumer greeted several of the men in the casual circle and then introduced Reese. While they were polite to him, they directed all of their conversation to Mr. Nussbaumer.

Reese glanced around the haphazard backyard garden. Some would say it was pretty, but it lacked something. He wasn't sure what, but Tessa would know. Too bad she couldn't join him. She'd enjoy a fine affair such as this with all of the ladies turned out in their afternoon finery.

His gaze swept the lawn and came to a halt on the dance floor. He wasn't much of a dancer, but for her, he might even give it a whirl.

Mr. Nussbaumer nudged him. "Don't you agree, Mr. King?"

"Uh, yes, of course." His eyes didn't leave the dancing couples. Was that—

A heavyset man chuckled. "I think your young friend is distracted by the bunny hug."

It wasn't the dance that distracted him, it was the dancer. More specifically, it was one girl. *His* girl. And in the arms of another man.

22

With her cheek pressed against Edward's, Tessa moved in time to the song with a ragtime beat. The bunny hug was such a silly-sounding name for a dance, but Edward said it was one of his favorites, so she'd accepted his invitation once again. Unlike the waltz or two-step, on this song the floor belonged to a spattering of the younger set.

As the dance dictated, they spun back to back with one another and linked arms, then Edward turned and placed his hands on Tessa's waist. With her back pressed against his chest, he lifted her feet from the floor and swung her like the pendulum of a clock.

She giggled at the giddy sensation and the gasps from some of the onlookers. Apparently this crowd hadn't witnessed the bunny hug often. When they whirled, she scanned the crowd for more shocked expressions.

Her steps faltered.

Only Edward's arm kept her from tripping. "Are you okay?"

"No, I don't think I am." She locked eyes with Reese across the lawn as the last notes of the song drifted on the wind. His face was awash in emotion.

Hurrying down the stairs, she hiked up the front of her skirt and raced across the yard.

"Tessa!" Edward called after her.

She ignored him. She had to make Reese understand.

As she neared, she slowed her approach, but Reese held up his palm, telling her to stop. He shook his head and mouthed the words "not now" before returning to his conversation with the men nearby.

Not now? He wanted her to wait to explain what he'd seen? She could only imagine what he was thinking. For his own good, she should march over there and insist he speak to her.

But he was standing with Mr. Nussbaumer. What would happen to Reese's possible advancement if they had some sort of public display?

Edward caught up to her and took hold of her elbow. "What's going on?"

She shook her arm free. "Don't touch me."

"Tessa, why are you acting like this?" Edward glanced over his shoulder, apparently following her line of sight. "Who's that with Fred Nussbaumer? Reese?"

She nodded.

"And he saw us dancing." His shoulders deflated. "I'll speak to him, Tessa."

"No, I'll take care of this." She turned to leave, but Edward caught her arm.

"Remember why you're here. You can't just take off."

"Edward, please."

"Let go of her." Reese's voice rumbled like thunder.

Tessa whirled. Mouth rigid, jaw flexing, Reese seemed ready to start a war. Cheese and crackers, was he going to hit Edward over the bunny hug?

Edward jerked his hand away from her. "I apologize, Miss Gregory. I've overstepped, but I wanted to express my thanks for the dance."

"I bet you did." Reese clenched his fists.

Tessa stepped between them. "You're welcome, Mr. Ferrell." Her voice sounded false, even to her. "You're an excellent dance partner." Did Reese catch her subtle emphasis on the word *dance*?

Dipping his head, Edward took his leave, and Tessa turned to Reese. His expression remained stony.

"Was he bothering you?" He crossed his arms over his chest. "And I want the truth."

"No! Edward's a perfect gentleman."

"It's Edward now?"

Her back stiffened. Tessa didn't like the tone of his voice, and she didn't like the accusation in his eyes. "I believe he's always been Edward. I think that's what his mother named him at birth."

"That's not what I meant, and you know it." His scowl deepened. "Wait a minute. Wasn't Edward the man you met for lunch the day you were late to the park?"

"Reese King, if you have questions to ask, then do so."

"All right. Who is Edward Ferrell, and why were you dancing cheek to cheek with him?"

Like an invading vine, jealousy had wrapped itself around Reese's heart, but that hadn't been what spurred him to action. When he'd seen Tessa being manhandled, he couldn't keep from intervening—even if it cost him the coveted position at Como.

Tessa glanced around and he followed her gaze. Several guests seemed to be watching the two of them. "Let's talk about this somewhere more private."

When they reached a garden bench behind a hedge of lilacs, Tessa sat down. Reese, however, remained standing. He steeled his heart. If the two of them couldn't trust one another, they had nothing.

"Like I told you, Edward and I are friends. He has a girl back at college—her name is Eve—but he does have a lot of connections. Since you said you had plans today, I took him up on his offer to escort me to this garden party. I couldn't afford to miss an opportunity to speak to so many important people about the conservatory."

"When I saw you, you weren't exactly talking to anyone."

She sighed. "It's a dance, Reese."

"I'm not socially incompetent. I've seen dances, and that wasn't a waltz."

Tessa rolled her eyes. "It's called the bunny hug. It's a new one."

"Like the turkey trot?"

"Yes." She smiled as if she thought she was making progress. "Reese, trust me. Dancing at these soirees is par for the course. It's what is expected of a young lady. If I want to fit in, that's what I have to do. I'd be an outcast if I refused. If it wasn't Edward asking me, it would be some other young man."

"So if you stay, you'll have to do that dance again with some other fellow?"

"If I'm asked. I could make up an excuse or . . ."

The chasm between their two worlds widened. Perhaps it was the difference in money or perhaps it was a difference in the roles of their two sexes, but either way, Tessa faced a whole new set of expectations he'd never considered. No wonder she bristled against all of the constrictions.

"I apologize for upsetting you." She lowered her face and seemed to study her shoes, which peeked from beneath her skirt. "I didn't know you'd be here."

He sat down beside her, took her hand, and traced circles with his thumb. "And I'm sorry I acted like a jealous lunatic. I'll apologize to Edward too, but no more bunny hugging with anyone except me, okay?"

She chuckled. "You know the bunny hug?"

"No, but I know how to hug. How hard can it be to learn the rest?"

As a dancer, Reese left something to be desired in his bunny hug, but as a man of his word, he figured he ranked among the best.

He apologized to Edward and solicited his help in keeping Tessa out of trouble. Out of the corner of his eye, he was certain he saw Edward and Tessa exchange a look, and he prayed she hadn't talked him into helping her with anything dangerous.

He was pretty sure he wouldn't be the first person who had told her not to do something. For starters, he imagined he'd have to stand in line behind her sisters.

"I need to get back to Mr. Nussbaumer." Reese glanced in his boss's direction.

"He's speaking to the host and hostess, Mr. and Mrs. Noyes," Edward said. "Why don't you let me introduce the two of you? I went to school with their son."

Tessa bit her lip. "But Reese, if Mr. Nussbaumer sees that you're with me—"

"I don't care, Tessa."

"But I do. I don't want to do anything that could jeopardize that position for you."

"If I may be so bold . . ." Edward cleared his throat. "Tessa, you came with me. Perhaps we can continue that ruse for now." He glanced from her to Reese.

Reese frowned. The thought of someone else claiming Tessa, even if it wasn't real, sent a fresh jolt of jealously writhing through him.

"I can open doors for Tessa and for the Como project. Just watch how Tessa works these people. It's amazing, and I promise I don't have any other designs on her."

Reese's jaw ticked, but it wasn't his decision to make. "Tessa can decide for herself. She's had people telling her what to do all her life, and I don't want to be another one. If that's what she wants to do, I'm fine with it."

Edward raised his eyebrows. "Tessa?"

She pinched the brim of her hat between her finger and thumb and pulled it down until it tipped alluringly. "What I want and what

I have to do aren't the same thing right now." She cocked a sassy smile at Reese, then slipped her hand in the crook of Edward's arm. "Shall we?"

For the second time today, Reese had to see Tessa with another man, and he didn't like it one bit.

Swallowing the distaste in his mouth, he followed the couple. Sometimes you had to make sacrifices when you loved someone.

But one thing was for sure, when it came time to leave, Tessa Gregory would be going with him—not Edward Ferrell.

23

Sam had not yet reached the front door when James Ferrell's Packard pulled into the driveway of her home. He'd ignored her entirely today at the capitol. It would serve him right if she refused to see him.

But that would be childish.

"Samantha." Jolly to a fault, he walked toward her. "I tried to find you after my speech, but we must have missed one another."

"You must need glasses."

"Why?"

"Because I was right in front of you." She put her hand on the doorknob.

He covered her wrinkled hand with his. "You're right. I did see you. Sometimes my position requires more in the line of duty than enjoyment."

She sighed. He was right, of course, but it hadn't felt that way today. Something inside her said there was more to it, but she hadn't been involved with a man for a long time. Perhaps her instincts were as rusty as her joints.

"Samantha, I've come over here to ask you to join me this afternoon at Fort Snelling. There's to be a military review in honor of the retirement of Brigadier General Walter, and I was asked to attend. Afterward I hope to visit the soldiers in the post hospital. I promise it won't be like today. I won't leave your side."

"I can handle being alone, and you know it."

"Then you'll go?"

She waited a few seconds before nodding.

He glanced at her attire and touched her suffrage sash. "You might want to change."

"Out of my bloomers or out of the sash?"

"I thought you might be more comfortable in a dress."

"These"—she tugged on the sides of her bloomers—"are very comfortable." She looked into his face. "James, what you meant to say was you'd be more comfortable with me in a dress. If we're to have any kind of relationship beyond friendship, perhaps you had better say what you're thinking."

"All right. I'd be more comfortable at this formal affair with the woman I am escorting wearing a dress."

"Very good. Why don't you wait in the foyer while I change?"

Samantha made quick work of selecting a modest violet walking suit Tessa had insisted she purchase at the beginning of the season. But at the last minute, she added one more thing to her outfit and descended the stairs.

James's eyes widened. He blinked not once but twice, as if he could make the suffrage sash lying diagonally across her suit disappear by sheer will.

She stopped in front of him. "Shall we go?"

"You're not going to, um, wear that, are you?"

Touching the rim of her hat, she feigned ignorance. "You don't like my hat?"

"No, I was talking about your sash."

"You still haven't learned to say what you mean." She slipped the sash off and laid it on the entry table. "Of course I wouldn't put you in that kind of position. This was a test, and you, Senator Ferrell, have failed."

He let out a hearty laugh. "What can I say? You've bested me, and I doubt it will be the only time."

Sam touched the sash as they left. Would he have taken her if she'd insisted on wearing it? They hadn't actually talked about where he stood on the issue of women's suffrage now, but they should. Surely James's eyes had been opened or he wouldn't be courting her. On their many lunch dates over the years, they'd always teasingly bantered about the topic. But what if he still held to an antiquated notion? Would he tell her the truth?

The drive to Fort Snelling took nearly half an hour, but Sam decided to put any suffrage discussion on the back burner for the time being. Instead, they discussed his speech that morning, their families, and a new education bill he was working on.

They were ushered to seats on an elevated platform to witness the military review. Another senator and his wife also attended and were seated beside them. How odd it felt to be there publicly as a couple. If she were going to do this regularly, she needed to say something to her family. She'd hate for them to learn she'd been keeping her relationship with James a secret from them but had let the rest of the world know.

Visitors lined the edges of the parade grounds. They grew quiet when the general and his staff galloped to the point of review.

James leaned close so she could hear him over the military band. "The first unit is the infantry corps."

Sam watched the soldiers file onto the field in perfect rows and display the flags with great pageantry. When the military band began to play, the troops paraded in front of the general. Then the rifle drill team wowed the crowds with masterful twists and turns of their weapons.

"It looks like the cavalry has arrived." James grinned. "Look at those mounts."

Although she was no judge of horse flesh, she did find the soldiers' mounts truly majestic as they rode across the review field. The sunlight glinted off the well-polished saber handles at the soldiers' sides. Why did a man on a horse somehow seem stronger?

After almost an hour, the artillery troops rolled in with their horse-drawn rocket launchers, field guns, and mortars mounted on carts. They were followed by what Sam believed to be two field howitzers, but she didn't recognize the odd-shaped thing to roll in at the end.

She leaned close to James. "What's that?"

"I'm not sure."

One of the lieutenants posted nearby turned to them. "Sir, ma'am, it's a carbon arc searchlight. The largest searchlights are permanently mounted, but this mobile one weighs almost six thousand pounds. That special rig behind it powers the light. It weighs another six thousand–plus pounds."

James leaned forward. "What kind of engine does it have?"

"A three-cylinder, water-cooled gas engine is connected to the generator, sir."

On the commander's signal, the artillery soldiers took their places and fired the rocket launchers into an open space. The display caused the spectators to erupt in applause, and then the general dismissed the troops for a late afternoon picnic.

After they'd eaten with the general, James directed her toward the fort's hospital. As James sat and spoke to each of the soldiers, Sam found her heart filling with amazement. His genuine concern and easy laughter made each man feel special. When he turned to leave the ward, he gave the men a final salute.

Sam took a deep breath to still the feelings stirring within her. Everywhere they went and every time he spoke to others, James garnered respect, and she'd always respected him as well. Even when they disagreed on something, he didn't resort to belittling her thoughts. But could she love him? Perhaps mutual respect was the seed of love that would eventually bloom. Still, if they couldn't agree on something as simple as suffrage, would resentment eventually choke out anything that grew between them?

She laughed to herself. Tessa must be rubbing off on her.

With Tessa's hand tucked in the crook of his arm, Reese walked with her along the back of the Noyeses' garden. Amid colorful Chinese paper lanterns, the crowds continued their merriment on the lawn, but he'd had enough of sharing Tessa with those people. Right now he wanted her all to himself.

"We made great progress today." Tessa slipped free and spun around. "When they vote on Monday, I'm sure Mr. Nussbaumer's conservatory will be funded."

He couldn't share her excitement. "Yeah, that would be good, I guess."

"What's wrong?" She tipped her head to the side.

"How do you do it?"

"Do what?"

"Put on that charade." He rubbed the kink in his neck. "Not only did you act like you'd been born with a silver spoon in your mouth, but you finagled those rich folks so that they'd end up having to side with you before they even saw what was happening."

"Little old me?" She pressed her hand to her chest and added a thick Southern accent.

"Tessa, I'm serious." He frowned. "I'm beginning to wonder if we're all simply pawns in your game."

She took his hands. "Remember, I was acting like when I'm in a play, but I never act when I'm with you. I'm always 110 percent Tessa Gregory with you."

"One hundred and ten percent, huh?" He looked into her hazel eyes, alight with fun, and his ire faded. Getting these people to commit to the conservatory was a game to her, a challenge. It made alarm bells sound inside him, but was that her fault? No,

Laura had put those doubts inside him a long time ago, and Tessa deserved to know the truth.

With her hand tucked against his side, they continued to walk while he considered his words. "Tessa, I need to tell you about someone."

He felt her stiffen beside him.

"Back in Chicago, I fell for a girl named Laura. She was good at manipulation, and I was young. I didn't see her for what she really was."

"I'm not like that, Reese. I'd never trick you."

"I want to believe that." He covered her hand with his own. "Laura drove a wedge in my relationship with my parents. She made me believe they were against me."

"How?"

"They didn't approve of her." He drew in a long breath. "She told me I had to choose, and I chose her. I'll never forget the look of anguish on my mother's face when I told them, or the disappointment in my father's eyes. In truth, my parents saw things in her that I didn't. In the end, I found out from an acquaintance that she was telling all of her friends how she had me under her thumb, and she'd keep me around until something better came along."

"Oh, Reese, I'm so sorry." She stopped and cupped his cheek, her voice thick with emotion. "I hate that you had to go through something like that, but I'm glad she didn't realize the treasure she had in you." She let her hand slide down to his chest. "I'm sure it will be hard, but please don't compare us. That isn't fair to me."

He smiled and settled his hands on her waist. "You're right."

"Besides, I rather like to fancy myself as unique." She slipped from his arms and walked backwards in front of him. "A one-of-a-kind, irreplaceable, distinctive soul."

She hiked her skirt and hopped onto the brick edge of a planter. With her arms extended, she began to skirt the edge.

"Tessa, what are you doing?"

"Living on the edge. You should try it. You could use more adventure in your life."

"With you, every day is an adventure."

She giggled. "Do you know what my favorite part of today was?"

He raised his shoulders.

"Having you talk to me tonight. Really talk to me. And—" She pirouetted and wobbled. "Dancing with you."

Reese hurried over and placed his hands on her waist to steady her. Catching Tessa was his job now, a full-time task he didn't mind one bit. "You can hardly call what I did dancing."

"Really? All I remember was the way you looked at me." She placed her hands on his shoulders. "Like you're doing now. It's as if—"

"As if I love you?" He lowered her to the ground. "That's because I do."

"But Reese, there are a thousand reasons why you shouldn't. I'm too impulsive, too dramatic, too—"

Reese pressed a finger to her lips. "God planted this seed of love, and I intend to nurture it"—he drew his finger along her bottom lip—"with infinite care."

Then he did something he would have previously thought impossible. He kissed Tessa Gregory speechless.

Tessa stepped off the streetcar and checked the address in her hand for Joe Walker's workshop. Since the streetcar stopped quite a distance from the address, she began what she guessed would be a ten-minute walk. Hopefully, Edward would already be there when she arrived. She'd never spent much time in the warehouse district, but she knew it was no place for young ladies.

Like fireworks on Independence Day, excitement burst inside her. She quickened her pace as she grew closer. Today she was going to learn to ride a motorcycle.

A twinge of guilt nudged her. When she'd left the park yesterday, she'd been careful to evade Reese's not-so-subtle questions as to where she was going. After all, a girl—even a girl in love—deserved a few secrets.

And she was most surely in love. A head-spinning, heart-pounding, mind-reeling love. At least she thought that was what she was feeling. She'd never been in love before, so how was a girl to know?

Since Memorial Day, she and Reese had been inseparable. Throughout the week, they'd talked at length about the garden party, the conservatory, his possible advancement, and Edward. Although Reese didn't like it, he said he understood her reason for needing Edward's connections, and after speaking with Edward, he was convinced the man's heart was held by the girl back at college like Tessa had said. She was almost certain, however, that Reese would have second thoughts about letting her learn to ride a motorcycle.

Then again, it wasn't up to him to *let* her do anything.

She turned at the corner and scanned the area. Edward stepped from one of the open doors and waved a dingy yellow rag in her direction before disappearing back inside. By the time she reached him, he had wheeled the motorcycle out of Mr. Walker's workshop. Tessa almost giggled at the loving way Edward drew his hand along the gas tank, where the word *Orbit* had been painted with a flourish.

Tessa placed her hand on the nickel-plated handlebar. "Where do I start? Do I just climb on?"

"No!" Edward's eyes widened in horror. "Tessa, there's a lot you need to know."

"Like what? I can ride a bicycle. How much harder can this be?"

"A lot." He placed his hand on the bicycle-type leather seat. "First, you need to understand how an engine works."

"Why? I want to ride a motorcycle, not build it."

He scowled.

"Cheese and crackers, then go ahead and tell me, Edward."

After five minutes of hearing about pistons, compression, belt drives, and other such nonsense, Tessa's ears hurt. She moaned. "Can we please start the first lesson now?"

"The second lesson." He pressed his lips firmly together, and his brows drew close. "What I was trying to explain was the first lesson, and I'm not sure you were even listening."

She covered her heart with her hand. "I promise I'll do better with the actual riding part." Then, for added effect, she dipped her chin and batted her eyelashes a few times. That usually worked on most men.

"Oh, all right." He motioned her to join him on the other side of the motorcycle. "We'll begin with how to start it." He showed her the lever to turn the gas on, the way to pump the oil into the crank case, and how to set the oil dripper. "You want two drops to fall about every seven seconds."

Tessa squatted to watch the oil drip inside the glass cylinder, then spotted a lever attached to the gas tank. "What's that lever for?"

"It tightens the belt and engages the engine." He paused and studied her apparel. "Good thing you wore those overalls. A skirt would get caught in the belt." He reached in his back pocket and pulled out a leather cap much like some motorists wore. "Here. Put this on. It will keep your hair from blowing. Now, I'll start the cycle the first time to make it easier for you to do on your own."

Tessa tugged the leather cap in place, tucked her hair beneath the flaps, and buckled the strap under her chin. Then, while Edward spoke, she kept a close eye on his hands. He explained how the rider turned the grip on the left handlebar all the way and snapped it into place to lift the exhaust valve and release the compression. "This left grip controls both the compression release and the spark advance."

"Sparking?"

He frowned. "See? I knew you weren't listening. The engine needs an ignition spark to start."

"Oh, that spark."

He rolled his eyes and mounted the cycle. With the kickstand lifting the back wheel about two inches off the ground, the motorcycle went nowhere when he began pedaling. "As I'm pedaling, Tessa, I'm going to tension the belt, then I'll move this left grip back so I'll have compression to start the engine and turn it for the spark. The right grip is the throttle."

"The throttle makes it go faster, right? See, I was listening."

"Naturally, you heard that part." He pumped his legs. The belt around the rear wheel turned the pulley on the engine, and the machine sprang to life.

The steady putt-putt-putt reverberated off the buildings. "It's quieter than I expected."

"I can change that." He grinned and flipped another lever. The putt-putt changed to a rumble, then he switched it back. "It has one setting for city driving and one for the country, where folks don't mind the noise."

To turn it off, he told her to release the throttle and then turn the left hand grip to discharge the engine's pressure. The thrumming of the engine died away. "Isn't she amazing? As quiet as a Harley, as fast as the Indian, and as dependable as the Excelsior."

"How fast can I go?"

"You can't go fast. Not yet anyway." He sighed. "Tessa, I'm not so sure this is a good idea. What if you get hurt?"

"A deal's a deal, and don't worry, I'll be fine."

"It's not you I'm worried about," he muttered. He swept his hand toward the machine. "Go ahead and get on."

Pulse pounding, Tessa mounted the motorcycle. It felt more bulky beneath her hands than a bicycle, and infinitely more powerful. "Can I take off and go now?"

"If you can start it." He chuckled.

Was this some kind of trick? She'd seen him do it with ease, but he didn't appear to believe she could do it. Maybe he'd kept some important piece of information from her?

She set her mind on the task at hand and followed each step. *Turn left grip until you hear a click. Get on. Release left grip. Start pedaling. Ease tension lever forward to engage the belt. Turn right-hand throttle to give the engine gas.*

Her heart jumped when the engine roared to life, vibrating her body. "Now what?"

"I'll lift it off the stand, and you can take it slow." He stepped into place. "Ease into it. Make a nice little loop. Got it?"

She nodded. Behind her, she felt the back end of the motorcycle raise and then touch the ground. She jerked the throttle to the right and the bike darted forward. The front wheel wobbled, and she struggled to keep the machine upright while maintaining the speed she needed.

"Easy, Tessa!"

After a few tries, she figured out how to manage speed, turning, and balance. Exhilaration fired through her as she upped the speed on her way back to Edward. What a heady feeling of freedom! No one could tell her what to do now.

"Slow down, Tessa." Edward's voice rose above the sound of the engine.

She eased back the throttle. No sense in upsetting him.

An automobile flew around the corner and drove in front of her. She gasped.

Lord, help me!

If Reese had not given in to that second cup of coffee, he wouldn't be standing here in the boardinghouse facing the Henderson brothers. Then again, he'd been praying for opportunities to show the young men Christ's love, so maybe this was the answer to his prayers.

Clem shoved his arms into the sleeves of his jacket. "Honest, Reese, we've got jobs, and we don't want to miss the first day. You want us to pay Mrs. Baxter, don't you?"

Reese frowned. They should have paid her weeks ago.

"And don't look down your nose at us." Albert put his cap on. "We need a ride this one time. We're not used to the morning streetcar schedule."

Of course they weren't used to the schedule. Neither of them had risen before noon for almost a month. Reese sighed. It was certainly much easier showing God's love to more lovable people, but he didn't recall reading any conditions on Christ's directions, so he might as well give the Henderson brothers a lift. Tessa had told him she was going to be delayed, and he'd already arranged with Mr. Nussbaumer to work later than usual to accommodate for a late arrival.

"Come on then." Reese opened the screen door and held it for the two brothers. "I'll drop you off on my way to work."

Riding with Albert and Clem was far from Reese's favorite way to start the day, but he did his best to keep a civil conversation going. By the time they reached the warehouse district, he had learned the young men had lofty ambitions to make a fortune in the city, and they had no intention of returning home to their father's farm.

From the beatings they mentioned, he didn't blame them, but he also had his previous observation confirmed. The brothers might want to make a mint, but they didn't plan on working hard to get it. Despite the compassion he felt for them regarding their upbringing, he couldn't let go of the frustration these two made him feel. *Lord, fill me with your love. Help me show them there's another way.*

"Take the next right," Clem said from the backseat.

Reese slid the throttle on the steering wheel downward, and the car slowed a bit. "It's good to see that you two have found work, and I hope you'll make the most of this opportunity."

Albert hit a pair of work gloves against his pants, and dust flew. "This job will have to do until something better comes along."

Clem clapped him on the shoulder and guffawed. "Or until your poker game improves."

"Is that where you're blowing your money? On cards?" Anger fanned to a flame inside Reese like the fire in a forge. Poor Mrs. Baxter was going without her rent so these two could live a life of leisure.

He gunned the engine as they rounded the corner.

Albert jumped. "Look out!"

Reese glimpsed a motorcycle hurtling in their direction and slammed on the brakes.

24

Tessa's mind whirled. She was going too fast. She needed to slow down, but where were the brakes on this thing?

Instinctively, she pushed the pedal backwards as if she were on a bicycle. The motorcycle slowed, but not fast enough.

She swerved to the left, narrowly missing the back bumper of the automobile, and came to a stop in front of Edward. Like he'd taught her, she let go of the throttle and then released the engine pressure.

Pulse still pounding, Tessa let out a whoop. "That was incredible!"

"Uh, you might want to turn around." Edward pointed toward the Model T she'd almost run into.

She twisted in the seat in time to see Reese jumping out of his car. Good grief, what was he doing here?

He jogged toward her. "Hey, mister. I'm sorry I turned the corner like that. I had no idea there were any motorcycles . . ."

Tessa turned away and steadied her breathing. *Don't look up. Don't look up. Don't look up.* Maybe he'd not recognize her in the leather cap.

He stepped closer and crossed his arms over his chest. "Edward, please tell me this rider isn't Tessa."

Edward stuffed his hands in his pockets and took a sudden interest in his shoes. "It was her idea. She wanted to learn to ride it, and a deal's a deal."

Traitor.

Tessa swung off the motorcycle and tugged off the leather cap. Her hair, loosened from its knot, tumbled about her shoulders. "Now, Reese, before you start in on Edward—"

"On Edward? I know better than anyone how you work. You probably hoodwinked him into letting you get on that thing. If I'm going to start in on anyone, it's going to be you. Do you realize how dangerous riding one of those can be?"

"Nonsense. I was perfectly safe"—she poked a finger into his chest—"until you came flying in. Why are you down here, anyway?"

"He gave us a ride." Clem Henderson waved his hand. "You remember us from the boardinghouse, don't you, Miss Gregory?"

"I do, gentlemen."

Albert's gaze swept over her in a less than gentlemanly way. "But I forgot how pretty you were, Miss Gregory."

Reese glared at him. "I think it's time you two got to that job of yours." After they'd gone, he turned back to Tessa. "If your lesson's over, I'll give you a ride back to Como."

"I'll take the ride if you promise to leave the lecture here."

"No promises." He swept his arm toward the Model T.

He didn't look like he was in the mood for her to decline his invitation. She handed Edward the leather cap. "Thanks for the lesson. It was fun while it lasted. Can I ride again another day?"

Edward looked from her to a red-faced Reese and gave her a weak smile. "We'll see."

The ride to Como was unbearably silent, and the air was thick. Every time Reese started to speak, he gripped the steering wheel so hard his knuckles whitened.

After he parked, he made no move to exit the car. "I don't know what to do with what I'm feeling. You scared me. I'm not used to that." He swallowed hard. "I only have one question. Why would you want to ride a motorcycle?"

"Why wouldn't I?" She closed her eyes and could almost feel the exhilaration once again coursing through her veins. "It was thrilling, Reese. You should have tried it." After all the time they'd spent together, didn't he understand her at all? "It was a—"

"A grand adventure."

"Exactly." So he did understand. His words had proven that. Right?

Reese climbed out of the car and came around to open her door. She fell in step beside him as they headed toward the park's barn, his shoulders stiff and his jaw set. Why were they here? It wasn't Reese's job to take care of the elk, moose, or two zebu cattle the park owned and kept fenced in one area of the park. Still, now wasn't the time to question him as to their location.

Without a word, Reese grabbed a pitchfork and headed outside. Tessa followed and watched as he hefted forkfuls of sweet hay over the fence. The humped cattle meandered over and began munching on the dinner. Reese continued to work without so much as a glance in her direction.

Moments seemed to stretch like warm taffy and fold in on themselves over and over. Did the cattle need that much food? Taking a seat on an upside-down bucket, she bit her lip against the temptation to speak simply to break the silence.

Tessa could take the tension no longer. "Reese, please, tell me what you're thinking. I can't help that I like to do wild and crazy things."

"I know you can't." He jabbed the pitchfork into the hay mound. "I think I can get used to you taking chances every once in a while. I might worry, but I know it's who you are. But I don't think I can ever get used to the idea of you hiding things from me."

"It wasn't so much that I was hiding it from you as it was not telling you about it."

He crossed his arms over his chest. "And that isn't the same thing?"

"No. Not really." She took a deep breath. "Okay, maybe it is. I'm sorry, Reese. I didn't mean to hurt you. I didn't think you'd approve, but Edward and I made this deal, and one thing led to another."

"Deal?" His brow furled. "What deal?"

"It's a long story."

His eyebrows lifted ever so slightly, but his expression remained stony.

"A story I'd be happy to share with you now." Doing her best to omit any unnecessary drama, Tessa explained how Edward had introduced her to board track racing and to his friend. She downplayed how angry she'd been at Edward that day, but it still bothered her to think he'd wanted Aunt Sam's money to fund his new company. "I really liked the motorcycles. They looked like so much fun to ride, and he offered to teach me if I help him out in return."

"Help him out how?"

She shrugged. "It's sort of an IOU in case he needs a favor, I guess."

Reese yanked the pitchfork from the hay mound and marched back into the barn.

"What's wrong now?" she called as she trailed him inside.

He heaved the fork into the corner. "Men like Edward don't simply grant favors, Tessa. He'll want something from you later."

Tessa's cheeks grew hot. "I don't think he's that kind of fellow."

"Not *that* kind of favor, but mark my words, someday he'll call in his marker." Reese let out a long, exasperated sigh. "I told you I can't live with you keeping things from me, so I need you to promise me something. If he asks you to do something that makes you uncomfortable, come to me."

She bristled. "You sound like my sisters. You don't think I could handle it myself. You think I need you to sweep in and rescue me."

"Tessa, that's not it at all." He rubbed the back of his neck.

"Sure, I'd want to protect you, but I don't want to control you or tell you what to do. You shouldn't have to handle these situations alone."

"But do you trust my judgment?"

"This isn't about your judgment. It's about us." He held his hands out palms up. "If we're going to have a future, I think we should get used to dealing with things together, don't you?"

She nodded but no words would come. Her mouth felt dry, yet her heart leapt. A future together? Was he implying what she thought he was?

Her heart screamed for her to promise she'd always tell him everything, but she also knew herself. This wasn't as easy as it sounded. She'd had a lot of practice at acting first and thinking later.

She licked her lips and swallowed. "Turning to someone for help isn't my first impulse."

"I'm not just anyone, Tessa." He stepped closer and drew his hand along the length of her arm before taking her hand. "I'm the person you can trust with your plans and your dreams. Promise me you won't keep things from me?"

She stared into his eyes, so full of tenderness, urging her to trust him in a way she couldn't describe.

She was like chaff on the wind, and he was so sure, so solid. Her father had been the same kind of man. He'd kept her grounded when the world around her was spinning. She could tell her father anything, even her wildest dreams, and he'd not laugh. Rather, he'd encourage her.

Reese had done the same. He'd come alongside her and offered his help. They'd taken her plans and created something truly beautiful. He'd believed in her from the start.

It was time for her to take a step of faith. If she wanted a life with Reese, they had to trust one another.

She drew in a deep breath and smiled. "Yes, Reese, I'll do my best not to keep things from you—even the things I know you won't want to hear. Remember, though, you asked for it."

Maps lay sprawled across Hannah's dining room table, and Tessa's sisters pored over them like military strategists. From their seriousness, it was hard to guess they were supposed to be planning an excursion for Aunt Sam's birthday, which would be fun for the whole family.

After a morning of plotting and planning, Tessa longed to escape, but she'd catch her sisters' ire if she dared. She'd tried telling them she had community gardens to tend to, but they'd simply told her she could work on them later. Even Reese could provide no distraction. He was at the shooting range today.

"If we stay in the States, we could go to California." Hannah pressed her finger to the spot. "What do you think about visiting San Francisco? Or maybe we should go to New York. I think they'll complete the Woolworth Building soon. I read it will be the tallest high-rise on the planet. Sixty stories tall! Imagine the view from the top."

"Imagine getting to the top." Tessa sat down, propped her elbows on the table, and leaned her chin against her fists.

Hannah frowned. "They have elevators, Tessa."

"Aunt Sam has been to both of those places." Charlotte picked up her map. "However, I don't think she's ever been to Italy. I'd love to try the food there, or better yet . . ." Her voice grew wistful. "We could go to France. There's nothing like French cuisine."

"Ooh-la-la." Tessa drew circles in the air with one finger. "I have one word for you two. Your ideas are b-o-r-i-n-g, boring."

"I don't think you can call New York or Paris boring." Hannah glanced at Charlotte. "But do you have a better idea, little sister?"

"Not yet, but I will."

"We could still go on a cruise on a passenger liner." Hannah set down her map. "And no, I haven't forgotten the *Titanic*, but we wouldn't have to go to the ocean. There are wonderful passenger cruises out of Chicago touring the Great Lakes."

Tessa feigned a yawn.

Charlotte placed a hand on Tessa's shoulder. "Do try to be civil. Remember, this trip is for Aunt Sam, who isn't exactly a spring chicken."

"But Aunt Sam likes adventure." Tessa swept her arm over the maps. "In this whole world there must be something that we'd all enjoy."

"She has a point." Charlotte sat down beside her. "Of course, areas with fine cuisine interest me, and Hannah has always loved anything that gets her up in the air. You'd probably love a trip to see European gardens or performers on the Russian stage."

"But this trip isn't about us." Hannah began to roll the maps. "It's about Aunt Sam and what she'd enjoy. We'll only be along for the ride."

"Hannah, wait." Tessa hopped up. "I think you're holding the answer in your hands right now. It has exciting new cuisine, gorgeous flora and fauna, lots of water, and even volcanoes. It's perfect."

"Volcanoes?" Hannah slipped the rolled paper into the tube. "Apparently your definition of perfect is different than mine or anyone else's in God's creation."

"Don't speak too quickly." A coy smile curled on Tessa's lips. "There are mountains too, and we could go there by passenger liner. Interested now?"

"Maybe."

"Jack London and his wife have been there."

"Okay, you've piqued my interest." Hannah pulled out a chair. "But I'd need to check out every detail."

Tessa rolled her eyes. "Of course you would."

Charlotte brought a plate of cookies from the sideboard and set it on the table. "So where is this perfect place?"

"The paradise of the Pacific—the Hawaiian Islands." Tessa broke a cookie and popped half in her mouth. "Not bad for your *little* sister, huh?"

"For once I think your idea has merit." Hannah smiled. "But I'll still need to—"

"Check into every detail." Tessa shook her head. "I know."

"Well, I think it's a splendid idea." Charlotte refilled her teacup. "Good work, Tessa."

Tessa's heart warmed. Finally, a smidgeon of respect from her sisters.

Snagging the envelope from the pile of mail, Tessa held her breath. Thank goodness it had come on a Saturday, and she'd found it before Aunt Sam. If her aunt had opened the letter from the University of Minnesota, Tessa's secret would be out.

She slipped her finger beneath the seal and opened the missive. Although the information inside was nothing new, it seemed stark and final in black and white.

The dean waxed poetically about the choices a young person makes, how willing the institution was to offer second chances, and the opportunities that might yet arise. He, of course, mentioned the mercy they'd shown in letting her finish the term, but the message was clear: she was not allowed to return in the fall.

It was so unfair. She'd done nothing worthy of expulsion—not really—and she'd not been allowed to defend herself. Now, if she didn't secure a job at Como Park, she'd have to defend herself to her sisters.

Maybe she should be up-front and tell them now. No, they probably wouldn't listen any more than the dean had.

What would Reese think if he knew the truth of why she needed this position so badly? Did he even need to know? Sure, he wanted her to confide in him, but if she was seeing him and working at Como, then there'd be no need to return to school and the problem would be solved.

She slipped the letter into her pocket and patted it. No, this secret was one she'd keep to herself for a long, long time.

25

Why did the people who most needed a sermon end up being absent on the day it was given?

Tessa glanced behind her and scanned the congregants for Hannah but saw only Lincoln and Ellie. Hannah must have been feeling poorly, which was too bad for a whole host of reasons. First, she didn't want her sister to suffer from morning sickness, and second, she really needed to hear this sermon about Leah and Rachel.

According to Brother Taylor, Rachel and Leah's problems began with good intentions. Jacob, he said, loved Rachel and worked seven years to win her hand, but her father had another plan.

Beside her, Reese squeezed her hand. "I'd work fourteen years for you," he whispered in her ear.

She bit back a giggle and turned to Charlotte, who sat on her other side with Joel. Wiggly Alice Ann finished filling the pew.

Brother Taylor held his Bible up as he preached. "Sisterhood is a precious bond, and this bond was severed by lies and jealousy."

He went on to declare that the Bible showed Rachel and Leah in a baby contest with one another about who could bear the most children. "When Naphtali was born, Rachel said, 'I've struggled hard with my sister, and I've won!'"

Tessa risked looking at Charlotte. Her glassy eyes told her the

213

topic was close to her sister's heart. Was Charlotte struggling with these feelings of jealousy?

Brother Taylor shared how even after Rachel's prayers were answered and the midwife told her not to despair, she named her second son Ben-Oni, which means "son of my trouble."

"Luckily for baby Ben-Oni," Brother Taylor said, chuckling, "his father gave him a different name, Benjamin, which means 'son of my right hand.'" The preacher stepped from behind his podium. "What these two women didn't see was that God's blessing was being poured out on both of them. God saw them both and he heard their prayers. He'd given them each other. That should have been their greatest gift, but they wanted something so much they were blinded to how God was already working in their lives."

As the congregation began to sing "Bringing in the Sheaves," Tessa noticed Charlotte dabbing her eyes.

As soon as the final "amen" was said, Tessa turned to Charlotte. "Are you all right?"

"I want a baby, but I want Hannah back more. She's been distant in an odd way—do you know why?"

Everything in her wanted to shout yes, but Tessa didn't dare. "Sorry, Charlotte, you'll have to ask her."

Reese touched her elbow. "Ready?"

She leaned close to her sister and whispered, "We're going to his friend's home for dinner. Wish me luck."

Charlotte smiled. "They'll love you. How could they not?"

From the moment she entered, Tessa could tell the Swenhaugens' home, though small, was rich with love. After introductions were made, Sonja wrapped Tessa in a hug. "We've been waiting to meet you. Reese, you didn't tell us how truly lovely she is. Shame on you."

"Momma, you're embarrassing the poor girl." Erik wrapped his arm around his wife's waist.

"But I think we should feed her. She's a mite skinny compared to our neighbor girl."

"Everyone is skinny compared to Inga."

Sonja slapped his arm while Reese and Erik shared a laugh.

"*Uff da!* Now look what you two have done. Poor Tessa doesn't know what all the laughter is about." Sonja took Tessa's hand. "Why don't you come with me? You can help me put dinner on, and I'll tell you some of my best Reese King stories."

"How can I refuse an offer like that?"

Sonja handed Tessa a lacy apron. "I'd hate for you to get flour all over your dress."

"Flour? I'm not a very good baker."

"We're not baking. We're making *potetlefse* to go with the sausages."

"*Potetlefse?*"

"Potato lefse." Sonja set a flat griddle on the stove and lit the gas burner beneath it. "Last night I riced the potatoes and added in the cream and butter while they were hot, so today all we have to do is add flour and roll them out."

"Roll them out? Like pie crust?"

Sonja nodded. "Only much more gently. Lefse is tricky, but you'll get the hang of it."

Tessa highly doubted she would. Charlotte's numerous efforts to make her into some semblance of a cook had not worked thus far, but she didn't want to hurt Sonja's feelings, so she'd give it a try.

Sonja added flour to the cold potato mixture and worked it through. She then passed Tessa a ball of dough. "Rub flour into your pastry cloth before you put this down. Then you can roll it."

"Maybe I should watch you roll it first."

"Ah, good idea." Within seconds, Sonja had the potato ball rolled into a thin, plate-sized disk. Then she eased a long, flat stick beneath the lefse, lifted it, and transferred it onto the hot griddle.

Immediately, the lefse bubbled up in places. When the first side had browned, Sonja flipped it over. "Grab that butter crock and the sugar bowl."

Tessa got the items from the Hoosier cabinet in time to see Sonja plop the lefse on a plate. "You should eat your first lefse the right way, rolled up with butter and sugar inside. Go on."

Tessa slathered butter over the hot lefse and sprinkled it with sugar before rolling it up. She bit into the item and moaned. It melted in her mouth.

"Hey, Sonja." Reese filled the doorway. "Are you trying to fatten her up already?"

"Be nice. It's her first lefse. Let her enjoy every bite."

Reese moved next to Tessa. "Don't I get a bite?"

Tessa shook her head. "I love you, but I'm not sharing this."

"You could roll out your own." Sonja handed him another potato ball.

To Tessa's surprise, he completed the task, even if his lefse looked more like a misshapen cloud than a dinner plate. After it had cooked, Sonja passed it to Reese. "Now, shoo. If you stay here, we won't have any left for the sausages."

Reese kissed Tessa's cheek. "I'll leave you in Sonja's capable hands."

Although Tessa did her best to convince Sonja she would be better at cooking the lefse than rolling them, Sonja would not be dissuaded, and Reese's cloud-shaped lefse looked perfect compared to her misshapen creations.

Sonja stirred the sausages. "Don't fret. They all taste the same."

There had only been a few times in her life that Tessa had felt an immediate connection to someone like she did to Sonja. They laughed and giggled as they worked, with Sonja telling a few funny stories about Reese.

Sonja waved her spoon in the air. "So, you've stolen our Reese's heart?"

Tessa drew in a deep breath. How did she answer that?

Sonja didn't seem to notice Tessa's lack of response. "From what he's said, I can tell you are a woman with great passion. That can be good, but it can also make you careless. All I ask is that you don't hurt him."

"I would never try to hurt him."

"I know." Sonja plopped the sausages onto a platter. "But even when we are not trying, we sometimes hurt others—especially those we love."

"But—"

"*Uff da.*" Sonja sighed. "What was I thinking? You'll hurt him. He'll hurt you. The question is, will it bring you closer or distance you? It's part of loving someone."

Tessa carried the plate of lefse into the dining room behind Sonja. Reese took the plate from her and brushed his hand against her cheek. "You've got a little flour there." He replaced the flour with a kiss.

Her love for him grew in that sweet moment. Falling in love with Reese hadn't happened all at once—it had grown over time. But was her new friend right? Would she inevitably hurt this wonderful man? *Please, God, don't let that happen.*

"Did you have to tell Sonja about the motorcycle escapade?" Reese yanked her car door open.

Tessa giggled as she stepped out. "I thought poor Sonja was going to faint."

He waited for her to start toward her aunt's mansion. Her antics, like a burr, had irritated him all the way there. "Why do you do that?"

"Do what?"

"Turn an innocent dinner into a stage performance. It's like you have to put on a show." Usually her theatrics didn't bother him in the least, but when his parents arrived in a couple of weeks, he knew they'd not be impressed.

"It's not a show." She turned to face him. "It's who I am. I thought you understood that."

"You're not like that with me. I watched you parade about at that party as if you were one of them, but then in the blink of an eye, you're a different Tessa for me."

"When I'm with a group, I'm one way." She held out her right hand, then her left. "With you another. Besides, you know why I was acting that way. It's for the conservatory."

"Maybe it's all an act. Maybe you're so busy pretending that you don't know the real you anymore—even when we're together."

"I've never pretended with you." Hurt tinged her voice, but anger flashed in her tear-filled eyes. "I'm not Laura."

She flew up the stairs and tore open the door.

"Tessa, wait!"

The slamming door echoed in his ears. Good grief, for a man who made his living making things grow, he sure knew how to rip a tender shoot out by the roots.

What a fool he'd been.

26

Tessa dashed into the parlor, and Aunt Sam immediately looked up from her needlework.

"I heard you come in with, shall we say, great force?" Aunt Sam passed her a handkerchief. "Is there a problem?"

Tessa crossed her arms over her chest. "Men are fools."

"Well, dear, it seems you've learned one of life's greatest lessons." Aunt Sam stuck her crochet hook into the ball of yarn. "The second part of that is even fools are right sometimes."

"Right?" Tessa huffed. "Are you taking his side?"

"No, of course not. You haven't even told me what happened."

"He accused me of playacting."

"You? I can't imagine." She bit back a smile.

"But it wasn't like that."

Aunt Sam patted the empty spot beside her. "Come sit. Tell me about it."

Between tears and sniffles, Tessa laid the whole afternoon before her aunt. Aunt Sam listened while Tessa told her about Reese's former girl, Laura, and how he'd been tricked by her.

Tessa blew her nose. "I understand that Laura hurt him, but it's not fair to get angry at me for what she did."

"No, it's not." Aunt Sam patted her hand. "Reese seemed like such a steady fellow."

"Oh, he is." She sighed. "Like an oak."

"And he didn't seem to mind your dramatic flair before, right?"

Tessa shook her head. "I don't think so."

"Then when he comes to speak to you, listen."

"Why would I do that? After what he said, I should—"

"You should listen." She released Tessa's hand and stood. "I believe there is something behind what he said to you today. Perhaps it's something that has been bothering him for some time, or perhaps it's a recent occurrence. Either way, you must get to the bottom of it. You cannot change who you are, and no man should ask you to. At the same time, he must decide if he can get past how Laura used him. It is a moment of decision for him." She stood. "But for now, I recommend what I consider the best therapy there is for an aching heart."

"What's that? Cake?"

"No. Bicycling."

"You want to go riding now?"

"It's for your own good, dear." She headed toward the door and turned. "Are you coming? If he returns, you won't want him to find you pining away." She raised her fist in triumph. "You want him to know you will go on living with or without him."

"But I can't."

"Oh, but you could and you would. It wouldn't be easy, but God is your source of joy, not a man." She lifted her hand and waved her fingers back and forth. "Now, go change. I'll meet you outside in five minutes."

Riding with Aunt Sam proved more of an athletic endeavor than Tessa expected. For a nearly sixty-five-year-old woman who'd suffered an apoplexy, she certainly didn't let anything slow her down.

She also enjoyed long cycling jaunts, so over an hour later, they neared the house once again.

Aunt Sam stopped her bicycle on the driveway and picked up a man's leather glove. "Is this Reese's?"

"I think so. He must have dropped it when he brought me home." Tessa took the glove and climbed off her bicycle.

"He might need it tomorrow. I could have Henry take it to his house. Do you have the address?"

"It's in Frogtown. I know the street but not the house number. Maybe I should go along and show Henry which house it is."

Aunt Sam grinned. "Sounds reasonable."

A few minutes later, Tessa sat in the back of Aunt Sam's Cadillac, holding the leather glove in her hand. Would Reese be home when she arrived? If not, Mrs. Baxter would certainly give it to him.

"What street, miss?" Henry asked from the front seat.

"He lives on Dale. It's a Queen Anne home painted in yellow, pink, and blue."

"I'm sure we'll find it, miss." Henry began to hum.

As they turned onto Dale Street, Tessa began to search for the boardinghouse. Nerves wadded her stomach in a ball. Reese might not appreciate her visit. Her heart flared as she thought about him, but she was quick to snuff it out. Reese could set things right or tell her goodbye.

"Please wait here, Henry. I ought to be only a minute."

She found the Henderson brothers sitting on the porch of the boardinghouse. The older one, Albert, had a shock of red hair and wore a faded yellow shirt. The younger one's hair was slicked back with far too much men's brilliantine pomade.

Albert stood up as she approached. "You're Reese's girl, aren't you?"

She chose not to answer. Right now she wasn't sure what the answer was. "Is Reese home?"

"Nope." Albert's gaze made her uncomfortable, and she wished she'd taken time to put on a skirt rather than wear her cycling outfit.

"But his car is here."

"Well, he's not." He leaned on the railing and nodded toward the street. "Who's that?"

"My driver, or rather my aunt's driver."

"Quite an automobile. Must be worth a penny or two."

She held out the glove. "I've come to bring Reese this. We found it on the driveway, and I thought he might need it. Will you see to it that he gets it?"

"Sure." He stepped to the side. "Bring it on up here."

A gentleman would have come down the stairs to retrieve it, but this man was clearly no gentleman. On the top step, she held out the glove again, but the young man took a step back, which forced her to step onto the porch if she wanted to deliver it.

"Sir, would you kindly stop playing games. Please take this so I can be on my way." She thrust the glove out.

But instead of taking it, Albert clasped her wrist. "What's your hurry? Why don't you spend a little time with Clem and me while you're waiting for your pansy lover to appear?"

She yanked her arm, but he held fast.

"Let go of me." She steeled her voice but kept it quiet, knowing that if she raised it Henry would come running.

"He's funnin' you," Clem told her. "Give him a little peck on the cheek and he'll let go."

"A kiss? Is that all?"

Albert leaned his cheek forward, ready to receive his prize, but instead of delivering it, she drove the heel of her shoe into his instep. He yelped and let go of her.

"Why, you little—"

"Uh, Albert, you'd better watch it." Clem pointed toward the sidewalk, where Reese was returning with Lafayette.

Tessa rubbed the place where his hand had clasped her wrist and willed her heart to calm. She met Reese's mica-hard gaze, and a whole new fear washed over her.

What if Reese didn't want to see her? What if coming here was a big mistake?

27

Reese's heart seized. Why was Tessa standing on the front porch of the boardinghouse, and what were the Henderson brothers doing with her?

"Come on, boy." He ran the rest of the way and stopped at the foot of the steps. "What's wrong?"

"Everything is fine." Tessa looked at red-faced Albert. "Isn't it, boys?"

Albert sent her an angry glare but clamped his mouth shut.

Reese looked from her to Albert, his ire growing. Something had happened, but before he could ask more questions, Tessa stooped and picked up a glove from the porch floorboards. "I found this on our driveway."

"So you came all the way over to Frogtown to return it to me?"

"I was afraid you might need it in the morning."

"You'll see me then."

She lowered her gaze to the glove in her hands. "Maybe."

"What do you mean?" His gut clenched. Was she saying it was over? Would she at least let him apologize for his callous words?

Clem chuckled. "It sounds like she doesn't plan to meet up with you tomorrow."

Reese glared at him and took Tessa's elbow. "Let's go in the parlor and talk."

"No girls in the house after six." Albert put his hand against the screen door. "You know the rules. After all, you made them."

"Then we'll go for a drive."

Tessa took a deep breath. "I was going to have Henry drop me off at Hannah's."

"This late?"

She nodded. "Remember, she wasn't at church this morning. I need to check on her."

"Then I'll take you. I'll let Henry know. You can wait for me here." He glanced at the Henderson brothers. "On second thought, why don't you wait for me at the car?"

When Tessa agreed, hope grew inside him. A few minutes later, he found her squatting next to the Model T, rubbing Lafayette's head. "I wish you could tell me what you and Reese were talking about on your walk, boy. What kind of bee got in his bonnet today?"

"I don't wear bonnets." Reese chuckled behind her. He helped her stand and opened the door on the Model T. However, it was Lafayette who bounded in first.

"Lafayette." Reese tried to sound stern. "I don't remember inviting you."

"I don't mind if he comes along." Tessa gave the dog another generous pat.

Reese flipped his hand. "Hop in the back then, you lucky dog. Tessa gets the front seat."

After Reese had started the automobile and climbed in, he eyed the large square box wrapped in brown paper and tied with a lopsided satin ribbon sitting on the seat beside Tessa. "Curious?"

She attempted to look disinterested. "It's a gift."

"Yes, it is, and it's for you." His lips curled as he watched her try to hide her excitement. "But why don't you wait until the Henderson boys aren't watching us before you open it?"

Conversation remained sparse on the way to Hannah and Lincoln's. Reese took the opportunity to ask if the Henderson boys had bothered her, and she insisted it was nothing she couldn't handle. He wanted to pry further, but she seemed to think the discussion closed.

He pulled the Model T to the side of the street and picked up the package. "I bought this a few days ago, but I decided to give it to you the next time I saw you."

Tessa tugged the ends of the ribbon, then peeled back the brown paper to reveal the pale blue, one-pound tin of Oreo sandwich biscuits. She traced the letters on the tin. "You remembered."

"But I forgot some things about you that are a lot more important." He drew in a long breath. He had to make her understand. "Tessa, I'm sorry for what I said today."

"Don't apologize for the truth. If that's how you really feel, then you don't have to apologize or give me gifts." Tears filled her hazel eyes. "Sometimes things don't work out the way we think they will. Sometimes a person is more of a handful than we bargained for."

"A person like you?" His voice was tender.

"That's right." She swallowed and pushed the tin in his direction. "I know I get too excited and too carried away. I know that as soon as I have an audience, I tend to put on a show, but not with you, Reese. Not ever."

"Tessa, I don't like what happened to me today." Staring straight ahead, he gripped the steering wheel. "Yesterday I got a letter that said my parents were coming for a visit."

"You did?"

He nodded. "After I learned they'd be coming, I started looking at you from their eyes."

She glanced at him. "And you knew I'd never meet with their approval either. I understand."

He whipped around to face her. "No, you don't. For as long as I can remember, I've wanted my dad to give me his seal of approval."

"I get it, Reese. You don't have to explain. As soon as we're done with the garden, you won't have to—"

"No!" He clenched his fist. "That's not what I want. I'm not good at this, I know, but I'm trying to tell you that I'm sorry. I love you the way you are, and they'll have to learn to love you too. Just because I made a mistake once doesn't mean I'm making it again."

She bit her lip. "Are you sure?"

"I've never been more certain. What do you say we go see how your sister is doing?"

"You're coming with me?"

"Unless you'd rather I not go." He came around the car and opened her door.

She set the tin of Oreos on the seat and took his hand. "It's up to you, but if you think getting your dad's approval is hard, wait till you try to get hers."

"And if she disapproves?"

"I'm used to it." She slipped her hand in the crook of his arm. "She doesn't approve of most of my choices."

That was his Tessa. And if he had his way, with or without his parents' approval, she'd be his forever. All the more reason he had to get that park promotion.

Two things had surprised Reese when he arrived at Como Park this morning. First, Mr. Nussbaumer told him the conservatory project would be put to a vote tonight, and he asked him to pray about it. Second, he asked Reese to go check on Indian Mounds Park, one of the parks in Saint Paul's system. The head gardener there had been ill for over a week, but Nels had been assigned to cover for him, a fact that made Reese wonder if Nels was the front-runner for the Como position.

The drive to Dayton's Bluff didn't take long, and his Model T managed the incline easily. Tessa, who'd never been to Indian Mounds Park, hopped out of the car as soon as they reached the

Hoffman Avenue entrance. An ornamental flower display with a collection of vivid yellows and reds greeted them.

"This looks to be in fine shape." She pressed a finger to the soil. "What was Mr. Nussbaumer worried about?"

Reese scratched his forehead. "The only thing he said was he wouldn't abide by his employees lying to him."

"How odd. Do you think he was referring to the current head gardener or Nels?"

"I'm not sure it's either one." Reese bent and pulled a dandelion from the edge of the planter. "I've never heard a bad word about either man, and as much as Nels irritates me personally, he's usually a good worker." He circled the planter, and once he was satisfied all was in order, he motioned to the Model T. "I'll give you a tour while we're giving the place a once-over."

They followed the paths until they reached the north edge of the park. Young trees dotted the landscape. He'd not yet been employed by the park service when trees and shrubs were planted in this park, but he'd spent many a day watering them.

He slowed on Thorn Street and stopped in front of an expansive three-story building. "That's the Mounds Park Sanitarium. It takes patients with both physical and mental problems."

Tessa glanced around. "What a beautiful place to recuperate. Look! You can see the park and the river from here." She leaned out the window. "Are those the burial mounds?"

"Yes. You look surprised."

"I don't know what I was expecting, but they look like little hills."

He chuckled. "Or mounds?"

"Point taken."

He headed toward them. "At one time, thirty-seven Hopewell and Dakota burial mounds dotted this area. Some are said to be nearly two thousand years old. There were at least nineteen mounds around here, and more around Carver's Cave. Some were excavated in the 1800s. More were destroyed when the rail yard was widened, and additional ones when the park commission bought the land."

"They destroyed the sites?"

"The park was bought for the view of the river more than for protecting the mounds." He released a long breath. "Some of the mounds blocked the view."

Tessa grabbed Reese's arm. "What are those people doing?"

"Collecting." His stomach roiled. "They're looking for pieces of pottery, mussel shells, arrowheads, and even bones—whatever treasure they can find."

"But these are graves. Can't you stop them?"

"I wish I could, but it's not illegal."

"I can't pick flowers in Como Park, but visitors here can desecrate graves?" She touched her fingers to her mouth. "It feels so wrong."

"You're right." He swung the Model T around one of the mounds. "Mr. Nussbaumer has forbidden his employees from participating in any collecting."

Tessa's eyes narrowed. "Maybe that's why he sent you here. One of the gardeners might be taking things even though Mr. Nussbaumer ruled against it."

Reese moved the throttle upward. "You're brilliant, Tessa Gregory. Do you know that?"

"Yes." She grinned. "But I still like to hear it."

When Sam entered the meeting place of the Minnesota Women's Suffrage Association, she could tell the new leaflets had arrived, for the whole room smelled of printer's ink.

She greeted a few of her fellow suffragists while waiting for the others to arrive. At last Clara stepped up to the podium. "Good morning, ladies." She laid her hand on the stack. "We have our work cut out for us today—five hundred leaflets with which we can blanket the city. After the successful Memorial Day parade, I think this will be a great follow-up. I hope you're all ready to do some walking."

A few of the young women moaned, making Sam smile. In her lifetime, how many miles had she walked for this cause? How many pamphlets had she passed out, and how many speeches had she given? How many times, like Sojourner Truth, had she shown up at ballot boxes only to be turned away?

Clara picked up a stack. "There are twenty-five of us present today, so if we each pass out twenty, we'll be done in no time."

The ladies fell into line, and Sam took her place with them. She accepted her pile of papers and read over the one on top. The leaflet listed ten reasons why women deserved suffrage, with each statement beginning with the word "because." She especially liked two of the points: "Because women suffer from a bad form of government just as men do" and "Because women are citizens whose government is *of* the people, *by* the people, and *for* the people, and *women are people.*"

She sighed. She'd heard all of the arguments listed on the paper before, but what would it take for other people to truly hear them? Sure, they'd made progress. Women were now allowed to keep their own wages, own land, and expect an education, but there was still much to do. Why couldn't the politicians see that until women were treated like citizens, with all the rights and privileges due to them, they were not truly free?

Every night she would pray for the politicians, especially those in Minnesota, to have the courage to stand up for what was right. They needed someone willing to risk their career on a cause that was unpopular among many male voters. For years she'd prayed James would be that person, but now? She wasn't sure anymore.

Heading for the stairs, she said a silent prayer, asking God to let her see the day when women and men could stand side by side and cast their vote. Gaining the right to vote for women was only the first battle. Persuading women to use it would be the true test of victory.

Excitement fizzed inside Tessa as the entrance to Carver's Cave yawned black before her. When she'd awoken this morning, exploring a cave was the last thing she expected to do.

Reese lit the lantern in his hand and held it aloft. "Ready?"

She nodded. They'd spoken to some of the park workers and asked about the mounds and the artifacts. Although none of the workers would give them a name, nearly all of them said they'd find what they were looking for inside this cave. Getting to the cave entrance, which was on a cliff face below the park, hadn't been easy, and she'd been grateful for her masculine apparel.

Reese took her hand, and they started to follow the path along the wall. The cave entrance opened to a huge domed area carved out of the limestone, so large it seemed to swallow the light of their small lantern. Immediately the air temperature dropped several degrees.

Her footsteps sank in the white sand, and the lantern's light glinted off the water of an interior lake.

She sucked in her breath. "Why haven't I ever heard of Carver's Cave? It's amazing."

"The railroad shaved off a big section of this place to widen the rail yard a long time ago." He came to a stop. "Hold up. Here's the boat." He passed the lantern to her and shoved the rowboat into the water. Once Tessa was seated, she asked him to continue his explanation.

"A man named John Colwell was charged with finding the entrance again. He traced the spring of water leaking from the bluff to find it. The park system's plans are to make it a lure for visitors."

"Do you think that's wise?" The steady sound of the oars slapping the water echoed in the massive chamber.

"Not really. Look at how people have treated the mounds." The deeper they went into the cave, the quieter his voice became. "There are supposed to be some rooms at the back of the cave. That's where we're headed."

About thirty feet into the cave, the dome began to slope downward until the limestone ceiling was only nine feet above them. The air was heavy with dampness, and Tessa's pulse beat harder as they lost sight of the entrance.

"You okay?" Reese asked.

"Of course." Her voice sounded tight.

"The Indians called this place *Waukon Teebee*, which means 'house of the spirits.'"

"Really?"

"Any ordinary girl might be a little afraid."

She cleared her throat. "Any ordinary girl might."

He kept a steady flow of conversation going, explaining things like how the back of the cave was nearly fifty yards from the entrance. Swinging the boat toward the lake's edge, he stilled the oars. "Hold the lantern up. Let's see if we can find any of those rooms."

Reese moved the boat slowly along the edge while Tessa peered into the darkness, hoping to catch a glimpse of something different than the limestone walls. "Reese, look." She pointed to an even darker area a few feet above the lake. "A room?"

"We have to get out of the boat to check. Do you see anything to tie it to?"

She swung the lantern around. "Nothing."

"Then you stay here and I'll go check."

"No!"

"So you want to be the one to go inside and see if there's anything there?"

Tessa bit her lip. Neither option made her happy. If she had her druthers, she'd stay in the boat, but would Reese think she was scared? How could he not? But if she offered to go, he'd refuse to let her. Then she could act irritated but still stay in the boat—safe and sound.

"Sure, I'll go." Using her best acting voice, she took on the confidence of a pirate. "You can boost me up."

He seemed to study her for a minute. "Are you sure?"

"Absolutely."

"All right, let's do it." He pressed his hands to his thighs and stood. "I know you like a thrill every now and then, and this one should be safer than riding a motorcycle."

"Truly?" She nearly choked, but she didn't dare tell him she'd been pretending. "You're going to let me do it?"

He hiked a shoulder. "Why not? I'll be here if you need me."

"What do I do?"

He took her hand and pulled her to her feet. "I'll lift you up to the ledge. Then once you're inside, I'll pass you the lantern."

She swallowed. Was she really going to do this?

"Ready, my little risk taker?"

She nodded. They moved slowly in the flat-bottomed boat until they were in position.

"Be careful." Reese's breath was hot against her ear. He placed his hands on her waist. "One, two . . ."

On three, he lifted her high enough that if she swung her feet upward, she could reach the opening. Thank goodness she was wearing overalls. At the last second, he gave her a little extra push, which made her land hard on the clammy stone floor.

"You okay?" he asked.

"Peachy." She leaned over the edge and took the lantern from him.

Even with the lantern illuminating the small cave room, the craggy rocks left eerie shadows she'd have to explore.

"What do you see?"

"A lot of crevices." She took a few steps away from the doorway and stopped. "Reese, can you still hear me?"

"Sure." He paused. "Listen, if this is too much, come back down, and I'll go up. I shouldn't have let you do it anyway."

"I'm fine." At least she was physically. Her nerves, on the other hand, were a bit shaky. She eased along the right side of the room. What if some creature made an appearance? Did snakes live in caves? She shuddered at the thought.

"See anything?" Reese's voice startled her.

"Nothing yet." Her light illuminated something wedged inside one of the crevices. "Wait. I think I found a sack." She set the lantern on the ground and pushed her hand past the cobwebs into the crack. Her fingers came into contact with a familiar itchy fabric. Burlap? She gripped it and yanked it free.

After grabbing the lantern, she hurried to the edge and hoisted the sack in the air for Reese to see.

"Great work, Tessa." He held up his hands. "Hand it to me, then pass me the lantern."

She did as she was told, then sat on the edge and waited for him to help her down. A noise behind her made her skin crawl. "Now, Reese, now!"

28

Reese tossed the sack in the bottom of the boat and whirled. The panic in Tessa's voice made his heart race. He yanked her off the ledge and set her down in the boat. "Are you okay?"

She wrapped her arms around herself and shivered. "All of a sudden I got the distinct feeling I wasn't alone up there."

He lifted the lantern in the air to see the opening. "I don't see anything." She'd probably gotten spooked. He certainly didn't blame her.

After tugging off his jacket, he wrapped it around her shoulders. "Better?"

"Much." She burrowed inside it. "Reese, not that I haven't enjoyed this little outing, but can we go back now?"

"Had enough adventure for one day?" He chuckled. "Now there's a first."

Half an hour later, they exited the cave with the burlap sack in hand. Reese untied the rope binding its top and gently poured its contents on the ground. A few fragments of pottery and arrowheads tumbled out first. He gave it another gentle shake, and a human skull rolled to the ground.

Tessa gasped and covered her mouth with her hand. "Reese, who would have taken this?"

"Only park employees know about the cave's back rooms."

"Nels?"

"Maybe." He put the items back in the bag. "But we don't know enough to accuse him."

"I don't understand. Why would anyone do this?"

"Collectors will pay a pretty penny for items like this. Whoever took this might be a collector themselves or might be looking at making some money by selling these artifacts."

"That's despicable. Whatever happened to honoring the dead?"

He pressed his hand to the small of her back. "We'll get to the bottom of this, Tessa, I promise. And we'll put these things back where they belong."

Tessa stood back and surveyed the garden she and Reese were creating. The perennials they'd planted were filling the areas in nicely with bright pink blooms. The shrubs had taken root, and the only landscaping left was to lay the pathways with paving bricks. In another two weeks, it would be complete.

She missed Reese's company at Como. Given Monday's discovery, Mr. Nussbaumer had requested his presence at the Indian Mounds Park both yesterday and today. She couldn't very well join them and keep her identity a secret, but she trusted him to do what he promised. He'd find out who was taking the artifacts and return the items to their rightful home.

After removing her straw hat, she wiped her sleeve across her brow and smiled. Rock-solid, honest, faithful Reese would take care of the situation there, while as his partner, she'd handle the one here.

She plopped her hat back on and returned to the wheelbarrow. Once she had these plants in, two of the three sections of the garden would be complete.

She paused. Like mercury in a thermometer on an August day, a creepy feeling rose inside her. Was someone watching her? Not wanting to scare away whomever it might be, she nonchalantly took the shovel from the wheelbarrow and glanced around. Movement in the trees caught her attention. She gripped the handle of the shovel. Why would someone be spying on her? Had someone discovered she was a woman?

She was probably overreacting. Too many stories filling her head. Besides, people came to the park to do all sorts of things. This fellow was probably hiking or enjoying the variety of trees in the arbor. Just in case, she'd keep her hat on and her head down.

When the figure moved again, she glimpsed something yellow out of the corner of her eye. That had to be a good sign. There was no way any respectable outlaw would get caught wearing yellow. But was it someone who was trying to out her disguise?

She couldn't worry about that now.

Shoving the interloper from her mind, she went back to work, planting several clusters of candy-colored lupines. The whimsical spires were among her favorites in this garden. When she finished, she looked up to see someone again watching her—only this time he was near the water fountain, a yellow kerchief hanging from his back pocket.

He was still too far away to be of any danger to her, but his presence unnerved her. If only she could see his face, she might be able to determine if he were friend or foe.

Stop it, Tessa. You're letting your imagination run away with you.

Sam patted her lips with her napkin. White linens and glittery chandeliers might make conversations more civil, but they did not make them any easier.

"James, I believe it's time to discuss the elephant in the room."

He looked around the tearoom at Field-Schlick's Department Store and chuckled. "I don't see any elephants."

Undeterred, she took a deep breath and pressed on. "You and

I are much alike. We are both strong willed and civic minded. We are dear, dear friends."

"And even a bit more?"

"Yes, a bit." A slight smile slipped through.

"Before you continue, why don't we walk while we talk?" He stood and pulled out her chair. "I believe you might enjoy the displays in the crystal shop."

"Even cut glass won't distract me. We need to discuss this."

"And we will." He directed her toward the elevator. It took three attempts before the elevator operator, an elderly gentleman who was hard of hearing, understood what floor they wanted.

After the elderly man closed the wire doors on the elevator car, Sam turned to James. "You know that suffrage is important to me. I have to know where you stand on the issue."

"Is it that important to you? Must we agree?" He took her hand and squeezed it. "Isn't this good enough?"

She pulled her hand away. "Why are you against letting women vote? Why do you want to deny women one of the fundamental rights of our democracy?"

Oblivious, the elevator operator stared at the floor indicator over the door.

"Samantha, it isn't that I want to deny women anything." The elevator came to a stop. "In fact, the reason I'm against women's suffrage is quite the opposite."

She stepped from the car and waited for him. "I'm listening."

He held up one finger. "First of all, women already have the right to vote in local elections, like that of the school board. I think it's best for women to be content with that."

"Why?"

"I don't want women to be drawn into the dirty pool of politics, and I can assure you it is an ugly place." He massaged the back of his neck. "Politics is a game of force, and women are not made to be that stern."

She raised her eyebrows. "Have you met Hannah?"

He motioned her toward the crystal room. Sam wandered among the goblets and bowls while James remained a few steps back. Apparently the idea of bumping a shelf kept him frozen in place.

She picked up a cake stand and ran her finger along the sharp edges of the cut glass. "Go on, James."

"Right now, many laws give an almost chivalric courtesy to women." He shifted his weight to his other foot. "They aren't required to serve on juries, and if they're charged with a crime, the punishment is much less severe. Equality will destroy these benefits to the fairer sex."

"So you're against suffrage for my own good?" She set the cake stand down.

"Yes, and for the good of the American family." He followed her to the stemware aisle. "I believe that in the majority of homes in America, a certain harmony exists between husband and wife. It is understood that the woman will care for the children, and the husband will provide for the family. Don't you worry that giving women the right to vote will wake in them a spirit of discontent?"

"They are discontented already because they do not feel like they have a voice." Her own voice rose as she spoke, and some patrons turned in their direction. She took a calming breath. "I'm sorry. Please continue."

"I have one more reason, and it's perhaps the most important one." He flashed a victorious smile in her direction. Did he honestly believe he'd win her to his side this easily?

"If women are allowed to vote"—he picked up a goblet and held it to the light—"someday they may be expected to bear arms in times of war." He leaned forward and lowered his voice. "Samantha, I've seen the horrors of war, and I do not wish for any woman to endure that."

"I can understand your reticence, but surely you can figure out a way around that."

"I could if I wanted to." He reached around her to place the goblet on the shelf, then settled his hand on her waist and gently pulled her back against his chest. "Women should rely on men. That's how it should be. You see, I can't vote for suffrage because it takes away my ability to protect the woman I love."

Sam's emotions whirled like a weather vane in a thunderstorm. The heat from his hand seared the flesh at her waist. Why had he gone and turned this civil discussion into a matter of the heart? How could she argue with chivalry—albeit misplaced—especially when he'd declared his love for her?

Love. She too had felt its heady stirrings. Knowing he loved her sent her heart pattering like a schoolgirl's, but those were emotions, and she was too old to believe love alone was enough to build a lasting relationship. It was a good start, one of the best, but alone it was not enough.

"Do you love me too, Samantha?" he whispered.

She turned in his arms to face him. "I believe I could."

"But you don't yet?"

"James." She placed her hand on his chest. "I won't let myself love you—yet."

"Because of suffrage?" Suppressed anger deepened the color of his cheeks. "You'd let this issue keep us apart?"

She swallowed hard. Could she love a man who didn't share her dreams? Didn't even support them? But he filled a hole in her life that she'd almost forgotten existed. After all she'd sacrificed for the cause, would she now give up love as well?

"James, the truth is that I don't know. I need time."

His eyebrows raised. "To change my mind."

"Perhaps." She allowed a smile to form on her lips. "It would make things easier."

"It would also make it easier if you weren't so stubborn." He exhaled a long-suffering sigh. "So what do we do in the meantime?"

She walked toward the door and heard the Field-Schlick Drum

and Glockenspiel Corps, the store's own percussion band, playing in the distance. "We can enjoy today."

"Let's enjoy the whole weekend—in White Bear at my cottage."

"James Ferrell, I'm ashamed of you."

"Not you alone." He chuckled. "Bring the whole family."

The corps must be in a department near them now. Like a music box, the tinkling sound of the glockenspiel fit in perfectly with the crystal.

"If I invited my family, they'd know about us."

"I think it's time they did, don't you?"

Her stomach dipped again. Was she ready for that? Perhaps she'd kept this from them long enough.

As if he sensed her giving in, he pressed on. "And from what you've told me, I think all of your girls could use a day at the lake."

That was true. The stress between Hannah and Charlotte had been palpable as of late, and Tessa was always game for any adventure. Maybe seeing how they got along with James would help her with her choice.

She slipped her arm in his. "For once I agree with you, but don't get used to it."

29

Having changed from her overalls, Tessa took the streetcar to Indian Mounds Park, hoping to see Reese. He'd not made it back to Como before she'd left for the day, but the chances of finding him in this expansive park were slim. Either way, the walk would do her good.

Near the largest mound, the view stole her breath. She sank onto a bench and drank in the vista. Like a ribbon of blue taffy, the Mississippi River wound through the valley. Beyond the river, the city of Saint Paul lay nestled in fields of green.

No matter how crazy her world seemed to be, connecting with nature—hands in the dirt, head in the sun—seemed to connect her to God. In moments like these, her soul almost wept for the beauty only God himself could create.

"This is certainly a pleasant surprise."

She looked up to find Reese studying her. "Are you all right?" he asked.

"More than." She scooted over on the bench and waited for him to join her. "This place is breathtaking. I was thanking God for his artwork."

"One of the blessings of park service." He took her hand. "I have some news."

"Good or bad?"

"I'll let you decide." He laced his fingers through hers. "You already know the park commission passed the conservatory project."

"And?"

He looked down at their clasped hands, the pause growing longer by the moment.

"Reese, tell me."

"Today Mr. Nussbaumer asked me for my opinion on his plans." He turned to her and a smile spread across his face.

"You're going to be his first choice for that position, I'm sure, Reese. You've done it."

"No, you did. It would never have passed without your help." He kissed her cheek. "But let's not get ahead of ourselves simply because he asked for my opinion." He pushed to his feet. "If you come with me to get my things, I'll fill you in on the rest of my day and you can tell me all about yours. Then we can go out and celebrate."

As they walked, Reese told Tessa about talking to the current head gardener, who was still recuperating from his illness. From him, Reese learned that the man had never personally been inside Carver's Cave, although he too had heard of the rooms at the back of the cave. He said his park employed five other workers besides himself, and he wouldn't put it past any of them to steal from the mounds while he was laid up.

"I asked him if he'd ever noticed anything being taken before he was ill, and of course he hadn't."

"What about Nels?"

"Some things I found out today could point in his direction, but nothing concrete." Reese motioned to the right when they came to a cross in the sidewalk. "The timing is suspect, and some of the other park workers thought he was odd and standoffish, but that hardly makes him guilty."

"Was he upset when he saw you here today?"

"He wasn't at this park. Mr. Nussbaumer sent him back to Como. Didn't you see him?"

"The only man I saw was wearing yellow and was spying on me from the trees."

Reese took hold of her elbow and stopped her. "Someone was watching you?"

She shrugged. "I was probably imagining it. Maybe the 'house of the spirits' spooked me more than I thought."

"What did you do?"

"I packed up early, went home and changed, and then came here." She twirled in a circle. "Didn't you notice the dress?"

"Oh, I noticed." He grinned. "And I saw the waves in your hair."

"I'm trying something new." She patted her coiffure. "*Ladies' Home Journal* says only young ladies can wear waves."

"They look good on you." His voice became serious. "Listen, Tessa, just in case there was someone watching you, I don't want you working alone anymore." He held up his hand when she started to protest. "What if that was Nels trying to figure out if you're a woman?"

"I thought about that, so I kept my hat on and my head down." She felt the blood drain from her face. "But what if Nels told Mr. Nussbaumer about me?"

"We'll cross that bridge when we come to it." He held the door for her. "Right now we have a celebration to attend."

"Ten thousand dollars for a kiss?"

"It's true." Tessa giggled at the incredulity in Reese's voice. The porch swing beneath the two of them, she waited for him to ask for the rest of the story. Their celebratory dinner had been capped off with a vaudeville show featuring Miss Inez Lawson.

"Sure, we enjoyed Miss Lawson, but it's hard to believe she received that much for a little smooch."

"Honestly, Reese. Don't look so doubtful." Tessa pushed back on the swing and set it in motion again. The sun had dipped long ago, but she didn't want the night to end. "I read all about her. Miss Lawson was in a taxicab when a party of young people piled in. One girl dared one of the fellows to kiss Miss Lawson."

"So he paid her ten thousand dollars?"

"No, while Miss Lawson was endeavoring to escape the kiss, she hit her lip on the taxicab." Tessa took a breath. "She couldn't perform that night, and she had to get three stitches in her lip. She sued the man for the ten thousand and won."

"Good for her." He brought the swing to a halt.

"Why are you stopping us?"

"First, I want you to know I'm proud of you and all the work you did to make this happen. Even if Mr. Nussbaumer doesn't know the debt he owes you, I do."

"Thank you."

He took her hands and pulled her to her feet. "And second, if I'm going to give you a ten-thousand-dollar good-night kiss, I don't want to do it on that creaky swing."

The wind shifted, and the cool evening air battled with the heat building inside her. "What if I refuse you?"

He wrapped his arms around her waist and drew her close. "Sue me." His lips brushed hers, teasing at first, then dominant and possessive.

Refusing him was the last thing on her mind. She melded to him, trusting him with her heart. How had she ever lived without this man in her life?

Reese stood on the stoop of the Swenhaugens' home, rubbing Lafayette's saggy ears. The air, Minnesota crisp and cool, made for the kind of night that should be enjoyed. The mosquitoes? Not so much.

The screen door scraped open, and Erik welcomed him. "It's good to see you, my friend, but what are you doing here?"

"You left a message at the boardinghouse that you had a branch come down and needed help cutting it up, so here I am."

"I see that, but I expected you'd arrive before the fireflies." He reached for a lantern. "Still, I won't turn away the help unless the neighbors complain."

Erik struck a match and touched it to the wick. The smell of kerosene surrounded them. As they approached the backyard, it was clear why Erik had telephoned. A dead tree, not a branch, had fallen. The tree's length took up most of the Swenhaugens' plot.

Erik removed a bucksaw and a small axe from his shed. "Choose your weapon."

Reese took the axe. "There are a lot of smaller branches to clear before we can get to the trunk." He hooked the lantern on the branch of another tree and set to work. While he began strategically hacking at the branches, Erik used the saw to cut some of the larger ones. Lafayette found a spot by the house and stretched out.

Erik tossed a branch out of the way. "What were you up to earlier this evening?"

"Tessa and I went to celebrate. The new conservatory project at Como was approved, and Mr. Nussbaumer asked me for my opinion on the new plans."

"Does that affect your position?"

"It might." Reese swatted a mosquito. "Mr. Nussbaumer will put one person in charge of it. He has that person narrowed down to Nels Anderson or myself."

"Sounds promising." Erik began to saw with a steady back-and-forth motion. "I'm sure the extra money would come in handy if you decide you wanted to take a wife."

Reese snapped to attention. "I didn't say anything about marrying Tessa."

His friend didn't miss a beat. "You didn't need to. I'm right, though, yes?"

Reese carried a load of small branches to the burn pile and

returned. "All right, yes, I have to admit marriage has entered my mind a couple of times. You've met Tessa. You see how great she is. How could I not be thinking about it?"

Erik chuckled. "It happens to the best of us."

Truth be told, Tessa permeated most of his thoughts these days. He found himself longing to be with her, which he figured was a good thing. Still, marriage was something else.

There was a lot to think about. Tessa made every day an occasion. She kept him thinking, growing, and changing. Most of all, she believed in him.

But she didn't know the entire truth about him.

He sat down on the log. "Erik, do you think you need to tell someone all about yourself—warts and all—before you commit to them?"

"If you're anything like me, you're growing new warts every day." He laughed. "If you're hiding something from her, then I think you'd feel better if you told her, but I'm guessing she already knows you have some flaws."

Everyone had a few flaws in their character. He had gaping weaknesses in his abilities.

Did she know he lacked the creativity she had in abundance? It had been obvious to his father. He could still hear his father's words on the day Reese proudly told him he wanted to be a gardener. "You're a hard worker, son. That should cover up your lack of creativity enough for you to be a good gardener."

Good. That was the word he'd used. Adequate. Okay. He wanted to be a great gardener like his father, and he wanted his father to see his success. With Tessa by his side, that reality was closer than he ever thought possible.

Erik broke off a branch. "One thing I know, Reese, is that our warts can be jewels in God's hands."

Or the wart could be the glaring ugly thing he knew it to be, and Tessa deserved to know the truth about why he'd partnered with her. It had been selfish of him to let her think it was all for her own good.

He sank the axe into the tree trunk. She deserved to know the truth. Why hadn't he told her all of it already?

Tessa couldn't believe what Reese was telling her. She stood before a boxwood bush with a pair of shears in her hand. "Mr. Nussbaumer really wants the garden completed in less than a week?"

"That's what he said." Reese thrust a shovel into the ground. "He said Nels and I were needed elsewhere."

"Do you think Nels told him about me?" Tessa pushed her straw hat up. "Reese, I don't want to get you in trouble."

"You didn't mind before." He dumped a clump of earth next to the hole.

"I've always cared, but maybe I care more now." She patted the earth around the plant. "If it would be better—"

"Tessa, now is not the time to bail on me." He leaned on the shovel. "I need you."

The letter from the university popped into her mind. If she didn't get a position here, her family would expect her to go back to her studies, so she needed this garden to be a success now more than ever.

She picked up the next plant. Once this garden was complete, Reese would finally be able to tell Mr. Nussbaumer about her and how she'd been helping them both.

"Tessa, did you hear me?" Reese asked. "I said you can't leave me now."

"I'm not going anywhere, except to White Bear Lake this weekend."

"*This* weekend?"

"Sorry." She wrinkled her nose. "It's a family thing. You're invited too."

"We'll have to see." He drew in a deep breath. "What's got you smiling now?"

"Remember what that policeman said to us that first day?"

"He said you were a polecat." He shot her a lopsided grin. "And he was right. Then he said, 'She's all yours.' Best thing that's ever happened to me."

Her heart warmed, and she could almost feel the roots of their love deepening.

Please, God, let this work.

30

A weekend without work sounded divine. A weekend without Reese sounded dismal.

Tessa rubbed the muscle on her aching arm and took in the view of White Bear Lake. She and Reese had worked hard to get the garden done, and he would be finishing things up in her absence.

Beside her, Aunt Sam fidgeted with her pocketbook in the back of the Cadillac while Henry whistled "Row, Row, Row Your Boat" in the front seat.

Tessa laid her hand on Aunt Sam's arm. "Are you worried about something?"

"Nothing of any significance, dear." She stilled her hand and took a deep breath.

"It was kind of Senator Ferrell to invite us up to his cabin for the weekend, but I admit it surprised me."

"Oh?"

"Well, I knew the two of you have been friends for quite some time, but I didn't know you'd seen him lately."

"You don't know everything about me, dear, any more than I do you."

"There it is." Henry pointed to a spacious two-story home with a wraparound front porch and a gabled roof.

Tessa sucked in her breath. Calling it a cottage hardly seemed accurate. Behind it, the azure waters of White Bear Lake stretched for miles.

Henry pulled into the driveway while Lincoln and Joel parked each of their cars on the street. Everyone tumbled from the vehicles, excitement in the air. Before they'd removed the last suitcase from the vehicles, Senator Ferrell arrived in his Packard with Edward in tow.

The family stopped and stared, first at him, then at Aunt Sam.

"Oh, did I not mention James and Edward will be joining us this weekend?" Aunt Sam smiled at the senator. "Pardon me. I must have forgotten."

Forgotten, my eye! For some reason, Aunt Sam had purposely omitted this fact.

"But don't worry." Senator Ferrell moved to stand next to Aunt Sam. "I'm staying at my son's cottage next door, so all of you will have full run of my house." He turned to Alice Ann. "And maybe you can even convince your mommy and daddy to take you to the fun house at Wildwood. We have quite a nice amusement park there, missy."

Tessa cocked her head to the side. Why was Senator Ferrell suddenly interested in making Aunt Sam's family so comfortable? Could he and Aunt Sam be . . .

No, she'd know about it. Then again, what had Aunt Sam said? That she didn't know everything about her?

The hair on the back of her neck tingled. A mystery to uncover? Perfect.

Where would Allan Pinkerton suggest she start? Observation? Tessa studied her aunt and the senator. As he swept his arm toward his home, he placed his other hand on Aunt Sam's back. A clue? Perhaps. Still, they were old friends. She'd need more.

Suddenly, this Reese-less weekend didn't seem quite so bleak. She'd dig up the dirt on her aunt's relationship with the senator before the end of the day.

Tessa eyed the shore of White Bear Lake. The gentle, lapping waves taunted her, begging her to dip a toe in.

"I dare you." Edward took three steps down onto the beach.

"Excuse me?"

"You were thinking about stepping into the water, so I said, 'I dare you.'" He sat down on the wooden deck chair beside her. "The water will be frigid this early. It doesn't get warm until July, but if you're afraid—"

"Hardly." Tessa moved her index finger in a circle. "Turn around."

"Why?"

"I can't very well remove my stockings with you watching." She clapped his shoulder. "So move it."

After he complied, she moved to the edge of her deck chair and eased her shoes and stockings off. She sank her toes into the cool sand and pulled her skirt down to cover them. "All right, you can turn around."

He glanced at her discarded accessories and grinned. "Change your mind?"

"No." She padded down the beach. When she reached the water's edge, she paused and hiked up her skirt.

"It's okay to turn back."

"I don't turn back, Mr. Ferrell. I'm a go-ahead girl. No risk too big." The wind whipped at her straw hat. She held it in place and submerged first one toe in the frigid surf, then her whole foot. She shivered and lowered the other foot into the water.

"Cold?"

"Not so much." Her voice quivered.

"Liar." He chuckled and moved down to the shoreline. "Okay, you proved you could do it. Come on out. There's something I want to ask you about."

Was Edward wondering about his grandfather and her aunt too? When he held out his hand, she took it, then followed him back up the beach. She longed for the warmth of her stockings, but the sand stuck to her chilled feet, so she'd have to let them dry.

"Are you thinking what I'm thinking?" she asked as they returned to their chairs.

"I doubt it."

"I'm serious, Edward. Haven't you noticed how your grandfather and Aunt Sam are looking at each other?" She glanced toward the house. "Look at them now. It's like the rest of us aren't even here."

"Good for them." Edward shifted in his chair. "Listen, before we get anyone else joining us down here, I want to ask you something."

"Okay."

"Do you remember when I agreed to give you motorcycle lessons?" He waited for her to nod. "You promised you'd do something for me in return someday."

"What do you need? Help in planning something for your girl back at college?" She giggled. "I have some excellent romantic ideas I'm sure she would love."

"That's not it." He stood and stuffed his hands in his pockets. "Tessa, you know Joe and I still need the funds for the motorcycle company—"

"I told you I wouldn't ask Aunt Sam."

"I know." His gaze shifted toward the house, then back to her. "I've been approached by a client who owns a building and glass company. They'd like to secure the bid on the conservatory."

"That's a wonderful idea. I'm sure Mr. Nussbaumer would love to grant the contract to a local business."

He sighed. "Tessa, if they are to win the bid, they'd have to submit the lowest figure. The park commission wants to know who will complete the conservatory for the best price. The only way my friends can win the bid is to know what other companies have submitted."

"How could they possibly know that?" Edward was acting quite strangely. What was he getting at?

"That's where the favor comes in." He sat down on the chair again and leaned close. "If you sneak into Mr. Nussbaumer's office, you can see what the lowest bid is and let me know."

Her back stiffened. "I couldn't do that."

"You could." His voice turned firm. "And you owe me."

She owed him? Her chest constricted and her breath came hard. She had to make him understand. "This wasn't what I thought you meant when I agreed to help you in the future. It's breaking the rules, and it's wrong, Edward."

"It's bending them, and you said yourself that you're the go-ahead girl. No risk too big, right?" He sat back.

"I won't do it. Figure out another way."

"If you don't, I may have to tell your family about what happened at the end of your college term."

Tessa's stomach lurched. "How did you find out about that?"

"Does the name Everett Ingersol mean anything to you?" Edward flashed her a checkmate grin. "I can tell it does. I believe he's a classmate of yours now. Well, he's an old friend of mine from high school. He told me all about your expulsion. I'm sure you've not said anything to your family. What would they think of the youngest Gregory girl getting herself in trouble once again? And what about Reese? What would a fine fellow like him think if he knew the truth about his girl?"

"I thought we were friends, Edward."

"We are, but a deal's a deal. Don't take it personally. This is business." He stood. "I'll need that information by next Friday."

Tessa wrapped her arms around herself as the cold vined from her feet through her body and wrapped around her heart. What was she going to do?

Soon.

Sam would tell her family about James and her at the first opportunity, but so far, no such time seemed to present itself. During the afternoon, James had taken various family members out on his sailboat. After dinner, the adults tucked the children in bed and gathered in the parlor around the fireplace for a rousing game of cards.

She laid her cards on the table with a flourish. "Gin."

"Again?" Edward chuckled. "Tessa, I think you should come join your sisters and me in this game. You're the only one who could possibly figure out your aunt's secret."

Tessa glanced up from the sketchbook in her hands. "I'm no match for her."

Something was amiss with her youngest niece. Had she figured out the reason for this visit to the lake? She'd been down on the beach with Edward. Perhaps the young man had shared something personal with her. She prayed that hadn't happened.

"You can come take my place." Hannah moved from the table to the davenport to sit between Lincoln and Joel. "I'm not feeling up to it anymore."

"It appears you've chased the competition away." James covered Sam's hand with his own.

Tessa seemed to eye the intimate gesture. She slapped her sketchbook shut. "How long are you and he going to keep this from us? Don't you realize what kind of damage secrets will do?"

"Tessa," Hannah snapped. "Hold your tongue."

"You're lecturing me? Of all people, you should be thinking about what you're keeping hidden."

Hannah visibly paled, and Charlotte laid a hand on Tessa's shoulder. "What's gotten into you?"

"It's not her fault." Sam locked eyes with Tessa. "I believe Tessa's detective abilities have helped her sniff out the truth." She steeled herself. *Soon* had become *now*. "Everyone, James and I have been keeping something from you." She shared a slight smile with the senator. "We've been seeing one another."

Lincoln withdrew his arm from Hannah's shoulders and leaned forward. "For how long?"

"A couple of months." James leaned back in his chair, apparently ready to be questioned. "As you know, we've been dear friends for years, but we've only recently let our feelings grow beyond friendship."

Grateful for his carefully chosen words, Sam squeezed his hand. "We've no plans for the future, but we didn't want to keep this from you any longer."

Hannah walked to the decanter of water on the table, hands trembling, and poured herself a glass. "Why didn't you tell—"

She swayed. Lincoln jumped to his feet and caught her a split second before her head hit the ground.

31

What had she done?

Tessa could only stare as Lincoln scooped Hannah into his arms and carried her up the stairs to the bedroom in which the two of them were staying. Joel snagged his doctor's bag from a hook in the hallway and rushed up behind them with Charlotte following.

If she hadn't forced Aunt Sam's hand, none of this would have happened.

Aunt Sam touched her arm. "It's not your fault."

"I upset her." She swiped the tears from her cheeks with the palms of her hands. "How could I do that, knowing her condition?"

"You knew?" Aunt Sam asked.

"Yes, I found out by accident, but she's never told Charlotte." Her voice hitched. "Charlotte will be devastated."

"For a while, maybe." Aunt Sam wrapped an arm around Tessa's shoulders and led her to the davenport. "Families might grow in different directions, dear, but their roots stay the same."

"I should go up there." Tessa stood and went to the doorway.

"I think there are enough family members in that bedroom." Aunt Sam's voice was calm and soothing. "And one of them is a competent doctor."

Rapid footsteps in the upstairs hallway drew Tessa's attention.

She glanced up to see Charlotte rush from Hannah's bedchamber followed by Joel.

"Charlotte, you know I couldn't tell you." Joel caught Charlotte's shoulder. When she turned, her face was streaked with tears, and he pulled her into his arms.

"How could Hannah not tell me?" Pain filled her voice.

Joel stroked her hair and pressed a kiss to her head. "She was worried about you."

"But I'm her sister."

So am I, and I didn't tell you either.

"I know you're hurting, sweetheart." He stepped back and took her hands. "But if Hannah doesn't avoid stress right now, she could lose the baby. Please, don't upset her any more than she is."

Fresh guilt washed over Tessa like the waves on White Bear Lake, and her heart felt battered by the storm. This was all her fault.

Tessa needed an anchor. If only Reese were here, she'd have someone to hold on to.

Never had Tessa been more excited to get back to Como Park than she was this morning. The situation between Charlotte and Hannah had remained tense throughout Sunday, and Edward's threat loomed like a dark thundercloud.

Given that the two gardens would be judged on Thursday, she'd work hard to keep Reese calm and his spirits high. Since Edward didn't need the bids until a day after the judging, she'd wait to tell Reese about her dilemma until then. She wouldn't burden him with her problems until later.

As soon as she arrived at the park, she walked to the garden she'd planted with Reese. She glanced around the area to see if she was alone and released a slow breath when she saw that she was. The eerie feeling of being watched had left her skittish.

She marveled at all he'd finished while she was away for the weekend. He had installed a two-bowl tiered fountain, trimmed every bush, and filled every urn. He must have worked day and night. Even the flowers they'd planted in drifts seemed to have already filled in under his care. It was as if they knew opening day had arrived, and they were ready to show off their blooms.

But would it be enough? This had begun as a project for her to get Mr. Nussbaumer's attention, but it had grown to mean so much more. It was a symbol of Reese's success as a gardener. It was a symbol of how well she and Reese worked together. Most of all, it was a symbol of how their love had bloomed.

By the end of the week, they'd have their answers. She prayed Reese would be the one to win the little competition between Nels and him. He could then inform Mr. Nussbaumer of her role in the garden's creation, and once her future was set, she could tell Reese exactly why she couldn't go back to the university in the fall.

She took a seat on one of the wrought-iron benches they'd placed, but even the mellow glow of the morning sun didn't quell the nerves jostling her inside. She'd lain awake for hours last night, thinking about her dilemma regarding Edward's request. Sure, she'd done lots of things that were a little risky, and this wasn't exactly illegal, but in her heart she knew it was unethical. How could she do something that felt so wrong? Her stomach spiraled at the thought.

But if Edward divulged her secret to her sisters, they'd be gravely disappointed in her, and it would put Hannah and the baby in danger. Did she really have a choice anymore?

Where was she?

Reese stood on the sidewalk near the area assigned to Nels for his garden and scanned the area for Tessa. Yesterday he'd asked her to meet him and his parents there at ten o'clock.

He glanced at his pocket watch and then at his parents.

His mother laid her hand on his arm. "You look nervous. I'm sure we'll love her, Reese."

But whether they liked Tessa was not the only thing making him on edge. Today Mr. Nussbaumer would make his decision about which garden he liked most. It would also be a day that his father would get to see what he and Tessa had done. Since she'd come back from White Bear Lake, she'd worked tirelessly beside him to make sure every element in the garden was perfect. Would it be enough to impress both Mr. Nussbaumer and his father?

"I thought you said she'd be here by ten." His father frowned. "Is she normally this unpredictable?"

Reese smiled to himself. *You have no idea, Dad.* "It's five till ten, and there she is now."

His heart swelled as she neared. *His* girl. If Mr. Nussbaumer offered him a new position in the conservatory, he'd then make enough to take a wife, and he planned to make her his forever.

Last night she'd teased him about wearing her overalls today to meet them, but her dress today was as feminine as could be. The cascade of roses down the front made it an especially appropriate choice. The dress's flowing material blew in the breeze. Had she called it chiffon?

Beneath the large-brimmed hat, she smiled at him, infusing him with confidence.

This was his day.

"Miss Tessa Gregory, I'd like for you to meet my parents, Samuel and Viola King."

"It's a pleasure to meet you, Mr. and Mrs. King." She dipped her head slightly. "You must be proud of all that Reese has accomplished here."

"He's a hard worker, our son." His father clasped his shoulder. "Thanks, Dad."

"And he's very talented too." Tessa smiled at him.

"Reese tells us that you share his love of gardening." His mother offered a warm smile. "He said you have been working with the City Beautiful Movement. A vacant lot garden?"

Tessa quirked a questioning look in his direction. He'd explain later why he hadn't told them about the Como garden they'd planted together.

"Uh, yes, but I'm merely helping. It's great to see the empty areas put to good use."

"Do you have other hobbies, Miss Gregory?" His father, however, seemed more interested in Nels's garden than her answer.

Reese's eyes widened as a grin spread on Tessa's face. She wouldn't dare tell them about the motorcycle, would she?

"I enjoy things that keep me moving." She shared a look with him. "I enjoy the arts too. Especially drama."

"Well." Reese took Tessa's elbow. "I see Mr. Nussbaumer. Shall we go take a look at Nels's creation?"

Tessa kept her distance when they met Mr. Nussbaumer at the entrance to the area, but he clearly didn't recognize her. Several other park workers had joined them to view the garden's grand opening. After he exchanged greetings with Reese's father, he motioned to Nels. "Shall we?"

Nels opened a wrought-iron gate, and the group moved down the paved brick walk. The formal-style garden featured simplistic, geometric designs. He'd used an existing boxwood hedge and trimmed it to line the pathway and make a pocket for the hydrangeas, astilbe, and hostas.

The linear designs matched Nels's character, much like Tessa's garden design matched hers. Nels's garden had a sense of order and tidiness. Only white flowers bloomed in his containers, and nothing seemed out of place. Symmetry reigned in every corner.

Reese risked a glance at Tessa, who wrinkled her nose. He chuckled. There were not enough bells and whistles to pique her interest.

Mr. Nussbaumer turned to Reese's father. "Would you care to offer your professional opinion?"

"It is well balanced and classic." He squatted next to a hedge and eyed it critically. "These are perfectly pruned. The work is skillfully done."

"I agree." Mr. Nussbaumer shook Nels's hand. "Very *gut* work, Nels. There is nothing wrong with your garden." He turned to Reese. "Now, shall we see what you have created?"

Mr. Nussbaumer fell in step beside him with his parents behind, leaving Tessa to walk beside Nels. Some of the other park employees trailed behind the group.

The closer they came to the garden, the more Reese's stomach twisted like an overgrown grapevine. Having his father there intensified the stress tenfold. What if his father didn't approve of their work?

They reached the entrance to the garden, an ornamental gate between two pillars, and stopped. Tessa called it the entrance to the enchanted garden. He motioned the others inside and hung back to gauge their reaction.

His father and mother paused to look at each of the garden rooms and whispered among themselves. Though not completely filled in yet, the flowers emphasized a display of color worthy of the Fourth of July. Mr. Nussbaumer stood in the middle by the two-tiered fountain so long that Reese feared he wouldn't explore the rest. Finally, he moved on, seemingly taking note of the basket weave design of the brick sidewalk.

Reese shot a glance in Tessa's direction. She too was watching the master gardener's every move. When Mr. Nussbaumer reached the *clair-voie*, an open gate that marked the next room, Reese smiled at her. This area held a sundial, and she'd chosen the piece because, according to her, gardens like this were timeless.

After nearly forty-five minutes, Mr. Nussbaumer approached Reese's father. "He is a *gut* gardener, *ja*?"

His father nodded. "I had no idea you'd embraced the Arts and Crafts movement with such enthusiasm and vision. You have a bright future before you, son."

Reese's heart soared. Finally. His father believed in him.

"I too am impressed, Reese." Mr. Nussbaumer held out his hand. "Congratulations. It is my pleasure to offer you the head gardener's position at the new conservatory. Not only are your plants in splendid condition, but your design is truly brilliant."

His design? No, this wasn't his design. Tessa was in every detail—the gate, the fountain, the sundial, the shrubs, and the flowers—but how could he speak up and say that now in front of this crowd? In front of Mr. Nussbaumer? In front of his father?

He looked at Tessa, excitement filling her eyes. She was smiling, waiting for him to tell them all the truth.

He tore his gaze away.

If he said something now, it would ruin any chance they could have for a future together. She would have to understand.

"Thank you, sir. I'm pleased you like my garden."

Tessa's heart shattered.

His garden?

She stared at him. Surely any second he'd turn in her direction and call a halt to this whole façade.

The plans were hers. The vision was hers. *Hers.*

Please, Reese, please, say something.

Nothing.

Tears seared her cheeks, and still she stood there. He didn't say a word or look in her direction. How could he do this to her? Had this been his plan all along? He'd said he loved her. Was that a lie too?

Like a weed in the garden, he'd yanked her heart out by the roots and tossed it aside to dry in the sun.

In her effort to prove how mature she was, she'd let a man use her and fill her head with romantic notions. What a fool she'd been!

Gathering the sides of her dress, she dashed down the sidewalk. She had to escape. She had to get away from Reese King forever.

32

Side aching, Tessa dropped to a bench and tried to catch her breath between sobs.

"Miss? Are you all right?"

She looked up to see the park officer, the same man who'd almost arrested her that first day, holding a handkerchief out for her.

No, I'm not all right! Even you should be able to see that.

She pushed his hand away and scurried toward the only building in the area. She needed a place to cry or scream or both, and right now, with everyone in the park fawning over Reese, the office would be empty.

As soon as she was inside, she slammed the door shut. More hot, angry tears spilled forth. Her chest felt as if it would explode. "This cannot be happening. It's not fair!"

Fair? What had been fair in her whole life? Was it fair for her parents to die? Was it fair to fall in love with a man who would betray her? Was it fair to be wrongly accused at the university? Was it fair for Charlotte to be unable to have a baby, while Hannah had no trouble conceiving?

Hannah. She had to get control of herself. Hannah needed her.

She sniffed and dried her eyes with her palms. Turning to Reese for help was no longer an option, and Edward was going to tell

Hannah about Tessa's school situation tomorrow if she didn't have that stupid information for him. She had no other choice.

Like the gates she and Reese had worked on, Mr. Nussbaumer's door remained ajar. She glanced around before hurrying inside. She didn't bother to shut the office door. Finding what she needed would only take a few minutes.

She picked up the first stack of papers and leafed through it. A second and third stack revealed nothing as well. Then a folder on the upper left-hand corner of the desk caught her eye. She opened it and read the top letter. It was a construction bid from the Ingersol Construction Company.

This was it! Now all she had to do was find out who had submitted the lowest bid.

Guilt swept over her and stilled her trembling fingers.

"I thought I recognized you." The park officer stood at Mr. Nussbaumer's door. "Care to tell me what you're looking at, miss?"

"Nothing."

"Then set that folder of nothing down and come out here."

Tessa heaved a sigh and did as she was told. The park officer grabbed her wrist and yanked out a pair of handcuffs.

"What are you doing?" She tried to pull away, but he managed to snap one side on.

"I'm making sure you stay right here while I go find Mr. Nussbaumer." He clipped the other end to a pipe on the wall.

"You're just going to leave me here like this?"

"Yep." He grinned. "Maybe you can figure out a better story before I return."

Could this day get any worse?

Reese scanned the hats of every woman in the park. Where had Tessa gone? He needed to talk to her.

One of the park officers hurried toward him. "Mr. King, I'm so glad I found you. Remember that lady I caught picking flowers who you said you'd take care of? Well, I found her going through papers in Mr. Nussbaumer's office. What do you want me to do with her?"

His heart lurched. "Is she still there?"

"Sure. I handcuffed her to a pipe."

What had Tessa been up to? "Give me the key."

"What?"

"Give me the key." He held out his hand. "I'll take care of her."

"She's trouble, Mr. King." He fished the key from his pocket and dropped it in Reese's hand. "Mark my words. She's trouble with a capital T."

Reese wrapped his fist around the key. "No, she's not. She's the best thing that's ever happened to me, and if I have to spend the rest of my life proving it to her, I will."

It seemed reasonable that the floors of a park office would be dirt covered, but Tessa had stood so long she'd finally had to sit down. Her rose-colored dress might never be the same. Not that she'd ever want to wear it again. When she got home, she might even burn it as a way to destroy her memories of Reese and this horrid day.

Tessa propped her arms on her raised knees and buried her head. After Mr. Nussbaumer came, any future at Como or any other park in the city would be over, but even worse, she'd failed in her task.

If she hadn't second-guessed herself at the last moment, she'd have had the figure she needed for Edward. His client could submit the lowest bid for the project, and most of all, Hannah and her baby would be safe.

The door handle rattled, and she jerked her head up in time to see Reese slip inside. He shut the door and latched it.

"What are you doing here?" Her voice came out icy.

"I could ask you the same thing." He dangled the key in front of him. "I ran into your favorite park officer."

"I'd prefer him over you." She moved her wrist, making the handcuffs clang against the pipe. "If you'll unlock me, you can be rid of me for good."

He crossed his arms over his chest. "Nope."

"You're not going to let me go?"

"Not until you tell me why you're here."

She rose to her feet and sent him a fiery glare. "That's none of your business."

"Anything that has to do with you is my business."

"It was. It's not anymore."

"I know I hurt you, and we'll talk about that later, but right now I want answers. Why are you here?"

"I had some papers to look at." Why give him a complete explanation when a partial one would do?

"Which papers?"

"The bids for the conservatory, but don't worry, I didn't see them. Unlike some people, I have a conscience."

"Why would you want those?" He ignored the barb and moved to unlock the handcuffs. He slid the one cuff off the pipe while Tessa removed the other from her wrist. "Wait a minute. You don't want those bids. Someone else does." He stepped back to look at her face. "Is it Edward? Did he ask you to do this? I told you—"

"That I was supposed to turn to you?" She rubbed her wrist where the handcuff had chafed. "Well, I had every intention of doing exactly that until you showed me that this whole time, you were the one putting on the act."

"Tessa, let me explain. I love you. I still care."

"Care?" Anger burned in her chest. "You care about your job. You care about impressing your father, but if you cared about me, you wouldn't have used me."

"Listen, Tessa." He reached for her hand, but she yanked it away. "I couldn't say anything about your part in the garden because I had to have that new position in order to have enough money to support a wife. It was so we could have a future."

"What future, Reese?" Fresh tears sprang to her eyes. The ache in her heart threatened to crush her. She put her hand on the door handle. "I may not have always told you everything, but I never intentionally hurt you. I can't love a man I can't trust with my heart."

33

The slamming door still echoed in Reese's ears. He stood in the park office, his chest heaving, clenching and unclenching his fists until they ached. He wanted to hit something or someone, but the only person he could be angry with was himself.

He headed into Mr. Nussbaumer's office to fix things. He didn't want to explain any of this to him.

When he stepped out of the room, the door opened and Nels walked in. Surprise at seeing Reese registered for a fraction of a second in the widening of his eyes. He quickly schooled his features. "Congratulations, Reese."

"Thank you." Reese swallowed. "Your garden was outstanding."

"But clearly not as remarkable as yours." Nels seemed to consider his next words for a moment before he crossed his arms over his chest. "You know, I saw her."

"Her?"

"The young woman disguised as a boy who helped you. I could have told Mr. Nussbaumer, but I chose not to."

"I appreciate it."

"Who is she?"

"Her name is Tessa Gregory. You met her a while back when we were having lunch together. Remember?"

"Hard to forget." He gave a wry laugh. "And you two are courting?"

"Maybe."

"Well, I wanted you to know, I'm not the kind of guy to take shortcuts. Besides, it wasn't like she designed it." Nels shrugged and offered Reese his hand. "The best garden won—fair and square."

Reese forced a smile and shook Nels's work-roughened hand, then watched the gardener exit the building.

First his father, then Mr. Nussbaumer, and now Nels—three chances to tell the truth about Tessa Gregory.

A cold hand gripped his heart. How could he do that to her?

Reese almost expected to hear a cock crowing in the distance.

The streetcar bell clanged as the conductor brought the car to a stop. Tessa forced herself to climb off at the corner and begin the short trek to Charlotte's house, but every step took more effort than it should have.

The steady *pop, pop, pop* of a motorcycle drew her attention, and she longed to hop astride one of the thrilling machines and feel the air in her face.

She considered going home to Aunt Sam, but that wasn't what she needed. She needed Charlotte to come with her to speak to Hannah. It would mean Charlotte would have to put aside her own hurt, like Tessa would have to put aside her pride.

Tessa prayed Aunt Sam had been right about a family being like a tree. *Please, Lord, let the roots of our love run deep.*

Charlotte greeted her at the door and immediately brought her inside, made her tea, and offered her a piece of chocolate cake. "Tessa, what's wrong?"

Although Tessa didn't intend to share every detail, amid tears and hugs, the story of the morning spilled out.

"Oh, Tessa. I'm so sorry that things are not going to work out at Como, but you can always go back to the university next term and finish your schooling."

Tessa's pulse quickened. The moment had come. "I can't."

"Why?"

"I only want to tell this story once." She squeezed Charlotte's hand. "Will you please come with me to Hannah's? I want you both to hear this from me. Please come. I promise it's a matter of life and death."

"Life and death?" Charlotte rolled her eyes. "I know you're distressed, and rightfully so, but really, Tessa, don't you think that's a bit much even for you?"

"We have to protect Hannah and the baby. So you'll go?"

"You're my sister, and if you need me, of course I will."

Fresh tears seared Tessa's eyes. The images on Hannah's parlor wall, two photographs in oak oval frames, blurred—a wash of gray and white.

"I smell cinnamon." Charlotte greeted the housekeeper. "Are you making those scrumptious cinnamon rolls, Mrs. Umdahl? In that case, I'm very glad we've come."

"Yes, ma'am." The usually somber housekeeper smiled at the praise. "Why don't you two have a seat while I let Mrs. Cole know you're here?"

Charlotte sat down in an upholstered chair, but Tessa remained standing. The cinnamon-scented air mixed with the cloying scent of lilies on the table and caused her roiling stomach to churn anew.

Tessa blinked to clear her watery vision. Momma and Daddy stared back at her from beneath the curved glass. Her heart squeezed. Her parents would have been so disappointed in her right now.

Mrs. Umdahl returned to the parlor. "Your sister will be down in a moment."

"Thank you." Tessa touched the cool wood of the frame containing her father's photograph.

After Mrs. Umdahl left the room, Charlotte joined Tessa at the photographs. "What's on your mind right now, Tessa?"

"Do you remember the big sycamore tree we had in the front yard?"

"Yes." Charlotte smiled. "I recall you were fond of climbing it, much to Mother's dismay."

"It was my playhouse. Sometimes it was a fort, and I was a nurse tending the wounded soldiers. Other times it was a castle, and I was a princess fighting off trolls. And my favorite times it was my home, where I could live with all of the animals and plants as my friends."

"It was a special place until it was hit by lightning."

"And it died." Tessa swallowed. "I came home from school one day, and Daddy had chopped it down."

"Our yard looked naked."

"I remember staring out the front window and thinking how strange the view was with the tree gone. I thought that tree was the strongest thing there was. I thought nothing could hurt it, but then it was gone. The roots were still there, but the branches and the trunk and the leaves were gone forever." Tessa closed her eyes and let her mind carry her back. She could still hear the leaves rustling in the wind.

Charlotte touched her arm. "What is it?"

Tessa's heart ached. She opened her eyes and looked at her father's face. "When Daddy died, I lost another tree. He was solid and true. I could count on him for everything."

"And now with Reese?"

"The axe has fallen yet again." Tessa sighed.

"Oh, Tess." Charlotte wrapped her arm around her sister's shoulders. "You still have us."

"After you hear my story, you may want to renege on that offer."

"What story?" Hannah, wearing a loose-fitting housedress,

breezed into the room. She stopped and looked at Charlotte. "Wait. Where are my manners? It's so good to see you—both. Mrs. Umdahl says she has coffee and cinnamon rolls set out for us in the dining room. Shall we talk in there?"

Once they were seated, Tessa peeled a piece of cinnamon roll from the spiral. With her thoughts so far away, she hardly noticed the sugar and butter melting on her tongue. Her sisters would never see her as an adult after they heard this story. Everything in her wanted to let Charlotte and Hannah continue with their small talk, but she had to protect the baby.

Where did she begin?

Charlotte took care of bringing Hannah up-to-date on Reese. She explained how he'd taken credit for Tessa's work, and how he'd ruined their plans to tell Mr. Nussbaumer about her skills.

"Tessa, I'm so sorry." Hannah reached across the table and squeezed Tessa's hand. "But you can return to college in the fall, and once you have your degree, you can create gardens everywhere."

"I can't go back."

"Honey . . ." Charlotte took a sip of coffee. "I know you don't feel like you can live without him right now, but it will get easier once you're away at school."

Tessa squared her shoulders. "I don't mean I'm not capable of going back. I mean I'm not allowed."

34

Tessa sent up a silent prayer, asking God to open up the floor and let it swallow her whole.

Hannah and Charlotte stared at her.

"What did you say?" Hannah set down her cup so fast the coffee splashed over the rim.

"Please, stay calm—for you and for the baby." Tessa slanted a glance at Charlotte. At least mentioning the baby didn't seem to upset her other sister. "I am not welcome to return to the university."

"Why? What did you do?" Hannah mopped up the spill with a napkin.

"Calm, Hannah. Calm."

"Don't tell me to be calm. You just told me you've been expelled."

Tessa stood. If she pretended to be an opposing attorney in a courtroom, maybe it would be easier to face Hannah.

No. No more playacting. It was time to grow up.

She placed her hands on the back of the dining room chair. "I broke the curfew for the girls' dormitory."

Charlotte's brow scrunched. "And they expelled you?"

"It might have had something to do with the way I got out of the dorm room."

Ever the attorney, Hannah shoved her coffee cup to the side and leaned back in her chair, ready to cross-examine every detail. "And how exactly did you get out of the dorm?"

"I crawled out the window and shimmied down a tree." She shrugged. "I guess all those years of climbing trees came in handy. The dean thought that was most unladylike."

"Imagine that." Hannah sighed. "I almost hate to ask this, but why were you climbing out the window?"

Tessa began to pace in front of the window. The more she thought about the whole affair, the more the embers of anger began to flame.

"Tessa?"

She faced her sisters, jaw set, back straight. "Every week, the horticulture department had a seminar on Monday nights. They talked about all sorts of important things, or at least that's what I'd been told by my classmates—my male classmates."

"You'd never gone yourself?" Charlotte asked.

"I couldn't. The meeting began at eight, which is the curfew in the ladies' dormitory. The men didn't have to be in until nine thirty." Her chest burned. Why did they have a curfew an hour and a half later, anyway?

"So you had to sneak out in order to go to a meeting?" Charlotte tore off another piece of her cinnamon roll. "Why didn't you simply explain the situation to the department chair?"

"I did." Irritation filled her voice. *Calm down. Be reasonable. Act mature. You don't want Hannah and Charlotte to think you were childish.*

She slowed down, choosing her words carefully. "I even made a petition and collected signatures from all of the women in the horticultural program, but Dean Shipley seemed especially annoyed by that. He told me I should let things remain as they were and not stir up trouble." She clenched her fists. "But it wasn't fair. I waited and waited, but when they were going to talk about aquatic gardens, I had to go. And they were going to address the Esopus Spitzenburg too."

"The what?"

"The Spitzenburg is an antique apple. Thomas Jefferson's favorite variety. It has a spicy flavor and it's susceptible to all kinds of disease." She licked her lips. "And it was delicious. I found out they had a fruit tasting at every meeting. Can't you see all the important things I'd been missing?"

She sank down into the chair. "I know it was irresponsible and you both probably have a hundred things you want to tell me, but I doubt that you'll say anything I haven't already said to myself. I thought if I could get a position at Como Park, then I'd have a perfect reason for not returning for the fall term, and neither of you would have had to learn about this whole ugly thing." Tears filled her eyes again.

Hannah walked behind Tessa's chair and placed her hands on her shoulders. "I can't speak for Charlotte, but I understand why you did what you did."

"You do?"

"I do too." Charlotte laid her hand on Tessa's arm. "It was unfair to make this seminar unavailable to the female students."

"But"—Hannah gave her shoulders a firm squeeze—"you should have told us right away so we could help. I'll draft a letter to the university in the morning, and if that doesn't change the dean's mind, Lincoln and I will be paying him a visit. Let's see him match wits with two attorneys."

"And Tessa, the worst part is you carried this burden alone." Charlotte passed Tessa a clean handkerchief. "Yes, it might have been hard to tell us in the beginning, but keeping it hidden only made it more painful for you." She turned to Hannah. "Didn't it?"

Hannah's eyes became glassy. "I'm sorry I didn't tell you about the baby, Charlotte. I didn't want to hurt you, but I hurt you more by keeping it a secret."

"You hurt yourself the most." Charlotte gently squeezed Hannah's arm. "Joel said he thinks the stress of keeping this truth hidden has affected you more than you realize."

Hannah laid a hand on her abdomen. "It isn't fair. You should be in the family way before me."

"I did feel that way—for about five minutes." Charlotte smiled and refilled her coffee cup. "I'm thrilled for you, Hannah. I don't know why God hasn't blessed me with a baby yet, but I've been asking him to help me understand this pain and walk with me through it."

"I wish I could fix the whole situation." Hannah swiped a finger under her eye.

"You mean fix me?" Charlotte held her coffee cup with both hands as if to warm herself. "If it were medically possible, I think Joel would have told me that, but it isn't. After what happened, I've had a lot of time to think."

She set down her coffee cup and walked around the table to join her sisters. She took Hannah's hands. "I'm not saying this is easy. I don't know what God intends for Joel and me through all of this. Maybe it's so I'll draw closer to him, or maybe he has other designs for our family. I do know he's not forgotten me. No matter what God's planned for me, Hannah, baby or no baby, I will rejoice in what he's planned for you."

They hugged for a long time, then opened up their circle and drew Tessa into their embrace. The ache in her heart eased, and her crushing burden lifted.

The Gregory sisters—rooted in love, grounded by faith, and watching their dreams grow and flower around them . . . together.

How could she have doubted her sisters' love for her or for each other?

Two days. Two miserable days without the woman he loved.

Sitting in the garden Reese had planted with Tessa brought him no comfort. Tessa was everywhere—in the shrubs she'd chosen for height and texture, in the flowers she'd claimed had their own countenance, and in the whimsical extras that she'd promised would surprise visitors.

Reese propped his elbows on his knees and pressed his brow into the heel of his hand. Lack of sleep had left his energy drained, but it was the empty hole in his heart that sucked the life from him.

Remorse, regret, and anger tangled inside him, making a crater in his stomach. He couldn't remember the last time he'd eaten. Poor Mrs. Baxter was beside herself with worry. She wanted to know what was wrong with him, but how could he tell her he was a coward and he'd betrayed Tessa?

"Hello, son." His father sat down on the bench beside him. "I thought I'd find you here."

Reese sat up. "You were looking for me? It's not lunchtime yet. I thought you and Mother were going to go to Minnehaha Falls this morning."

"She's going with your Tessa's aunt. I believe she said her name was Samantha Phillips."

"Mrs. Phillips? When did you speak to her?"

"Yesterday. Your mother insisted we go over and talk to Tessa to see if we were the cause of the sudden rift between the two of you."

"Was Tessa all right?"

"She wasn't there. Mrs. Phillips said she was at her sister's home." He took a deep breath. "She also said Tessa was deeply wounded, but that most wounds can heal."

Reese rubbed his thumb over the raised zigzag on his left index finger. "And leave a nasty scar."

"Some do." His father stood and walked around the sundial. "This is truly a beautiful place, Reese. As I told you before, it shows a great deal of vision."

"Go ahead and say it, Dad. You know it isn't my design. Remember, you already told me I lack creativity."

"What?"

"Dad, don't pretend. We both know the truth." Reese pushed

up his shirtsleeves. "I'm a hard worker, but I don't have what it takes to be a gifted garden designer."

"Did I say that?"

"More or less."

His father leaned against one of the brick pillars. "Apparently I was wrong."

"No, you weren't. Didn't you hear me? Tessa did all this. You can see her touch all over the garden. I know you can."

"You're right." His father moved to the *clair-voie* and placed his hand on the metal spindle. "I could tell, and before you panic, your secret is safe. I didn't say anything to Fred Nussbaumer. But son, hers is not the only hand I see at work in this garden."

Reese cocked his head to the side. "What do you mean?"

"I see you here too." He swept his arm toward the pillars. "You made those. I can tell by the strong, bold lines and solid structure. Those will be standing long after the last bloom fades. Maybe you can't see it, but you bring a richness here, where Tessa brought the element of joy." His father looked at him and chuckled. "You look surprised. Didn't you think I could tell you selected the shrubs, knowing what would tolerate Minnesota's cold winter? And you're one of the only gardeners I know who could make everything look established after only a few weeks. You are truly gifted in husbandry."

Reese stared at his father, unsure of what to say. He'd heard more words of praise in that minute than he had in his lifetime. Had his father actually used the word *gifted*?

His father again joined him on the bench. "Reese, I'm not sure what I said to you that day long ago, but I can tell that you remember it word for word. I can also see you are a skilled gardener. You and Tessa make a brilliant team."

"I have to tell Mr. Nussbaumer the truth about Tessa's help in all this."

"It isn't going to change his mind." He squeezed Reese's shoulder. "I've known Fred for a long time, and he isn't going to hire a woman, so don't be the hero. You'll be putting that new position you earned on the line for nothing."

Reese pushed to his feet. "No, Dad. It will be for something. It will let me sleep at night, and it will let me look Tessa in the eyes and promise her I'll live the rest of my life trying never to let her down again."

His father stood and studied him for a second. Reese lowered his gaze. He couldn't bear to once again see the disappointment in his father's eyes. Then, before he knew what was happening, his father pulled him into a hug.

"I'm proud of you, son."

Reese had waited his whole life to hear those words, but they could barely penetrate the hedge of guilt around his heart.

Lord, please forgive me.

The stubborn weed refused to budge. Tessa wrapped both hands around it and gave it a firm yank. She was rewarded with the sound of a snap as the roots let loose.

She sat back on her knees and tipped her face to the sun. Pulling weeds was exactly what she needed right now. If only it were as easy to rip out her thoughts of Reese.

After slipping out of the house earlier, Tessa had made her way to Aunt Sam's garden. She'd neglected it terribly. At the rate Hannah and Charlotte were going when she left, Tessa imagined they'd still be giggling and talking when the moon came out. Thank goodness the children were taking Sunday afternoon naps.

While she loved her sisters, Tessa didn't feel up to laughing with them right now. Sure, she was glad it seemed the tension between them had evaporated and her conscience was now clear, but the pieces of her heart still felt scattered like dandelion fluff in the wind.

She plucked a fluffy dandelion from the ground. Once, when

she was a little girl, she had sat on the porch steps with her mother holding a similar dandelion in her hand. She'd had a bad day, with her sister constantly telling her what to do, so her mother told her to make a wish and blow the dandelion seeds in the air.

Tessa smiled at the memory.

She'd wished to be an only child.

But now that she was an adult, she knew the truth. Blowing dandelion fluff only made more dandelions. Wherever seeds fell, they grew.

An *awooga* horn of a Model T startled her. She whipped her gaze toward the street. Reese?

No, the driver was honking at a motorcycle. Now that she'd ridden a motorcycle, she seemed to see them everywhere.

What if it had been Reese? Her blood ran fast at the thought. A part of her wanted to see him, but another part burned at the idea. She jerked another weed from the soil. He'd used her and he'd lied to her. After all his talk about Tessa's acting, he was the one who'd put on the best show of all.

A clanging sound in the corner of the garden made her look up. It sounded as if the gate was closing, but no one was there. Perhaps the neighbor's kitten was out prowling again, or maybe it was Edward wanting his information.

She jumped at the sound of footsteps behind her. Turning, she spotted Aunt Sam approaching.

"Hello, dear." She sat down on a nearby bench. "I thought you might need some company. Is there a reason you're pulling those weeds like they're the enemy?"

"I'm pretending they're pieces of Reese's hair." Tessa giggled. "Not really."

"I'm sure you're angry with him."

"Do you and the senator ever argue?"

"Yes," Aunt Sam said softly. "We did."

Tessa sat back. "Is something wrong between the two of you?"

"We had a long talk again about suffrage." Dark circles rimmed Aunt Sam's eyes, and the wrinkles on her brow appeared deeper. She seemed to have aged overnight. But was it overnight? How long had this been going on? Had Tessa been so wrapped up in her own troubles that she'd missed Aunt Sam's?

"What happened?"

"When the vote came up the other day in the legislature, he voted against it—again." Her voice broke. "He'll never change his mind, but worse, he still wants to change mine. So I told him we would have to go back to simply being friends."

"You don't think you could work around this? Agree to disagree?"

"He enjoys my company and I enjoy his, but he doesn't truly understand me. Not really." The breeze blew a strand of gray hair free from her bun, and she patted it back in place. "I wouldn't be true to myself if I traded what I believe for love. I'd be living a lie."

"Oh, Aunt Sam, I'm so sorry."

"Thank you." Aunt Sam forced a smile. "But I've spent too many years fighting for this cause to marry a man who won't be celebrating with me when the day we can vote finally arrives. I can't be with a man who doesn't support my dream."

"I know exactly how you feel."

"No, dear, you don't."

Tessa quirked her head to the side. "But Reese—"

"Made a mistake. A grave one. I believe you too have made a few."

"Did Hannah call you?"

Aunt Sam nodded. "You should have told me. I would have understood better than anyone."

Tessa's eyes burned with tears. "I know."

"And you should have told Reese."

"I know."

"Tessa, I don't believe for a minute that he doesn't support your dream. He risked a great deal in even allowing you to work alongside him."

"I'm so confused. I thought Reese was solid and honest and strong."

"You're a gardener." Aunt Sam stood. "Take a look at the seeds Reese has sowed in his life. That will tell you what kind of man he really is." She reached down and cupped Tessa's cheek. "While you're at it, you might think a bit about where your hope has been rooted—or rather, in whom."

Tessa watched her go. What did Aunt Sam mean? Where was her hope rooted? In whom?

She'd put her hope in Reese and he'd let her down.

Something tugged on her conscience—a few words from a sermon. The mustard seed of faith. She closed her eyes, and the preacher's words came back to her. *Brothers and sisters, the burden is not on Christians to muster faith, but to have enough faith to focus on the One who has the power to perform whatever needs to be done.*

Her heart pounded against her ribs. Where had her faith been in all of this? Though she'd never been as virtuous as Charlotte or as well-versed as Hannah, she'd always believed God was central to her life, but now, when the odds seemed insurmountable, she'd not turned to him to help her. She'd turned to a man—a good one, but still a man. Worse than that, she'd turned to her own devices to get what she wanted. Not once had she turned to the One who could truly handle the situation.

Her chest heaved under the weight of the discovery. She gathered her knees against her chest, and with the sweet scent of roses hanging in the air, she wept.

Lord Jesus, I'm so sorry.

"Miss Tessa, you have had two telephone calls."

"Oh?" Tessa smiled at the butler. Since she'd spent the early morning in her bedroom praying, she hadn't heard the telephone ring.

"Mr. Reese King called first thing this morning."

"He did?" Tessa's stomach somersaulted at the mention of Reese's name. She had so much she wanted to talk to him about. She owed him an apology, and she needed to tell him the whole truth about why she wanted to work at Como Park.

"Yes, miss, and Mr. Edward Ferrell called. He says it's urgent he speak with you. He left his number." Geoffrey frowned. "But of course, as a young lady, you are not required to return the call."

For once, playing the female card might prove to her advantage. The last thing she wanted to do today was speak to Edward Ferrell.

She picked up her purse. "Geoffrey, will you let Aunt Sam know I'm going to Como Park this morning? Since my sisters are supposed to be coming over, I'll return by one o'clock."

"Should I call for the car?"

She waved her hand. "No, no. I'll take the streetcar. I like the ride."

He opened the heavy front door. "Very well, miss. Enjoy your day."

A sky as blue as a Minnesota lake greeted her. Billowy white clouds dotted the expanse, and a breeze kissed her cheeks. It was as if God was smiling on her.

Even though she and Reese had a great deal to work out, Tessa sensed a peace about all of it. She'd placed the whole situation in God's hands.

As she neared the neighbor's hedge, she heard a mewing sound. The neighbor's kitten again? She was constantly getting herself stuck in one place or another.

Tessa stepped off the sidewalk, slipped around the back of the bush, and pushed back the branches. "There you are." Her collar had gotten caught, so Tessa reached into the bush and unsnagged it. She scooped the feline into her hand, hauled her out, and stood.

Nuzzling the dove-gray kitten against her cheek, she stroked her velvety fur. "You really know how to get yourself in a jam."

A twig snapped behind her, but before she could turn, someone covered her mouth with a cloth. She dropped the kitten and fought against her captor, clawing at his strong arms.

The sickeningly sweet smell of ether engulfed her.

Don't breathe!

Her lungs burned and she had to take a breath. The man pulled her tighter against his chest. One breath. Two. Three.

Fight, Tessa. Fight.

But her body wouldn't obey, and the mews of the kitten grew fainter and fainter.

35

Reese had waited long enough to speak with Tessa.

After pulling his Model T to the curb, Reese climbed out and began the trek to Tessa's aunt's mansion. The walk had never seemed so long.

He knocked on the door, and the butler greeted him. "Would you please tell Tessa I'd like to speak with her?"

The butler frowned. "Mr. King, please come inside."

Reese complied.

"Please, wait here."

How odd. Geoffrey had never seemed so abrupt. If even the servants hated him, he was in trouble.

But instead of Geoffrey returning, Tessa's aunt, Hannah, and Charlotte hurried in to meet him. Great. This was not getting any better.

"Tessa isn't with you?" Hannah pressed her knuckle to her lips.

"With me?" Icy fear jetted up his spine. "No, I haven't seen her. Mrs. Phillips, what's going on?"

"She left here this morning and was to return to meet with us at one o'clock." Worry creased the elderly woman's brow. "But she never came."

Reese glanced at the grandfather clock. She was two and a half hours late. "Maybe she lost track of time."

"She'd done some serious soul searching, and she was coming to talk to you." Mrs. Phillips spoke with such earnestness that her words chilled him further.

"Mrs. Phillips, I had no idea."

"Under the circumstances, I believe you should call me Aunt Sam. Until we find her, we're all going to be seeing a great deal of one another."

Reese nodded mutely. His mind raced and his breath came hard. He had to stay calm. If she was in trouble, she needed him. Had she changed her mind? If so, where would she go? If not, where was she?

"Have you asked the neighbors if they saw anything? Contacted the police?"

"Lincoln is doing that now." Hannah rubbed her forehead and swayed.

Charlotte took her elbow. "You need to sit down and relax as much as you can. Reese will find her." She glanced at him. "Won't you?"

He nodded. He'd find her or die trying.

A haloed pinprick of light appeared and then expanded in Tessa's vision. Her stomach churned, and her head felt as if it had been stuffed with cotton batting. She pressed her palm to her forehead and moaned. Where was she?

"Well, you finally decided to join the living." Her captor held a lantern above her prone body, but the light blinded her and she couldn't see his face. "I was beginning to think we gave you too much ether. You've been sleeping for hours."

Hours? Her family would be frantic.

She struggled to sit up but, still too foggy, fell back onto the sand. Sand? She felt the ground around her. It was definitely sand, but the lantern cast a reflection on a stone ceiling of some kind.

A cave? She drew in a deep breath. The dank air had a familiar musty staleness to it.

Wait a minute. She recognized this place. Turning her head, she caught sight of the underground lake only a few yards away. She was in Carver's Cave in Indian Mounds Park.

Her second attempt at sitting up worked. When she finally saw who held her against her will, she sucked in her breath. "Albert, why did you bring me here?"

"Money, of course." Her captor lit a cigarette. "You're going to write a nice note to that rich aunt of yours, telling her where to leave the ransom money."

"I'm not writing any note."

"Oh, I think you will." He came closer to her and ran a filthy finger down her cheek.

Tessa shivered and glanced at the doorway. If she timed things right, could she make a run for it?

"Don't even think about it. Clem's outside standing guard." He pulled a piece of paper, an envelope, and a pencil from the pocket of his shirt—his yellow shirt—and thrust the items toward her.

"You write it." She glared at him. "Or maybe you don't know how."

"I know how to write," he sneered. "But I want it in your hand-writing to prove I have you."

Tessa's mind whirled. What would the famed detective Allan Pinkerton advise her to do in this situation? If she couldn't escape, he'd tell her to find a way to signal her family. Could she somehow get a message to them inside the ransom note?

"Well, I can't very well write in here." She grabbed the paper and pencil from his hand. "It's too dark. At least let me write on a rock by the entrance." When he hesitated to agree, she pressed on. "You said yourself Clem was standing guard. What trouble could I possibly be to the two of you?"

He motioned with his head toward the entrance. "Go on."

With her shoes sinking into the sand, walking was difficult. There'd be no way to make a run for it. If only she had her work boots. She paused at the cave entrance and took a deep breath. The sun was sitting low in the sky. It would be dark soon, and she'd be forced to spend the night in this cave with Albert and Clem.

Albert pointed to a flat rock. "Now, write the letter and put it in the envelope."

Tessa took her time. There had to be something that would let them know where she was. *Lord, help me see it.*

"Hurry up." Albert shoved her to her knees.

She spread the paper on the rock. "What do you want me to say?"

"'Dear rich aunt—'"

"I am not saying that."

"Then write whatever you call her." He held his hand up to shield his eyes from the setting sun. "Tell her we want five thousand dollars. She should leave it at Como Park, in the rose garden. Tell her to put it in a flour sack. You rich folks have those, don't you?"

"Yes, we have flour sacks." She began to draft the letter, pausing every few words to stall for more time to think.

"You done?"

"Almost."

"Let me see it." He yanked the paper out of her hand, sending the pencil rolling from the stone desk. Tessa watched it roll right onto a tubercled rein-orchid.

She gasped. That was it!

The tubercled rein-orchid was rare. Maybe, just maybe, if she could get it into the envelope without being seen, her family would show it to Reese. Then, if she were truly blessed, Reese would recall seeing it. It was a lot of ifs, but it was her best chance.

She inched toward the plant.

"What are you doing?"

"Getting the pencil. It rolled off."

"Be quick about it." He went back to reading the note.

Tessa ripped a tiny orchid from its stem and closed her fist around it. Thank goodness this plant had such tiny flowers. Any larger and Albert might figure out her plan from the thickness of the envelope.

Her back itched, and when she scratched it, sand fell. She must have sand in every fold of her clothes. What if she added a few grains with the flower?

"Sign it." Albert thrust the letter at her. "And put it in the envelope."

She folded the paper and skillfully slipped the letter and the flower into the envelope. Reaching into the waistband of her skirt, she pinched a bit of sand and then dropped it inside the pre-gummed envelope. She licked it and scrunched her nose at the bitter taste of the glue.

A shrill whistle made Albert look up at Clem. Tessa caught a glimpse of someone coming down the hill. A woman? If she could get her attention—

"Get back inside." Albert yanked her to her feet. "Now."

Tessa deliberately stumbled. She fell to the ground and grabbed her ankle. She'd seen enough girls play the role of damsel in distress to know exactly how it was done. "Oh, my ankle! I think I've twisted it."

Albert's eyes fired daggers in her direction. "Do you really want me to carry you?"

Her ankle made a miraculous recovery. She added a limp, though, to give her story some credibility. Once inside, she found a rock on which to sit.

Albert picked up a piece of rope and walked behind her. "Put your hands back here."

She crossed them over her chest, and he yanked her wrist, twisting her arm behind her until she surrendered the other hand as well. "That's better."

Once her wrists were bound, she watched Albert use the flame of the lantern to light up another cigarette. Odd. He should have been concerned about the newcomer.

"Are you in there, Albert?" a lady called in a high-pitched voice.

"Yep. Got our rich girl right here." He leered at Tessa.

The woman, who was clearly in cahoots with these two, stepped into the glow of the lantern.

Tessa gasped.

"You look surprised, Miss Gregory." Marjorie Walker removed her straw hat. "And before you ask, no, Edward is not part of this, and neither is my husband Joe. If you had simply helped Edward when he asked for it, then I wouldn't have had to resort to this." She sighed. "But I refuse to be poor again, and my Joe is dead set on this motorcycle company. I met these two enterprising young men at my husband's shop shortly after he hired them and decided their skills could be put to good use. My husband needs five thousand dollars for his company, and these young men would like to become investors. See, the plan is perfect." She turned to Albert. "Did you have her write the note like I told you to?"

He patted his pocket.

"Good." She smiled at him. "Take the Ford and leave me your motorcycle. Leave the ransom note on Edward's front seat. He's at the Motordrome now. You know his car, right?"

"The silver American Underslung."

She nodded. "He'll see the envelope as soon as he gets in, and once he reads it, he'll deliver it to her family."

"What will you do when you get the money?" Tessa heard a note of panic in her voice and willed herself to calm it. "I know who you all are. You can't simply let me go."

Marjorie gave Albert a knowing look, then her eyes flicked to the lake.

Tessa swallowed. Fear cinched around her chest and squeezed the breath from her lungs.

"After you deliver the envelope, go watch for the ransom money to be delivered. I told Joe I was staying with a sick friend tonight." She smiled at Tessa and pulled a derringer from her purse. "I'm sure you're feeling quite ill right now, aren't you, dear?"

Between the ether and this unsettling news, Tessa thought she might indeed be sick, but she wouldn't let this woman have the pleasure of seeing that happen.

"It will never work. Samantha Phillips isn't really my aunt."

"What do you mean?" Albert's brows knit together.

"She's my brother-in-law's aunt, and she was kind enough to let me live with her. That's all." Tessa crossed her arms. "She won't pay a thing for me. I'm not even a blood relative."

"Maybe we should deal with her now and get it over with." Albert tipped his head toward the water. "I've got the rope."

"No, not yet." Marjorie squatted in front of her and stared into Tessa's eyes. "I want her to see she's wrong. These rich folks think they know everything, and I want her to die knowing we bested her."

All her life, Tessa could figure out a way around, over, or through any situation.

Until now.

Helpless. Alone. Totally undone.

Lord, my faith is as small as a mustard seed, but I'm putting it all in you.

Not one clue.

Reese crumpled the piece of paper in his hand and heaved it into the fireplace at Tessa's aunt's home. Aunt Sam and Charlotte had taken Hannah up to lie down, leaving him alone with Joel and Lincoln.

"You checked all of the places she likes to go?" Lincoln pressed.

"I checked the vacant lot garden, her favorite store to shop at, and every crevice of Como Park. I even checked the theater that was showing a moving picture she said she wanted to see. She's not anywhere."

"People don't just vanish." On the davenport, Joel leaned forward and clasped his hands.

Lincoln nodded. "I think it's time to consider someone might have taken her."

"Kidnapped her?" Reese rubbed the back of his neck. "Why?"

"My aunt has money." Lincoln squeezed Reese's shoulder. "If that's what's happened, there will be a ransom demand soon."

"And?"

"And I'll pay." Aunt Sam breezed into the room. "No matter what the cost. Her safety is what matters."

"I'm not so sure about that," Lincoln said.

Reese glared at him. "How can you say that?"

Lincoln sighed. "Paying money still doesn't guarantee her safety. Most kidnappings don't end with the return of—"

"Stop right there." Aunt Sam held up her hand. "We are not going down that road. We are not going to give up hope. Tessa will be back with her family, and that's that."

Reese would have hugged the woman, but the arrival of the butler stopped him.

"Mr. Edward Ferrell is here to see you, ma'am. He says it's urgent."

Edward! Reese's blood boiled. He had been the one to try to force Tessa into helping him. He had to be in on this. Why else was he here?

Following Aunt Sam into the foyer, he balled his fists. Edward stood with an envelope clenched in his hands.

Aunt Sam nodded a greeting. "I'm surprised to see you so late. What's so urgent?"

He held out the envelope. "This was on my car seat when I left the Motordrome tonight. It's about Tessa."

Reese stepped close as Aunt Sam opened the missive. She withdrew the letter, and even though he knew it was rude, Reese read it over her shoulder. He recognized Tessa's handwriting from the scrapbooks she'd shown him and from the garden designs. Someone had taken her, and if they ever wanted to see her again, Aunt Sam would have to pay.

"Why was it in *your* car?" Lincoln asked from behind Reese.

Suddenly, it all made sense. Tessa hadn't helped Edward, but he'd still needed the money. What better way to get it?

White-hot rage consumed Reese. He grabbed Edward by the shirt collar and thrust him against the wall. The picture frames rattled. "Where is she?"

Lack of sufficient oxygen darkened Edward's face. "I don't know. I promise!"

Lincoln clamped a hand on Reese's arm. "Let him go."

"Do you know what he did to Tessa?"

"Yes. Hannah told me." Lincoln pulled on Reese's arm. "It doesn't make him guilty. Besides, if he is in on it, we'll never find her if you kill him."

After giving Edward another shove for good measure, he released his hold on the man's shirt.

"Reese, I believe Tessa has sent you a clue," Aunt Sam said.

"Me?"

She held up a flower. "I don't know who else she'd hope would get this."

As if it were a treasured jewel, Reese cradled the tiny blossom in the palm of his hand. "It's an orchid."

"Come now, Reese." Aunt Sam placed her hands beneath his. "You know our Tessa. She wouldn't send you a common orchid. What's special about it?"

Pressure welled in his chest. If this was a clue, what if he couldn't figure it out? No, he wouldn't think that way. He refused to let Tessa down again.

He met Aunt Sam's gaze. "I need better light."

In the parlor, she directed him toward the Tiffany gas lamp on the end table. He dragged an armchair over and sat down with the flower pinched between his thumb and forefinger.

"What can you tell?" Joel loomed over him with Lincoln by his side. Edward, thankfully, stood on the other side of the room, still insisting on his innocence.

"Gentlemen." Aunt Sam nudged them aside. "Please step back and let Reese have some room."

Reese looked at the flower. Like all orchids, this one had three sepals and three petals. "See this?" He pointed to the lower petal. "This one is oblong. The base is shaped like an arrowhead."

Lincoln leaned in close and squinted. "If you say so."

Reese prayed to recall all that he'd learned, then studied the flower again. There was a thick tubercle on the upper surface near the base. That was it! That alone separated this flower from all the look-alikes.

"Do you know what it is?" Joel asked.

"It's a tubercled rein-orchid, and it's hard to find. Very hard." Reese turned the flower over in his hand. "It prefers wet meadows and prairies or sandy areas in marshes."

"Sand?" Aunt Sam held out the envelope. "Look inside."

Reese poured the contents onto a copy of *Redbook*. The white sand sparkled against the black letters on the cover.

"It's another clue." Aunt Sam smiled.

"White sand is everywhere in Minnesota." Joel raked his hand through his hair.

"But not white sand and that orchid." Aunt Sam locked eyes with Reese. "The clue is for you. She knew you'd be here. She knew you wouldn't let her down. Where could she be?"

Reese closed his eyes. He had to think. He saw hundreds of flowers every day. How could he remember just one?

The image of the flower came to his mind. He'd seen those flowers, but where?

He was certain there were some by Cozy Lake in Como Park, but there wasn't any of this white sand there that he recalled. Besides, where would they keep Tessa hostage?

In the back of his mind, he recalled Mr. Nussbaumer once pointing out a cluster at Phalen Creek in Swede Hollow, and there were some old shacks that would make a good place to hide Tessa, but the two of them had never visited the area.

Still, she believed he'd recognize the flower. Why? Where had they gone where this orchid might have been present?

A thought hit him like a medicine ball to the gut. He sucked in his breath, his heart racing.

Please, Lord, let me be right.

"I think I know where she is."

36

Sleeping with your hands tied behind your back is impossible. Tessa would know. Add the threat of imminent death looming over her head, a rock for a pillow, and a crazy woman holding a gun, and it made for a long night.

On the bright side, Albert the letch was gone.

Clem had come in a few times and whined about the job he'd been assigned and how hungry he was. Marjorie had promptly sent him back out. Tessa had to agree with him on the hungry part. These three had thought of nearly everything they needed to pull this off—except food and water.

She added starvation to her list of reasons she couldn't sleep.

She might as well strike up a conversation with Marjorie. Maybe she'd learn something useful. "You ride a motorcycle?"

"Of course I do."

So much for chatting. "How long have you three been planning this?"

Marjorie shrugged. "I guess I hatched the idea about two weeks after the boys started working for Joe."

"You know, you don't have to kill me. I'm a good actress. I can tell them I don't know who held me captive."

Marjorie snickered. "Like I believe that."

Tessa sighed and tried a different tactic. "How did you and Joe meet?"

"We went to school together. He noticed I didn't bring a lunch on Tuesdays and Thursdays, and he started sharing his with me on those days." She got a far-off look in her eyes. "I've got five younger brothers and sisters. We didn't have enough money for food for all of us, so we took turns on who got to eat."

"Joe sounds like a great guy." Tessa licked her dry lips. "I'm sorry you had to go without. I know how hard that is."

"What does a rich girl like you know about going hungry?"

"Remember, I told you I'm not her real niece. I grew up in Iowa. After my parents died, we lost the farm. It seemed like we lived on beans for weeks." Tessa chuckled. "Have you ever had bean pie? My sister was trying something new. I wouldn't say it was her best recipe."

Marjorie stood up. "It isn't going to work. You're not going to make me change my mind about killing you with some sob story about beans. You already said you're a good actress."

"I'm not acting." Tessa closed her eyes and leaned her head against the rock. "But what's Joe going to say when he finds out the truth about all of this?"

"He won't."

"The truth always comes out, Marjorie. Always."

How had Reese gotten stuck with Edward?

He brought his car to a halt at the bluff top, near the path to Carver's Cave, and Edward pulled in behind him. After he'd told Lincoln and Joel about the three areas where he thought Tessa might possibly be, they'd decided that each of them should take one spot. Lincoln was convinced Edward wasn't involved, and since this site was the most likely, he told Reese to take Edward along as backup. He also promised to update the authorities on the ransom note and the orchid.

Reese and Edward drove separately in case one of them needed to go for help.

Climbing out of his car, Reese sighed. This was crazy. Who took the person who might be the perpetrator of the crime to the rescue?

"Stay here," Reese barked. He reached in his backseat and pulled out his Remington Pump.

"I should come with you."

"You don't know the way, and it would slow me down." He stuffed a fistful of shells in his jacket pocket. "It's better if you stay up here. See those two motorcycles in the brush? Keep an eye on them. Why would they be here this time of day?"

"What if you need help?"

He shut the door. "You hear shooting? Come running."

Tessa felt something warm on her wrists. She'd been rubbing them against the rock for almost an hour and only now could feel the rope begin to fray.

At some point in the night, Marjorie had decided to bind Tessa's feet as well so her captor could sleep. While it frustrated Tessa, it also gave her a chance to work on the ropes binding her wrists without being noticed.

Through the cave entrance, she spotted a glimmer of light. Was it dawn already?

Then she saw a shadowed figure step into view.

"Tessa?"

Her heart leapt at the sound of Reese's voice. "I'm here!"

Marjorie bolted from her sleep. "What's going on?"

Another shadowy figure jumped to the earth behind Reese. Clem?

"Reese! Look out!"

But Reese didn't have a chance. The other man struck Reese over the head, and he crumpled to the ground.

"No!" Tears sprang to her eyes. Had the man killed him?

As he began to drag Reese inside, Tessa saw that it was indeed Clem. Tessa watched Reese's chest rise and fall and sent up a prayer of thanks. He wasn't dead—yet.

"Who's that?" Marjorie demanded.

"Reese King. Her fellow."

She whirled toward Tessa. "How did he find you?"

"I have no idea." Tessa shrugged. "He works for the park service. Maybe he saw the motorcycles up top."

"Tie him up." Marjorie pointed to the rope.

"We need to get out of here. He may have already alerted the police."

"I said, tie him up."

"Clem, you're right." Tessa felt the ropes on her wrist finally give way. "You need to get away now if you ever want to see a dime of that money."

"Don't listen to her," Marjorie said. "We have a plan, and we need to stick to it."

Clem spun and ran toward the exit.

Marjorie fired the pistol in his direction. It missed, and he kept going.

Tessa continued to hide her hands behind her back. "Listen, Marjorie, I know that's a one-shot gun, and the way I see it, you're two shots short of taking care of Reese and me. If I were you, I'd be hightailing it out of here before Clem and Albert take off with the ransom money and you never see a cent."

Panic flickered in Marjorie's eyes. She gave Tessa a final glare, hiked up her skirts, and bolted from the cave.

Tessa undid the rope around her ankles and hurried to Reese. She patted his cheeks and called to him. He groaned and slowly began to rouse.

"Reese?" Someone was calling for them. It sounded like Edward. Did she dare answer?

"Tessa, are you all right?" He entered the cave, picked up the shotgun Reese had been carrying, and looked at Reese. "Is he okay?"

"I think so." How had Marjorie not seen the gun Reese had carried? God had indeed moved a mountain, but was she now facing another accomplice in Edward? Why else was he here?

She hated that he now had the gun. If he was on their side, she was in trouble again. "Did you see Marjorie?"

"I saw someone, but they weren't on the path. I was trying to get down here to you. Reese said if I heard shots—"

She heaved a sigh of relief. He was with Reese. "Did Aunt Sam pay the ransom?"

He nodded. "She insisted. Listen, Tessa, I'm sorry for what I did."

"Save it for later." She pushed to her feet. "Stay with Reese. Is your car up top?"

"Yes, mine and Reese's, but where are you going?"

"To catch the bad guys."

About two-thirds of the way up the hill, it occurred to Tessa that she didn't know how to drive an automobile, but how hard could it be?

She topped the bluff and scanned the area. Edward's silver Underslung was nowhere to be found, but Reese's white Model T remained parked. She started toward it, but the sun glinted off something shiny in the brush. Surely Clem had taken one of the motorcycles, but had Marjorie taken Edward's car and left the remaining motorcycle? It made sense given how difficult it was to start a motorcycle alone.

She hurried over and nearly cheered when she saw the fender of the cycle. Perfect. This she knew how to drive.

She worked it free, mentally going over all that Edward had taught her. She remembered which lever turned the gas on and that she had to pump the oil into the crank case. He'd said something about an oil dripper and two drops every so many seconds. She set it, hoping she guessed correctly.

Eyeing the belt that engaged the engine, she cringed. She was wearing a skirt today. She'd have to raise it to a scandalous degree. Oh well, it wouldn't be the first—or the last—time she shocked someone.

She recalled that Edward had started the cycle the first time for her by spinning the back tire hard while it was still raised on the kickstand. After three tries, she gave up on that method. She simply wasn't strong enough to give it a sufficient spin. However, riding down the bluff should certainly do the trick.

With her skirts raised to her knees, she climbed on and pushed the bike off the stand and began to pedal down the hill. To her great delight, everything worked as it should. The engine sparked, the belt tension engaged, and the machine roared to life. The smell of the exhaust was a sweet perfume. She twisted the right hand grip, pushing the throttle as far as it would go and the roads would allow.

Zigzagging through the streets, she hoped to make up some of the distance between her and Marjorie, but she had no idea what she'd do once they met up. She ignored the drivers who honked at her, and one time she had to swerve to miss a delivery wagon when she didn't see him barreling through an intersection.

Nearly half an hour later, she reached Como Park. At least she knew where the rose garden was. She prayed that Marjorie was still wandering the footpaths. No bicycles, and especially no motorcycles, were allowed on the sidewalks, but some rules were made to be broken. Still, she had to go slow in case of pedestrians.

She spotted Albert, Clem, and Marjorie in the garden with a motorcycle a few feet away. Apparently she wasn't the only rule breaker.

Since this path wasn't wide enough for an automobile, she

guessed both the Ford that Albert had driven away and the Underslung that Marjorie had stolen were parked somewhere. So when the time came for them to leave, which crook would drive what?

They seemed to be fighting, all three crooks tugging on a satchel. Suddenly Clem turned toward her, and the gaze of the others followed. The rumble of her motorcycle must have alerted them. Why hadn't she stayed farther back?

Albert yanked the satchel from Marjorie and climbed on the motorcycle behind Clem, leaving Marjorie no escape.

No! This couldn't happen. After what they'd done to her and to Reese, she couldn't let them get away. Not with Aunt Sam's money.

Nerves pulled taut, she made a decision. It was now or never.

"Where's Tessa?" Reese sat up and gingerly touched the knot on the back of his head.

Edward kept a steadying hand on Reese's shoulder. "She went after Marjorie and the Henderson brothers."

"Alone?" He moved too quickly and the cave tilted. His stomach fought to upend itself. He swallowed the bile in his mouth.

"She told me to stay and help you." Edward gripped his upper arm. "And it looks like it's a good thing she did. Besides, she'll never catch them. She was at least fifteen minutes behind them."

Reese stumbled to his feet. "Take me to her."

"The only place you should go is a hospital." He slung Reese's arm over his shoulder.

"I'll be fine." Except that his head throbbed and he was seeing two Edwards. "Please, Edward, she needs me."

They started for the cave's entrance. "Tessa doesn't seem like she needs anyone. She does quite well on her own."

"It's a charade." Reese chuckled. "Mostly."

"You sure you want her? She's always going to be a handful."

It hurt to smile too, but he did it anyway. "She sure is."

If Clem and Albert were able to start their motorcycle, they'd get away. Excitement coursing through her, Tessa twisted the throttle and the motorcycle raced forward.

She intentionally clipped the front tire of the crook's cycle, spilling the motorcycle and its riders. But now a planter loomed in front of her. She pushed the pedal backwards to stop her momentum.

Still, she was going too fast.

In a split second, her front wheel hit the planter, and she flew off the motorcycle and came down hard into a rosebush.

Whistles? Why was she hearing shrill whistles? Had she hit her head?

"You again!" The park officer loomed over her. "I should have known."

Tessa struggled to get up, thorns digging into the tender flesh of her hands. She jabbed a finger toward the crooks. "Catch them!"

"*They* aren't in a planter."

"But they rode a motorcycle in *your* park!"

"Don't worry." The officer extended his hand and pulled her up. "My buddies have them, and you're all going to jail. Look at these roses. This is a lot more serious than picking a few dead pansies."

The other park officers handcuffed Clem and Albert. Both Marjorie and Tessa were marched back to the park office in the custody of an officer. None of the officers seemed interested in hearing the whole story. She'd need Reese's help to get this sorted out.

Her heart grabbed. Was Reese okay? What if he'd needed more help than Edward could provide? Maybe she should have gone for Joel instead of chasing after criminals.

Would she ever learn not to be so impulsive?

The park officer came to an abrupt stop. Tessa followed his gaze, and a thrill shot through her.

Reese.

The park officer sighed when Reese approached. "Let me guess. You want me to leave her in your care."

Reese picked a rosebush stem from her hair. "I certainly do."

37

"Tessa, hold still!"

"I am perfectly capable of brushing my own hair." Tessa yanked the brush out of Charlotte's hand and stared at the image of herself in the dresser mirror. Scratches marred her skin, and dark shadows rimmed her eyes. She needed about two days of sleep, but every time she closed her eyes, she saw Albert or Marjorie hovering over her.

"But Tessa, honey." Charlotte made a grab for the brush. "There are rosebush leaves and stems everywhere."

"And there are thorn pricks and tears too." Hannah pointed to the holes in Tessa's dress. "I don't think this one is salvageable."

"I doubt if I'd ever wear it again anyway." Tessa tugged a stick from the front of her dress. "Too many unpleasant memories."

Charlotte gave up on the hair brushing and sat on the bed. "Can you talk about it?"

Tessa started at the beginning and relayed the story. To her surprise, neither sister interrupted or asked questions. They simply let her talk.

"You were so brave." Charlotte took her hands. "I'm so proud of you."

"And they'll never hurt you again, Tessa." Hannah plucked another stick from her dress. "Lincoln and Edward returned from the jail a little while ago. They said Marjorie, Clem, and Albert have been charged with kidnapping. All three of them will be going to prison for a long time."

Tessa expected to feel satisfied at that sort of news, but instead a profound sadness swept over her.

"Are you all right?" Charlotte asked.

"It's such a waste. Joe really loved Marjorie and she really loved him, but now they'll be separated for years."

Lincoln knocked on her door. "Edward wanted me to tell you he's sorry he ever introduced you to Marjorie Walker, and he regrets all that he's put you through." He frowned. "I'm not sure what he means by that, but if you want me to kick him out of the house for good, I will."

"No. We all make mistakes." She sighed. "I know I certainly have."

"All right, I'll let him stay." Lincoln started to leave, then returned. "I almost forgot. Joel said Reese will be fine. He's asleep now, and Joel wants him to stay that way for an hour or two." Lincoln glanced at her clothes. "I'm not sure that will be enough time, though, for you to make yourself presentable."

Tessa tossed a bed pillow at the door frame, but Lincoln dodged it.

She and her sisters giggled, and it had never felt better to laugh.

Tessa eased the door open to one of Aunt Sam's guest rooms. Reese, propped on a plethora of pillows, smiled at her.

"May I come in?"

"Of course."

She left the door ajar, padded across the thick rug, and set the vase of lemon-scented verbena on the nightstand. "Joel said you'll be fine, but you need to take it easy for a day or two." She fingered one of the long, glassy leaves. "What will Mr. Nussbaumer say about that?"

Reese hiked a shoulder. "I'm not sure I even have a job at Como anymore."

"Why? Because I wrecked the motorcycle in the planter?"

"No, not because of that." Reese chuckled and took her hand. He brushed his thumb against the bandage on her wrist. "I told Mr. Nussbaumer everything, Tessa. I told him about you and your plans, and I told him how you helped garner support for the conservatory project."

She stared into his denim-blue eyes. "Why did you tell him?"

"I couldn't live a lie."

"What did he say?"

"He said he needed some time to consider everything." Reese swallowed. "I'm so sorry that I hurt you, and I will support you in whatever you choose to do. If you still want to go back to the university, I'll wait if you'll have me."

She looked down at their entwined fingers and pulled away. "Reese, I wasn't completely truthful with you either." As briefly as she could, she explained her expulsion from school. "I wanted so badly to prove myself that I justified my own lies. But there's more."

"Go on."

"When you're being held captive, you tend to have a lot of time to think."

"Soul searching?"

She nodded. "I was putting my hope in you, and as good a man as you are, you are still a man, and it was only a matter of time before you let me down." He started to speak, but she held up her hand. "What I'm saying is, I should have put my hope in God. Only he has the ability to move all the mountains in my life."

He grinned. "We make quite a pair."

"We certainly do."

Footsteps in the hallway were followed by a knock on the door-jamb. Aunt Sam stepped inside. "There's someone who'd like to speak to you both."

Mr. Nussbaumer entered, his hat in his hands, and Aunt Sam slipped back out. "It is *gut* to know you are okay, Reese."

"Thank you, sir."

"I wanted to personally tell you that I've given Nels a new position."

Reese cleared his throat. "I understand, sir."

The master gardener pointed to an empty chair. "May I?"

"Yes, please." Tessa reached for the coffeepot beside the bed and poured him a cup. "If you prefer tea, I can have it brought up."

"No thank you, Miss Gregory." He accepted the cup, then turned toward Reese. "When Nels went to check on Carver's Cave after your experience today, he caught a park employee delivering another artifact."

"Who?" Reese sipped from his own cup.

Mr. Nussbaumer's brow furled. "The current head gardener at Indian Mounds Park, the man who was ill."

"I should have known." Reese pushed himself up in the bed. "I thought it was strange that he said he'd never been inside Carver's Cave when it was in his own park."

"Yes, that would be odd." The superintendent crossed his arms over his chest. "I cannot tolerate dishonesty, so Nels will be replacing him."

Tessa clenched her hands in front of her. He couldn't tolerate dishonesty. That didn't bode well for Reese.

Mr. Nussbaumer stood. "So I will expect you, as my employee, to always tell me the truth."

"You want me? I still have the job?"

"*Ja.*" The master gardener smiled. "Anyone who risks everything to clear his conscience is a *gut*, honest man." He turned to Tessa. "And you agree?"

"Yes, sir." She flashed Reese a triumphant grin. He had probably lost any chance at the head gardener's position, but at least he didn't lose his job.

"Reese tells me I owe you a debt of gratitude. He said that without your help, my conservatory might still be a dream."

"I was happy to help." The old Tessa might have taken advantage of this situation and pressed Mr. Nussbaumer to give her a position, but the new Tessa refused to do anything that might hurt Reese.

"The garden you designed, it is *gut*, *ja*?"

"I think so, but Reese deserves as much credit as I. Even more so."

He nodded. "Yes, I can see his hand throughout the garden, but the soul of the garden is yours."

Tessa didn't know what to say to that. He didn't seem to mean it as a compliment. It was more of a statement of fact.

"Miss Gregory, I have been hardheaded about many things, but I like to think of my artistry as progressive. You worked alongside Reese and handled the job well. You also clearly see a garden as a canvas, and there are any number of places where you could work. However, if you are still interested, I believe you and Mr. King make a formidable team."

Her heart soared. "Are you offering me a position?"

He laughed and placed a hand on Reese's leg. "If you can handle working with this sloth."

"Oh, I can."

"Very well. Then your first task is to get him up and about. It wouldn't bode well for the conservatory's new head gardener to miss the groundbreaking."

After they'd profusely thanked him, Mr. Nussbaumer said his goodbyes and left the two of them alone.

Dazed, Tessa walked to the window and watched Mr. Nussbaumer leave. Clouds had rolled in during the afternoon, and a soft rain pelted the window. "How did this happen, Reese?"

"God moved your mountain."

The creaking of bedsprings made her turn. "What are you doing out of bed?"

"Kissing the woman I love."

He closed the distance between them and took her hand. Raising her bandaged wrist to his lips, he kissed the sensitive flesh above it. For the first time, she noticed a scar on his forefinger. How had it gotten there? She wanted to know. She wanted to know everything about Reese King.

"Better?" His voice was thick.

"I think I hurt here too." She pointed to her cheek, then to her ear. "And here."

He brushed kisses as soft as pussy willows in the places she'd indicated. Heat pooled in her stomach. Had her heart ever beat so fast?

"And here." She drew her finger along her lower lip.

He placed his hands on her waist and brought his lips to hers, kissing her again and again. He tasted of coffee and happiness, and Tessa's heart swelled.

This was an adventure she never wanted to end.

Epilogue

SUNDAY, NOVEMBER 14, 1915

Tugging on the pearl-studded neckline of her peach-colored dress, Tessa glanced at Aunt Sam and the rest of her family. The fragrance of myriad flowers filled the humid air inside the conservatory while huge palm fronds hung overhead.

"Stop fussing." Charlotte batted Tessa's hand away from her dress. "You'd think this was your wedding day."

"It's nearly as important." Tessa scanned the crowd inside the conservatory for Reese. "Where is he? It's almost time to cut the ribbon."

Spanning sixty thousand square feet, the conservatory was a marvel of steel and glass. Its purpose was twofold: first, to provide a year-round area to display the flora and fauna, and second, to provide an adequate site to winter hot-weather plants like the palms and ferns.

Arched wings extended out from the conservatory's center section, giving the crystal palace an airy, elegant feel. Today Superintendent Nussbaumer would personally guide visitors on their maiden tour of the exhibits. Reese had raised chrysanthemums in sixty-seven varieties, and Tessa had supervised the arrangement of potted plants in the hourglass bed and at the edge of the curving path to the aquarium. They'd set up rough pine tables and lined the straight walkways of the conservatory with hundreds of mums.

Tessa turned toward Aunt Sam. How different her life might have been without her. She'd become their tree of strength, and today she beamed with pride.

She glanced at her sisters too. Charlotte, ripe with child, settled her hand on her stomach while Joel jostled the toddler they'd adopted only nine months ago. Alice Ann beamed at her daddy and new brother.

Tessa's gaze locked with Hannah's—the sister who'd taken on the university and gained Tessa the right to return if she so desired. But to Hannah's dismay, Tessa decided not to finish her formal education and to remain here at Como Park with Reese, where every flower was her teacher.

Hannah smiled at her, and Tessa blinked threatening tears away. When their parents had died, it was Hannah who had been the one to make them all promise to support each other's dreams. Since then, Hannah had become an attorney, Charlotte a chef, and Tessa a gardener, but were those ever their only dreams? Tessa didn't think so. They'd also dreamed of love. Each sister had her heart's desire fulfilled—at least for now.

With the Gregory sisters, who knew what they'd decide to tackle next.

"There's the man of the hour." Lincoln lifted his son, now almost two, from Hannah's arms. "And he's looking quite dapper."

Tessa spotted Reese too. He wore the new pinstriped suit and felt hat she'd purchased.

Her husband—and he was entering with Mr. Nussbaumer.

Last summer she and Reese had married in the Arts and Crafts garden they'd planted together at Como. They'd watched as the panes of glass were added to the conservatory's dome following the ceremony, and they'd honeymooned with their family in Hawaii.

Brother Taylor's words still echoed in her mind. *For a seed to grow, it must become completely undone. The shell cracks. The insides must spill out, and everything changes forever. What comes next is a miracle, and it happens over and over in the gardens of the earth, as well as in the gardens of our hearts so that love can bloom.*

Taking her hand, Reese drew her onto the podium beside him. Mr. Nussbaumer addressed the crowd, welcoming those who came, talking about this building—his dream—and thanking all those who had a hand in making the dream a reality. As Mr. Nussbaumer concluded, the orchestra struck up a waltz.

Reese pressed his lips to Tessa's ear, making chill bumps rise on her neck. "Congratulations, Mrs. King. You did it."

"*We* did it."

Joy exploded inside her. God had blessed them beyond anything even she could have imagined, and everywhere she looked, love had bloomed.

Author's Note

Thank you, my reader friends, for joining me on the Gregory sisters' journey. Your readership means so much to me, and I thank God for each of you. I thought you might enjoy learning a little bit more about this book's unsung hero.

By the turn of the century, parks had taken the forefront in municipal planning. Not only did cities want to present themselves as beautiful and cultured, but they also wanted to offer inexpensive recreation to the citizens. A few cities in America led the way in this effort, including New York, Chicago, Saint Paul, Des Moines, Saint Louis, and San Francisco.

History books cannot possibly acknowledge all of the men and women who contributed to making America what it is today. One of those unsung heroes was Fred Nussbaumer.

Born in Baden, Germany, in 1850, George Friedrich Nussbaumer learned to be a landscape gardener in his father's greenhouse. He lived and worked in London, Paris, Russia, and Germany before coming to America in the late 1870s. He was superintendent of parks for Saint Paul in 1891. He served until his retirement in 1922, over thirty years later.

H. W. S. Cleveland, Nussbaumer's predecessor, thought that the park's main objective was preservation. Cleveland felt that parks should be a place for citizens to escape city life and get in touch with nature. He believed in interfering with nature as little as possible.

Nussbaumer agreed with Cleveland's philosophy, but he also strongly advocated for a wide variety of free or reasonably priced recreational activities, services, and educational opportunities for park visitors. He understood the importance of having both floral displays and untouched natural areas. He knew the people paid for the park system and wanted it to be available to everyone.

Under his direction, parks became recreational and cultural centers, and his model was copied throughout the country. His crown jewel, the conservatory, is one of the few remaining Victorian-style glass houses still in existence today.

Every year, thousands of visitors flock to Como Park, the Como Zoo, and, of course, the restored Marjorie McNeely Conservatory. This year in November, the conservatory will celebrate its centennial. I can't wait to attend.

For more information about Como Park Zoo & Conservatory, visit www.comozooconservatory.org.

Fan favorite **Lorna Seilstad** is the author of the Lake Manawa Summers series, *When Love Calls*, and *While Love Stirs*. As a history buff and antique collector, she brings history back to life using a generous dash of humor. She has won several online writing awards and is a member of the American Christian Fiction Writers. She lives with her family in Iowa.

Visit

LornaSeilstad.com

to Stay Connected

Don't Miss the First Books in
THE GREGORY SISTERS
Series

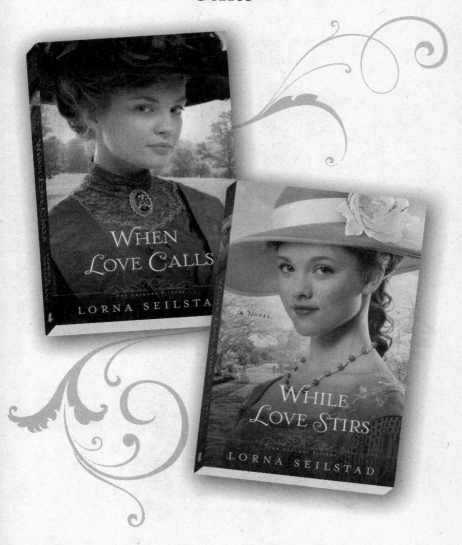

Revell
a division of Baker Publishing Group
www.RevellBooks.com

Available wherever books and ebooks are sold.

Lake Manawa Summers Series

"Buckle up! With a sparkle of humor, heart-pumping romance, and a writing style that is fresh, fun, and addictive, Lorna Seilstad takes you along the fun-filled shores of Lake Manawa."

—JULIE LESSMAN, award-winning author of the Daughters of Boston and the Winds of Change series

WITHDRAWN

R Revell
a division of Baker Publishing Group
www.RevellBooks.com

Available wherever books and ebooks are sold.